COWBOY'S SECRET SON

ROBIN PERINI

THE DEPUTY'S BABY

TYLER ANNE SNELL

MILLS & BOON

First Published in Great Britain 2018
by Mills & Boon, an imprint of HarperCollins*Publishers*
1 London Bridge Street, London, SE1 9GF

Cowboy's Secret Son © 2018 Robin L. Perini
The Deputy's Baby © 2018 Tyler Anne Snell

ISBN: 978-0-263-26588-0

0818

MIX
Paper from
responsible sources
FSC™ C007454

FSC
www.fsc.org

This book is produced from independently certified FSC™ paper to ensure responsible forest management.

For more information visit: www.harpercollins.co.uk/green

Printed and bound in Spain
by CPI, Barcelona

COWBOY'S SECRET SON

ROBIN PERINI

This book is dedicated to my family. I'm blessed to experience unconditional love every single day. You are my strength, my heart and my world. I love you all.

Prologue

The Texas night sky broke open with the boom of thunder and sizzle of lightning, splitting the heavens with a malicious hand. Oblivious to the violent rainstorm, Jared King stood on the end of the pier at Last Chance Lake, a large duffel at his side. Peering through the curtain of water streaming off his Stetson, he searched for any sign of his wife. Was this just another cruel twist in the kidnapper's perverse game?

Where was she? Where was Alyssa?

His phone rang, piercing the roar of the torrent. He grabbed the cell and tapped the screen. "King," he snapped.

A spine-chilling and all-too-familiar chuckle sounded through the line. "You look upset, Jared."

His chin shot up and he spun in a 360. The guy was watching.

Jared squinted into the darkness, searching for any indicator to the kidnapper's location, shunting the full-blown terror that had gripped his heart and soul in a dark place.

Why had he ever left her alone?

When she'd taken the chance of marrying him and coming to live in the middle of nowhere, he'd promised to take care of her. Always. And look what had happened.

She'd been taken by a madman.

Another quick flash illuminated the large lake and his heart picked up the pace, thudding at the clip of a galloping stampede. Was that a boat near the swimming platform at the center of the lake?

Was it them? It couldn't be the sheriff. He'd agreed to stay out of sight until Alyssa was safe. Jared refused to take chances with her safety.

Before Jared could focus, the world went dark again. He could see nothing. The entire lake had morphed into an endless black hole.

"Where is she?" he asked, desperate to keep his voice steady.

"Do you have the money?" the kidnapper countered in a guttural whisper.

Jared snapped on his flashlight and lifted the duffel, sweeping the beam along the large bag.

"Good. I bet that emptied out your bank account. Did you follow my instructions?"

His unwavering focus probed the storm. If only he could catch a glimpse of the kidnapper or Alyssa. "I told you I would." Jared ground his teeth at the taunting tone, but inside a niggle of something not quite right set off alarm bells. "Where is my wife?"

"You sound nervous. You should be." A low laugh filtered through the phone. "I told you not to lie to me. You failed. You didn't follow *all* of my instructions," the man said, his voice unidentifiable. "You contacted the law. I warned you I'd be watching."

Jared stilled. Oh God. How had the kidnapper found

out? He clutched the duffel's strap with a death grip. Jared had called Carder, Texas, sheriff Kevin Redmond when Alyssa had first been kidnapped. He'd had no choice. He couldn't raise the cash the man wanted. Not after sinking everything into that new quarter horse stud last week. With no time to liquidate, he'd needed help. He and the sheriff had been careful, though. They'd never met in person.

Obviously they hadn't been careful enough.

What had he done?

Jared's knuckles whitened around the phone. "Please—"

"Too late for apologies. You broke the rules. Now you pay the price."

"Wait!"

"Just remember, this is all your fault."

The line went dead.

"You hear that, Kevin?" Jared whispered into the small microphone hidden beneath his shirt, fighting against the panic squeezing his heart.

"He could be bluffing," the sheriff said, through the earpiece.

But Jared recognized the uncertainty lacing Kevin's voice.

A motor roared to life from the middle of the lake.

"That's got to be him," Jared shouted. "He's on the water."

"N-no! Please!" a woman's pleading cry sounded from somewhere in the inky darkness.

"Alyssa?" Jared shouted.

"What the hell—?" Kevin cursed.

A splash sounded. The motor kicked into gear.

"Sounds like he's heading to the far side." Jared

squinted, trying to make out any movement in the night. "I can't see a damn thing. Alyssa!"

She'd called out to him. She had to be close.

"I'll head him off." Another motor rumbled. The sheriff's boat. "Keep the comm open," Kevin yelled over the engine.

Jared had no chance of beating the boat to the other side of the lake in his truck, but he had to try. He shined his high-powered flashlight across the water to catch the direction of the boat's wake. Maybe, just maybe.

The beam swept past the old wooden platform and he jerked it back. He froze. Two pale hands gripped a post, blond hair shining against the water.

Alyssa.

"I see her," he shouted.

He tugged off his boots, dove into the icy water, and sprinted toward her. He made it to the structure in record time and stopped, treading water in the twenty-five-foot-deep man-made lake. He spun around, desperately searching for her, barely acknowledging the engine from Kevin's boat closing in.

She was gone.

"Alyssa!"

Jared dove beneath the surface, but with no moonlight shining down, he couldn't even see his hands in front of him, he could only feel. Frantic, he whirled in the water, reaching out, searching for something, anything to hold on to, to bring her to safety.

Something long and thin brushed his side. He clutched at it. His fingers clasped the rough surface of bark. A branch. He shoved it away.

His lungs ached. Just a few seconds more and he'd find her. He could feel it.

The water burned his eyes. His mind grew fuzzy. Damn it. He had no choice. He needed air. If he drowned, he couldn't save his wife.

He kicked to the surface, sucked in a large breath, and submerged beneath the water, but all he could feel was cold, dark and empty. He had no idea which direction to search.

A circle of light illuminated the darkness above him. The sheriff. Thank God.

An odd blue-green aura lightened the water around him. At least Jared could make out shapes and shadows.

A flash of white caught his attention. Nearly out of air again, he swam toward the unusual object.

His heart skipped a beat. Gauzy white material floated past him in a ghostly blur. He lunged at it but grasped nothing but fabric.

It must have come off her.

He swept his arms right and left, each movement more and more desperate. She *had* to be here. He bumped into something and clutched at it. Another branch?

No. Not rough wood, but soft skin. A hand. An arm.

He grabbed at Alyssa and tugged. She wouldn't budge. He pulled again.

Still nothing.

Panic rose in his throat. Lungs nearly bursting, he propelled himself lower, running his hands over her torso and legs until he grasped a thick braid of rope. Sliding his hands down the line, he followed the trail to a large tire.

The bastard had weighted her down.

Jared shoved his hand into his pocket and gripped his knife with numbing fingers. Holding it with a death grip, he snapped it open and sawed through the hemp.

In his head, the seconds ticked by. He couldn't see. He

needed to breathe. The knife slipped and sliced across his thumb. He hardly felt the sting.

After what seemed an eternity, the last fibers of rope gave way. Alyssa didn't move.

He clutched her close. Kicking with everything he had, he catapulted toward the light above.

Jared broke the surface a few feet from the sheriff's boat. He sucked in more air. "Help her."

Kevin Redmond leaned over the edge of a small boat. "Got her." He pulled Alyssa in.

Jared crawled on board.

"Guy took off in a truck," the sheriff said. "I lost him."

Didn't matter. Jared would kill the guy later. With shaking hands, he turned his wife over. Her eyes were wide-open, sightless, the white gown draped across her gently swelled belly.

"Don't die on me, Alyssa!"

Jared leaned down and rested his cheek against her mouth, his finger on her neck, but no breath escaped, no pulse throbbed under her skin. Rain pelted them. He ignored it. He pressed his hands against her chest, rhythmically, frantically trying to revive her.

He'd heard her call out just moments ago.

"We'll get her to the hospital," Kevin shouted. "Keep at it."

The boat skidded across the surface of the lake toward the pier.

A crack echoed through the night when her ribs gave way. Wincing, Jared hesitated for a bare second but kept going.

He pressed his lips to hers and pushed one breath, two breaths into her lungs.

The boat stopped. An ambulance would never make it way out here in time.

"Get the truck started," Jared didn't even look up until he heard his beat-up Chevy purr. The headlights shined at them.

He gazed into his wife's face, ghostly white. His body went numb. This wasn't happening.

"Fight, Alyssa. Please, fight." He pressed his lips to her cold, wet mouth and puffed in once, twice, praying she'd cough up water.

She remained still, unmoving.

Jared scooped her into his arms and raced down the pier. "Don't give up." He jumped into the back of the truck and continued performing CPR, willing her to live, willing the family he'd always longed for to survive.

"Don't give up. Please, Alyssa. Don't give up on me, and I promise, I'll never give up on you."

Chapter One

Present day

If today's clear skies had reflected the turmoil twisting Courtney Jamison's heart into a quivering mass of uncertainty, the forecast should've indicated hurricane-gale winds, kiwi-sized hail and lightning slicing between skyscrapers across the city.

Instead it was a perfectly wonderful day. For most.

Courtney loved New York. The twenty-four-hour energy, the fashion, the events and especially her position as curator of her grandmother's legacy—one of the most prestigious art museums in the city.

She never would have anticipated the last eighteen months, but she'd found a joy she'd never expected. Then, one week ago her world had capsized. Whatever happened in the next hour, she had no doubt her life would never be the same.

The heavenly scent of brewed coffee laced with a touch of cinnamon wafted through the shop's air. The churn of blenders and mixers cut through the sounds of engines and horns piercing the door. She waited in this very ordinary setting for news that could destroy her world.

Maybe she'd been mistaken. After all, she hadn't been thinking clearly that night eighteen months ago. Just feeling. Maybe her memory of his face, the contour of his cheek, the quirk of his lips when he smiled…maybe the man she'd seen on the news hadn't been *him* at all.

It could happen. No need to borrow trouble when there was enough to be found in the world. The valuable advice had been one of the last bits of wisdom her mother had imparted before cancer had stolen her away from a ten-year-old who'd still needed those loving arms. Unfortunately, today was too critical *not* to worry.

Hers wasn't the only person whose life could change forever.

A bell's ring announced another patron. Courtney glanced up and her stomach flopped. The man's military haircut screamed his thirty-year Marine career. She'd hired him because he didn't frequent her family's social circles. No one would think Courtney, Edward Jamison's high-society daughter, would hire a private investigator who didn't boast a Fifth Avenue pedigree.

That fact alone made Joe Botelli precisely who she needed.

He gave her a quick nod and crossed the room toward her. "Ms. Jamison." He placed the folder between them and slid it across the table. "I found him. You were right. He stayed at the Waldorf that night."

She closed her eyes briefly, bracing herself for the rest. "Tell me."

The PI flipped open his notebook. "The highlights?"

She nodded. She could read the rest later, in the quiet of her penthouse, where she didn't have to maintain such rigid control on her emotions.

"Jared King, thirty-two years old. Until about three

years ago, desperate to keep his family's Texas ranch in the black by training rodeo horses and raising stock."

Jared. She rolled his first name around a few times, attaching it to the all-too-sensual dreams that invaded her sleep much too often. The moniker suited him. From what she'd seen on television, his apparent career was anything but expected.

"Jared King." She tested it aloud for the first time. "So he really is a *cowboy*?" Courtney sagged in her chair, her body going limp with disbelief. That's one she wouldn't have guessed until she'd seen his image a week ago. And definitely not based on the Armani suit he'd worn all too perfectly that weekend at the Waldorf Astoria. The Stetson, flannel shirt and well-worn jeans had been her one holdout of hope that she'd been wrong.

"Yes and no. He lives on a ranch that's been in his family for generations. It's on the outskirts of a small town called Carder in the southwestern part of Texas." Joe Botelli shifted in his seat. "Several years ago oil was discovered on his property. He went from scraping by to being one of the wealthiest men in Texas. The money didn't change his lifestyle much from what I can tell. He still spends most of his time working the cattle ranch and supplying stock to rodeos."

She could hardly wrap her brain around his words. Cattle, rodeo? The closest she'd ever been to either was flipping through channels on late night television and landing on an old 1940s Roy Rogers movie.

"Is…is he married?" she asked, trying not to reveal her nerves—or her fear. After her mother had died, she'd learned never to expose her thoughts or emotions, to maintain control and dignity at all times. Hopefully the skill would keep Botelli with the discerning gaze from realizing her true vulnerability. She'd taken a huge risk asking a stranger to investigate Jared King. Right now she had to wonder what she'd opened in the proverbial Pandora's box.

"Widower."

Jared had lost his wife. Her heart quivered in sympathy—and foreboding. What if he wanted…? She couldn't let her mind go there.

The PI leaned back in his chair as if he couldn't care less about her or the devastation his information had caused. "Do you want me to continue digging?"

Courtney gripped the folder in her hand as if her future depended on its content.

In truth, it did. Every fact she digested from the dossier would make Jared King more real. More dangerous. But she couldn't fall apart here. "His address is inside?" she asked.

At the man's nod, Courtney opened her three-year-old Prada purse and slid an envelope of cash across the table. No need to create a record of this transaction. She didn't plan on seeing the private investigator again. She'd shred his card when she arrived home. "Thank you."

The PI's brow arched, but he pocketed the money and stood. "If you need anything else—"

"I won't."

At her terse response, he gave a sharp nod, rose from the table and exited the coffee shop. Courtney barely noticed him leaving. She couldn't stop staring at the folder. For so long she'd dreaded—and wished for—this day.

Her phone dinged. A text came through.

Come home. Trouble.

The oddly curt message from her housekeeper closed her throat. Courtney clasped her neck. She couldn't breathe. The barista called out her order, but Courtney ignored the announcement. She had to get home. Without a backward glance, she raced out of the coffeehouse and flagged a taxi.

Panicked, she dialed home.

No answer.

Without a second thought she called her assistant to inform her she wouldn't be returning to the museum.

The cab swerved through traffic. Courtney took in a slow, deep breath. Perhaps she was overreacting. Since recognizing Jared, she'd been a rigid ball of nerves.

Despite logic trying to convince her everything was fine, her heart raced, slamming against her chest. She fought through the dread and clutched the door handle.

Luckily traffic was lighter than normal. The moment the taxi stopped in front of her building, she threw a hundred-dollar bill at the surprised cabby and jumped out.

"Good day, Ms. Jamison," the doorman commented, holding the heavy glass open for her.

Unlike normal, she couldn't muster a smile or chitchat. Ignoring Reggie's furrowed brow of concern, she hit the button for the elevator.

She slipped the key card into the penthouse lock, but the familiar click didn't sound. The door silently eased open.

"Marilyn?" she called. "What's wrong?"

Courtney skidded to a halt. Her sitter lay on the living room floor, eyes staring unblinking and lifeless at the ceiling. Blood pooled around her head, seeping into her gray hair.

She dropped to her knees, her finger slipping through the blood when she searched for a pulse.

Nothing.

Only a split second passed before the shock leached into Courtney's throat. "Dylan!" Courtney tore through the living area, searching frantically. Where was her son? She grabbed the fireplace poker and gripped it tight before racing into her baby's bedroom.

She froze.

The crib had been overturned, the chest of drawers upended, clothes strewn across the floor.

Courtney whirled around. Her gaze landed on the closet door. Her stomach rolled and bile rose in her throat. Was the murderer still there? Did he have her baby?

She picked her way through the chaos, clutching her makeshift weapon with both hands. She reached out, barely able to breathe.

Terrified of what she'd see, unable to stop the horrifying images flying through her mind, she yanked open the door and flipped on the light.

Her knees gave way.

Empty.

"Dylan, where are you?"

She begged for a jabber a laugh, even a cry, but nothing. Within minutes she'd searched the rest of the apartment. Only one room left. *Her* room.

She slammed through the door and froze. In the center of the perfectly pristine bed lay her nine-month old son, pillows penning him in a makeshift crib on the bed.

He wasn't moving.

Courtney's heart stopped. She raced over to her heart and soul, terrified of what she might find. She leaned over the peaceful countenance and her body went limp.

"Dylan?" Courtney's hand shook. The fireplace iron thudded to the floor. She reached out to touch her baby boy's face.

Her son's chest rose and fell. He was alive.

Choking back a sob of relief, Courtney scooped up her son with noodle-like arms. The movement caused Dylan to screw up his face and let out a loud yell.

"What happened, baby?" She glanced around the room, but nothing else appeared to be out of place.

Her gaze landed on Dylan's stuffed lamb sitting on one pillow. A sheet of paper was pinned to the toy. She scanned the words in horror.

If we wanted to kidnap him, your son would be gone.

If we wanted to kill him, your son would be dead.

When we come back, we WILL take him. We WILL kill him.

Unless we receive $3,680,312.00.

We will call you with instructions.

If you contact the police or FBI, he will die.

If you don't get us the money within 72 hours, he will die.

Don't try to be smart. You can't hide from us.

With a shuddering breath, Courtney tried to comprehend what she was reading. The strange amount of money, the taunting threats. Nothing made sense.

She gazed into Dylan's one brown eye and one green eye, trying to smile with reassurance, all the while backing toward the door. "We have to get you out of here."

Bundling up the diaper bag, Courtney raced out of

the apartment with one last sorrowful glance at Marilyn. What kind of monster would kill the sweet woman who loved Dylan so much?

She hugged her child close. "I'll keep you safe, Jelly Bean. I promise."

ALMOST TWO HOURS LATER, the car service's Mercedes pulled up in front of her father's Greenwich, Connecticut, mansion. Courtney turned her cell phone over and over in her hand. Her thumb hovered over the emergency key. For the thousandth time on the ride there, she considered calling law enforcement.

Something had stopped her once again. Maybe it was all those television programs that showed how easy it was to hack a phone call. She couldn't take the risk. Not with Jelly Bean. The kidnapper had come into her *home*. Had touched her baby boy. Had killed Marilyn.

A shiver vibrated down her arms. Part of her kept telling herself this couldn't be happening. Threats like this were the stuff of crime novels and television shows, and yet every time she reread the note and pictured poor Marilyn lying on the floor of her penthouse, she knew it was her reality.

Which was why she was about to make an unprecedented request. Courtney rubbed her eyes. She'd never gone to her father with an open hand, but she didn't know where else to turn. Her job, the penthouse, everything but her salary was part of her grandmother's trust specifically created to fund the museum. She didn't have the money to pay the murderer what he wanted.

She had to believe her father would give her what she needed. He had to. Even though he'd been furious—not to mention disappointed—when she'd found herself pregnant and had refused to name the father.

She'd been too embarrassed to tell him she didn't know the man's name.

"You getting out or what?" the driver asked from the front seat.

Courtney nodded and unbuckled the car seat. She rounded the vehicle to retrieve Dylan, and the driver met her at the door. He opened it and she grabbed the carrier, careful not to jar the baby.

"How much do I owe you—?"

The man shook his head. "It's been taken care of. I was asked to give you this when we arrived." He handed her a padded envelope. Before she could open it, he jumped into the Mercedes and screeched out of the driveway.

One look and her gut sank. She recognized the handwriting on the label. She lowered Dylan to the ground and gently tore open the envelope. She pulled out a phone with a sticky note attached.

Keep the phone with you.
Keep your silence. Especially from your father.
And don't forget, you can't hide from us. We'll always find you.

The note crinkled in her grasp. How did he know so much? The words blurred on the paper. Her knees shook; her legs quivered. She nearly sank to the ground. Her gaze whipped to the now empty driveway. Was the driver blackmailing her? She shook her head. Somehow she doubted it. He wouldn't have wanted to show his face. Besides, he'd said someone else had paid him.

The blackmailers had made their point clear, though.

She'd better follow his instructions exactly. No police, no law enforcement. She couldn't imagine what the cops would think when they found Marilyn. She'd considered phoning in an anonymous tip, but she couldn't risk being arrested. Not before she was certain Dylan was safe.

"Okay, you can do this. You can do anything for Dylan." She shoved the phone into her pocket and stumbled through the front door of the mansion. The eight-thousand-square-foot home had been in the family for four generations, the money originated from more than a few deals with Andrew Carnegie.

Courtney had never ruminated on her family's money much. It had always just been there. She'd never been more thankful for the privilege than she was today.

She glanced at her son. Today the money she'd always taken for granted would save Dylan.

She refused to consider that the first payment wouldn't be enough to get rid of the blackmailer. One step at a time.

The foyer's Baccarat chandelier glittered high above her, though the butler didn't appear out of nowhere like he usually did.

"Fitz?" she called.

No response. How strange.

"Clarissa? Burbank? Anyone here?"

Her footsteps echoed on the marble floor. Where was the rest of the staff?

A horrific possibility hit her squarely in the chest. What if the killer had come here. Oh God.

She started to run from room to room. No. This wasn't right. Bare rooms, boxes, paintings missing.

"F-father?" she called, her voice shaky. She opened the door to her mother's old sitting room. The blank space on the wall slammed into her. The Degas painting her mother had purchased just before her death was gone.

"Father!" she shouted again.

"In the library." Her father's voice filtered through the deserted hallways.

Something was wrong. He sounded strange, his words slurred. Courtney hurried through the double doors. A stack of boxes littered the floor. He huddled behind his mahogany desk, staring across the room as if in a trance. A half-empty bottle of cognac sat at his elbow, an empty old-fashioned Waterford glass directly in front of him.

Carefully, she set Dylan down on the floor and ran to her father. "What's going on?" Was he actually leaving their family home? It didn't make sense.

He shoved his hand through his already mussed hair and cleared his throat. "I should've called you sooner." He let out a long sigh.

She studied his bleary gaze. Drinking again. Why wasn't she surprised? "Father, I don't mean to be rude, but right now I need your help. For Dylan. We need three million dollars."

He blinked up at her, confusion lacing his eyes. He reached for the century-old bottle, poured four fingers and swigged it down. "No."

She couldn't have heard him right. "You don't understand. Please. I'll move out of the penthouse. I'll find somewhere else to live. But I need that money." Panic raised her voice. He had to help. She didn't want to reveal the threat. She couldn't afford for her father to contact the FBI or the cops. He always wanted to fix everything. Had made it his mission to protect her from the time her mother had died.

"It wouldn't matter," he said. "I'm sorry. So very, very sorry."

"What are you talking about?" She gripped the lapel of his coat. "I haven't asked for anything since I started working. I make my own way—"

He pressed a finger over her lips and gazed at her with bloodshot eyes.

"I'd give you the money if I could, Courtney. You don't know how much I wish I could, but I can't." He looked away. "All the money is gone."

Chapter Two

Spring didn't bring new beginnings to Last Chance Ranch; it choked 'em dry in the West Texas sun. Jared King had learned long ago that his family's cattle spread richly deserved its name. It had for six generations.

Now, he even had to fight his north-side neighbor, Ned Criswell, for water that was rightfully theirs. A never ending feud he'd tried to escape for years.

When Jared had volunteered for the Army at eighteen, he'd been convinced he would never succumb to the ranch's bad karma. What a young fool he'd been. After being discharged he'd brought home a beautiful young wife and pretended he could find hope where only despair had dug in roots. After Alyssa's death, he'd finally given in to whatever mojo the half-million acres possessed. He wouldn't try to buck destiny again.

He tilted his Stetson against the afternoon glare and hooked his boot on the sturdy rail of the bull pen. He leveled the dead-cold stare that would have sent his ranch hands quaking and running for cover on Ned Criswell and his no-good son. The two burley men refused to back off. "You can't keep that river dammed up. Last Chance Lake is down several feet already."

Ned's face turned beet red, and he stuck out his barrel chest. "The water stays on my side of the property line until you stop those company men from traipsing across my land."

Jared head throbbed. They'd replayed this scene countless time over the years. The bad blood between the families stretched back decades, but Ned Criswell had become even more ruthless. And relentless. He might actually do it, just to get back at Jared's father, even though he'd passed away years ago.

The son, on the other hand, Chuck Criswell was all about the money. And the power.

"The water's running low for my cattle," Jared said, fighting to keep his tone reasonable for the moment. "You don't want to take this fight any further, Ned. You know I'll win."

"My father has as many friends in Austin as you do. We want what's coming to us." Chuck spit a wad of tobacco on the ground.

"Shut up," Ned said, glaring at his son.

Even with the same goal, the two men couldn't show a united front. A sure way to lose. Jared was fine with that.

A loud snort sounded from the enclosure next to them. Chuck scooted away from the fence. "That bull is a menace." He frowned. "You shouldn't have saved him."

Sometimes Jared agreed. Angel Maker had earned his name. He'd nearly gored a half dozen of Jared's best hands. The black bull from hell pawed at the dirt, giving Jared the evil eye. He'd saved the bad-tempered beast from being put down after a deadly episode at the San Antonio Rodeo earlier this year. The bull's bloodline would solidify Jared's place as the premier stock supplier for the Professional Bull Riders rodeo circuit. His money might come from oil and gas now, but at his heart he was still a rancher, and the rodeo was in his blood.

Besides, Jared had a penchant for lost causes…at least those that didn't touch his heart.

Angel Maker butted his head against the fence. This time Ned joined his son, away from the pen. Jared bit back a smile. If the animal had wanted to do any real damage that pen wouldn't stop him. "He likes you."

The older man bit out a curse. "You gonna say something to those oil guys or not?"

"You signed a contract. They have a right to cross your land on the road."

"I changed my mind."

Yeah. He wanted more money. Jared recognized the gleam in Ned's eye. The Criswells had a weakness for gambling—and Chuck had developed a rep for being particularly unlucky. Rumor had it that between the football play-offs, Super Bowl and the latest NCAA basketball tournament, the Criswells had cleaned out their bank accounts.

"If you don't knock down that dam, Ned. I'll do it for you."

"I don't like threats. You're worse than your old man, King. And he was an SOB."

"You took advantage of him and nearly cost Dad our land," Jared said, with a bite. "But I'm not the pushover my father was. The Army taught me how to fight."

Ned's face paled, but like most cowards, he didn't face a battle, he ran.

"This isn't over." He turned to his son. "Start the truck."

Chuck ran over to the brand-new F-350 and jumped

in. Ned followed and heaved himself into the front seat. "I'm keeping the dam."

Chuck gunned the accelerator, leaving a cloud of dust in their wake.

Jared rubbed his brow where the headache had erupted just beneath the surface. Ned had to know he was on thin ice diverting a waterway that flowed across more than his own property. Problem was, bureaucracy could take months to deal with it and the spring livestock needed that water.

"I say we send some equipment in and bust a hole in the dam." Jared's foreman sidled up to him. "The Criswells won't give in," Roscoe Hines said under his breath. "They're getting desperate." He glanced at their newest hand. "Tim, try to distract Angel Maker."

Jared kneaded the base of his neck in exasperation. "Ned was a bully when he screwed my dad. He hasn't changed. He won't back off even if it's in his own best interest. Using water as a leverage to change our deal is a mistake. He's doing a lot of damage and he won't win. Our contract is ironclad."

The clatter of wooden planks and the banging of metal clamored from Angel Maker's pen.

"Speaking of bad blood…" Roscoe raced to the bull's pen. "Get out of there, Tim."

The eighteen-year-old hand jumped over the fence and out of the pen. Angel Maker rammed the wood, and it creaked under the two-and-a-half-ton bull's weight.

Tim's freckled-face had gone red with exertion. He bent over and sucked wind, but his eyes gleamed with challenge.

Roscoe shook his head in incredulity and sauntered

back over to Jared. "That kid's either going to be a hell of a good hand, or he's going to wind up dead."

"I'm betting the former," Jared said. "Reminds me of Derek the first time you guys drove up to the ranch after Dad hired you."

"That son of mine was some daredevil, that's for sure." Roscoe smiled, that proud grin only a father could have for his son. "He said he'd come visit soon, but every time he makes plans, work interferes."

"We need to get him out here, see if he's forgotten how to ride."

Man, they'd had fun together as kids on a ranch with no fences, no boundaries. The moment Derek had arrived on the ranch he and Jared had been inseparable. There'd been hard work and a lot of chores; they'd gotten into their share of trouble, but Jared hadn't minded. They'd faced the discipline together. From junior high rodeo through high school football, up through and including enlisting at the Army recruitment office. Strange how life had taken them in different directions. Their paths had diverged so much, he hadn't seen Derek in a couple of years.

"He likes his new job?"

"He seems to. Makes more money than I ever dreamed." Roscoe shook his head in befuddlement. "Not sure how exactly. Something to do with computers."

"He was always book smart," Jared said. He'd have to give his old friend a call. Roscoe had been looking a little under the weather lately. Jared couldn't convince his foreman to see the doc. Maybe Derek could.

The roar of an engine broke into his thoughts just as a baby blue Mustang drove up to the main house about fifty or so feet away.

"You expecting someone?" Roscoe asked, eyeing the vehicle.

"Not that I know of." Who'd drive a dang fool car like that onto his ranch?

"Maybe someone else on the hunt for all those greenbacks you got stashed in the bank."

Jared scowled at his foreman. A few five-times-removed relatives had come out of the woodwork once word of the oil went public. Jared had tried to help until they'd made it clear they hadn't wanted a leg up, but a perpetual handout. Once he'd cut off the money, they'd disappeared once again.

The car stopped and the engine went quiet. It sat there for several moments until one long, shapely leg, then another, stepped out.

The woman ran her fingers through her hair. The sun gleamed off the blonde locks. Roscoe let out a long, slow whistle.

Jared couldn't move. He blinked once. Then again.

It couldn't be. Not her.

She stood still, in her four-inch heels and tailored dress, looking like a city girl who had been dropped into a foreign land. She tucked her short hair behind one ear and hesitated, turning in a circle, taking in the lay of his ranch.

He fought the urge to wash the dirt away and waited, his breath quickening as the lines of her back then the curves of her front came into view. It was her, all right. He didn't know her name, but what he did know made his libido perk up and his heart thud to attention for the first time in the eighteen months since he'd held her in his arms.

Unable to stop himself, Jared crossed the yard. The

closer he got, the more he noticed the fidgety movement of her hands.

At least she couldn't hide her nerves. Made him feel a bit better, because *his* damn hands were shaking too.

About ten feet away from her, he paused.

She faced him and lifted her gaze to his.

His breath caught. It *was* her. She was here. On *his* land. Exactly like he'd dreamed more times than he could count.

Her cobalt blue eyes widened as if she couldn't believe it was him.

Well, ditto.

The rumblings of a tractor, the whinny of the horses, the snort of Angel Maker faded into the background. The world melted away; his heartbeat whooshed inside his head.

She blinked and glanced over her shoulder into the vehicle.

Her movement shocked him back to reality. He strode toward her, forcing himself not to hurry too fast.

"I'm surprised," he said, determined to keep his tone nonchalant.

"As am I," she said.

Her voice was a bit huskier than he remembered. He studied her face and detected tension around her mouth, redness staining her eyes.

They stared at each other, the awkward silence continuing far too long. What was he supposed to say? *I came back to the hotel room but you were gone?* Or maybe the more appropriate, *So, we slept together a year and a half ago and the earth moved. What's your name?*

At that moment, Velma marched down the steps of the main house, wiping her hands on a dish towel. Not much gave away her age, except her silvered-auburn hair and her devil-may-care curiosity. She wasn't shy about inserting herself into almost any conversation either.

She shot him a piercing stare and tilted her head. He could see her interest building. A small curse escaped under his breath. His housekeeper was more like his grandmother than anything. She'd worked for the King family as long as Jared could remember. She knew him too well, and unfortunately, she'd developed a sixth sense whenever Jared found himself in a situation that could turn awkward at any moment.

Her gaze alternated between him and their visitor. "Quite a set of wheels, boyo. You must be drooling."

She sent him that knowing gaze she'd used when she knew he wanted something in the worst way. She had no idea. Unfortunately, Jared could feel the heat flooding his cheeks.

"And who might your friend be?" Velma asked with a satisfied grin, walking boldly over and sticking out a hand to introduce herself.

"I'm Courtney Jamison," the woman responded. A nervous smile tilted their visitor's lips.

Courtney Jamison. He let her name settle across his mind. It suited her. It screamed New York and the Waldorf Astoria where they'd met. It definitely didn't suit the Last Chance Ranch. Not by half.

A cry sounded from the car.

"You have a little one?" Velma asked, her smile lighting as bright as the West Texas sun on a clear day.

"His name is Dylan." Courtney reached into the backseat, fiddled with something in the car and pulled a baby from the vehicle.

"Almost a year?" Velma asked.

"Nine months," Courtney said softly, looking straight at Jared.

"A big boy then."

Nine months. That meant she got pregnant about eighteen months ago. New York.

It couldn't be. It was just one night. One…

As if in a trance, he closed the distance between him and Courtney. He stared into the little boy's eyes. One brown. One green. The baby had heterochromia. Just like him.

Jared held out his hand. It shook. Dylan leaned against his mother's chest and dipped his face into her neck.

"Dylan," Courtney whispered. "This is your daddy."

The words struck Jared harder than Angel Maker's most vicious charge. His mind whirled in denial even as the truth peeked at him from beneath long, baby-fine lashes. He couldn't deny that he stood face-to-face with the one thing he'd never believed he'd have.

Dylan tilted his head and a smile lit his face. He leaned forward with outstretched hands. Jared bent closer. The baby grabbed his hat and threw it to the ground, chuckling.

"Takes after you, boyo," Velma said. "That's plain to see."

A strange white noise buzzed in Jared's ears. He shook the static away. "How did you find me?" he asked, barely able to croak out the words.

He didn't want to say more. Velma and Roscoe both had big ears, and they were obviously curious. He'd be fielding a whole lot of questions before sunset hit anyway.

Jared picked up his hat and held it toward Dylan. He couldn't take his eyes off the baby. The little guy grabbed the brim and tugged.

Strong grip, his son had.

His son.

What was he supposed to do about that?

"I saw a news story about the bull you saved. That's how I found you." Courtney nodded toward Angel Maker, who appeared to be eyeing Tim for a second soul-fearing battle. "That's him?"

"In the flesh."

He wouldn't be diverted by that animal. He had a million questions, but he'd start with one. "Why are you here, Courtney?"

Her name caressed his tongue, and he lingered on the taste for a moment.

She glanced away, not meeting his gaze. Something didn't feel right. The hair on the back of his neck stiffened to attention. She chewed on her lip and seemed to be searching for the words.

"You could've called," he said. "Or had a lawyer contact me. Instead, you traveled halfway across the country with our son with no way of predicting my reaction. Why?"

She straightened her back and lifted her chin. At this angle, he could take in every detail of her reddened eyes and tightly drawn lips. Something was definitely wrong.

"I came for your help. Someone has threatened to kill our son."

COURTNEY HAD NEVER seen anyone react so fast. The words had barely left her lips when Jared's gaze scanned the perimeter. The muscle in his jawline pulsed, and a flat, dangerous stillness settled through his body.

"Come with me," he said, gripping her arm with a firm hand.

He didn't take a second look at Dylan, didn't hesitate. He pulled her toward the sprawling ranch style house and glanced over his shoulder. "Roscoe, check in with the hands. I want to know if anyone's seen anything…off."

"But we've already doubled security because of—"

"Triple-check everything," Jared snapped.

The grizzled cowboy didn't hesitate. He gave a curt nod and hurried into a huge barn past the pen holding the angry-looking bull.

Courtney had never experienced a more surreal moment. Jared didn't question her; he didn't look at her like she was crazy. He simply acted.

He shuffled her up the steps and across the wide wooden porch. He opened the screen door and held it while she disappeared inside. She couldn't quite accept the foreign place where she found herself. On an actual Texas ranch in the middle of nowhere after a too long drive from an airport that had taken all of ten minutes to walk from one end to the other.

Not to mention she currently stood only a short city block away from a vicious-looking bull, several stereotypical cowboys, a bevy of horses and a large barn. If it hadn't been for the beat-up pickup truck she'd parked besides, she'd have wondered what century she'd landed in.

"Velma, lock the front door, shut the curtains and stay inside," Jared ordered the woman hurrying behind them. "I don't want either of you out in the open until I know exactly what's going on."

The housekeeper didn't pause or argue, but moved in a whirlwind to follow his instructions. Jared tugged on Courtney's arm. Normally she would have resisted the manhandling, but he'd stunned her. She hadn't even showed him the note yet.

"My luggage—"

"I'll bring it in later."

The curt words brooked no argument. At Jared's tone Dylan squirmed in her arms, whimpering a bit. She bounced him, holding him closer. "It's okay, Jelly Bean. We're going to be fine."

She could only pray she wasn't lying.

Courtney kissed his forehead and breathed in his baby powder scent. She touched her cheek to Dylan's soft hair and closed her eyes. The blackmailer had forced her to keep his cell phone. She wasn't stupid. He had to be tracking her. He had to know she'd flown to Texas. She'd believed him when he'd promised she couldn't hide.

She'd needed help and law enforcement was off the table. She'd risked everything coming here. The blackmailer had been perfectly clear. He wanted money. Since she didn't have any and neither did her father, she had no choice. Jared was her only option to protect her son.

After a glance through the shutters in the front window, he faced his housekeeper. "Velma, show Courtney into my study. I'll check the back door."

Brow furrowed, Velma crossed the stone foyer to a set of large mahogany double doors. "Come along, dearie."

Courtney followed, trying to keep her increasingly unhappy son calm. She rubbed his back in slow, circular motions. Velma snapped closed the curtains on three large windows before flipping on a series of track lights to brighten the wood paneled room.

Dylan clutched at the neck of Courtney's Louis Vuitton dress, his mouth drooling, his face reddening.

"I know what you want," she whispered, gently pushing his light brown hair off his forehead. She settled into a large leather sofa and zipped open the diaper bag, pulling out a teething biscuit.

Dylan grabbed the treat in both hands and stuffed it into his mouth, gnawing with gusto. He sagged against her, content for the moment.

"You know your boy well," Velma remarked with approval.

"He's my son."

"And mine." Jared stood, outlined by the dark wood door frame, a rifle crooked over his bent arm. "The house is secure. I've instructed four hands to keep watch. Velma, I could use some of that coffee cake you made yesterday."

"Go easy, boyo," she cautioned with a small pat on his arm.

Courtney shivered at the warning. Jared didn't respond, but firmly closed the doors behind Velma's retreating figure. The catch clicked into place.

Slowly he faced her, his tall figure and broad shoulders shrinking the large room. Most New York apartments would fit comfortably into a tiny corner of his home.

She squirmed in her seat, feeling at a distinct disadvantage. If Dylan hadn't been so comfortably settled on her lap, she would have faced Jared standing instead of him looming above her. The weapon didn't help.

As if reading her mind, he propped the gun in the corner, squatted down in front of her and stared unblinkingly at Dylan. The baby gazed back, still working on his biscuit. Jared thrust a hand through his short dark hair. It shook slightly and a flash of insight struck Courtney. He may have gone all alpha on her, but their son had Jared King spooked.

Cautiously, gently he touched Dylan's leg, then clasped

his tiny hand. The little boy grabbed his finger and squeezed. A small smiled tilted Jared's lips. A sad sigh escaped him and reluctantly he pulled away.

"Who wants to hurt our son?" he asked with a frown, his focus still glued to Dylan.

Despite some misgivings, Courtney had no choice but to trust Jared. That's why she'd come. She tugged a sheet of paper from the zippered pocket of the diaper bag and handed it over. "I found this pinned to one of Dylan's stuffed animals yesterday. Someone was in my apartment. They k-killed…"

Her voice broke as she relayed what little she knew.

He read the note and with each word of her explanation Jared's eyes grew icier. His jaw muscle pulsed. "Did you call the police?"

She shook her head. "I couldn't risk their involvement with that note. I had to protect Dylan."

"I see." Jared stared at the floor, his gaze thoughtful. "Leaving was your only option."

His words were a statement of fact, not a question and the vice around her heart eased a bit. Maybe she'd done the right thing after all.

Who else could she trust after everything that had happened? Her entire body shook as her mind rewound yesterday's horror.

"I left Marilyn. On the floor. Alone. Her family lives in Maine. They don't even know what happened."

Courtney pressed the heel of her hand against her eyes to keep back the tears. The guilt tore through her. "I was so afraid they might come back, I went to my father's house. I thought I'd be safe there, but whoever did this knew I'd hire a car. The note warned me, and I believe them."

She'd never felt so alone.

On the drive from the airport, each time she'd passed a police car, she'd considered flagging him down, and every time she'd let the vehicle pass her by. "I couldn't stop looking over my shoulder the entire trip here. I kept imagining every person I encountered was following me."

She clutched Jared's arm. "I won't involve law enforcement. It's too risky. He knows too much."

Would Jared agree? Was she being foolish? They'd killed Marilyn in cold blood. She couldn't bear it if Dylan… A stark shiver skittered through her. No, she was doing the right thing. She had to be.

"Hey there." Jared touched her knee and squeezed gently. "I understand, more than you know."

Relieved Jared seemed to see the situation her way, Courtney's shoulders relaxed, but only slightly. "Good."

"Courtney, do you think the blackmailer knows who I am? Is he aware Dylan is my son and that you've come to me?"

"They can't know. *I* didn't know your name until a week ago." She bit her lip. She had to tell him everything, but if he turned her away… She let out a long, slow breath. "I only learned where you lived yesterday, but…" Her gut twisted and she pulled the cell phone from her purse. "They ordered me to keep this phone with me at all times. If they can track it, they know exactly where I am."

Jared didn't speak for a moment. Courtney held her breath, every muscle in her body taut with apprehension.

"There goes any advantage we might have had." He shot to his feet and paced, "Okay. Let's minimize your exposure as a precaution. Where did your plane land?"

"San Antonio." She rubbed the bridge of her nose.

Why hadn't she thought this through more? "I should have driven, shouldn't I? I used our real names to board."

"It's not easy to get passenger lists unless you're with law enforcement or a hacker," Jared said, his voice calm and reassuring. "Most rental company cars have GPS tracking, though."

She slapped her hand over her mouth. "I didn't even consider that possibility."

"Why should you? One of my hands will return the vehicle to the airport, but we should still assume they know you're here and will contact you."

Jared settled across from her and leaned forward. "Let's get down to the real question. Are you asking me to help catch whoever wrote the note or do you want to pay the ransom?"

Panic rose in her gut and she clutched tighter at Dylan. "I'd do anything to protect him." Courtney avoided his piercing gaze. "The thing is, I could scrape together maybe fifteen percent of it, but I don't have the kind of money they want."

"They were very specific in their request. Are you telling me that not only does the ransom amount hold no meaning to you, you don't have enough to pay?" Jared stilled. "I don't know much about New York fashion, but that's a very expensive designer dress you're wearing and the Waldorf doesn't come cheap. What kind of game are you playing?"

His narrowed look pinned her to her seat. She averted her gaze.

"It's not a game." She twisted the button on Dylan's clothes, struggling to ignore the suspicious tone in his voice. "I thought my father could give me the money, but his situation has…changed. Last week the bank ran out of patience."

"So that's why you're here." Jared stiffened and pulled away from her. "You don't need me. You need my money."

His tone indicted her, and she couldn't blame him. Most people would've been insulted and deep down the tone stung, but she understood. How many people had come into her life to get what they could? She'd learned a long time ago not to trust so easily. Or let anyone in. It was one of the main reasons she'd chosen not to live off the family money.

That didn't stop her from bristling at the accusation. "I came here to figure out what to do," she said. "I can't deny that you're the one person who can help me pay the ransom, but you're also the only one who has as much to lose as I do. I'm out of options to keep my…our son safe."

Our son. She'd have to get used to saying that.

Jared didn't speak for a moment. His reproachful gaze burned into her. She met it with unblinking eyes. Obviously he didn't doubt Dylan was his son. How could he? Their matching eyes were the tell. But the threat, the money, that could be an elaborate hoax. If Jared didn't believe her, she had no plan B.

She gnawed on her lower lip considering her options. There were none.

"We're not paying." The muscle in his jaw pulsed. "I refuse to be blackmailed. They'll just keep coming and it will never end."

She opened her mouth to speak, but he shook his head. "This is nonnegotiable. I'll do whatever it takes to keep our son safe. Giving into a blackmailer isn't the answer. I know—" His voice cracked. "Excuse me."

He quickly rose, scooped up the rifle and strode out of the room, shutting the door with a soft click.

Courtney stared after him. She wasn't quite sure what had just happened. She rocked Dylan against her, staring at the closed doors. Jared King wasn't what she'd expected. He definitely wasn't the suave man she'd encountered in the bar of the Waldorf, but she didn't need that man. She needed a fighter, and she'd witnessed the fury in his eyes.

For the first time since she'd walked into her apartment she felt a slight easing in her breath. Jared King was a warrior. A warrior with money.

A warrior willing to help them.

Whatever he thought of her, something in the set of his jaw gave her a glimmer of hope that Jared wouldn't fail.

She had to believe that. For Dylan's sake…and her own.

JARED SAGGED AGAINST the heavy doors of his study, his entire body shaking. The idea someone might kidnap his son… This couldn't be happening. Not again.

Though unlike Alyssa, who had been taken without warning, the threat to his son had put them on notice. He would do whatever it took to prevent the abduction.

This time, the outcome would be much different. Only one question ate at his gut. Was Courtney Jamison telling the truth. Was she a victim, or was she after his money? And how could he be sure?

He'd find out which, but it didn't impact his actions. Whether she was trying to play him or not, he'd never forgive himself if anything happened to Dylan.

The rest…well, the truth would come out. It always did.

Velma exited the kitchen carrying a tray. "What's wrong?"

"Someone's threatened to kidnap my son. They demanded a lot of money or they'll take him."

She gasped, set the tray on the foyer table and walked over to him. She pressed her palm to his chest in comfort. "This isn't five years ago."

"You're damned right it isn't. I'll be smarter this time." Jared shoulders knotted as he stood there. He couldn't meet Velma's gaze. He gritted his teeth. "It feels the same. I'm shaking, Velma. Like the moment I walked into the nursery and found the message."

"It's not the same. It's not *him*. This doesn't have anything to do with you or your past. You didn't even know about the boy until she arrived."

"Maybe." Jared shot Velma a sidelong glance. "Did you see him, Velma? He looks like me."

She patted his cheek. "I know, boyo. No doubt about who his daddy is."

Jared stared at the scuffed toes of his boots. "I'm going to lose him, you know. Even if we catch the person threatening my son, Courtney won't stay. They don't belong here."

"Just because Alyssa didn't fit in—"

"Like you always say, the past is over." He gently eased away from her. "Have Tim quit messing with Angel Maker so he can bring in Courtney's luggage. Put her in the room across from mine. I want to be close at all times." The staccato words came out harsher and more clipped than he intended. He bent down and kissed her cheek in apology. "I'll be back. I have some plans to make."

He turned on his heel.

"Jared?" Velma called out. "He needs a safe place to sleep while he's here."

He slowed his pace, but didn't stop.

"Don't let the past rule the present, boyo. You'll regret it."

Did she think he didn't know that? Did she have any idea how tempted he was to grab that little boy and hug him tight. To take Courtney into his arms and convince her that they could make a city girl–country boy relationship work like a Hallmark movie.

Except life wasn't a movie. There were no happy-everafters. Not in his world.

There was only reality. And bad guys won way too often.

Determined not to let history repeat itself, he strode down a barren hallway. His first order of business was to take care of his son. He veered from the door of the brand-new wing he'd completed just last year and made his way to the end of the original house's hallway.

He hadn't opened the door separating the old part of the house since he'd renovated, though Velma kept the place spotless. He stepped through, into the past. A white door loomed at the end of the corridor. His heart pounded, rushing through his ears. He forced his boots to cross the decade-old carpet to the end. For a moment he stood there. With a deep breath, he turned the knob and walked inside.

A never-used crib rested in the corner of the room. A yellow crocheted blanket lay abandoned on the floor. As his gaze took inventory of each item, one after another, pain twisted his heart. He would have bent over in agony if he'd allowed himself to feel. This room represented his failure to protect his family. And the threat that still loomed large over his life, a threat he would never deny.

He let his attention settle on a large hole in the drywall, marring the perfect paint job. A sledgehammer lay beneath the opening, a tool he'd swung with anger and fury and unrelenting grief.

Jared hadn't ventured inside the room in five years. He almost hadn't climbed out of the dark abyss after losing Alyssa and their unborn daughter. He couldn't go through that kind of pain again.

Jared would make it impossible for the blackmailers to harm his son. To do that, he needed to identify the person who wrote the ransom note.

Actually, it was more like a blackmail note. A demand before the kidnapping. Strange. Dylan hadn't been taken, but he could have been.

Why? What was the end game? To take a nine-month-old baby? To hurt Courtney? The more he considered the note she'd shared with him, the more he kept coming back to the unusual ransom amount. The number had to be the key.

He'd do whatever it took to find out who had threatened his son, and make them pay.

And then what? Jared closed his eyes. The moment he'd recognized Dylan as his child, his soul had threatened to reawaken.

He couldn't allow it.

After it was over he'd send both of them away, back to the city, where they belonged.

And when they left, Jared had no doubt what was left of his heart would crumble to dust.

Chapter Three

A bright beam of afternoon sun slipped through the closed curtains and cut a shard of light across the study's rug. A few muffled shouts echoed from outside, but they were orders, not panic.

No way anyone could have followed her already... right? Jared was just being cautious. Exactly as she'd hoped.

Courtney glanced down at Dylan. The biscuit had fallen from his hand. He'd succumbed to sleep. At least someone felt safe after the last twenty-four hours.

She brushed his hair off his brow. "Oh, Jelly Bean. What have we gotten ourselves into?"

Her mind whirled with confusion. She didn't know what to think. On the one hand Jared appeared to be enamored with his son. On the other, he'd obviously felt used because of his money and had vanished out of the room as if he wanted nothing to do with her.

In any other situation, Courtney might have stalked out and headed back to the airport, but she didn't have that option. Neither of them did. Not when the most important person in their lives was so very vulnerable.

Dylan sniffed and turned his head against her breast.

He snuggled in closer and she closed her eyes, just holding him.

Nothing could happen to him. She wouldn't let him be harmed. No matter what the consequences.

She'd already made too many mistakes. Whoever had threatened her knew enough about her habits to recognized that she hired cars from a single trusted vendor. They'd obviously been watching her for a while.

She'd resigned herself that the blackmailer would follow her and find her. She had no choice but to see her plan through.

A soft knock sounded on the door.

Velma walked in and set a tray down on the coffee table. "I brought coffee and cake," she said in a whisper, a frown worrying her brow.

The housekeeper glanced from Courtney to Dylan and back again. She shook her head slowly and clicked her tongue. "This isn't good."

Courtney stiffened, frowning at the woman who'd seemed almost too friendly outside. "I'm only here for Dylan. Believe me," Courtney retorted in a tight whisper.

"Calm down, dearie. I'm not judging you." Velma studied her with an eerie gaze, as if she were trying to peer directly into Courtney's soul.

After several moments, Velma nodded. She'd obviously made a decision. "You were right to come. Jared will protect you and your son, and he needed to know about young Dylan. It's just…" Velma poured a cup of coffee, and a bit sloshed over the side.

"Bother." She mopped up the spill, then gave up and sat in the chair opposite Courtney.

"I'm sorry for snapping. My nerves are frazzled," Courtney muttered. She chewed on her lower lip. Dylan shifted against her chest, and she cradled the baby protectively. "All that matters to me is him."

"As it should." Velma twisted her hands in her apron before raising her chin and meeting Courtney's gaze. "I'll say this only once, and we'll never speak of it again. If you hurt Jared, I won't let it pass. You'll find me a formidable enemy."

Courtney didn't know how to respond. She opened her mouth to speak and Velma held up her hand.

"*But*, if you are who I believe you to be, I'll stand beside you and fight the powers of hell to protect Jared's son." She clasped Courtney's hands. "I'm just afraid the two of you will break my boyo's heart."

Velma's unexpected words slapped Courtney in the face. "I'm not trying to hurt him."

"I believe you, but you will anyway. Jared might appear as impenetrable as a rock and too strong to wound, but he's been injured to the core of his soul. He sealed off his heart. You represent every dream he ever had and a nightmare he's barely survived."

The enormity of Velma's statement gave Courtney chills. "What happened?"

"It's not my story to tell." A marked sadness glistened in Velma's eyes. "Ms. Jamison, you brought trouble here. Jared will give his life to save you and Dylan without a second thought. Please don't pierce his armor. Leave him be. He doesn't deserve to be hurt again."

Before Courtney could process the cryptic words, Jared strode into the room. "We need a few moments, Velma. Alone."

The housekeeper left with a last pointed look. Her words made Courtney examine Jared's expression more closely. She recognized the tension tightening his mouth and the worry in his eyes. But also a caution that she might have interpreted as suspicion before she'd spoken with Velma.

He sat across from them and pinned her gaze with his. "You'll stay. I'll help Dylan all I can, but you need to be honest with me. About everything. Deal?"

"I expect the same."

"That goes without saying." He crossed his arms, building a thick and solid wall between them. "So, who do you think is threatening you?"

She'd known he would ask. She wished she had an answer. "I have no idea."

His frown deepened. "You must have some theory. You have to have been thinking about it from the moment you read the note."

"Of course I have." She raised her voice slightly. Dylan squirmed in her arms and she forced herself to relax, lower her voice. "My life is simple and mundane. It's just me and Dylan. I can't imagine who would see me as an enemy."

He didn't respond but she could see the skepticism in his eyes.

"I'm telling you the truth."

He cleared his throat. "I've never heard of a ransom note *before* a kidnapping. Not to mention the unusually specific amount. Is it connected to your home, your family, your job?"

"The only numbers in my life matching over three million dollars are items from the gallery and my grandmother's trust."

Those words had him straightening is his chair in clear interest. "Trust?"

"It may sound promising, but it's not what you think.

The money is specifically earmarked for the running of the gallery. Even the penthouse where I live is reserved for the gallery curator. I have no access to the money."

She stroked Dylan's arm and the baby's breathing evened again. "There have been a few protests and threatening letters at the museum because of the Native American exhibit. The artifacts were collected during the nineteenth century, but the museum is in the process of returning the authenticated pieces to the original tribes."

"What are they worth?"

She understood the real question behind his query. "In total, a lot more than three million."

"So it doesn't explain the exact dollar amount." Jared rubbed his temple. "How about one piece?"

"I'll contact my assistant and have her look at the insurance values to know if any single artifact would match."

"It's a place to start," Jared said.

"But why would they threaten my son and kill Marilyn?"

"Marilyn was collateral damage, as harsh as that sounds. Dylan is a way to guarantee the money, but the amount *has* to mean something." Jared was silent for a moment. "What about relationships?"

The questions cloyed at the base of her neck. She recognized why he asked, but each query felt like an underlying accusation. "Don't you think I've racked my brain, gone through every possibility? And just so we're clear, I haven't dated anyone since I learned I was pregnant with Dylan. He's my only focus."

"And before? Maybe someone who didn't want to break up? A stalker?"

"I hate to go against the stereotype of what you see

about New York women on TV and in the movies, but I was more focused on my education and proving myself in my career than in serial dating." Sarcasm dripped from her voice.

The more she justified her life, the more the fury bubbled deep in her belly. "This is getting us nowhere."

He winced. "You're right. I'm not a cop, I'm a rancher. We need professional help."

Courtney tightened her hold on Dylan. "Why am I afraid I'm not going to like what you're about to say? Please don't tell me you want to call the police."

"Not the police, but a friend. He works for a company called CTC. Covert Technology Confidential. They're local. I trust them, and they take…unusual jobs. On the down low. CTC has the expertise we need to identify who wrote that note."

Her entire body shivered. Were they really going down this path? "What if all the guy wants *is* the money? What if we gave him the money and he *does* go away? Wouldn't that be safer?"

"Do you really believe that?"

"I want to. I know you don't want to give in to blackmail, and part of me agrees. But the part of me that's desperate to protect Dylan thinks we should pay." There. She'd finally spoken the words aloud.

With a solemn nod of his head, Jared contemplated her quietly for a few moments. "I understand. But I have to ask this. Could you live knowing he threatened to kill Dylan, wondering if tomorrow is the day the abductor might come back with more threats, more *requests*? Or that he'll succeed?"

Jared's words were stark and harsh. She couldn't stop the chill settling at the base of her spine. "Of course not.

I don't want to look over my shoulder the rest of my life. I don't want to be terrified Dylan won't come home from school one day. You see it on the news and wonder what you'd do if the worst happened to you. Yesterday the fear became all too real. It's a nightmare I can't escape."

He didn't respond, and she realized it was her call. She twisted her hands in her lap. Both were such a huge risk. "You really think your friends can help?"

"I do. From what I've seen, they have experts working for them that I wouldn't bet against."

She studied his face, his strong jaw. She recognized the determination in his eyes. She might not know Jared well, but something in that intense gaze, in the loyalty Velma had showed him convinced her to believe in him. She sucked in a long, slow breath. "Okay. We're in this together. Call them."

Jared gave her a comforting pat on the shoulder, strode across the room and picked up the landline. He dialed a number. "Ransom. It's Jared King. I need your help. And I need your word you'll keep it very quiet."

While he spoke to the man he'd convinced her to place her faith in, Courtney shifted Dylan in her arms. Poor baby. He was down for the count. She slipped his blanket from the diaper bag and placed it on the thick rug before laying him down. His face looked so sweet, so innocent. She shuddered at the flash of the memory of yesterday. She could have lost him. She almost did. Right now, she'd never felt more vulnerable.

Part of her wanted to run away from the world, just disappear, but that would solve nothing.

A loud knock sounded at the door. Roscoe walked inside. She placed her fingertips on her lips and nodded down at the sleeping baby.

"The men have surveyed the immediate area. Nothing suspicious," Roscoe said in a low voice, eyeing her with skepticism.

His loyalties were clear. She didn't blame him. But she wouldn't allow him to get in her way, either.

Jared held up his hand and finished his conversation. "I'll see him when he gets here." He hung up the phone and turned to Roscoe. "Léon from CTC will be here later today. Make sure he has everyone's full cooperation."

Roscoe straightened, a scowl twisting his countenance. "Can I talk to you for a few minutes? Alone."

Jared gave the man a quick nod. He pulled out a Glock from the desk drawer and slipped it into his waistband. "I'll be right back."

They disappeared through the door. She had to wonder if he had a weapon hidden in every room. Right now, that didn't seem to be a bad idea.

"I don't think Jared's foreman likes me," she whispered at the sleeping baby.

Velma hovered in the open door. "Faith isn't Roscoe's forte, and he's definitely not subtle. He doesn't like anybody he doesn't know, but if he takes your side, he never wavers. He was foreman for Jared's daddy, and when Mr. King passed on, Roscoe watched the place until Jared could come home from the Army to take over the ranch. He's made it his job to keep the boy from working or worrying himself to death like his father. He'd do anything to protect Jared."

"And I'm someone who came here with trouble in my wake. I get it," Courtney said.

"You don't know her!" Roscoe's shout filtered from the other side of the house. "She's after the money. Just like—"

A door slammed shut and the angry words muffled. Velma gasped.

Courtney's eyes widened. Just like who? Dylan squirmed on the blanket, letting out a small cry. Within seconds his lungs burst into a scream.

She scooped him up, but he had that I'm-not-happy-and-you-can't-placate-me-'cause-I'm-hurting look. She dug into her bag for the numbing cream for his teeth and rubbed some on his gums, then slipped him some baby pain reliever. "There you go, Jelly Bean. It'll be better soon."

Just as Dylan calmed a bit, Jared burst into the room.

"What's wrong with him?" he asked, his voice edged with worry. "Does he need a doctor?"

The front door slammed. Dylan howled.

Courtney winced. "He's teething. It's normal, but uncomfortable. The medicine should start working soon." She met Jared's gaze. "Is there a safe place I can put Dylan down for a nap? I think you and I need to settle a few things."

"About more than you realize," Jared said.

He glanced over at Velma. "See if you can't do something with Roscoe. I'll show Courtney their room."

"Old coot," Velma muttered, slipping out of the room.

With a sigh, Jared picked up the blanket from the floor and grabbed the diaper bag. "Let's go."

He led her down a wide hallway. She placed her hand on his arm and he paused. "Am I going to be a problem for your foreman? I could talk to him."

The tic returned to Jared's jaw. "He'll get over it." He nodded at a door on the left. "That's my room. You're across the hall."

He clearly didn't want to continue the conversation.

Courtney would have preferred to leave it, but she had to ask. "If I'm going to stay, I need to know that Dylan will be protected."

"Roscoe's got a hot head, but he's never let me down. He won't now."

"Forgive me if I reserve judgment." Truthfully, the man's feelings didn't matter. She wouldn't be letting her guard down around anyone. Not until the blackmailer was caught.

"I wouldn't expect anything less." With a quick push, Jared opened the door to a perfectly decorated, perfectly neat and tidy guest room. Her luggage and Dylan's car seat sat in one corner. The queen-size bed dominated the space, but it would definitely do.

"There's an attached bath," he said, stepping aside so she could enter. "If you retrace our steps and hang a right, you won't miss the kitchen. When I'm not around, Velma can help you find anything you need."

Courtney entered the room. "It's lovely." She pushed the comforter toward the end of the bed. Dylan still whimpered in her arms.

She sent Jared a sidelong glance. "It may take a while to get him to sleep. He's pretty fussy."

He backed away from her and settled in the doorway, with his shoulder propped against the jamb. She paced back and forth. Slowly Dylan grew limp in her arms. She expected Jared to get bored and leave, but he simply stood and watched her every move.

What was that expression on his face? Longing? Sadness? A little of both?

Once Dylan's breathing evened out, she laid her son in the center of the bed and slipped pillows beneath the fitted sheet on either side of him to create a makeshift crib.

"You're resourceful."

Courtney shrugged. "I can't take credit for the idea. The hospice nurse who took care of my mom used the trick to keep her from rolling out of bed."

"I'm sorry. Did you lose her recently?"

"A lifetime ago. I was ten. Brain cancer."

"Losing a mother is hard," he said, his voice laced with understanding.

"You, too?"

"Car accident when I was just a little older than Dylan. That's when Velma came to live here." He paused, his gaze focused on his son. "I guess we both know what it's like to live without a parent."

"Seems so." Courtney sent him a sidelong glance. His hooded gaze reminded her of that night at the Waldorf. She'd been sitting alone, not intending to speak with anyone, and when he'd entered the bar, her heart had skipped a beat.

He'd been everything she'd dreamed of in a fantasy. One too many drinks had given her the courage to sit on the barstool next to him.

He'd been wary at first, but something about him. She'd asked him a simple question. His favorite drink. The rest of that night they'd simply talked. He'd asked her about her favorite New York attractions and why. They'd connected about the important things. The importance of family ties, of honesty, of how they both felt as if they'd been born in the wrong era. How disposable the world seemed.

That night she'd felt…complete. For the first time.

She placed Dylan's favorite blanket on top of him, reassured herself he was safe. She shifted her weight. "I know we need to talk more, but I can't leave him. I'd be checking on him every five minutes."

"What if you could watch over him from the other room?"

"You have a camera?"

He returned a few minutes later with a small wireless device and pointed the lens at the bed.

After a few seconds he held the phone up to Courtney and an image of Dylan sleeping filled the screen. "Better?"

Courtney gripped the cell. After Dylan's birth she couldn't count the nights she'd spent watching over him, terrified of making a mistake. Of missing something, of not being enough for him. She'd felt so alone. Eventually she'd worn herself out. That's when Marilyn had stopped her on the elevator. The grandmother of nine had held her hand and told her it was going to be fine. Courtney had burst into tears, and Marilyn had saved her sanity, agreeing to watch Dylan every day. From that moment until yesterday Courtney had felt confident that her baby was in good hands.

And now… Marilyn was gone, losing her own life protecting Dylan.

Courtney was alone again. Except for Jared, and she still didn't know exactly what that meant.

With a tight grip on the phone she followed him to the study. He gestured to the couch and she sat down.

"Before you start, I want you to know I was planning to tell you about Dylan," she rushed to explain. "I tried to find you when I realized I was pregnant, but the hotel wouldn't give me your name."

Jared grimaced. "They wouldn't give me yours, either."

"You tried to find me?" Courtney couldn't quite believe it. They both knew what had happened that night.

"I went out to get us breakfast. When I returned, you were gone. The concierge wouldn't say anything."

She flushed. "I thought you were sorry… Why didn't you order room service?"

"I needed to think. What happened between us was…"

"Unexpected?" she finished with a small smile.

"Very." Jared shifted in his chair. "My accountant forced me to buy that suit to meet with some bigwigs from a company who wanted me to sell off half the ranch. I hated that suit. It wasn't me. I needed some air to figure out how to tell you that the man you drank tequila with wasn't the man you thought."

She smoothed her dress. "I have to admit I was surprised when I found out where you lived, what you do for a living. When I met you in New York, you fit right in."

"Maybe for a day or two. I missed the sky the moment the plane landed," Jared admitted. "Are you disappointed? In me?"

How was she supposed to answer that? She could only be honest. It was all they had between them. "More like stunned. You acted like you belonged at the Waldorf as much as here."

"The tequila didn't give me away?" he asked.

"I wasn't drinking white wine, now, was I?" She settled back against the chair, foggy memories of the night filtering through her mind.

His hand touching hers on the bar. The moment he'd tucked her hair behind her ear and her breath had caught. The second she'd leaned into him and when she'd turned her head he'd kissed her for the first time.

The racing of her heart when he'd whispered an invitation she couldn't refuse.

Even now she flushed. She could never have imagined herself falling for a man in a few hours, and yet, she had.

He grinned, his eyes crinkling as the smile reached his eyes. "Hardly."

This was the Jared she knew. Quick wit, give and take. He'd challenged her that night, seducing her with something special, something she'd never felt with the men she'd dated. Only now did she realizing it was the cowboy in him. Who knew a big city girl could melt for a country boy the way she had. She'd wanted him, and she hadn't been disappointed. In anything. "I'm a quick learner," she said. "That was a first for me."

"Doing shots?" Jared raised a brow. "Or falling into the arms of someone you didn't know."

She winced at the truth. "Both."

"Me, too," Jared said. "We couldn't be more different."

She glanced from her Chanel dress to his jeans and Western shirt. "True. But the moment I found the note I was relieved you lived across the country and nowhere near my world. Dylan is safer here than in New York. We're both safer with you."

"I wish I were sure about that."

JARED LOOKED AWAY and the room went silent with shock. He hated seeing the uncertainty on Courtney's face. He hated revealing the truth.

She clutched the phone. "We are safe here, aren't we?"

"It's complicated, but we committed to being honest with each other."

From the moment she'd told him Dylan was in danger he'd mulled over the idea that he should send her and

Dylan to CTC. Ransom had protected his location with the security of a military complex. They didn't know who they were dealing with. Whoever it was, they were dangerous.

He leaned forward in his chair, resting his arms on his jeans. "I've been having some trouble with the guy who owns the ranch north of here. I don't think he'd go so far as to drag you into our family feud, but he's unpredictable. Last week someone dug up the posts on a fence bordering the property. Several dozen of my cattle wandered onto his land. He's a loose cannon, volatile even. His goal is to drive my family off this land."

Courtney's knuckles whitened on the phone and she stared at her son's image through the screen, not meeting Jared's gaze.

"I have the sheriff looking into the vandalism, but the investigation is going nowhere."

His statement jerked her head up. "If the blackmailer finds us here, if he sees the sheriff—"

Jared held up his hand. "I'm withdrawing my complaint. I'll give the sheriff some excuse and deal with the Criswells on my own. Who knows, maybe if I back off, they'll get bored with these destructive pranks."

Jared was 99 percent certain the Criswells were responsible. He wasn't sure if it was Ned or Chuck or both, though. Ned had always been a greedy SOB. The bad feelings between the Kings and the Criswells had been going on since Ned and Jared's father competed for the quarterback position on their high school football team.

After his father's death, the feud hadn't died. When they'd discovered oil on the King property, the old animas had reignited with a vengeance.

Too much money made enemies of acquaintances as well as friends.

Jared should probably have dealt with the Criswell issue on his own in the first place. Too much like five years ago, when Alyssa had disappeared, he'd counted on the law. After the vandalism, he'd called Blake Redmond, who'd taken over as sheriff for his father. Blake had investigated. Ned, of course, had denied any involvement in tearing down the fences between the two properties. There'd been no proof.

There still wasn't, but the Criswells were the only ones who had anything to gain.

Courtney rose from the sofa, pacing back and forth. "Maybe coming here was a mistake." She turned the phone around, providing Jared an unfettered view of his son. The baby lay sound asleep, and completely vulnerable. "I just don't know. There are too many variables. What am I supposed to do, Jared? I don't have anywhere else to go. But I have to ask. Can you protect us?"

Her words sliced at his gut, much too close to the five-year-old wound that had never fully scarred over. This time would be different. This time he had friends who could do more than law enforcement ever could. He crossed the room, took her hands in his and looked deeply into her eyes. "I know you have no reason to believe in me, but I promise you, we'll get this guy. I'll do whatever it takes to make certain you and Dylan are safe."

She clutched his hands hard, her nails biting into his skin. "Whatever it takes?"

"Without hesitation."

Courtney found the intensity in Jared's gaze oddly reassuring. She unfurled her fingers and stepped back from him. "I believe you."

"I'll call the sheriff and ask him and his deputies to

avoid the Last Chance Ranch for a while." He rounded his desk and picked up the landline.

Courtney glanced once more at the image of Dylan on the cell phone screen. Still sound asleep. She'd have to time his nap correctly or tonight would be a nightmare, and she couldn't afford a bleary-eyed day. She needed to keep sharp.

She walked over to the curtains and peered through the small crack between the light-colored panels. She didn't doubt that if she'd stayed in New York, Dylan might already be in a kidnapper's hands. Or worse. Within a few minutes she witnessed four men wandering outside with rifles in hand. The firepower made her feel better. At least for now she was safe. Dylan was safe.

They couldn't hide in the house forever, though. The only way to regain any semblance of a normal life would be to figure out who had written that note. Courtney knew of only one thing she could do. Review every person in her life to try to figure out who could be responsible.

Despite what she'd told Jared, she had to believe that somewhere in the back of her mind she'd seen something or done something that would point them to the person threatening to kidnap Dylan.

She pulled out a notepad from her bag and sat down. She'd start with the night at the Waldorf. The answer would come to her. It had to.

A phone rang. She dug through her purse. It was *his* phone.

Her entire body trembled. She picked up the cell. "Hello?"

"Did you really think you could hide by visiting your

baby's father?" The sound of a mechanized voice chilled her to the core.

She gasped. No one knew about Jared. No one except the private investigator she'd hired.

"I know more about you than you know about yourself, Miss Jamison. You picked a man with a lot of zeroes in his bank account to sleep with. I'm sure on purpose. That's what all women want, isn't it? A man with money."

Her grip tightened until her knuckles paled with the effort. She motioned with frantic movements at Jared before tapping the speakerphone on. He hustled over to her and grabbed his phone from the table.

"You think you deserve what Jared King can buy you, don't you?" the inhuman voice taunted.

She glanced over his shoulder. Jared was sending a text asking if CTC could trace the call.

Keep him talking, Jared mouthed.

"Please—"

"Don't bother to beg. So, you discovered your father's broke, hmm. And now you're begging another man for my fee."

Courtney met Jared's gaze and she could see the shock in his eyes. Could he have been responsible for her father's financial meltdown?

"Well, time's up. Can't have anyone tracking my location, now can we? But, Miss Jamison, don't forget, you can't hide, no matter where you are."

A gunshot rang out from outside. Courtney's heart seized. "Oh my God. Dylan."

She raced down the hallway, Jared on her heels.

"Courtney, let me—"

She wasn't about to wait. She slammed open the door. Her baby lay sound asleep. Her knees buckled.

Roscoe raced into the room. "Angel Maker's loose! He took down Tim and he's on a rampage."

"You'll have to corral him." Jared clasped Courtney's arm. "I can't leave them alone. Angel Maker may have caused trouble but he didn't get out of that pen without help. It's a diversion."

Roscoe gave Jared a frustrated look and ran out the door.

A diversion. Courtney strode over to the crib. A small stuffed bull sat propped against the side, not far from her soon.

She scooped him up and thrust the stuffed animal at Jared. "He was here. He was in this room."

Chapter Four

Jared pushed Courtney behind him. His pulse raced so fast his heart slammed into his chest. Impossible. The house was as secure as he could make it. The guest room had only three ways in and out. The door and two small windows. Jared gripped the Glock. While the orange-red setting sun glared at him, he checked the latches, but both locks were secure. He scanned the room. Nothing appeared out of place.

He searched the bathroom, under the bed and the closet. All clear.

"Dylan's not going to be without one of us. Ever," Jared said, tapping on his phone. "Roscoe, I need a report. Where'd the shot come from? Was the shooter one of ours or a trespasser?"

"It came from behind the barn. I don't know who," Roscoe said. "Damn. All hell's broken loose."

Understatement of the year.

Shouting peppered the phone call's background. He could hear Roscoe questioning the others. Jared fought back his frustration. Normally, he would've been out there with his men, but he'd have to trust his foreman to take care of things. Courtney and Dylan needed him there.

He glanced over at her. She hovered in the doorway,

poised to run, holding Dylan against her chest, her protection unflinching. Damn, she was brave. Their son whimpered and she jostled the baby in an attempt to calm him.

"In here." Jared covered the phone's speaker and motioned to her. "Stay in the corner away from the windows."

She couldn't take her eyes off the small stuffed animal he'd tossed on the floor but followed his instructions anyway. For now, as far as Jared was concerned, this room was the only safe place on his ranch because he'd checked every inch.

"None of the hands fired," Roscoe said. "It had to be someone else. Frank said he saw some large tire tracks behind the barn. I'll check on it."

With an eye on his son, Jared mouthed a harsh curse. Criswell's F-350 was a big truck. Could the Criswells be behind this? "I want everyone on guard duty to stay at their posts. Don't let Angel Maker distract the hands if it compromises security. You got it? And find out who's trespassing on my land."

"On it."

"Velma!" Jared shouted down the hall.

Within seconds the housekeeper appeared in the doorway, her chest heaving. "What's wrong?"

"Someone was in the house. He made it to the guest room. Did you see anything? Hear anything?"

Velma slapped her hand over her mouth. "Is Dylan okay?"

"The baby's fine," Courtney said, her voice husky with emotion. She pointed at the stuffed blue bull. "The intruder left that."

"Oh my." Velma sagged against the wall. "I'm sorry, Jared. I didn't think you'd—" She cleared her throat. "I brought that toy to him, dearie. I picked it up at the rodeo a few years ago. Since the little guy didn't have anything to play with…"

Jared wanted to sag to the floor in relief. The blackmailer hadn't penetrated the house.

"It was you?" Blindly, Courtney sank onto the bed, blinking back tears. "He wasn't here. He hasn't found us?"

Velma rushed across the room and patted Courtney's knee. "I'm so sorry, sweetie. I didn't mean to frighten you."

No one could fake that response. Jared's doubt that Courtney had orchestrated an elaborate scheme for money faded to almost nothing. Which ratcheted up his concern. They were in danger from two fronts now.

He couldn't afford to make the assumption the blackmailer wasn't outside, not with the cell phone a homing beacon. The Criswells may have freed Angel Maker, but Jared didn't believe in coincidence either. The chaos that bull caused would make the perfect distraction for either the blackmailer or the Criswell's.

Damn it. Jared resented being under siege. With Courtney and Dylan so vulnerable, his hands wouldn't be enough. "Bring Dylan," he said to Courtney. "No one's alone until I secure the house."

He entered the kitchen. A large pot of Velma's famous Texas chili bubbled on the stove. She hurried over to give it a stir before turning down the heat.

Jared opened the back door and checked the double lock he'd recently installed. "No sign of tampering." One of his hands gave Jared a brief nod. The man's rifle was handy and he stood at the ready with a good view.

After inspecting the front door, Jared headed to the

cellar's steps, Courtney and Velma behind him. He made his way down slowly, cautiously, every so often looking back at the two women standing at the top of the stairs.

He flipped on the light. It flickered against the inky darkness of the root cellar. Light glinted off the small glass window just below the ground level. "We're vulnerable here," Jared said. "A man could just squeeze through if he kicked in the glass."

Jared studied the shelves holding Velma's canned fruits and vegetables. They lined the room. He'd never wired this room for security. Huge mistake. He grabbed a couple of two-by-fours that leaned against the wall and climbed the stairs. After locking the door he jammed one plank under the brass handle and braced it with the other piece.

"That should hold for now."

"You think he's out there?" Courtney asked. "The man who threatened Dylan."

"I don't know. But I don't believe in coincidences, so until I'm convinced this house is completely secure, I'm not letting either one of you out of my sight."

JARED HATED WAITING more than anything. It had been over an hour, and here he sat at the kitchen table, his hand resting lightly on the Glock. Just across from him Courtney fed Dylan. At any other time, the picture in front of him might have made Jared smile. More food ended up on the baby's face than in his stomach. But he couldn't get the tight feeling from balling in his gut. The stuffed blue bull had been a hit, but whenever Jared glanced at the toy, another what-if ping-ponged through his mind.

Velma had apologized several times for not asking if she could give Dylan the toy. It wasn't her fault, of course.

It was the blackmailer's. His note would keep them all on edge until he was caught. For now, they waited.

A too quiet Velma hovered near the oven. After a fight with bread dough she had two loaves rising and a batch of Jared's favorite cookies in the oven. Snickerdoodles.

The sweet scent of cinnamon and sugar wafted through the house. The picture should have been the epitome of a blissful home. Instead, the house had become a fortress.

Jared's leg bounced beneath the table. He'd rounded the rooms a half-dozen times, letting Roscoe and the hands take care of the pandemonium outside.

Courtney fought to convince Dylan to eat another bite of mashed potatoes.

"Jared never did like anything white, either," Velma said. "He'd spit it out. I finally added bacon bits and cheese and he'd scarf those down."

"Potatoes are boring," Jared said, willing to go along with Velma's attempt to keep things normal.

"Dylan's favorite is spinach." Courtney made a half-hearted attempt at a smile. "I don't know where he gets it from. I like raw, but not cooked."

A loud pounding rattled the back door. Jared rose, weapon drawn. Courtney and Velma froze. Dylan grabbed the spoon and shoved it partway into his mouth.

"It's me," Roscoe's voice shouted.

Jared inched open the door. When he saw only his foreman, he stepped aside. "What the hell took so long?"

"First we had to corral that damn beast. After we finagled Angel Maker back into his pen and calmed down the horses, I still had to figure out what happened." Hat in hand, Roscoe limped into the kitchen and sagged into a chair. "Someone let the son of Satan out. Nearly broke Tim in two when the idiot tried to stop the beast, got me in the hip. I'll be lucky if I can get out of bed tomorrow. Frank's taking the kid to the clinic in town and I've got Lloyd watching the east side of the house until they get back."

"Did someone just waltz in and open the gate?"

"Oh, whoever did this was smarter than that. We found one of the pins missing. Could've been done anytime. Angel Maker had to hit the fence just right to take down the gate. Hell, the Criswells could've pulled the pin days ago." Roscoe shook his head. "That shot spooked him just the right way. This was way more than digging up a few posts."

Jared stared out the window, running through the last month and the last day in his head. "Maybe that's why Chuck was so jumpy today. He knew the gate could give way at any moment."

"You really believe letting the bull loose was about your ranch and not Dylan?" Courtney asked.

"Not everything's about you, city girl." The foreman scowled.

"Roscoe," Jared warned. "If the blackmailer wanted to create a distraction to leave Courtney and Dylan alone, he failed." Jared tapped his fingers on the table. "Right now, my money's on Chuck Criswell being stupid enough to fire that shot. Who else but a cowboy would use a bull as a weapon?"

"Sheriff needs to throw Criswell in jail and let him stew for a while," Roscoe said, frowning. "I bet he can take pictures of the tire tracks behind the barn and match 'em up."

Jared cleared his throat and met Courtney's gaze. "About that. Take the pictures yourself. I've asked Sheriff Redmond to back off the investigation for a while. We'll handle it ourselves."

The foreman let out a loud curse.

"We got a kid here, Roscoe."

"What are you thinking?" he said. "The Criswells will just keep coming. They could hurt someone. Or worse."

"You're right." Jared turned to face his foreman. "So, I want everyone armed until CTC brings in extra security. Identify who's willing to stand guard. Get back to me on the schedule. My highest priority is a 24/7, 360-degree view on the house. I don't want one foot in a blind spot. Whoever's left will keep an eye on our critical buildings. Have the men eat and shower in shifts until further notice."

"We've got stock scheduled for delivery," Roscoe reminded him. "If we don't meet those obligations we'll take a huge hit to the ranch's reputation."

"Send an armed contingency with them. If Ned or Chuck let out Angel Maker, they're willing to do anything."

"Got it." Roscoe rose from the table, shot Courtney a sour look and limped away.

"I don't think he likes me much," she said.

"He doesn't like the situation. He likes you just fine," Jared said, locking the door behind his foreman.

She gave him an astonished look. Jared shrugged. "Well, he's just not all that fond of citified women."

"Citified?"

"That's one way of putting it." Velma let out a small guffaw and pulled the cookies from the oven.

"Life on a ranch doesn't always agree with city folks." Jared peered over Velma's shoulder at the cookies. "Tell me the truth, Courtney. It's hours to the nearest museum, symphony or even a traveling Broadway show. How happy could you be in a small town where the biggest excitement is a barn raising or the annual July Fourth barbecue?"

"Touché." She sent him a considering look. "It's not exactly what I'm used to."

Even though Jared had expected her agreement, it didn't stop the small pang in the region of his heart. Where was his head? He had to remember she wouldn't be staying.

So why did he have to keep thinking and hoping she might? And why did he have to like her so much?

She'd ignited something in him from the moment they'd met. A smile lit her eyes. Even in New York, something genuine exuded from deep inside her. He'd been drawn to her immediately.

She was confident, beautiful and passionate. He'd known that from the start. Now he recognized so much more. She valued their son over her own safety or comfort. Nothing citified about her love for Dylan. That was pure country.

"Roscoe has his reasons." Velma set a plate of warm snickerdoodles in the middle of the table interrupting his thoughts. "He met a girl in Dallas at a stock sale and fell head over heels. He brought her to visit the ranch. She took one look at the place and hightailed it out of here so fast her feet didn't touch the dirt. Kind of soured him. Not saying it's right. It just *is*."

The housekeeper sent a pointed glance to Jared. He knew what she was thinking. No need to mention Alyssa's first step onto the Last Chance Ranch. His wife had been shocked when he'd brought her home. Roscoe and Velma had both been skeptical, but Alyssa had tried to fit in. Prejudice went both ways. Jared would never know if she would've come to love the ranch like he did.

"No." Dylan closed his mouth and turned away from the spoon.

"He's finished." Courtney wiped his face. "I need to change and feed him. Is it safe to use the bedroom now?"

Jared rubbed his temple. "More than likely, but I'm not taking any chances. Until CTC beefs up the security." He stood up. "Until then, I'll go with you."

Courtney stood and hitched Dylan on her hip. "You know I'll be feeding him, right?"

"He just ate." What was she talking about?

"*I* need to feed him." Her cheeks reddened and Jared realized what she'd been trying to say. "Oh, I see. We'll figure it out. But I'm not leaving you alone."

He followed her toward the guest room. He couldn't remember a time when he'd been more uncomfortable around a woman in his life. What had he gotten himself into? If he hadn't been terrified for her safety, he would have disappeared into the barn.

"Don't close the door," he said, planting himself in the hallway.

She nodded and disappeared inside the bedroom, shutting the door behind her halfway.

Jared hovered in the hallway tempted by her soft whispers and quiet laughs. He knew nothing about babies unless they were the four-legged, barnyard variety. Had no idea how long changing Dylan would take, much less feeding him, but he clearly was the outsider in this endeavor.

He didn't know how long he stood waiting when a flash of movement caught the corner of his eye. He jerked around, hand hovering over his Glock.

Velma jolted and raised her hands in surrender. "Dinner's ready. I took a pot of stew out to the barracks for the men."

"She's still with Dylan," Jared said, avoiding her gaze.

Velma gave a soft smile. "Have you held him?"

Jared cleared his throat. "He doesn't know me. And when this is over they'll go back to New York. I'll be here. It's better not to confuse him."

"At first I thought you should stay away from her, too, but she's got guts, boyo. I like her." Velma crossed her arms and frowned. "A son needs his father."

"A child needs to be safe."

Tears welled in her eyes. "I know, boyo, but—"

Jared tamped down the emotion threatening to well from deep inside. He had to maintain control. He couldn't allow his feelings to color his judgment or his thinking. "I'm not taking any chances. Not with them. Not with anyone I care about."

"And that's why he won," she whispered under her breath.

NIGHTTIME PEEKED OVER the horizon. Jared caught a glimpse of the moon through the study curtains. He'd come up with a lame excuse to avoid Velma. Courtney had already found an ally in his housekeeper, but Velma lived her life wide-open. Always had, always would.

Courtney stuck her head in the door. "Are you busy?" she asked. Dylan sat on her hip and appeared utterly satisfied to be close to his mother.

Who wouldn't be?

She placed her tote bag next to the sofa and tucked her feet beneath her before letting her head fall onto the cushioned back. Dylan grabbed for her necklace and tried to stuff it in his mouth. Courtney played tug-of-war for a bit with him, smiling with an expression of adoration that made Jared's throat thicken with emotion.

The baby giggled and threw himself into her arms. She wrapped him in her embrace and rocked him back and forth. "Mama loves you, Jelly Bean."

"He's definitely energetic," Jared said.

"He likes to play, especially at this time of night." She gave Jared a considering look. "Do you want to hold him?"

Jared stiffened and nodded to his laptop. "Work."

"You're missing out," Courtney said softly.

He knew, oh God how he knew, but if he fell in love...

Dylan wiggled in Courtney's lap and slid to the ground. She pulled out the stuffed bull and gave it to him. He threw it across the floor and crawled to retrieve it.

"Maybe he'll be a baseball player," Jared said, watching how every step or so Dylan would place one foot on the floor instead of his knee.

"He keeps trying to walk," Courtney said. "He can stand if he holds on to the edge of a couch or chair."

Soon, Dylan had situated himself beneath a wood coffee table and happily played with his animal having a conversation that Jared couldn't decipher.

Jared would've been content to sit and watch the baby all day, every day. He couldn't lose himself in his own wants. And he couldn't let Courtney and Dylan get to him. He had a job to do.

Courtney pulled out a notepad from her bag. "I've started a list of every person I can think of who I came into contact with since we met. I even added the car service. They can tell you who delivered the blackmailer's phone so CTC would have something to work with."

"That's a great idea."

Jared joined her on the sofa and glanced over at her list. There weren't that many names.

She flushed. "I told you my life was pretty mundane."

"Do any jump out at you?"

"That's the trouble. I can't imagine any of these people wanting to hurt Dylan."

Jared glanced at his watch. CTC should be here soon. Waiting had never been his strong suit. He preferred being in the middle of the action, and right now he felt more like a quail waiting to be flushed into the open and shot for dinner.

"How are we going to protect Dylan if we can't figure out who wants to hurt him?" she said, her gaze fixed on her son.

He understood her frustration more than she could possibly know. When Alyssa's murderer had never been caught, Jared had shoved aside any possibility of risking another serious relationship. He'd even tried to run Velma and Roscoe off, but they wouldn't leave. He couldn't understand why they'd be willing to take the chance, but they hadn't budged. Hadn't even moved to town.

For five years he'd prayed the man who'd kidnapped Alyssa would make a mistake, that he'd somewhere, somehow reveal his identity, but the man had vanished. The case had turned ice-cold. And unsolved.

Jared wouldn't let that happen again.

The doorbell rang, followed by a loud knock. Courtney jerked in her seat.

"It's probably CTC," Jared said.

Despite knowing the hands guarded the main house, he pulled his gun before walking to the door. He opened it.

Ransom's operative faced him. Jared couldn't hide his

surprise. The guy could've escorted Courtney to a New York gallery opening or crawled next to Jared on the battlefield. His blue eyes were clear and piercing, with a decided edge that spelled danger.

No doubt about it, Jared would want Léon on his six, and not in the opposite camp.

"Rafe told me what you did for him and Sierra at the San Antonio Rodeo." Jared shook Léon's hand. "I hope you can help us."

"Rafe wanted to be here, but he can't leave Sierra. She's close to delivering the baby."

Jared could make out a slight accent, but couldn't place it. Didn't matter. If Ransom trusted Léon, so did Jared.

"So I heard." Jared led Léon into the study and brought him up to speed.

The man didn't take notes, but Jared had studied Léon from the moment he'd entered the house. The operative took in every detail of the room. He'd taken inventory of the gun case and the vulnerabilities in the study.

Of course Jared had clocked Léon's ankle holster, his sidearm and the knife sheath.

"Miss Jamison, may I see the phone you were given?" he asked the moment he sat down.

Courtney handed it over, and Léon cracked open the case. "GPS tracker. He knows your current coordinates—or at the least the phone's location."

"He implied as such on the phone," Jared said.

"He's smart and tech savvy." Léon snapped the case back together. "He blocked our tech from tracing the last call, so we have no idea where he is. Zane's working on a maneuver around the problem. He'll find it."

The headache that threatened earlier in the day intensified behind his eyes. "What if we take her and my son to CTC. Leave the phone here, and I'll answer when it rings. They would be safe."

"On the surface the idea seems plausible," Léon said, "but we'll lose our chance to set a trap. Without any leads we're thin on options until he calls again. The truth is, if someone wants you dead, they only have to be on target one time. To prevent him from attacking, we have to be on point *every* attempt. The odds are in his favor."

An ice-cold chill skittered up Jared's spine. From his training he knew Léon was right. Much easier to hit a mark than prevent an attack. If he had any confidence the blackmailer would leave Courtney and Dylan alone, he'd pay the money in a heartbeat.

Léon returned the phone to Courtney. "He hasn't tried to contact you again to give you a drop location?"

She shook her head.

"Interesting. What's he waiting for?" Léon mused. "It's more than just the ransom." He crossed his boot over his leg and tapped the leather for a moment. "If all he wanted was money, he'd have asked you for a million or two million, not that exact amount. It obviously has meaning for him, and that's his mistake. Once we find out how the number connects, we'll know what he wants."

Jared shoved his hand through his hair. "Courtney made a possible list of suspects."

"I don't think it'll help," she said, handing it to him.

"Every bit of information helps, if nothing else as part of the elimination process. Our blackmailer wants you to wonder about him. He wants you dangling at the end of his string as his plaything."

Jared ground his teeth in an attempt to maintain control over the fury ramming through his body.

"He's sending a message. We just have to decipher

it." Léon met Courtney's gaze. "CTC is going to dig into your life and try to discover how that non-ransom ransom note ties to you. Are you okay with that?"

She nodded. "Whatever it takes."

"Whatever you need," Jared added.

Léon rose. "Until then, I agree you need additional security. Ransom will send several operatives to work with your hands. Now that I've verified the phone number, we can track the cell, and hopefully triangulate our guy's location when he calls you. And he will."

"So we sit and wait? That's your plan?" Jared frowned. "How about you take the phone and lead him away from here?" Anything to keep a distance between the tracking device, Courtney and his son.

"I hear you, Jared. Believe me. But he's got the leverage. He wants to communicate with Courtney, and we need to let him."

Courtney glanced over at Jared. He fought against the desire to scoop her up, grab Dylan and take off to the mountains. Hole up in a cave for the foreseeable future. The Guadalupe Mountains were an unforgiving range he knew well. If he wanted to stay hidden there for months, he could. Instead, he gave her a slight nod. He might have a bad feeling about this plan. Anything putting her and Dylan in danger didn't sit well in his gut, but Courtney deserved her life back.

"If we're going to do this, how do we keep Dylan safe in the meantime?" she asked.

"I'll make sure neither one of you is ever left alone," Jared said.

"And we employ basic battlefield strategy," Léon said. "Establish a perimeter and no one gets in or out without us knowing. Then, we wait." The operative's eyes grew hard. "When he calls, Courtney, you'll need to keep him on the phone as long as possible. If it goes well, we'll be able to bag him before he makes any kind of move."

She chewed on her lower lip, but it was her white knuckles that told Jared how scared she really was. "You'll keep this low-key. No cops, no feds."

"I agree," Léon said. "Whoever did this is smart and organized. In fact, you need to take me out to the barn and introduce me to one of your stud bulls, because I'm supposedly here to negotiate a price."

Jared took Courtney's hand in his. "You okay?" She sent him a tense nod and he squeezed. "We'll make this work."

He walked Léon to the door and they crossed to Angel Maker's pen. The bull snorted.

Léon made a show of examining the animal. "This demon's got the perfect name. The devil's in his eyes."

Jared rubbed his chin. "You need to know I'm dealing with a saboteur, too. The sheriff was investigating, but I called him off. I think one of the Criswells took a shot to cause chaos. It complicates things. I'm worried about Courtney and Dylan staying here."

Jared didn't acknowledge his greatest fear. That he couldn't protect them. If anything happened to Courtney or his son, he'd never forgive himself.

"You were Army. We need intel. Right now that phone is our only link to this guy. Zane will start on the deep dive into her and her family's finances. Maybe we'll get lucky. Until then, we don't have a choice. Not if you want to find this guy."

"I know." Jared's jaw ached with tension. "Damn it."

"We'll ramp up your surveillance system and install

cameras along the perimeter. The main yard and house will be secure. Your outbuildings, less so."

"But the best way to catch this guy is to follow the money." Jared walked Léon to his vehicle. "I don't like him holding all the cards. We're like apples in a barrel waiting to get shot."

Léon opened the door of his truck. "Not for long."

Chapter Five

The day had been an unqualified success.

Stars blanketed the West Texas sky.

His prey was holed up like cowards inside the main house on Jared King's ranch.

She'd come running to Jared just as he'd planned. The note, the ransacked penthouse, her dead babysitter, they'd all pushed her into Jared's life.

Now, they were good and trapped and exactly where he wanted them.

She'd let Jared take her. She'd given birth to *his* baby. She would have to be punished for her mistake.

Oh, Jared had made the game a bit challenging, but a few hired guns would make no difference in the long run. The cameras would be dealt with soon enough. They had no idea who they were facing.

Money was the root of all evil. Wasn't that the proverb?

Except, it wasn't true. Being poor, being desperate, being without, losing every hope and dream, that's what changed a man. Made him into something less than human.

It was a hard lesson those barricaded inside the house would learn.

He would strip everything away, then they would understand.

They truly were nothing.

STEAM ROSE IN the bathroom and clouded the mirror. Hot water pummeled Courtney's aching shoulders and pounding head. Nothing could have prepared her for today. When she'd imagined informing Jared about Dylan, she'd pictured inviting him to her New York apartment, proving to him how settled she and her son were, how Jared could be involved in their life if he wanted to be, but that she'd be okay if he didn't want to be. She didn't need anything from him.

Fast-forward to now, and she found herself two thousand miles from home with not a coffee shop or taxi in sight, stuck in a ranch house complete with a killer bull fifty feet away, a murderer threatening to steal her baby, no money to pay off the threat, and her son's father glued to her side for the foreseeable future.

Even more astonishing, he'd never let any doubt stop him from protecting Dylan; he'd simply taken action. He'd done everything and more than she could've asked, including bringing in CTC.

Léon—he'd refused to provide last name—had been brutally honest, and dangerous. He'd warned her about snooping in her life. She had nothing to hide. Her father, she wasn't so sure about him. Since he'd lost the entire family fortune, he'd obviously made some bad business decisions or the bank calling the loans due in the last week wouldn't have mattered. Whatever Léon found out was worth a little embarrassment if it brought the murderer to justice and protected her son.

She just hoped they found answers soon. Her entire body throbbed with unabated tension. She could feel every nerve ending pulsing with pent-up disquiet.

If she let herself, she'd collapse into the tub in a blob of putty. Of course, that wouldn't do Dylan any good so she turned off the water and reached for a towel. There was no evidence the blackmailer was there. They had armed men walking the perimeter.

She had to believe they were safe with Jared. She had no other choice but to have faith.

The door was closed, but unlocked. On the other side, in the guest room, Jared had volunteered to watch Dylan, which might have made her nervous if Velma hadn't winked at Courtney and said she'd watch over the boys. Knowing the older woman would be within calling distance had been a bit of a relief. Enough to sooth the tension from her neck and back temporarily.

Courtney slipped into ivory pants and a soft rose linen shirt. Completely inappropriate for bedtime, but her baby doll nightgown would've been even worse. She'd been limited to what she'd left the last time she'd visit her father and what was in Dylan's diaper bag. Now that she'd arrived, she recognized she was completely unprepared.

A low, deep voice filtered through the closed door and Courtney cracked it open. Jared sat in a white rocking chair, swaying to and fro, his son in his arms, staring at the baby's face.

He toyed with the baby's fingers, counted his toes. She understood. The moment he'd been born, she'd done the same.

They didn't notice her, and she didn't move. She could

only watch, stunned. Jared had avoided holding Dylan since they'd arrived. Now Jared's expression had softened into adoration, even as his jaw throbbed in stress.

Courtney recognized the feeling well. When she'd brought her baby home from the hospital, no one had been waiting for her. Panic had settled deep in her gut. Heck, she still experienced the feeling every day, usually after Dylan had drifted to sleep and she lay alone in her bed staring at the ceiling with the street noises of the city lulling her to sleep.

What if she failed him? Dylan had only her, no one else. The last twenty-four hours had exploded those emotions into heart-suffocating fear. She could hardly breathe; her entire body vibrated on the verge of tremors. Every horrifying outcome replayed in her mind like an endless loop, unwilling to stop.

Seeing the utter contentment on her Jelly Bean's face, for a brief moment she could breathe again. Dylan loved nothing more than being rocked. Especially if he were held tightly, and Jared, if nothing else, had a strong, firm embrace.

She knew that from the night spent in his arms.

The rocking chair creaked a bit beneath his weight until his surprisingly in-tune hum gave way to words. Courtney didn't know a lot about country music, but who hadn't heard "Mamas Don't Let Your Babies Grow up to Be Cowboys."

She rested her shoulder against the doorjamb. The only thing consistent about Jared since the night they'd met was the unexpected.

"You're not gonna want to be a cowboy, are you, Dylan? Not when you can be anything. I didn't have much choice. This dirt had bored into my blood by the time I could walk. You won't be brainwashed by the Texas sunset or the smell of fresh hay or the power of a quarter horse beneath you as you gallop across the summer grass."

"Sounds like a little boy's dream come true," Courtney whispered.

At her intrusion, Jared jerked his head up and grimaced. "In the movies, maybe. I almost lost the ranch until they discovered oil."

He slowed the rocking chair. "I think he's asleep."

"You can hold him awhile longer if you want to."

He hesitated then shook his head. "I shouldn't." With care, he stood and handed Dylan to her.

Courtney took the baby, expecting Jared to escape through the bedroom door and retake his place in the hallway where he'd spent the last few hours. Instead, he hovered, an enigmatic expression on his face. She shifted her weight and looked down at her son. Even in sleep she could see Jared, from the shape of his mouth, to the tilt of his head, to the slight smile as he slept.

"Léon didn't waste any time waiting for morning. CTC's men are updating the cameras and installing a perimeter alarm tonight. By morning we'll know if anyone unidentified sets foot beyond that two-hundred-yard point."

"That's a relief." So, they were safe. For a while. She needed some time. To breathe. To think. She wasn't sure what she'd expected from today, or this trip, but her entire body ached with fatigue. She needed rest. She glanced over at the bed. They would make do. If he'd just leave. "Dylan and I will be fine for the night."

She gave him a pointed stare, trying to get across the message.

"Where will Dylan sleep?" Jared asked, either immune or impervious to her insinuation.

"With me. I'll use the pillows. We'll be fine."

Jared rubbed his neck. "Would a baby bed help?"

"Of course, but where—?"

"I'll be back in a few minutes."

He left the room and his footsteps faded down the hall. When he reappeared, he carried a good quality wooden crib. Roscoe gripped the other end, the old cowboy's jaw tight with tension.

"The sheets are clean. Is over there okay?" Jared asked, pointing across the room.

She nodded, stunned.

Jared and Roscoe placed the crib flush with the wall. Before Courtney could thank them, Roscoe disappeared.

Still holding Dylan, she ran her hand along the smooth wood. "It's beautiful. I don't understand. It looks brand-new."

He didn't respond for a moment. His face frozen, Jared finally met her gaze. The pain in his eyes twisted her heart.

"Will it do?" he asked, his voice husky and so low she could barely make out the question.

"I'll sleep better knowing he's safe." She placed Dylan in the crib and pulled a yellow blanket over him.

"Good night." Jared's soft words filtered through her. Before she could follow, he left, partially closing the door.

She couldn't let him leave. His words and actions didn't make sense.

She exited the bedroom. A passage of closed doors greeted her. Velma hovered at the end of the hall. She tilted her head toward Jared's room and then made her

way to Courtney. "I'll watch the baby." She pulled a revolver from the pocket of her apron. "He'll be fine."

With a deep breath Courtney turned the doorknob.
Jared stood, stiff, his back toward her. "Leave it alone,
Velma," he said.

"It's me."

Jared's back stiffened. He didn't turn to face her. "It's
been a long day. How about we call it a night. Please."

The rough tenor of his voice pulled her into the bedroom. With tentative steps she crossed to him. She placed
her hand on his back. A shudder vibrated between them.

"How can I help?" She rounded him and looked up
into his face.

He swiped at his eyes and gave her a halfhearted grin
laced with pain. "A flash from the past. Just go back to
your room, Courtney."

His voice pled with her to go, but she couldn't leave.
She threaded her arms around his waist. For a moment
he stood stock-still, stiff and unyielding. She lay her head
against his chest. His heart thudded, strong beneath her
cheek.

Finally he slipped his arms around her. "This is
wrong," he whispered. "I can't let you stay."

"But you want me." She had no doubt of that. She
pulled slightly away and placed her hand on his cheek.
"I know you do."

His thumb caressed her cheek, following the line of
her jaw. He swallowed. "You are so beautiful. You make
me hurt. I dreamed of you so many nights."

Her heart skipped a beat. She'd wanted to lose herself
in his arms from the moment she'd awoken in that hotel
room without him. She called herself stupid at the time.
People didn't fall in love in a few hours. They didn't

know each other well enough to define whatever was between them as love.

A connection, certainly. She could feel the tug between them.

Before she lost her nerve she raised up on her tiptoes and pressed her mouth to Jared's. Maybe everything between them had been part of a dream? That night couldn't have been as amazing as she'd remembered.

The moment their lips touched she knew she was wrong. A flash of shock swept through her and settled low in her belly. She pressed harder, searching for a response.

What if he didn't respond? What if he—

A groan rumbled in his chest. He cupped her cheeks and his lips moved against hers, opening, searching for those memories.

He pulled her close, plastering her softening body against the hard planes of his. Against her, his body trembled. Courtney clung to his shoulders.

This wasn't what she'd expected.

He pulled away, his breathing harsh and shallow. She blinked once, then again, still in shock at the intensity of her response.

"You shouldn't have," he said, his voice husky.

He wasn't wrong. She'd complicated everything. She'd been selfish, thinking of herself, and not Dylan.

He gripped her shoulders. "I can't do this to you, Courtney. In the end, we'll both be hurt. I know you don't understand why, but I *need* to keep you safe. From the present, and the past. I couldn't live with myself if something happened to you. Or Dylan."

Gently he stepped away.

"Jared—"

"Watch over our son. Please. And I'll watch over both of you. It's all I can do."

His body rigid with tension, he led her to the door. She had no choice but to walk through. Her entire body hummed with unfulfilled longing, but he was right.

Until they could be sure Dylan was safe, nothing else mattered.

JARED STOOD FROZEN as Courtney's bedroom door snicked closed behind her. His entire body shuddered. My God how he wanted her. He rubbed his face with his hands and cupped the back of his neck.

Resisting her might very well be as challenging as identifying who was after her.

He'd failed that night in New York. He'd entered the bar longing for a shot of tequila and to disappear in his room, get out of his suit and into some jeans.

Instead, with her first simple question, he'd been enthralled. She'd exuded elegance and sophistication until their conversation had shifted, and he'd caught a glimpse of her heart. He'd convinced himself that their differences didn't matter. At least for the night.

Her devotion for their son, her fierce protectiveness. She obviously put him first. He admired the hell out of her. And that terrified him.

His cell phone rang and he looked down at the screen. CTC. Already?

"King."

"Jared, it's Zane Westin."

The CTC computer geek. "You found something."

"I need to speak with Courtney," he said. "And she needs access to a computer."

Well, hell. "We'll call you back in a few."

Jared ended the call and shook his head in disbelief as he forced himself to cross the hall. Was God laughing at him? He tapped lightly on Courtney's bedroom door.

She cracked it open, her eyes red, exhausted and emotion filled. "What could you possibly want now?" Her expression challenged him that any request better be important.

His brain went sideways, though, when his gaze veered down. She wore a silky, sapphire-blue, very short, very flowy scrap of material that cupped her breasts in a way that made him groan.

She glanced down at her attire and flushed bright red before disappearing behind the door and slipping on the shirt she'd worn earlier. It didn't help. "What do you want, Jared?" she asked, her voice tired and defeated.

He'd done the right thing, hadn't he? He was trying to protect them both from being hurt. Surely she could see that?

"Zane Westin from CTC wants to speak with you."

She buttoned the top up to the neck and closed the bedroom door quietly behind her. "You have the phone so I can see Dylan?" she asked, her chin held high as if she weren't half-naked.

He handed her his phone.

"We need to get on the computer," he said and led her into the study.

He pulled up a second chair and they sat side by side at his desk. He tried to ignore the flowery scent emanating from Courtney while the computer booted up. Hell, it took all the strength he possessed to keep his distance. He'd give almost anything to touch her.

She hovered beside him and he dialed CTC.

"We're both here and the computer's up," Jared said.

"Go to Courtney's social media page."

She logged in and a lively website displaying photos of Courtney at the museum and a few of a grinning Dylan greeted them. They looked happy and carefree. Courtney had created a good home for Dylan.

"I'm not sure I understand." Courtney clicked around the site, searching for anything unusual.

Jared had to agree. He couldn't decipher anything worrisome.

"Hold on. I'm sending you a link," Zane said.

A private message popped up and she clicked on it. The computer page shifted and a short text appeared. She blinked at the angry words.

When you play with people's hearts, they aren't the only ones who get hurt. Your time will come and the agony will come back on you tenfold.

Jared's shoulders tensed at the words. "Who does this guy think he is?"

"That's why I called," Zane said. "People say things on social media they would never express face-to-face. I need to know if this is someone who's just a hothead online so I can strike him off the list, or if you believe he could be a threat."

Jared turned to her. "Did he hurt you?"

She shook her head and he recognized the shock in her eyes.

"No, of course not." Courtney covered her mouth with her hands. "I never even saw the message. I didn't know I'd hurt him so badly."

"Who is he?"

"Desmond Hanover. We dated for a few months a couple of years ago. He got very serious very quickly. At first I was flattered, but soon his real interest became all too clear."

"Sex?" Jared asked.

"Something far more seductive. Money. He was more interested in what he assumed was my trust fund not the gallery's, and a job with my father than me."

"So you dumped him," Jared said.

"He was using me." She shrugged. "He came by a few more times. I threatened to call the cops and that was that."

"Some men don't handle rejection well." Jared would have liked to teach this guy some manners. A swift kick down Fifth Avenue would've felt good.

"But most don't concoct elaborate blackmail schemes requesting bizarre amounts of money, and they definitely don't commit murder," Zane commented.

Courtney tucked her legs up under her. "What if I just call him and ask," she said.

"I've done a credit search on him," Zane said. "He owes the bank over two million dollars and is about to go bankrupt." The clicking of speed typing sounded through the phone. "The numbers don't add up to our target, but he's a good candidate."

Jared reread the post. "The guy definitely has some anger issues."

He sent Courtney a sidelong glance. "You look skeptical."

"I can't imagine him killing Marilyn in cold blood. He never did like to get his hands dirty. I remember him going ballistic over a little dirt on his cuff. Let me call him."

"What do you think, Zane?"

"If I can eliminate this guy through a phone call and move on to other suspects, I wouldn't argue. If we don't like the sound of him, I'll keep digging."

Jared handed over his cell phone to Courtney. Zane read off Desmond's number and she put the call on speaker.

"What?" a sleepy voice answered.

"Desmond?"

"Who is this?"

Someone groaned in the background.

"Desmond, this is Courtney."

There was silence on the phone. "Courtney? Courtney who?"

Jared lifted a brow. Either the guy was a great actor or he'd forgotten the last name of the woman he was blackmailing.

"Courtney Jamison," she said.

Desmond let out a small laugh. "Heard your old man went belly-up in the markets. Guess I dodged a bullet when you wouldn't introduce me."

Courtney shook her head. "And thanks for reminding me why I dumped you, Desmond. Sorry to bother you."

Zane chuckled through the landline. "I'm putting a big red *x* through Desmond's name. Sorry I had to bother you."

"I want to help," Courtney said. "Whatever I can do."

"I appreciate the offer. I'll be in touch."

"Zane. How's it coming?"

The man sighed. "The fact that I just called you about a loser like Desmond is a good indication I've got doughnut holes right now. Courtney, honey, except for this blackmailer thing going on, you're one boring chick."

"Gee, thanks."

Jared shot her a quick glance. Her face had paled to almost porcelain.

"Don't you worry," Zane said. "This isn't even close to my toughest search. Besides, it's always darkest before the dawn. There's a light at the end of the tunnel, et cetera, et cetera. I'm doing the dive into your father next. No offense, but your dad's data looks to be much more interesting."

The phone clicked off and Jared shook his head. "Computer nerds are a different breed."

Courtney didn't say anything, just stared at the computer where an image of her and Dylan took up most of the screen. She wrapped her arms around her knees.

"Don't let this discourage you." Jared rotated her chair to face him. "They'll find him. They're just getting started."

"I'm afraid."

Her stark words tugged at Jared's heart. He stood and pulled her to her feet. "Come here," he said softly.

He wrapped his arms around her and she leaned against him.

A visible shiver went through her. "If someone hates me so much they'd threaten a baby, why don't I know who it is?"

Her voice caught in her throat. The pain of her words reached into Jared's soul and twisted, jerking forward memories of confusion and despair.

He didn't know how long they stood there, clinging to each other, holding on as if they were about to be torn apart.

She gripped his shirtfront and finally lifted her head. He cupped her cheek and looked down at her.

"Better?"

She didn't say a word, but nodded.

Her gaze met his. Her curves pressed against his torso. Awareness flared in her eyes. Her breathing grew labored and his own body grew heavy with desire.

No doubt the fire that burned between them eighteen months ago had flared to life.

"I should go," she said. "It's too much right now, you know what I mean?"

He stepped back, his entire being missing her closeness, leaving a bereft emptiness where only loneliness remained.

She crossed the study and at the door looked back. He could have followed her, could have probably seduced her with one kiss, one touch.

He let her go. She was right. It was simply too much.

Chapter Six

Dawn filtered between the slats of the blinders in Jared's room. He sat in a chair in the open doorway of his bedroom, rifle within arm's reach, and stared unblinking at the cracked-open door to Courtney's bedroom. She hadn't really slept. Every time he'd checked on them, her eyes had been open, staring at her son.

He hadn't slept, either. Not that he could have even if he'd wanted to. Memories of losing himself in Courtney's kiss warred with the risk. Even if the Criswells were arrested and the blackmailer caught, he couldn't let his guard down. Each moment of Alyssa's kidnapping played over and over in his mind.

He couldn't come up with a win for the long term that included Courtney and Dylan.

Short term…he had to find a solution. Throughout the night he'd tried to work out alternatives. Léon had been right. Jared couldn't send them back to New York alone; but they couldn't go into hiding forever, either, especially without knowing the identity of the murderer. Jared knew better than most how much an unsolved case paralyzed life.

Someone had better find a lead fast, because they

needed a plan. Jared hated sitting there waiting for some lunatic to make the next move.

A baby's cry sounded from beyond the door, at first tentative, followed by an ear-numbing scream. Jared jumped to his feet and slammed into the room across the hall.

In the doorway to the bathroom, Courtney stood in all her nude glory. She was gorgeous.

She shrieked and whipped a towel around her naked body. "What are you doing?"

Fighting against temptation, Jared averted his gaze from her damp skin and walked over to the crib. Dylan stood in the crib, clutching the wood edge, his face twisted and red. The kid could use those lungs full force, that's for sure.

"Whoa, little guy, what's got you so mad?"

Jared turned his attention to the baby to avoid Courtney's tempting shape. Dylan looked up at his father. Huge tears fell from his glistening eyes. His mouth pouted and the crying wouldn't stop.

Jared slid his hands around the baby's torso and lifted him against his chest, then above his head. The shocked baby stopped crying for a moment and looked down.

"Quite a different view from up there, huh, Dylan?"

The baby screwed up his face.

"It's not working, Courtney." Jared could feel the panic rising within him. "What do I do?"

"He's hungry and wet," she said, tucking her towel under her arms. She reached into Dylan's bag. "I ran out of diapers last night and am running low on wipes. I need to get to a store."

"You can't leave the ranch," Jared said. "Not until we know more."

She crossed her arms in front of her in an image he would never forget. An absolutely livid expression dressed in a too small towel.

"Well, Dylan can't do without the supplies. Can we send someone? Maybe Velma or Roscoe?"

There was a more immediate solution. Jared sighed, knowing he had to take her to the one room in this house he hadn't wanted her to see. The room he'd entered less than a handful of times in five years. But since he didn't know what she'd need or what sizes would fit his son, he had no choice. "Throw some clothes on and come with me. Please."

She must've heard the strain in his voice, because she didn't argue with him, she simply disappeared into the bathroom.

When she left, Dylan reached toward the closed door and screamed as if Jared were torturing him. He tried bouncing the baby up and down. Tried flying him like an airplane. Nothing worked.

Roscoe appeared in the doorway holding his ears. Jared shrugged.

"I'm going outside to work on the tractors where it's quieter," the foreman shouted.

The baby squirmed in Jared's arms. He was ready to bang on the bathroom door when he tried one last time to lift Dylan over his head.

The hard crying stopped. The baby chortled and smiled. Jared brought him down to face height. Up, and a smile. Down, and a frown.

After a few more push-ups, to Jared's immense relief, Courtney appeared in the doorway, dressed. Jared handed over the fussy baby. He should have been pleased to give his son to her, but the emptiness in his arms lingered.

He enjoyed those chubby legs and belly, and that laugh. Dylan's laugh could light up any dark day.

"Let's go." Jared led them through the convoluted hallways to the old part of the house and the nursery door.

With one last look at her, he slipped the key in the lock and opened the room.

Courtney gasped.

He knew why. She saw a finished nursery with a few missing pieces and one huge hole in the wall. A changing table sat on one side of the room. The crib and rocking chair he'd delivered yesterday were gone. The walls had been painted yellow in a Noah's Ark theme, though the missing drywall marred the happy color.

Deliberately avoiding the scar, he opened several drawers and stood back. "Take what you need."

Her steps tentative, Courtney leaned over and looked in the drawers. Dylan balanced on her hip, she pulled out a few onesies. "These are for a newborn. Too small."

Jared cleared his throat. "Try the closet."

She slid open the door and viewed stacks of cloth diapers and washcloths which sat untouched.

"Who—?"

"Take what you need." Jared picked up the never-used diaper bag and handed it to her. He knew each word was clipped and angry, but every moment in this room sent a tsunami of pain through him.

Courtney balanced Dylan and filled up the bag. The baby whimpered, then let out a full cry.

"I need to change him."

She lay the baby on the table and covered his midsection with a washcloth.

"Where are the pins," she muttered, wrestling with the square cotton diaper.

Jared's mind had gone numb, but he forced himself to look. He dug into a drawer and pulled out some animal-styled fasteners.

"Not quite a disposable," she said, holding Dylan down with one hand. "I'm learning more and more to appreciate stick-on tape."

Dylan grinned up at her. He bounced with a laugh, kicking his feet in the air and sending the washcloth flying.

"You're an exhibitionist, Jelly Bean," she chuckled before fastening the last pin. She looked over at Jared. "Are there any rubber pants in the closet that would fit him?"

Jared scanned the room. He remembered storing a ton of unidentifiable supplies after Alyssa had gone crazy in the baby store. She'd bought items for up to a year old. He squatted down and opened the bottom drawer.

"How about these?" He handed her two plastic-looking briefs.

Courtney took them. "Even an extra. We should be fine for a while."

Good. Then maybe he wouldn't have to come back here. He fought to breathe against the suffocating flood of memories. "I'll send one of the hands to Carder for whatever you need. Or better yet, maybe have someone from CTC buy what you need. Less cause for talk."

"Who would care?"

"There's no superstore in Carder. Just a general store. Everyone knows everyone's business. If someone from the ranch starts buying baby supplies, the entire town will know by lunch."

"I can't imagine having that many people interested in what I do or say."

"Small towns," Jared said. "Not a lot of distractions."

Courtney lifted Dylan. "I noticed a few toys in the back. Can I bring some with me? We left in a hurry."

"Take whatever you want," he said in a rushed voice. The room had begun to close around him.

Courtney piled a ball, some blocks and a stack of brightly colored rings in the large bag. She paused at the two-foot-diameter hole in the wall Jared had been avoiding staring at since they entered the room.

"Let's go," he said, and lifted the bag over his shoulder before she could ask about the center of the wall he'd destroyed with a sledgehammer.

With a slight hesitation and one last regretful stare, they walked back to her bedroom.

He braced himself for the question, because he didn't want to tell her. Didn't want her to know how badly he'd failed.

She sat Dylan on the rug and rolled the ball to him. He giggled and stuffed the edge in his mouth.

"Whose nursery was that?" she asked.

A DEAFENING SILENCE engulfed the bedroom. Courtney had been shocked by a lot of events over the last few days, but finding a fully stocked nursery in Jared King's house confused her as much as anything.

Dylan banged a ball on the floor, obviously enjoying his new toy almost as much as the stuffed bull Velma had given him. Courtney smiled at her son, but the expression faded when she saw Jared's devastated face.

Obviously the Last Chance Ranch hid a lot of painful secrets.

Jared stood quiet and unnaturally still, staring at their son with an intensity that made Courtney shiver.

She closed her eyes. She'd been so relieved to find

supplies that Dylan could use, she hadn't really thought what it meant until they'd returned. She shouldn't have asked. How could she take it back?

"You asked about the nursery—"

"Everyone has a right to some secrets, Jared." Courtney tried to give him an out. The pain in his eyes was hard to look at.

"You more than anyone have a right to know."

Dylan crawled across the floor and pushed the ball at Jared's feet. It bounced against his boot and the baby grinned. Jared hunkered down and returned the ball to his son.

"I was married before."

She'd known. His wife had died. That much her private investigator had told her. As he spoke, Courtney wished she could retract the question. She didn't like the direction her mind took her.

"You don't have to—"

Dylan shoved the ball back at his father. Jared sat on the floor and focused on the game, avoiding Courtney's gaze.

"You remind me of Alyssa a bit," he said finally. "You both exude class when you walk into a room. You both look out of place on a working ranch."

Jared turned the ball over and over in his hand until Dylan grabbed for it. He let the baby take the toy.

"We were happy. Mostly. But she got bored with small town life. We hoped having a family would fix the problem." Jared shrugged. "It might have. I'll never know."

He glanced over at the baby's bed. "I made the crib for our daughter. I spent weeks wanting it to be perfect. She never slept in it. She died with Alyssa."

Courtney couldn't stop the choked sob from escaping.

He'd lost his wife, and his unborn child. She couldn't imagine the agony. She crawled to Jared's side and placed her hand on his arm. "Please, don't relive any more. I'm so sorry I asked."

He didn't move away from her. Instead, he lay his hand on hers and after a few moments lifted his gaze to hers. She'd never witnessed so much pain behind a man's eyes. He broke her heart.

"It's important you hear this," he said after a long, deep breath. "I was busy trying to keep us out of bankruptcy. We couldn't afford enough help so I drove the cattle to the far end of the ranch to graze. Took me a day and night on horseback. When I got back Alyssa was gone. There was a message painted on the wall of the nursery. They wanted money in exchange for her safe return."

Courtney shivered at the similarity. "You've been through this before? Like me?"

"Not like you. I had no warning. When I came home, Alyssa had simply vanished. I didn't receive a note. The message was spray painted on the wall of the nursery I'd just finished painting."

Nausea rose to her throat. Please no. Not that.

"The guy knew exactly how much would break me. But he didn't know I'd just used all my cash to purchase a new stud. No way I could liquidate by his deadline so I called the local sheriff. I told myself I had no choice."

Jared's tone went flat. "The guy taunted me, made me think I could save Alyssa. I didn't follow his instructions and she paid the price. She died along with our unborn daughter."

Courtney leaned up against him and slipped her hand into his. "Did they catch him?"

Jared rubbed the back of his neck. "After it was over

the guy vanished. He's still out there somewhere." Jared sent her a quiet, devastating glance that tore her up inside. "Even if we catch the blackmailer, the threat against me will still be out there. I can't risk anyone else getting hurt because of me."

What could Courtney say? She'd do the same thing. For a few moments, she rested against Jared, wanting him to feel her support. Nothing could be said to comfort him. A little human contact was all she could offer.

Across from them, Dylan gripped the ball. He pressed one of the sides and tinny music started to play. He giggled and rolled over toward them, shoving the toy at his father.

Jared's jaw throbbed and Courtney realized how much he strained to maintain control. She could see he wanted to let himself open up to their son. She understood more than ever why he couldn't.

"I'm so sorry for what you've lost. If I'd known—"

"You would've come here anyway because you'd do whatever it takes to protect Dylan."

Yes. He understood like no one else in the world ever could or would. "You're right."

"So would I."

The stark words reignited the connection between them. She wanted to say more, to help him, but she had no idea how.

Before she could work up the courage, Jared's phone sounded. He rose, relief written on his face at the distraction. Courtney had to agree, though she missed the warmth of his touch. Jared had faced and lost more than she could ever imagine. Nothing she could ever say or do would make it better.

"King," he said into the phone. Within a few seconds he tapped the speakerphone. "It's Léon."

"Miss Jamison?" The operative's voice sounded very solemn, causing her stomach to knot a bit. "Did you hire a private investigator to look into Jared's life and finances?" The rustle of papers shuffling reached through the phone. "A man by the name of Joe Botelli?"

Her gaze flew to Jared's. A cloud of fury darkened his expression. "Why would you do that?"

She swallowed deeply. "When I recognized you on the television, I needed to know who you were, Jared," she blurted out, knowing how the facts must appear to Jared. She would've taken it the same way. "You were his father, but I knew nothing about you. It was never about money. I had to protect Dylan."

Jared's expression had frozen into a mask. "Go on, Léon. Does he have any insight?"

"I'm at your front door," the accented voice said. "I think we should talk face-to-face."

The doorbell rang. Courtney scooped up Dylan and his toy, and sidled up beside Jared. "I wasn't trying to find out your bank balance." The words raced out. "You have to believe me. I needed to know if contacting you was the right thing to do for Dylan."

Jared rubbed his temple. "I get it. I really do."

Did he, though? Had contacting Botelli ruined the trust between them so soon?

Velma reached the door before them. She hesitated. "Should I open it?"

"It's CTC," he said.

Léon walked into the house, his face solemn. "We need to talk."

"Maybe I should watch the baby?" Velma said, holding out her arms.

Courtney hesitated. Every instinct in her screamed to keep Dylan tight in her arms.

"Are the perimeter alarm and cameras active?" Jared asked.

"Done," Léon said. "And we're constantly monitoring."

"It's up to you, Courtney."

She glanced at the operative's intense expression. He gave her a curt nod. "I think it's best."

With reluctance she handed over Dylan. Velma patted her hand. "Don't worry. I'll be right in the kitchen giving him a cookie. If I hear anything strange, I'll hightail it right back to you."

Courtney nodded and followed Jared and Léon into the study. "What's wrong?"

"You may want to sit down," Léon said.

"Just tell me."

"Botelli's dead. He was mugged two days ago around three in the afternoon near his office."

Courtney slapped her hand over her mouth. "That can't be. We met at lunchtime in a coffee shop just near there."

"Whoa. Hold it. Mugged?" Jared paced back and forth and finally came to rest toe-to-toe with Léon. "Coincidence?"

A dismissive huff escaped the operative. "That's what the murderer wants the police to think. I'm not seeing a lot of investigation going into it, but I don't buy it. He was a Marine. Tough SOB from what I hear. No small-time punk took him out. Not from what I can tell. I have our forensic expert pulling the preliminary autopsy report."

"You can do that?" Courtney asked.

"CTC can do a lot of things. We have friends who owe us. They believe in paying it forward."

Léon took a seat next to the coffee table. "Sit down. Both of you. There's more."

Courtney couldn't imagine how much more there could be. Her mind had gone numb. First Marilyn. Now this. Who had them in their crosshairs?

She sat down on the sofa and Jared settled in next to her, leaving a good two feet between them.

"This is a copy of Botelli's file on you, Jared. Nothing shocking. A few articles, financials, information about your wife." The CTC rep placed a folder on the table. "We have to assume whoever is after your son has this information, as well."

Jared glanced at the pages. She could read the fury in his glare along with a we'll-talk-about-this-later message. "Are you saying Dylan's kidnapping is because he's my son?"

"I started in that direction. Until we found this." Léon lay two more files in front of them.

Courtney glanced at the name on the folders. "Me and my father?"

Léon cleared his throat. "Some of this is a bit intrusive, but it couldn't be helped."

"Go ahead," she said, bracing herself. Her father had shocked her already when he'd revealed he'd lost their family fortune. She didn't think she could be any more surprised.

"Your net worth isn't anywhere near enough to pay the ransom since you don't own the penthouse where you live. Your grandmother's trust is tied up, as well. Anyone wanting you to pay a ransom could figure out those facts easily and know they'd have to go elsewhere for the money."

"To me?" Jared asked.

"You aren't the first obvious source of money. Ms. Jamison is." Léon opened up her father's folder. A long list of numbers appeared.

"These are your father's most recent loan requests and lines of credit. All rescinded within the last week, by the way, which forced him to sell everything. He's broke. Take a look."

She winced. She'd hope her father had been exaggerating, but the evidence didn't lie. "There are some large numbers here, but none of them match the number in the note," Courtney said.

"We haven't found the correlation yet, but our current hypothesis is that your father's finances might be at the root of the ransom."

She sagged against the sofa's back. "Someone's using my son to get back at my father? Why?"

"We don't have the details. Not yet. Zane's working the issue." Léon met Courtney's gaze. "We're headed back east to see your father. We think we might get answers more quickly in person. And Zane can dive into his computers."

"I should come with you," Courtney said. "He'll talk to me."

Jared shot to his feet. "No way. The guy murdered an ex-Marine in New York. You're not going anywhere near that place."

"I agree," Léon said. "I don't even want you to call him. I'd like to see his face when I ask the question. Once we correlate the money to something specific, we'll be able to narrow down the list of suspects. We won't be shooting blind in our protection."

"I didn't tell him what was happening. The note warned me."

"You may have saved his life. Joe Botelli had opened a file on your father. That could be why he was eliminated."

Stunned was too limp a word to describe Courtney's emotions. "What about you and your team? Will you be putting yourselves at risk if you talk to my father?"

"That's our job. And we're better than good at it." Léon's expression turned cold and dangerous.

"Keep us in the loop, Léon," Jared said.

"And you keep your guard up," the operative warned. "You never know who the guy could hire, but my gut tells me this is personal and specific. That makes him less predictable than I'd like. We'll know more when we speak with Mr. Jamison."

"We need the answer soon," Jared said, and placed his hand on Courtney's and squeezed.

"There is one more wrinkle I should bring up," Léon said. "I left this one for last."

Despite Jared's reassuring touch, Courtney gripped her pants leg with a fist to shove down the foreboding rising inside her. "What is it?"

"The cops found your nanny's body, and they have your fingerprints in her blood. They've put out a BOLO on you and named you a person of interest in her death."

Chapter Seven

Today marked the second day Jared hadn't taken Mulligan for a long gallop across the ranch. He might not be able to take the quarter horse as far as usual, but with the cameras and perimeter alarms in place, he could at least stretch their legs with a walk around the paddock.

The ranch house's walls started closing in on Jared. He was going stir-crazy. He wasn't meant to be inside all day long. If he'd ever wondered how he'd do with a city job, he had his answer.

At just after noon his phone pinged a text message. The last of the alarms were in place. Thank goodness. He picked up his tablet to view the new camera angles CTC had installed. He tapped through the live images a half-dozen times. He didn't see anything out of place.

Unlike his study.

Jared had to smile at the chaos. Dylan had littered the floor of the study with toys. Courtney lay on her stomach playing with him. They were in a holding pattern at the moment. After CTC's preliminary investigation, Jared was more convinced than ever Courtney's father was the key to the ransom demand.

They should know more soon. CTC's private plane

had landed in New York and they were on their way to see Edward Jamison.

"Okay, I've had it," Jared said. He snagged his son into his arms. "How about you and I go outside?"

Courtney looked up at them. "Outside?"

"The alarms and cameras are up. There's nowhere the blackmailer can hide. The guards are on duty. Dylan and I are going down to the barn to look at the animals. We'll stay close."

The baby tilted his head and threw his arms around Jared's neck.

His chest tightened at his son's response. Dylan didn't have any pretense. He was so refreshing.

"Would you like to come?" he asked Courtney.

"I have to get something from the bedroom. I'll meet you down there."

Jared hesitated, but she gave him an encouraging smile. He could see what she was doing. She wanted him to bond with his son. Well, it had taken all of a smile for Jared to want more than anything to throw all caution aside and give the baby the world.

Every moment he was around Dylan he fought against those instincts. So what was he thinking spending more time with the child? He could blame cabin fever. Why not? It was better than the truth. That he wanted to get to know his son, his quirks, his sense of humor, what made him laugh and cry, what made him angry.

"This may be a big mistake, Dylan, but we're doing it anyway." He strode out of the study and out the front door.

The porch stretched to either side. Jared walked to the corner of the house. The men walking guard duty appeared shocked to see him with a baby in hand. Well, they'd have to get used to it. Until this was over. Tim was brave enough—or young enough—to approach Jared. His arm was in a soft cast. He smiled at the baby.

"Cute kid."

"How you doing?"

Tim shrugged. "Angel Maker just clipped me. I'm fine."

"You're not on pain meds are you? You need to be alert with that rifle at your side."

"Just some ibuprofen. I swear."

Jared nodded. "You see anything unusual?"

"Except for the bull going AWOL?"

"Except for that."

Tim shook his head. "It's been real quiet. Everyone's on guard, Mr. King. Nobody wants nothing to happen to your boy and your lady."

His lady. The words made his gut ache, but he forced a smile. "Get back to your post. The kid and I are going to explore a little. See if you can't find time to walk Mulligan a bit sometime today."

With a half-baked salute, Tim rushed over to the other side of the house.

"It's hard to find good help, Dylan. When I was about twelve, I thought I'd be running this place with my best friend, but he didn't love it like I did. He likes computers. Frankly, I'd recommend following Derek's lead. That's where the money is. Unless you happen to get lucky and a few dinosaurs died a million years ago under the dirt."

Jared stepped onto the road and walked toward the barn and stables.

"This is my ranch, son." Jared swallowed past the thickness in his throat. His legacy. "The Last Chance Ranch, because it was my ancestors' last chance at redemption for a few too many wild adventures. The Kings have been here for six generations. Mostly causing trouble. You're too young to hear those stories. Maybe someday."

Dylan tilted his head and patted Jared's cheek. He rubbed against the stubble and giggled before stretching out to try to grab Jared's Stetson.

"You're a cowboy at heart, aren't you, little guy?"

Jared's heart filled with pride. He'd never dreamed he'd be here, with his son. Courtney had given him an unimaginable gift. He leaned low and nuzzled Dylan's cheek. "I love you," he whispered softly. "You may not remember, but I always will."

He reshuffled his son and together they headed toward Angel Maker's pen. The gate had been fixed and reinforced. The bull Angel Maker snorted his red eyes staring down the baby. Dylan's gaze grew wide. He reached out a hand.

"Oh no you don't, my boy. He's dangerous. You can't go near any of the animals without me or your mama or Roscoe or Velma, but Angel Maker in particular. He might be a mean one, but his genetic material is going to create some excellent stock. You know what, kid, maybe someday I'll take you to the rodeo…"

Jared's voice petered off. That wasn't going to be happening, not once he sent Dylan and his mother back to New York. For their own safety. Until Alyssa's killer was caught, Jared wouldn't take the risk.

The idea made his gut ache. He shook off the feeling and pushed through the double doors on the horse barn. "See all that hay. That's what horses eat."

Jared chuckled. He didn't know exactly what Dylan

understood but that look on his son's face made him wonder if he wasn't horrified at the idea of eating straw.

"I'll give you a hint. Velma's cookies are *way* better than a horse's diet."

He walked down a row of stables. "Let's go see Mulligan. He'll like you." He walked across the hay to the stall where his favorite mount chomped on feed. Jared pulled out a carrot from the barn stash. Dylan reached for it.

"I don't know if you can eat this, little guy. I'm pretty sure I'd have to turn it into mush, but it's one of Mulligan's favorites."

Those big brown eyes blinked, then the beast looked away.

"Unless he's pouting." Jared reached over the gate to pat the horse. "I know, boy. It's been too long since your ride, and we can't go today. So how about that carrot?"

The horse didn't reach for it. Jared shrugged. "I could take it away."

He left his hand open and Mulligan chomped down the vegetable. "I thought so."

He patted the animal's neck.

"Okay, boy. Be still. We have a visitor." He shifted Dylan in his arms. "Son, this is Mulligan. He's my horse."

Jared gently guided Dylan's hand to the horse's soft nose. His son's mouth opened in awe and he patted the animal's fur, then turned a bright grin on his father. "I thought you'd like him."

The baby squirmed in Jared's arms. "You want down? Sorry. Not in here. Not until you're older."

Dylan screwed up his face.

"Don't give me that. How about we go see the tractor."

Jared exited the barn and rounded the building. A large green tractor was parked, waiting for a rider. He eyed one of the CTC guards and sent him a questioning glance. The man sent him a go-ahead signal so Jared climbed up and sat in the seat. "We're high up here, aren't we?"

Dylan rubbed his eyes and buried his head against Jared's chest. "Are you shy? Did I scare you?"

Had he done something wrong?

"He's just sleepy," Courtney's voice said from down below them. Tim had followed her, and Jared gave him an appreciative nod before the young man returned to his patrol.

She was gazing at him with an expression he didn't want to recognize. They both had to be careful. They shared one night and a child. Emotions and feelings had ruled one night. They both needed to keep their heads on straight for now.

"You're very good with him."

"Kids and ranches go together. There's nothing hard about it."

Dylan blinked and reached his arms down to his mother. She smiled. "You ready for a nap, Jelly Bean?"

The baby frowned, but Courtney simply chuckled. "I think you are."

Jared climbed down from the tractor and handed his son to her, leaving him empty. And not only his arms.

"I want to try to keep him on his normal schedule as much as possible," she said. "Even though nothing about right now is normal." They made their way into the house.

"I understand. But I'm still your shadow. For now at least."

"Are you sure? I'm feeding him again."

Jared's gulp echoed through the air. Courtney bit back a grin. They returned to the house to the bedroom and she settled in the rocking chair. Jared took his place just outside the door, but looked away when she nestled Dylan to her breast. She covered them both with a blanket and eased back and forth.

"See-saw, rocky-daw," she hummed softly.

Jared peeked out of the corner of his eye. She toyed with the hair falling on Dylan's forehead. Jared had never really considered the intimate relationship between mother and child. Even if he were part of their life, he could never have the kind of relationship Courtney had with Dylan. Their bond excluded him. Did other fathers feel the same way?

She swayed to and fro, her eyes closed. At least she felt comfortable enough to relax. The discoloration beneath her eyes revealed her need for sleep. The last couple days had been tough.

Her eyes opened and she met his gaze. "He's asleep." She fiddled with her clothes under the blanket and removed it. His son's eyes were closed, his small mouth slightly open in sleep.

"You're exhausted," Jared said, stepping into the room. "I know you didn't sleep much last night. You should get some rest."

She shook her head. "I wouldn't feel comfortable." She rose and lay Dylan in the crib.

Jared held his breath. If he'd learned one thing in the last twenty-four hours it was that Dylan could go from sleep to awake in a split second. The baby shifted a few times, nestling down into his blanket, then finally settled on the mattress with the fuzzy blue bull clutched in one hand.

Courtney sighed in relief. "Another cup of coffee will hit the spot."

She veered toward him and Jared reached out his

hand, stopping her. They faced each other and he couldn't breathe. Her eyes softened and melted his heart.

"You're an amazing mother," he said. "Dylan's a wonderful little boy."

She shook her head. "I don't know what I'm doing half the time."

"You fooled me, because I don't see how you could have done better with him." Jared tucked her hair behind her ear, just as he had that night. "The night we met, you said you longed for something permanent in your life, that wouldn't be disposable."

"And I got Dylan." She frowned. "I can't lose him, Jared."

"We're safe enough for now. Take a nap."

"I can't. What if I fall asleep and something happens?" She swiped at her eyes. "What's wrong with me? I'm not usually this weepy and I've been like a faucet since I arrived."

"No sleep and stress will do it every time. Believe me, I know. Lean on me. That's why I'm here." Jared pulled her into his arms and held her close. She rested her head against his chest. "Come to bed. I'll watch over you both."

She gripped his shirt tight and he walked her backward toward the bed. She let him push her onto the mattress. He knelt in front of her and pulled off her ballet flats.

"If you hang around much longer, we need to get you some boots." Jared rotated her legs on the bed and stared down at her.

She gripped his hand. "Stay with me." Her eyes were pleading and vulnerable. "I can't do this alone, Jared. I know you're trying to protect us from your past, but right now the present is scary enough. Can't we deal with one crazy person at a time?"

Her words didn't allay his fears, only reminded him of the threats. "I don't want you hurt, Courtney."

"Me, either. So, stay with me. Just for today. I'm tired of being alone in this, Jared. I need you."

The three words twisted his heart. He sat on the bed and pulled off his boots, shifting until he lay beside her. He pulled her back against him and lifted the quilt over them.

They lay spooned, facing the crib so he could watch over Dylan.

"Thank you," she whispered.

The room went silent save for their breathing. The heat between their bodies cocooned Jared in warmth. If someone weren't trying to destroy everything around him he would have said he was experiencing a slice of heaven.

He didn't know how long they lay there together, but he knew she hadn't drifted off to sleep. Her breathing hadn't fallen into that deep, regular pattern.

"The noises here are so different from New York," she whispered.

"No traffic, no horns, no impatience."

"I hear some muffled shouts and a bit of puttering around the house, but it's so quiet."

"Is that good or bad?" Jared whispered in her ear, trying to keep himself from nuzzling her neck. All he'd have to do would be to turn her toward him and he could kiss her. He didn't think she'd say no.

"I'm used to blocking out noise. It's hard to fall asleep without it."

As if she'd read his mind she turned in his arms. "I

can't fall asleep," she said, staring at his lips. "My mind keeps dwelling on horrible possibilities."

She placed her hand on his cheek. "I want to forget, Jared. Just for a few minutes. Can you help me forget?"

HER ENTIRE BODY TREMBLING, Courtney clutched his shirt. Would he pull away from her? Her stomach flipped with nerves. What had she been thinking? Could she laugh it off, blame her insane offer on lack of sleep?

"Courtney. Look at me," Jared said, his voice low and deep.

She forced herself to raise her head and meet his gaze. His eyes had darkened with intensity. He turned her hand over and kissed her palm, lightly, gently.

Her heart thudded in response.

"Does that help you forget?" he asked with an infinitesimal smile in his voice.

"No," she said breathlessly.

His lips touched the top of her head. "How about now?"

"Not yet."

He shifted his weight and her head rested against his shoulder. His ran his lips along her temple. "Now?"

Courtney closed her eyes, leaning into him. The pine scent of his soap intoxicated her. "No. Please."

His finger tilted her chin up and he kissed her cheek, moving along her skin until he came ever so close to the corner of her mouth.

"Jared," she groaned.

He pulled back and stared deeply into her eyes. His callused hand toyed with her hair. "It's like spun gold," he said quietly. "Almost unreal."

His fingertips followed the line of her cheek to her

throat. Courtney held her breath, anticipating his next touch, terrified he would stop, that he would allow her to think again.

He simply stared at her, silent. Her body trembled in anticipation. He touched her lip with his thumb tugging gently, then traced her mouth, teasing the sensitive nerve endings until she wanted to scream.

"Please," she breathed. "Please kiss me."

"I dreamed of you," he whispered. "Too many nights."

"Me, too. Sometimes I didn't think it was real."

"Except you had our baby."

"And he's proof that the entire night wasn't all in my imagination."

"Are you sure about this?" he asked carefully. "Emotions ruled that night. I have a feeling they are again."

"I don't care," she said. "I've been waiting a year and a half to feel alive again. Don't make me wait any longer."

With a force that surprised even her, she tugged at his lips and he opened his mouth, tasting the salt of her skin. Courtney closed her eyes against the overwhelming emotions. For the first time since she'd awoken in the lonely bed in the hotel room she didn't feel utterly alone.

He swallowed deeply. "If I kiss you, Courtney, I won't stop."

"I don't want you to."

He lowered his mouth and his lips touched hers. She wrapped her arms around his back and pulled him closer, wanting to feel his body on top of hers.

"Jared!"

Roscoe's shout tore them apart. Jared wrenched his lips away from hers and catapulted off the bed.

The foreman rushed into the room, his gait off-kilter from his earlier encounter with Angel Maker. "A brush fire popped up from the north near the oil rigs. It's been dry the last few months and we've got a twenty-mile-an-hour wind. It's heading for the quarter horse facility."

JARED GRABBED HIS boots and sat on the edge of the bed. He refused to look at Courtney. He could imagine the invitation on her swollen lips and passion-filled eyes.

Dylan whimpered and stood up in his crib. Courtney crossed to him and whispered to him, calming the baby.

"Lightning?" Jared asked, facing Roscoe. He didn't appreciate the arch of a brow on his foreman's face.

He shoved his feet into his boots. Roscoe didn't say a word, only tossed his shoulder holster at him.

So much for being discrete. Roscoe knew exactly what they'd been about to do.

"No storms, no clouds. It came out of nowhere."

"Man-made, then. Could be an accident. Could be one of the Criswells." Jared strode across the hall and grabbed his rifle. "Velma!"

At his call, the housekeeper rushed into the bedroom. He handed her the weapon and gave Courtney the keys to his truck. "Stay locked in this room with Dylan. If the fire gets out of control, I'll call and you two head for CTC. Velma knows where it is. Got it?"

The housekeeper pointed the barrel toward the ground and nodded. Courtney gripped the keys tight.

Jared tried to give her a confident smile. "It's part of living in the middle of nowhere. You gotta do for yourself. By the time the volunteer fire truck arrives, we'll have this thing out. Right, Roscoe?"

"Sure, Jared." The foreman studied Velma, his features looked pale and nauseous. "You don't take any chances, woman. You hear me?"

"Oh, quit your sweet talkin'. Besides, maybe one of the hands flipped a cigarette," Velma said, the perpetual Pollyanna. "Some of 'em got no more sense than a bullfrog."

Roscoe stared at her like she was crazy.

"It could be," she protested.

"Get your head out of the dirt, woman. You know what's happened. Criswell is upping his threat. He's trying to force Jared to give in."

"There is another option," Courtney said. "What if it's *him*? What if he's here, on this ranch."

Jared thrust his hand through his hair. "We'll review the video footage after we take care of the fire. In the meantime, do what you have to do to protect yourself," he ordered. "I'll leave as many men to guard you as I can. The CTC operatives are out there and I'll make certain more are on the way. You're not alone." He sent Velma a stern look. "Just don't shoot me on the way back in."

"Get out of here, boyo," Velma said. "We women can take care of ourselves. Been doing it all my life."

She gripped the rifle with the very determined look on her face he recognized so well. She would do whatever it took to protect her family. So would Courtney.

Jared paused, then pulled her close and gave her a hard kiss on the lips. "You take care of our son. I'll be back soon."

He took one last look at his unhappy son before racing out of the room. Roscoe headed for the truck and Jared locked the door behind them. He took in a quick sweep of the guards.

"No one gets in that house except me or Roscoe," he ordered.

They nodded. Angel Maker snorted in his pen as if in agreement. Crazy bull.

"Let's go," Jared shouted and jumped into his truck. Several hands leaped into the back. Jared pushed the truck as fast as he could, heading north. He could see the smoke rising. There was a lot of it.

Once or twice, though, he caught himself glancing in the rearview mirror. "I don't like leaving them," he said to Roscoe.

"Get your head in the game, Jared. If the fire gets past those buildings, the wind'll bring it to the house way fast. The whole place will go up in flames, and we might not be able to get back in time," Roscoe said. "We gotta stop it up here."

The truth of his foreman's words chilled Jared. As they got closer thick smoke settled on the air making it tough to breathe.

"Break out the masks the minute I stop," he said.

"The men know what to do," Roscoe said. "I trained 'em. And you. So let them do their job."

Jared skidded to a stop a few hundred feet from the barns. He looked on in horror. The crackling fire had licked its way up the backside of the large structure.

Roscoe exited the truck and started shouting orders. The men piled out of the vehicle and grabbed a pile of white smoke masks. They weren't anything like what firefighters wore, but they'd keep their lungs clear in the short term.

An explosion made the ground shudder. Thick smoke billowed from the top of the barn. Okay, that wasn't normal.

Jared tapped his phone to speed dial CTC.

"What's going on out there, Jared?" Ransom asked. "I got an emergency page from my men.

With a curse, Jared's grip tightened on the phone. "Is everything at the ranch okay?"

"So far, we're status green."

"Keep it that way. I left Courtney and Dylan at my house, but I've got a bigger mess here than I thought. Either the Criswells have gone nuts or someone with a much bigger agenda is trying to burn everything on my land."

"Or, it could be a diversion, Ransom countered. "Do you get the feeling it's as if the guy has a view into exactly what we're doing and thinking?"

Jared spat out a curse. "Exactly. I'm going home."

"We'll keep them safe and I'll contact you if the situation changes," Ransom said. "But that fire needs to be contained before it spreads."

Ransom was right. Jared ended the call and shoved his phone into his pocket. When he slammed open the door a wave of heat hit him. He could hear the horses whinnying from inside the structure.

"Sanderson, take the back. You two—" he pointed to a couple of hands "—work the hoses. The rest of you, get the animals to safety. I want this fire under control before the Carder Fire Department arrives."

The men scurried off. At least he'd had the money to purchase the mobile firefighting unit. Its two hoses would give them a fighting chance of getting this thing under control.

Jared rushed into the building. Brownish-tinged smoke billowed around him, the air thick with soot. He squinted. Roscoe fought one of the quarter horses and pulled him out. "They're spooked bad," he coughed.

Jared grabbed a rag from a bucket and opened the stall to his prized mare. She snorted and reared up. "Easy girl," Jared choked out. Grabbing her bridle, he covered her eyes with the rag and tied it over her ears.

The blindfold calmed her and he led her out, handing her off to one of the hands. "Get them to the east pasture," he shouted.

Jared rushed to the fence when he caught sight of the fire leaping from the roof of the barn to the barracks. Off in the distance the siren of Carder's single fire engine headed their way. It might not be enough.

A shout rang out from inside the vacant winter barracks.

"Stop!" a hoarse voice called out.

"What the hell?" No one was supposed to be staying here. Jared ran to the building and threw open the door. The fire had dropped down from the roof and had created a wall of conflagration. He scanned the ceiling. The timbers would give way soon.

Eyes burning, lungs scorched, he could barely make out the long hallway, but a familiar blue shirt on the ground caught his eye.

"Roscoe!"

Taking a deep breath, he leaped through the fire and hurried to his foreman. A wooden beam lay beside him, and blood trickled from the wound on his forehead. The fire behind them roared. Flames consumed a curtain at one of the windows.

Jared grabbed Roscoe beneath his arms and dragged him to the other end of the building. In just the few seconds since he'd entered the structure, the fire had doubled in size, sweeping across the wood floors as if it were in a conflagration race. The flames licked up the walls, closing in on them.

Above, the wood creaked. Desperate, Jared searched

for a means to escape. He tugged Roscoe toward one of the windows, but the fire outran him and suddenly the last opening was barricaded by flame.

"Roscoe? Can you hear me?"

The man's eyes fluttered.

He was still alive.

One wall remained fire-free. For the moment. Slowly sparks soared toward the wood. It would ignite at any moment. Without a sledgehammer or something large and heavy he'd never break through. Spinning around, searching for a way to survive, Jared's gaze penetrated the smoke. He grabbed a chair and ran toward the fire-engulfed window, slammed the wood through, and then raced to pull a blanket from a lower bunk.

He wrapped Roscoe in the blanket, making sure it covered his arms, and shoved his foreman through the opening and dropped him to the ground. Flames licked against the back of the shirt. Heat moved in closer. Jared dove through the opening, twisting in the air to avoid landing on Roscoe, and rolled in the grass. Pricks of heat peppered Jared's back. He yanked the smoking shirt from his body and ground it into the dirt.

They weren't safe yet. Roscoe was too close to the building. He grabbed the man's hands and dragged him away before collapsing backward onto the ground.

Smoke exploded from the opening as oxygen fed the fire. The smoke rose in a plume, darkening the sky. Jared lay there for a moment sucking in air. His eyes burned.

He was alive.

With a groan he sat up and bent over Roscoe. The man's eyes were closed, his jaw slack.

Hand shaking, Jared placed his fingertips on Roscoe's carotid. A faint beat pulsed against him. He tore off the smoke mask and rested his cheek close to the man's mouth. No breath.

"You're not doing this to me, Roscoe. Not today."

He unmasked himself, closed his foreman's nose and puffed a couple of breaths. Then waited.

"Breathe, damn it."

Two more puffs.

Roscoe heaved, Roscoe rolled over, and coughs shuddered through his body. He swiped his mouth. "That's enough. I'm awake, I'm awake," he choked out. "No reason to keep kissin' on me."

Jared sagged, a slight chuckle escaping him. "Don't scare me like that. Breathing isn't optional."

Roscoe wiped his mouth and propped himself up. His eyes widened. "We gotta run."

Jared followed his gaze and let out a loud curse. He grabbed Roscoe by the arm and practically carried him.

The building behind them groaned and shuddered, wood cracking under the heat. The fire roared with intensity sounding like a tornado.

After twenty feet, Jared and Roscoe collapsed on the ground.

Not a moment too soon.

Glass windows exploded; the roof imploded.

Both men turned over and covered their heads.

Debris shot over them, a fire rain bombarding them. When it subsided, Jared stood up and looked around.

Several men were dousing the shrapnel. He bent over. "That was close."

Roscoe looked up at Jared.

"I saw someone. He had a gas can. This was sabotage."

Chapter Eight

The ranch house felt like a prison. Courtney paced back and forth and peered out the small window of the bedroom. She should be *doing* something. Gathering food, water, bandages. Instead, because of the threats, she was stuck here, like the citified woman Roscoe believed her to be.

Plumes of dark brown smoke drifted from the north over the ranch, its acrid scent poisoning the fresh air. An hour ago the sirens of a fire truck and ambulance had screamed across Jared's land.

Still, they waited.

Unaware of the dangers outside, Dylan had discovered energy to spare. He crawled around the room, exploring everything. She'd shut the bathroom door to keep him from getting into trouble. Right now, he'd discovered the closet and a small cubby underneath a short table sitting inside. It was just his size. He threw his stuffed bull out of the closet and crawled to retrieve it before repeating the process a second, third and fourth time.

Courtney would normally have been on the floor enjoying her son, but instead, she recorded every fact she could remember from the time Marilyn had called to warn her. With one eye on him and on Velma, she filled page after page.

The housekeeper sat on the bed holding the gun and staring at the door.

"How much longer do you think?" Courtney asked, her legs bouncing with nerves.

"No telling. Fires are tricky, especially as dry as it's been lately. No news is good news as far as I'm concerned. Nobody tried to get in this room, and Jared hasn't called to evacuate. To me, that's a win."

Dylan crawled between her legs and grabbed on to her pants. He pulled himself up and grinned at her, oh-so-proud of himself for standing alone.

"Look at you, Jelly Bean," she said with a smile. She chucked him under the chin. He hugged her and then scooted beneath the crib, lying on the floor and staring up at its base.

Courtney planted herself cross-legged on the bed. "Jared told me about Alyssa and their daughter."

Velma's eyebrow popped up. "I'm surprised. He doesn't talk about them. Ever."

"I can't believe they never caught the man who killed her."

Velma clicked her teeth together. "That was a bad business. I thought Jared might waste away to nothing. He blamed himself for so long, not being able to save Alyssa from drowning. For months he called out her name in his sleep, promising he'd save her this time."

"She drowned?"

"The murderer pushed her out of the boat at Last Chance Lake and weighed her body down with a tire. Jared did everything humanly possible, but she was under the water too long. He's never forgiven himself."

"I didn't understand how much he must have gone through," Courtney whispered. "And he was never caught. He could still be out there."

"That's Jared's fear. It's why he's built an impenetrable wall around his heart. The truth is, the murderer could easily be dead. He hasn't shown his face since. The ranch has done well. And we haven't had any trouble until the last few months when the Criswells started causing trouble because they want to bleed more money out of Jared."

The sabotage on the ranch couldn't be about Dylan and her. A month ago, she hadn't known Jared's name.

"Jared won't move on, will he?" Courtney twisted her hands in the fabric of her pants.

"He won't take the risk. He can't. Not with anyone. And especially not with his son."

A phone rang and Velma pulled it out of her pocket. "Jared? Is that you?"

She nodded her head and looked over at Courtney giving her a thumbs-up. "We're fine. Barricaded and safe."

She let out a sigh.

"Is he going to be okay?" The worry lines on Velma's brow deepened.

Courtney leaned in and Velma moved the phone so they could both hear.

"Roscoe's sitting in the ambulance now," Jared said. "They're giving him oxygen, but he refuses to go to the hospital."

"Stubborn old coot. Bring him home and I'll make up a room for Derek, too."

Velma ended the call.

"What happened?" Courtney asked.

"Roscoe done and got himself almost killed, but they put out the fire. Jared's bringing him home. And I'm calling his son." Velma's face held a certain amount of glee. "Derek will give his father hell for not taking care of himself. We may finally convince that boy to come home."

"Finally, we can leave this room."

"Not so fast, honey. Until Jared walks through that door, you and I are staying put."

With a scowl, she returned to her notes, but another half hour didn't provide any insights. A familiar rhythmic knock sounded softly on the door.

Velma grinned and Courtney yanked it open.

"Glad you didn't shoot me through the door, ladies," Jared said.

He looked like he'd been through a war. Soot smeared on his face, his clothes reeked of smoke. Shirt torn and coated with dried blood.

She ran her hands up and down his body, checking for injuries. "Are you hurt?"

Jared quirked a half smile. "You should see the other guy." The smile didn't reach his eyes, though. He shoved his hand through his hair. "I need a shower. I put Roscoe in the old guest room. One of the hands is helping him."

"I'll check on him and make you a dinner that'll stick to your ribs. Both of you," Velma paused and clutched the rifle. "I'm keeping this with me."

"Good idea."

Jared crossed the room and peered underneath the crib, watching Dylan quietly for a few moments. "Slept through it all, did he?"

"He had an adventure but wore himself out a few minutes ago."

Jared picked up the stuffed bull and set it next to his son.

Courtney studied his face. "How bad is the damage?"

"We got lucky. The volunteer fire department and some of my men are staying to finish up. They'll make certain there aren't any live embers to reignite the fire."

"Could they tell what started it?"

"That's a complicated question." Jared rubbed his eye. "A cigarette ignited the burn near the oil derricks, but once the flame reached the barn, someone used an accelerant."

"So it *was* deliberate."

"Not only that, someone hacked into the surveillance cameras' signal." Jared kneaded the back of his neck. "Someone wanted my whole place to burn to the ground."

COOL WATER SLUICED down Jared's back, soothing the heat. He winced as he passed over the scraped skin. He was getting too old to jump through windows. He pressed his hands flat against the shower's tile and bent his head down so the water would do its magic. Roscoe had almost died. He'd almost lost the horses. Several men had been injured. And for what?

They'd disabled the cameras until they could identify the vulnerability. He wanted to scream and shout, "What do you want from me?"

A quick squeeze of shampoo and he lathered up his hair. He had no time for asking questions without answers. He had some decisions to make and actions to take.

He rinsed and turned off the water. After drying, he wrapped a towel around his waist and rubbed his hair as he stepped into the bedroom.

Courtney sat on the king-size bed, waiting for him. Her eyes widened, but she didn't look away.

"You need something?" he asked and pulled a white T-shirt from his drawer then slipped it over his head.

"Sorry. I thought you'd be dressed." She hesitated. "I better go."

"Don't. We need to talk," he said. "Wait here."

He grabbed a pair of briefs and jeans and disappeared into the bathroom. His mind whirling with concern, he slipped them on. When he returned, she sat still, her hands folded in her lap, appearing as proper as a woman could sitting in a man's bedroom.

He didn't quite know how to begin.

"Is Dylan with Velma?" He ran a brush over his wet hair, bringing the short cut to order.

"She's his new favorite person since he discovered her snickerdoodles."

"The way to a man's heart—"

"Is through a sweet tooth in Dylan's case."

Jared tried to smile, but he couldn't. He sat down next to her. "When you arrived on the ranch, you turned my life upside down."

She bowed her head. "I know. I'm sorry."

He lifted her chin with his finger. "I'm not. I'm just sorry I haven't been able to live up to my promise." He let out a long breath. "Whoever's doing this is a step ahead of us. You're not safe here. Every instinct tells me we're sitting in the bull's-eye of a target, and I have no idea who from. If the Criswells are willing to use fire as a weapon, and maybe even hire someone to sabotage security equipment, they're out of control. I can't call the sheriff or Dylan could suffer. If whoever is blackmailing you caused the fire, he's already here. Either way, we have no choice but to act."

"We need another option," she said.

"Unless CTC comes up with a good suspect in the next couple hours, I want us to take you and Dylan into the mountains while they do their job. I probably should have made the move yesterday." He clasped her hands. "I thought I could protect you. I really did."

"You have. We're safe. Dylan's here," she said squeezing his hands in return. "It's not your fault."

"My battle with Ned has compromised your safety. That *is* my fault, but I'm done playing by the rules, because our enemies sure as hell aren't."

"What are you going to do?" she asked.

"See that you're safe, then have a long, serious conversation with Ned so CTC can focus on the man who's threatened you and my son."

A soft knock sounded on Jared's door.

"Come in," he said.

Velma peeked inside. Dylan was balanced on her hip gnawing on a cookie. "Roscoe wants to see you, Jared. And Derek said he could make it here by morning."

"Good. He's the only one I'd trust to keep this place running with Roscoe down. And maybe he can convince his dad to see a doctor."

She frowned. "I wouldn't count on it. He seemed pretty set he's not letting a doctor touch him." Velma looked from him to Courtney and grinned before closing the door softly.

A blush tinged Courtney's cheeks. "I wish there was something I could do," she said softly.

"Maybe there is. Léon left a copy of the files he showed us. They're on my desk. Go through them again. Perhaps you'll see something they missed. I better go see Roscoe."

"Give him my best," she said.

Jared left her and made his way to the old part of the house. Roscoe had refused to get into bed and sat at a makeshift table eating a bowl of soup. He scowled. "That woman's feeding me like I'm an infant," he groused.

"Let her pamper you or she'll make your life a living hell."

"Don't I know it." Roscoe winced when he lifted his arm.

Jared let out a curse. "You need a hospital."

"I need to be here. I saw the guy, Jared. He was wearing a mask, but I saw the triumph in his eyes when he poured the gasoline. He was about five-ten, medium build, brown eyes."

"So not Ned Criswell. Or Chuck. Nobody would call them medium build."

"Maybe one of his hands?"

Jared sat across from Roscoe. "I'm taking Dylan and Courtney into the Guadalupes, up to the old hunting shack. You and I are the only ones who know about it and I can keep them safe."

"You gonna let Ned Criswell destroy this ranch for good?" Roscoe said with a frown.

He lifted his chin, and Jared winced at the scrapes and bruises his foreman sported.

"Look, I'm just going to say it. What if she's making the whole thing up, Jared? What if that woman Marilyn never died. What if this is a big plot to insert herself here and get your money."

"Careful, old man."

"Hear me out. The private investigator could've been mugged. Or she could've hired some thug to kill him. She could have an accomplice who's calling that cell phone. Hell, it could even be a recording. We don't have any proof the threats against that boy are real. Except maybe in her mind. We *do* have proof someone's trying to destroy this ranch. Seems to me you should be worrying about the King legacy and not some elaborate fairy tale spun by a woman you don't know except to take her to bed."

Jared jerked to his feet and grabbed the neck of Roscoe's shirt. "If you hadn't almost died a couple hours ago, I'd slug you for that. Do you think I never considered the possibility? Well, of course I did. The moment she mentioned she needed money for the ransom I suspected her."

A gasp sounded from behind Jared. Courtney stood in the hallway, her face pale. She turned and ran.

"Courtney," he shouted. He glared at Roscoe. "Damn it. If anything happens to them because of this, I don't know if I can forgive you. Ever."

COURTNEY SPED DOWN the hallway, away from Jared. She didn't veer into her bedroom. It was the first place he'd look. Did he really believe she'd planned this whole thing? They didn't know each other well, but she'd trusted him with her son. She'd put her faith in him. His words stabbed at her heart, a betrayal like she'd never experienced.

She made it to his study. This was *his* room. The last place he'd search for her. She walked the room, noticing for the first time the wall of antiques mounted near the stone fireplace. An old horseshoe circa early nineteenth century. A barbed wire wreath. An Apache medicine bundle and an array of Apache knives from different eras. Some with stone blades, some with steel.

Several newer knives were displayed in Jared's gun cabinet. Everyone on this ranch carried a gun of some kind. Courtney had never shot one, but she was tired of depending on others to defend her.

She reached inside and pulled out a sharp knife in a sheath. She slid it from its leather case and the blade glinted in the light.

"You going to gut me with that?" Jared said quietly.

"Maybe." She faced him. "Do you still believe I made this all up to somehow gain control of your money?"

"I considered it."

The words were a slap in the face.

"And dismissed the idea when you responded to the threat to Dylan when Velma left the stuffed bull in his crib. You may be from New York, but you're no actress. Your emotions come through with every expression."

"Roscoe doesn't trust me."

"He's scared. He almost died and he doesn't know how to stop what's happening any more than I do."

"I'm done trying to convince him, Jared."

"You don't have to." Jared took the knife from her. "What's made you so curious about the weapons?"

"I have to be able to defend myself."

"A knife is more difficult to use than a gun," he said. "But it can be hidden and used to surprise someone. Try this one. It's a folding knife with a five-inch blade. Legal in Texas. You can slice someone across the belly and run like hell."

She turned it over in her hands and opened and closed it several times.

"If you're going to carry it, stand so you protect your vital organs. Bend your knees and keep your nondominant hand in front of your neck. Your heart and lungs will be harder to reach."

She stood as he instructed. It felt strange. Jared took

his position about an arm's length in front of her. "Stand up straight and hold your arm out. See how you can barely reach me."

Nothing she could do at this distance.

"Okay, now go from the other position and slash at my neck or chest. The angle gives you better coverage. The goal isn't to kill me. Just to stop me and get away."

"Let's try it."

He took her through a series of moves at least a dozen times. She bent over and took in several deep breaths. "I don't know if I can do it."

Jared put his hands on her shoulder. "If you're not going to use the weapon, don't carry it. I'll put it away."

She gripped the knife and shoved it into her pocket. "If it's a choice between me and Dylan and someone else, I can use it."

"Have you ever fired a gun?" Jared asked.

She shook her head.

"It's easier to use, but you have to be willing to pull the trigger."

"For Dylan, I'll do whatever it takes."

"Let's go to the root cellar," he said.

Before she could question the bizarre statement, he disappeared out the door and returned with a large target.

"With the cameras hacked, I'm not risking going outside."

He pulled out his Glock and grabbed her hand, leading her downstairs. He set up a backstop then added several bales of hay. Finally Jared pulled over a small table and placed the gun down on it.

"You ready for this?" he asked.

She took a deep breath and nodded.

"This is a Glock. They don't have a traditional safety

that will stop you from pulling the trigger. However, there are internal safeties that will stop it from firing unless you actively pull the trigger. So if you drop it or throw it, it's not going to fire."

He picked up the weapon. "There's an eject button on the side. Flick it and the magazine will come down. That's where the bullets are located."

The magazine fell into his hand and he placed it on the table.

"The other important thing you should know is how to pull the slide back. When you pull the slide back, you can verify there aren't any rounds in the chamber."

He tugged and the Glock clicked open. He gave it to her.

"So, right now, we have an empty, safe weapon."

Jared pulled out a box of bullets. "Load the magazine one bullet at a time." He showed her one. "Now you try."

Seemed easy enough. Courtney pressed a bullet into the magazine and added a second by pressing the first one down and sliding the second one back. Before long she'd filled the magazine.

She could do this. She had to. For Dylan.

"Excellent."

"Push the magazine into the bottom until it clicks."

"It's more simple than I thought."

"Now you pull the slide back. When you do that, you'll have loaded and cocked the gun. It's ready to fire."

Very gently she tugged it back and the weapon clicked in place.

"See how the trigger is now forward. You're ready to shoot. All you have to do is point downrange and pull the trigger."

Courtney squeezed and the gun jerked in her hand. By

the time she'd emptied the magazine she had better control. She set the weapon gingerly on the table. "There's quite a bit of kick."

Jared nodded. "Remember, it's not like the movies. Don't plan on shooting farther than ten feet or so. You probably won't hit the target."

"Can I try again?"

"We can practice as much as you want to."

Courtney began loading the Glock again. "I don't want to practice, but I need to. I just hope I don't have to use it," she said.

"If we're faced with life and death, I plan to be there so you don't have to."

Jared stared down at her. "Are we okay?"

She grimaced. "We have to be. Dylan's all that matters." Courtney turned away from him.

Jared opened his mouth to say something but his cell phone interrupted. He tapped the speakerphone. "You have us both, Léon."

"We met with Jamison. Your father is somewhat… indisposed."

"You mean he's drunk. He'd started when I arrived the other day."

"Well, I don't think he's stopped since. He was passed out. We took him to the hospital."

Courtney rubbed her eyes.

"Zane's going through his computers, but he didn't keep great records. His emails are more informative. He was trying desperately to save your family home. Doing anything he could."

"Where do we go from here?" Jared asked.

"I'll send what we have," Léon said. "Can Courtney

review the documents? Maybe she'll see inconsistencies we don't."

"Whatever you need," she said.

"Zane will keep searching. There's nothing more I can do here, so I'm heading back. When your father regains consciousness, we can hopefully catch a break." Léon paused. "Ransom informed me about the hack. There are other options, you know. We can make Courtney and her son disappear. We've done it for others."

Jared met Courtney's gaze. She shook her head.

"We're not ready to turn our backs on solving this yet, Léon. But we'll keep it in mind."

Jared hung up the phone. "What do you think? Would you want to change your identity, leave behind everything and start fresh?"

Courtney folded her hands. Could she and Dylan give up everything? "If I thought he couldn't be safe, I'd consider it."

Jared nodded. "Me, too."

"But like you said, I'm not ready to give in to this guy yet." She strode over to his desk. "Can you check your email?"

He smiled at her. "Let's do this."

On a tablet, Courtney reviewed the documents one by one, line by line. She sifted through the notes from CTC and then returned to the documents. Her eyes went blurry.

"There's not enough tying the numbers to a particular person or group," she said. "And nothing that matches the number in the blackmail note."

Courtney retrieved her notepad. She transcribed all the numbers that were smaller than the total. Soon a prick of excitement tingled at the back of her neck.

"Jared. I think I found something. These four numbers add up exactly to $3,680,312.00."

He leaned over and gave her a huge smile. "What do they correspond to?"

"These four entries. I recognize one of the names. It's a Pennsylvania bank."

"Does your family have business in Pennsylvania?"

"I remember my grandmother talking about a mill that had been in the family since the Industrial Revolution. At one time it was the flagship of the company."

Jared typed the information into a Google search.

"Bingo. A mill owned by your family was shut down without notice five days ago. Several hundred people lost their jobs." Jared picked up his phone. "I'm calling Léon. You may have just solved the mystery."

HIS CAMPOUT WAS well hidden, out of view of the cameras. No one would find him there.

The plethora of computer equipment in the trailer had come in handy. He hadn't expected the challenge of CTC.

They'd been good. They were better than him, but he'd had years to prepare.

He'd faced a few hiccups, but nothing he couldn't handle.

After pressing the jamming signal he searched the smoky remains of the buildings.

No one had died.

Pity.

Unfortunately, the destruction hadn't forced Jared's hand. Yet.

One window of opportunity, that's all that was

needed. He scanned the horizon and his gaze lightened on a fresh target.

Yes. That would do. That would do nicely. Jared would never be able to resist.

Chapter Nine

Jared spent the evening in the office with Courtney researching the Pennsylvania textile mill in a small community outside of Allentown. The picture was grim. When Jamison had finally closed the doors, it had decimated the community. There was little left.

There had been numerous protests and they came up with a list of over a hundred suspects, then narrowed it down to those who had been arrested. CTC split the list with them. Unfortunately they'd come up empty.

"This doesn't make sense. Why focus on me and Dylan?" Courtney asked, throwing down the papers in disgust. "It's an awfully convoluted way to make their point. Even if we give them the money, it won't bring the mill back."

"Feels wrong to me, too," Jared said. "Maybe your father has more insight."

Courtney curled up her legs under the sofa. Dylan was safely in bed with the camera monitoring his every breath. She still carried the knife in her pocket and she and Jared had formed a truce of sorts.

Roscoe was another story.

"Until my father sleeps it off," she said, "he won't be able to help us. I've seen him out of it for a couple days."

The picture she painted was one of a very lonely little girl. "How often did it happen?"

"After my mother died, a lot." Courtney shifted on the couch. "He didn't know how to handle her illness, and I didn't make it any easier."

Jared joined her on the sofa.

"Until I was thirteen or so, I didn't know most dads didn't have that sour smell of alcohol coming off their skin."

Jared stretched his arm across the couch's back, behind Courtney's head. "It must have been hard."

"Not as much as you'd think. My dad had worked all the time anyway. Losing my mom was the hardest thing I ever went through, but our housekeeper made sure I did my homework. I spent weekends with her working for different charities. Cooking at soup kitchens, building homes, that sort of thing."

"Not the childhood I would have guessed," he said.

"What, you thought I went to boarding school and spent all my time shopping?"

He grimaced because she'd absolutely nailed it. That's exactly what he'd thought. He twisted in his seat. "You are a constant surprise and it's very intriguing."

She leaned her head back, resting it on his arm, and turned toward him. "It's funny. I don't think anyone who knows me, knows about that part of my life. Not even my father."

Her words tugged at Jared's heart. She might reside in New York, but the more he learned about her, the more he recognized she didn't *live* there. Not really. Possibilities niggled at the back of his mind; possibilities he shouldn't even consider. But he wanted to.

Courtney shifted in her seat and moved closer to him.

"If things were different. If no one was out there trying to hurt us, do you think… I mean, would you…"

She glanced away from him but not before her cheeks reddened. He leaned into her.

"If things were different, nothing would keep me from seducing you in every way I know how until you never wanted to leave."

The words left his lips before he could stop them.

Her eyes dilated and she eased closer. "I'd like to pretend. Just for tonight."

Jared's body tensed and he stilled. "The future—"

She pressed her finger to his lips. "The future is tomorrow. We were interrupted once. I want tonight. I want all of you tonight, Jared."

He saw no hesitation in her eyes, just like that night a year and a half ago, but this time their senses weren't dulled by tequila. He tugged her into his lap and wrapped his arms around her. She turned to face him and cupped his cheeks in her hands.

She brought her mouth down to his and unleashed the passion. She straddled his hips and ground her pelvis against him. His body hardened under her.

Jared thrust his hands into her short, silky hair and pressed open her lips. His tongue dueled with hers in an age-old ritual. Unlike the last time, he knew exactly where she longed to be touched.

He nibbled at the base of her jaw and let his hands slip to the sides of her blouse down to her hips and tugged the material from her waist. In one easy movement he removed her shirt and lowered his mouth to the curve of her breast. She arched against him and her soft groan urged him onward.

Soon she was nude from the waist up and he feasted on her curves, evoking shivers of ecstasy from her.

Her hands clutched at his T-shirt and she pushed it over his head, her hands exploring the muscles of his chest. She pressed him back against the sofa and he let her touch him, her gentle fingers outlining the scrapes and burns from the fire. He didn't feel anything but pleasure, though.

His body hardened under her and when he couldn't bear it any longer he lifted her up and stood.

He could hear his labored breathing and hers. She explored his skin and slipped her fingers beneath the waist of his jeans. She flicked open the button and lowered his zipper, but he stilled her hands.

"Not so fast," he whispered. "You're overdressed."

In no time, he'd removed the remainder of her clothes and she stood before him. Her body had changed since having Dylan. If anything, she was more beautiful than ever. He shirked his jeans and pulled her back into his arms, lowering her to the rug on the floor.

She tugged him closer, then shifted her weight with a laugh, reversing their positions. She propped herself up on his chest and smiled down at him.

"I like pretending."

"So do I." He flipped her over and urged her legs apart. Once he'd slipped on a condom he paused, looking deep into her eyes.

"You're certain."

"Very."

Whereas before their movements had been frantic and heated, Jared didn't want their lovemaking to end. Slowly, tenderly, he pressed inside her until he was buried deep. His head dropped onto her shoulder and he sighed.

He was home.

A STRONG ARM rested on Courtney's bare skin. For a moment, she couldn't quite figure out where she was. Morning sun spilled through the curtains in Jared's study.

She lay cocooned in his arms, covered by a soft quilt.

Last night she'd told him they could pretend. She'd lied. She didn't want to pretend. She wanted last night to go on and on. She wanted every kiss, every touch to be real, but she knew she could never convince Jared. And how could she argue? She'd do anything to keep her family safe. Even at the expense of her own happiness. Or her own life.

As would he.

He'd proven it, and it was one of the reasons she… she loved him.

Oh God. She loved him.

Her chest tightened. She could hardly breathe as the truth settled over her heart. But she couldn't doubt her feelings. She shared parts of herself with him no one else knew. He'd gifted her with his own heartbreaking past.

She'd give anything to be able to heal him, to make the hurt go away. She cuddled down deeper against him.

Jared tightened his arms around her.

"Good morning," he whispered, kissing her hair. He let his fingertip travel down her arms and she shivered at his touch.

A loud cowbell rang outside. He let out a low curse. "Breakfast for the men. It must be six."

Courtney glanced at the phone Jared had laid beside their makeshift bed last night. Dylan had started squirming a bit. He'd make his presence known soon.

She sat up and searched for her clothes. They were strewn near the sofa.

"We probably can't make it to our bedroom without someone seeing us."

"We can try," she said.

Jared grabbed his jeans and tossed her clothes to her. Quickly they dressed and Jared stuck his head out the door.

"Clear," he said and led her into the hallway.

They rushed toward their bedrooms just as Velma appeared from the kitchen. She took one look at them, grinned widely and turned back the way she'd come.

"So much for sneaking around."

A loud pounding sounded on the front door.

"I'll get it," Jared said, tucking his shirt into his pants.

Courtney hovered out of sight. Maybe CTC had uncovered something.

Jared opened the door to a blond-headed man wearing an expensive suit and a wide grin.

"J.K.!" he shouted.

"Derek." Jared grinned and embraced the man. He shut the door and locked the dead bolt. "I'm glad you're here. Roscoe will be thrilled. And surprised."

So, this was Roscoe's son and Jared's childhood friend. She'd never seen such a welcome on his face.

Derek's gaze paused on her. He smiled at Jared. "Have you got something to tell me?"

Jared followed his line of sight. For a moment he paused. Courtney froze. Maybe he didn't want her to meet his friend. Maybe—

"This is the mother of my son," Jared said, holding out his hand to her.

Hesitantly, she made her way over to him and took her hand. He entwined his fingers with hers.

"Your what?" Derek's expression turned from a smile to shock.

Courtney held out her hand. "I'm glad to meet you."

Derek grinned and pulled her in for a tight hug. "Anyone who got this guy to return to the land of the living deserves more than a handshake."

She smiled at him.

"You done good, J.K. I can tell she's a class act."

Courtney tucked her hair behind her ear. He was more like Velma than Roscoe, that was for sure.

Derek crossed his arms in front of him. "I should've come back sooner. "Dad's been emailing me and he didn't say a thing about you two. Of course he didn't say a word about the fire either."

Courtney met Jared's gaze before he responded to his friend "It's one of the reasons I'm glad you're here."

At Jared's solemn tone, Derek stilled. "The same reason you're wearing a Glock?"

In a clipped tone, Jared brought his best friend quickly up to date on everything. Derek whistled under his breath. "And the fire?"

"May be related to Courtney. Maybe to the Criswells. We just don't know and I need another set of eyes to keep everyone safe. Someone who knows this land like I do."

Derek glanced down at the floor, avoiding Jared's gaze. "I haven't lived here for a long time, J.K. I'm not sure I'm the best choice."

"That's bull. You care about this place as much as I do. You always have."

For several moments Derek didn't speak. Jared waited. Courtney could only hope his friend agreed. They needed all the help they could get.

The furrow cleared from Derek's brow. "You've got me. I'll do whatever I can. Now, how's Dad doing? Really."

Jared squeezed her hand tight and a light settled in his eyes. Courtney leaned into him. Piece by piece things were looking up.

"Roscoe's about like you'd expect," Jared led them into the study. "Stubborn, but improving. He's staying in the old wing of the house while he's recuperating so Velma can keep an eye on him."

Derek grinned. "I'm sure he likes that. A lot."

"Please." Jared shuddered. "Just don't go there. I pretend I don't know what's going on between them, and I like it that way."

The expression on Derek's face slipped a bit. "First I need to see Dad, then put me to work."

Jared slapped Derek on the back. "You bet. Go visit, and then we'll figure it out. Man, I'm glad you're here."

Derek grinned at his friend. "Me, too. It's been much too long."

AFTER A QUICK SHOWER—which he would have much rather shared with Courtney—Jared exited his room with a new attitude. Maybe their luck was changing. Derek had come home to help out. They'd discovered a connection between Courtney's father and the money.

The only problem with that was Courtney and Dylan would leave soon, and Jared would miss them. More than he could have imagined.

He walked into the kitchen and poured a cup of coffee. Velma grinned. "Derek the wanderer is back."

"He certainly is."

"Did I hear my name taken in vain?" Derek asked.

Velma raced over to him and hugged him close. "Roscoe's missed you. You need to come home more."

"Business has me hopping," Derek said. He turned to Jared. "I'm heading to my room and get a shower and change out of my work digs into jeans and boots. Burberry and barns don't mix."

"I'd agree with you there. Not to mention those shoes. Italian?"

Derek nodded. "I checked in on Dad. He's resting, so for now I'll check in with Frank about where he wants me to stand guard. See you later?"

Jared nodded. "Hey, Derek. Thank you. It means a lot that you're here."

"I wouldn't be anywhere else."

Derek disappeared into the old part of the house, and Jared scooped up an egg sandwich from the tray Velma had stacked on the sideboard. He sat down at the table and munched on his breakfast. Velma eyed him for several minutes before finally sitting across from him.

She grinned with that knowing, scary expression that had terrified him from the time he'd gone through puberty.

"What do you want to know that I'm not going to tell you?" he asked between bites.

"I can't believe he came home. His father's been trying to tempt him for two years. I didn't think I'd succeeded."

Jared eyed the coffee cake across the room. He rose and fetched the plate before returning to his seat. He took a large bite of the cinnamon and sugar treat and followed it with a large swallow of coffee. He nearly rolled his eyes in pleasure.

With a shrug he took another bite. "I texted him after

you called and let him know I needed him to convince Roscoe to the doc for a full physical."

Velma frowned at that. "The cough?"

Jared nodded. This time his cake tasted almost like sawdust. "It doesn't sound good."

"I know. I've been worried, too. Whatever the reason, I'm glad he's here."

"Can you believe he jumped right in to help with the guard duty. With Tim injured, we could use all the help we can get."

Velma folded a napkin and took a deep breath. "Which brings me to another topic of conversation."

Jared flushed. "If it's about this morning—"

"I'm not a prude, boyo, but I am worried about you. And about Courtney and Dylan. Are you going to ask them to stay after this is all over?"

Jared stared down at his cup. "I wish I could, but it's not possible."

Velma shot to her feet. "I think what you're doing is wrong. That little boy needs a daddy. Courtney needs a partner. And you, Jared, need someone who loves you more than anything in the world. Don't let that SOB who stole your family five years ago win again."

Velma's eyes went wide in shock and she spun away from him. She headed toward the laundry room and slammed the door.

Courtney walked in and let out a low whistle. "I think you're in trouble."

Jared flushed. "I'm sorry you had to hear that. She doesn't understand."

Courtney stole a small piece of coffee cake from his plate and popped it in her mouth. "She understands perfectly. She doesn't want you to live your life in fear."

"I explained to you what happened. I can't risk your life or Dylan's, not when the person who hates me is so willing to kill those closest to me.

One sharp push and Courtney shoved her chair back. "I understand, Jared. And maybe once we've caught the blackmailer I'll feel differently, but right now, I need you by my side, and I'm getting used to it. The truth is, I'm not so sure I want to give you up when this is over."

She stalked out of the kitchen. Jared watched the sway of her hips as she turned the corner to head back to her bedroom. Was he a fool for paying attention to the past?

A sudden wave of shouts hit just outside. Jared shot to his feet and raced to the front door. He met Tim coming up the stairs.

"What's wrong?" Jared asked. Tim's recent cast had already taken on a shade of Texas dirt.

"Frank and I were doing rounds on the west pasture. We found a slew of dead cattle and even more with tremors and convulsions. I've never seen anything like it."

Jared's face turned to stone except for the pulsing at his jaw. Tim took a step back and Jared forced himself to calm down.

"What caused it?"

Jared had a bad feeling he knew exactly what the culprit was.

An older cowboy pushed in. "Someone salted the water."

The worst thing you could do to animals. And it wouldn't only affect the cattle.

"What's the damage?" Jared asked.

Tim shook his head. "No telling how many we lost. Or how many wild animals were poisoned. We blocked the watering hole but ever since Old Man Criswell dammed up the water, fresh is hard to come by. The cows were a bit dehydrated anyway, and that salt did them in."

Jared paced back and forth. Was this Criswell again? It had to be. Why would a blackmailer from Pennsylvania want to poison cattle in Texas? It didn't make any sense.

Jared faced Tim. "Take care of the carcasses," he ordered. "We'll need samples to send off to the lab to prove the cause. And I want you to keep an eye out for tire tracks, human tracks, bottles, anything that could point to the person who poisoned the water."

"I saw tire tracks. Like the ones behind the barn where the shot was fired. Same tread."

Jared rubbed his chin. "Really? We thought it might be a large truck. Like an F-350, didn't we?"

Tim nodded.

Jared slammed his hat against his jeans. "You know what, Criswell has gone too far this time. I don't know if it's Ned or Chuck or both, but I've had it." He turned to Tim and Frank. "What are you two waiting for? Get back out there."

The two men hurried away and Jared glanced over his shoulder. Derek stood near the house and Courtney stood in the foyer of his house.

He strode over to them. "Derek, keep watch here. I'm heading over to the Criswell ranch. I shouldn't be more than an hour or so. This feud has gone on long enough. Besides if they don't stop meddling, we'll never be able to narrow our investigation long enough to catch the blackmailer."

She grasped his arm. "Be careful. Please. I have a bad feeling about your leaving."

"Don't worry about me."

"Of course I'll worry." she said. "You're a stubborn

man who doesn't have the sense to grab on to what you have, but I must admit I'm fond of you anyway."

"Fond?" Jared rested his lips against her cheek.

"That's all you get until you're back safe and sound."

Jared cupped her cheek. "I'll have my phone and radio with me. If you hear anything from CTC or the blackmailer, call immediately."

"That's what terrifies me, Jared. Why haven't we heard?"

HE PUT DOWN his binoculars and smiled. Jared's beat-up pickup had left the property. Everything was going according to plan. Well, maybe not everything. There'd been more collateral damage than he'd wanted, but in the end, his victory would be worth it.

Jared had no idea what was in store for him. He might have clawed his way back the last time, but this time... this time he'd understand everything.

He opened the back of his SUV. The supplies had been easy enough to steal.

Before night fell, it would be over. The Last Chance Ranch would have no more chances.

Chapter Ten

Courtney watched Jared drive toward the north, her heart filled with trepidation. The guards acknowledged her one by one. She wasn't alone, even if it felt like it. She'd become used to having him around.

Probably not a good thing.

She went back into the house and into the kitchen. Velma had jerry-rigged a high chair for Dylan and she was tempting him with cereal.

"Everything okay?"

"The little one and I are doing fine." Velma glanced over at her. "How are you?"

"I've never seen Jared so angry," Courtney said. "You don't think he'll go too far with the Criswells, do you?"

"I couldn't say. Especially if they killed his cattle and he can prove it."

Courtney sat next to her son and tried to tempt him with some melon. "Velma, who on the ranch knows the most about watering cattle?"

The housekeeper turned away from the stove with an inquiring expression. "Roscoe. Why do you ask?"

"No reason." Other than it had become clear over the last couple of days that whoever had sabotaged the ranch was one step ahead of them. "Could you watch Dylan for me? I think Roscoe and I need to clear the air."

Courtney kissed Dylan on the forehead and headed to the old part of the house. She entered the hallway where the nursery was located. She didn't really know which room was Roscoe's.

Slowly she walked down the hallway. She passed the old nursery door. She knocked on a closed door very lightly.

No answer. Gingerly she cracked it open. Empty and abandoned.

She made her way to the next one and rapped on it.

"I told you I'm not hungry, Velma."

Something clattered inside and a loud curse echoed through the door. Courtney pushed inside and gasped.

Roscoe lay on the floor, his body bandaged, bruised and battered, the contents of a breakfast tray strewn all around the room.

When he recognized her he flushed. "What do you want?"

"Do you need some help?"

He braced himself on the bed and rose to his feet. "I can handle it."

"Everyone needs help now and then."

Pretending to be calmer than she was, Courtney knelt down and scraped the ruined toast, sausage and eggs back on the tray. Luckily the carafe of coffee was sealed.

"The coffee looks to be intact," she said. "Would you like a cup?"

Roscoe scowled and slid back into bed. "Doc said 'no' with the medication he gave me."

Courtney winced. "Ouch."

The foreman raised a brow. "You an addict, too?"

"I'm not human until my fourth cup, usually. I had to cut back when I found out I was pregnant."

"How hard was it?"

"The first few weeks weren't pretty. Between morning sickness and caffeine headaches no one wanted to be around me."

Roscoe chuckled. "When Velma learns I'm off coffee and decaf is little more than hot colored water so she's going to force tea down my throat. I hate stuff that tastes like watery weeds worse."

Courtney stared at the wiry old man and laughed. "Hard to argue with that." She placed the tray on the too small nightstand. "Why don't you like me?"

"I don't know you," He frowned. "But Jared changed the minute you stepped out of the silly car you rented. That's not good for the ranch." He cleared his throat. "But I was wrong. Jared set me straight about a few things. And Velma told me that boy of yours is a pistol just like young Jared."

"Did you know him when he was a baby?"

"Nah. My son and I moved to the ranch when he and Jared were boys. After my wife passed from leukemia."

"I'm sorry. My mom died of a brain cancer."

"You know how it is, then. Derek took it hard. She understood him. My boy's too smart for his own good, that's for sure."

Roscoe stretched out a shaky hand. "Truce?" he asked.

"How about we just start over?"

"Deal. Why did you come see me after the things I said about you? I thought you'd avoid me at all costs."

"I probably would have except for what happened to the cattle last night."

"What's going on?"

Roscoe straightened up tall in bed.

Now Courtney wondered if she hadn't made a big mistake. Too late now. She told him about the salt in the water.

Roscoe's face turned alarmingly red and a flurry of curses exploded from his lips. "I wouldn't have thought Ned Criswell would go that far."

"Jared's going to see him and have it out. I'm worried."

"He go alone?"

She nodded.

"Damn it. That isn't good. Ned Criswell's a mean SOB, but he's a good rancher and he values water and the livestock. His son, on the other hand, has no honor. Ned might have ordered his guys to dig up the posts so the cattle could escape and stampede, but if I had to bet, I'd say Chuck salted the water."

"Why would he do such a thing?"

"Because he hates ranching and he knows if his dad can convince Jared to pay them off, he's set for life. He hates living in Carder, and he'd love for his old man to keel over so he can take the money and head to the big city. You aren't gonna live in or around Carder if you can't tolerate the main business in the community. Everyone in the area except those CTC guys make a living off the land or off those who work the land." Roscoe picked up his phone. "I'll get Sheriff Redmond to go out and check on them."

Courtney grabbed the phone from his hand. "You can't."

"What the hell's wrong with you?"

"The man who threatened Dylan said if I contacted the police, they'd hurt him."

Roscoe leaned back against his pillow. "So that's why Jared called off the sheriff. Why didn't he just say something?"

"He was trying to protect you, I guess."

"The boy's lost a lot in his life. He's always trying to protect everyone." Roscoe put out his hand. "Give me that phone."

She hesitated to place it in his hand.

"I'm sending Derek to the Criswells to watch Jared's back. Jared won't jump down his throat. Hell, I'd go if I could, but even I'm not stupid enough to try to drive all the way out there like this."

"Jared wanted Derek to stay here, to watch us."

"We've got plenty of guards," Roscoe frowned." And my boy will keep Jared safe."

"Thanks, Roscoe." Courtney kissed his grizzled cheek. The tension in her shoulders had eased a bit knowing Jared had backup. "I'm glad we aren't enemies, anymore."

"Go on, get out of here. I'm afraid once things get back to normal, I'm going to fall for you just like Jared and Velma have."

Courtney smiled at him. "That's the way I like it."

THE SMELL OF bacon drifted through the house. Courtney carried the empty breakfast tray back to Velma. "Roscoe and I aren't at war anymore."

The housekeeper turned to her with a huge smile. "I knew he'd grow on you."

Velma lifted the bacon from the skillet and rested it

on paper towels. Courtney peered at the scrumptious-looking meat. She couldn't resist and snagged a piece.

"How's Dylan?" She munched on the treat.

Velma placed another half-dozen strips in the pan and the crackling of frying and the delicious scent filled the room. "Oh, the boyo has sure taken to that little blue bull considering all the trouble the animal caused."

Courtney knelt down and kissed her son's head. "Are you having a good time with Miss Velma, Jelly Bean."

Her son tugged the blue bull and babbled at it.

"I wish I knew kid talk. No doubt he and that bull have had some very interesting conversations."

Velma's eyes crinkled at the corners. "He's a good boy, Courtney. You've done a wonderful job with him. Such a good disposition."

"I got lucky."

"Don't kid yourself, sweetie. In spite of being on your own, that baby's not nervous around strangers. He's lovely and happy. That doesn't come from luck. It comes from his mama's confidence and love."

"Thanks, Velma. That means a lot."

Courtney kissed Dylan's nose. Most of the time when she looked at him she saw Jared, but his dimples, they belonged to her father.

"Velma, do you think you could watch him for a while longer?"

"I thought you'd never ask."

"I'll be in the study talking to my father. Hopefully he's feeling better."

"Don't you worry about a thing." The housekeeper waved Courtney away.

Leaving her son in good hands, she pushed open the mahogany doors and entered Jared's study.

They'd left the room in chaos this morning. The quilts they'd slept on were still strewn on the floor. Courtney folded them and placed them on the couch, grabbed the CTC folders and rounded the desk.

If they were ever going to catch this guy, they needed a break, and her father was the only one who might be able to help.

Sinking in the suppleness of Jared's leather chair, she picked up the cell phone he'd loaned her. She dialed her father's number. One ring, two rings. Four rings. No answer. She debated whether to leave a message when a voice filtered through the earpiece.

"H...h...hello?"

Slurred but coherent.

"Father?"

"Courtney? Courtney, what's going on? These men grabbed me from my hotel and forced me into a hospital. I'm lucky they didn't confiscate my phone."

How long had it been since she'd heard him in such a state? Years. "Father, do you remember me coming to visit?"

The phone went silent.

If he'd blacked out, he really may not be able to help them. Then what would they do?

She forced her voice to stay calm. "I visited you a couple days ago. Remember. I brought Dylan. It was the day you had to leave the house."

He let out a harsh laugh. "You mean the day they stole our things and kicked me out of our home? The day they took the paintings, the furniture, the china, the crystal. Everything."

Courtney winced. He wasn't doing well at all. "That's.

I need to ask a few questions, and I need you to try hard to remember."

"You can say it, Courtney. You need me to not screw up again. Like the day I failed you and Dylan. I didn't have any money." He let out a low sob. "And I drank the entire bottle of Cognac. I blacked out."

"Are you feeling better now? Are they taking good care of you?"

"I'll survive. We've been here before, haven't we?" He coughed and it turned into a fit. Just hearing the congestion in his lungs reignited the worry. "Of course life will be different. I'll have to find a job when I get out of here."

"How about you take things one day at a time for now?" Courtney spoke slowly and patiently, but inside she wanted to grab hold of him and get answers. She composed herself and tried to refocus him. "Father, I need your help. Can you concentrate for me? It's very important." She leaned forward in Jared's leather chair, her pen poised on her notebook.

"Those men have been picking my brain since they woke me up," he groused. "I don't know about any three million dollars and change. Except I wish I had it."

"Father, I need information concerning the loans you took out for the mill in Pennsylvania. They add up to over three million dollars. It's a very specific amount of money."

Her father laughed out load. "Well, of course it is. I split the loans up so I'd be able to keep the mill going and have a little flexibility. Lot of good that did."

"That's it? No, there had to be more to the blackmail note. It was personal. They'd threatened her son.

"Was there anyone who caused a lot of trouble while you were working on getting the loans for the mill?"

He laughed. "Of course not. It kept the mill afloat, but out of the blue last week the bank called them all in. I couldn't pay. Had to close the mill. End of story."

She rubbed her temple. "Who would have been the most upset? The workers? The town? Local politicians?"

"All of the above."

Courtney stared at the sheet of paper and sank back into the desk chair. Her father rambled off a few more random details, like an interview he gave to the local town paper, but they didn't seem relevant. The number in the ransom note represented the loss of the mill, but they'd punished her father already. Who would gain by threatening to kill her son? Did they simply want the money?

This felt wrong.

Maybe Jared would see an angle she didn't. She dialed his number and he picked up right away.

"Are you okay?" he asked, his voice crackling.

"This is a terrible connection." she said.

"I'm heading into a valley. I might lose you for a couple of minutes."

Sure enough, his voice dropped off.

She dialed again, but he didn't answer. She redialed several times then waited a few minutes. When she picked up the phone again, several strange hits of static sounded, then no signal. That was odd. It had never happened before at the ranch.

Courtney stilled. She perked her ears to listen carefully. She could hear discussions and laughter outside. Nothing worrisome. And yet, a tingling took up residence at the back of her neck, a foreboding that tasted sour at the back of her throat. She rose from behind the desk and strode across the study, checking her phone in different parts of the room. Still, no service.

She made her way to the mahogany doors. Instead of hurrying through, though, she eased them open. She peered into the foyer.

It was deserted. And silent. Everything looked normal.

Then her gaze landed on the front door dead bolt. It was unlocked.

Against Jared's rules.

Her throat closed off. Her gaze darted behind her to the gun rack.

She backed up.

"Oh no, you don't," a voice whispered from just behind the door.

The strangely quiet tone he used to speak made it impossible to identify his voice. Maybe that was the point.

Courtney whirled around, but a man in a ski mask grabbed her by the arm and shoved her against the wall just inside the study and closed the door behind them. He pressed his forearm against her throat. "I decided not to call," he whispered. "This time, I came in person."

She froze. It was *him*. She had no doubt, but she couldn't figure out how he'd managed to sneak through the security. How was it possible?

"Are you going to behave or cause trouble?" he whispered. "If you're good, I may let your son live. If not, I have no trouble killing him as soon as I see him."

He pressed harder against her windpipe. Spots circled in front of her eyes.

"P-please," she gasped.

He released his grip slightly.

"I—I'll do whatever you want."

If she could only delay enough, maybe Velma would

escape with her son. Maybe Jared would get there and save them all. He wasn't that far away.

"I thought you might," he whispered. "You haven't figured out the game yet, though. None of you have." He chuckled, a satisfied arrogant laugh that burned fury in Courtney's skin.

"Hold your hands in front," he said softly. He bound them, cinching the knot tight.

He paused, his brown eyes narrowed. "If you don't follow all of my instructions," he whispered, "I will kill everyone in this house, including your son. Just like I killed your babysitter in that penthouse."

If she'd had any doubts this was the man they were looking for, she didn't anymore.

He opened the study door and stood at her back, his body touching hers. She shuddered. He bent toward her ear. The knit mask brushed against her cheek. "Don't speak, don't cry out. Walk where I guide you in complete silence. Do you understand?"

"Yes."

He slapped her face. Hard. Her head whipped to the side. "I told you, no talking. Just nod your head. Do you understand?"

She nodded.

"Excellent."

His perpetual whisper creeped her out each time he spoke. It was as if he were less than human. He pushed her through the study door and down the hall to the guest room where she'd been staying. She said nothing. She couldn't risk Dylan's life. Or anyone else's.

"You've never been helpless a day in your life, have you? Well, you're going to find out exactly what it's like to feel that way."

She tried to move her arms and get at the knife in her pocket, but when she adjusted her shoulders, he slapped her again.

"Don't play games, Courtney. I can see your moves coming a mile away."

He shoved her into the bedroom and kicked the door closed. There had to be a way to warn Velma. The cameras were no help. The app was on Jared's phone.

Unless he looked at it. A small sprig of hope ignited until her captor pushed her face down onto the bed.

"Turn over."

Oh God. What was he going to do? She had no choice. She complied.

"Stay there. And remember what I said. If you move, they are all dead."

He gripped her throat, and she could tell without a doubt, he could snap her neck if he so chose. He loomed above her. "Will you obey me?"

She nodded.

"Don't worry, Courtney," he said with a slight smile. "I'll be back soon."

He left her lying there. She stood up and scanned the room. Her eyes fell on a picture. If she broke the glass she could use it to break free. When he came back, she could stop him, as long as he didn't have Dylan with him.

She grabbed the photo frame. How much noise would it make if she slammed it against the bathtub?

Before she could decide a loud crash clattered from somewhere near the kitchen. Velma shouted in terror. "You're not taking that baby," she screamed.

Dylan squealed in terrified cries. Panicked, Courtney ran to the bathroom and threw down the frame.

The noise was drowned out by a horrific crash. Then a loud thud.

A gunshot rang out.

God no.

Footsteps raced across the floor.

"Courtney! Jared!" Léon's voice shouted.

"I'm here!" Courtney replied.

After what seemed forever, he opened the door. He held Dylan in his arms.

He whipped out a knife and cut through the rope.

She reached out for Dylan and pressed him against her breast, patting his back to calm down her terrified baby. "Shh. Jelly Bean. Mama's here. You're safe. I promise."

"When did you get back?"

"Just arrived. Lucky thing. You okay for a minute?" Léon asked.

"Did you get him?" Courtney asked. "Please say you killed him."

Léon shook his head with a scowl. "He got away. I'm not sure how, but he's gone."

Her head fell on top of Dylan's. "Then it's not over."

Léon shook his head. "Take care of your son. I have to help Velma. She hit her head pretty badly protecting Dylan."

Courtney followed him to the kitchen. She gasped in dismay. Velma lay on the floor in the midst of shattered glasses and dishes. Blood oozed from a head wound. Her eyes were shut, her skin pale.

Courtney knelt down beside her. Léon felt for a pulse.

"She's alive, but we need to get her to a hospital as soon as possible. Where's Jared?"

"Driving back from the Criswell ranch, I hope. I tried calling but there was no service."

"Jared has his own tower. He rarely loses service."

"*He* did it."

"That's my guess."

Léon rose and wet a rag to clean some of the blood away from Velma's injury. "She was hit hard."

He glanced over his shoulder. "Keep trying the phone. We need to warn Jared to keep an eye out for someone suspicious on the ranch."

Courtney hit the redial button. Over, and over, and over again.

Finally she had four bars.

Jared answered. "What the hell happened? I've been trying to reach you for a half hour."

She could hardly speak. "He was here, Jared. He broke in and tried to take Dylan."

Chapter Eleven

Jared pressed the accelerator to the floor. The beat-up truck bounced over the dirt roads. He wiped away the blood at the corner of his mouth. Thank God for Derek, Courtney, and Velma. Dylan was safe, but damn it, Jared should have been there to protect his family.

His family. He'd come to think of them that way in just a few short days. He slammed his hand on the steering wheel. "Come on. Faster."

He glanced in the rearview mirror. He looked like hell. Ned could throw a few good licks for a man old enough to be Jared's father. Chuck had cowered. He'd also admitted to sabotaging the fence posts, stealing the pin on Angel Maker's gate and flicking the cigarette near the oil wells. He'd denied firing the shot, dousing the stalls with gasoline and salting the water, though.

For some reason, Jared believed him.

Chuck would pay for what he'd done. The man was just lucky no one had died.

But his denial begged the question, was Courtney's blackmailer also responsible for the destruction on Jared's land? Or was there someone else still out there?

One thing at a time.

He drove onto his land and closed in on the ranch

house as fast as the truck would allow. He didn't hesitate when he reached the perimeter alarm system. The sirens sounded and his men scrambled, their weapons at the ready.

Jared slammed on the brakes and the tires skidded in the dirt in front of the house. Courtney met him at the door, Dylan in her arms. She ran to him and he hugged them close.

"Are you okay?" He pulled back and studied her face. He touched her cheek lightly. "He hit you?"

"I'm fine. He threatened to kill everyone in the house if I didn't obey him." Her face went pale. "I didn't know what to do, so I followed his instructions."

Jared placed his hands on her arms. "You did the right thing. There are times to fight, and situations where it's best to bide your time. We know he's killed before. You and Dylan are alive and safe."

Jared kissed her forehead, so as not to hurt her bruised face. "How's Velma?"

"She hasn't regained consciousness. Tim took her to the hospital and Roscoe went with him," Courtney said. "She wouldn't let him have the baby. She and Léon saved Dylan from that man."

"Where's Derek?" Jared could feel the fury rising in his chest. Had his friend let him down? "He was supposed to watch you."

"He went to help you. We thought we were safe."

"He never showed." Jared's gut sank. "We have to find him." His gaze snapped to Courtney. "Is there any clue as to his identity?"

"He wore a ski mask and he whispered. All I can tell you is that his eyes are brown."

"So, we're no closer to identifying him, and now Derek's missing." Jared ran his hands over Courtney to make certain she was all right. "This wasn't supposed to happen." Jared turned to Léon. "No more games. No more trying to draw this guy out until we have actionable intel. I want Courtney and Dylan out of here. Now."

The operative winced and nodded in agreement. "Ransom has his plane gassed and waiting for you at the airport. We're not filing a flight plan or revealing the destination to anyone until you're in the air." He scanned the area surrounding them, his gaze piercing. "Come inside. No telling when or if the guy will come back."

Holding Courtney close to his side, they walked in the house.

"You're taking my truck. There's no way to track in, even for a hacker. You'll leave the kidnapper's phone here. When you leave, you'll keep your hat pulled low and your face down," Léon said. "I want it to appear as if you're still here."

"What about me and the baby?" Courtney asked.

"I have an equipment box that you'll fit in. Jared can carry Dylan in a duffel and we'll stow the car seat in a garbage bag. You'll all go into the back end of the SUV until you arrive at the airport. The perp will expect us to be hunkering down for a while. Hopefully long enough for you to get away.

Jared nodded. "I like the idea."

"Then let's do it."

A half hour later, Jared started Léon's SUV and pulled down the road leaving Last Chance Ranch. The tinted windows hid the luggage area from view.

The vehicle rumbled over a cattle guard. The rough ride shook the SUV waking Dylan. The baby let out a cry that made Jared wince.

"Just a minute, little guy. Mama will get you soon. I promise."

Jared's voice calmed Dylan a bit, but it didn't last long.

Once they were off his property, Jared called out to Courtney. "Clear."

She pushed open the metal case. Dylan lifted his arms. "Ma."

"Stay hunkered down," Jared said. "We can't take any chances."

"I will." Courtney pulled Dylan into her arms and cuddled him. Jared kept his eyes on the road. The small airport got very little traffic. They shouldn't run into anyone.

They reached the outskirts of Carder. The ribbon of asphalt cut through the landscape. A bright blue sky met the horizon. It would be good flying weather.

Jared reached a dip in the road and a white vehicle drove toward them. His hands clenched on the steering wheel.

"Car coming. Keep low."

The sheriff's lights took shape on top of the SUV the closer they got. Blake Redmond would recognize one of CTC's vehicles. It shouldn't be a problem.

Jared whizzed by the sheriff. Almost there.

A squeal of tires came from behind him and a siren started screaming.

"What's wrong?" Courtney asked.

"Nothing. I'll pull over and get rid of Blake. If I was speeding he can write me a ticket."

Jared pulled the vehicle over. The sheriff's car stopped behind him. Blake rounded the car and Jared rolled down the window.

"Look, Blake—"

The sheriff whipped off his sunglasses. "Where do you think you're going, Jared?"

"Since when do you go all official on me?"

"Don't go there." Blake shook his head. "I gotta ask. Do you have a gun in the vehicle?"

"Of course. I'm wearing it. I have a conceal carry permit."

"Nine millimeter, right? According to your permit."

"Yes." Jared didn't like the wincing expression on the sheriff's face. "What's going on, Blake?"

"I need you to step out of the vehicle."

He glanced behind him and met Courtney's frightened gaze. He gave her a quick nod. If he could keep her hidden, even from a friend, that was one less person who knew where they were. "Look, Blake. Whatever it is has to wait. I've got a plane—"

"I'm sorry, Jared. You're not going anywhere. Not until we straighten a few things out."

"I have no idea what you're talking about."

"You got a nice-sized bruise on your chin, and that eye's not looking so good. You get into a fight?"

Jared didn't like where this was headed. "So what if I did? Since when's that a crime."

"My information says you took a drive out to Ned Criswell's house? Is that true?"

From Blake's expression, Jared had the distinct impression the sheriff wanted him to deny the allegation. Trouble was he couldn't.

"Ned's wanting to renege on an agreement we made. I thought we should talk it out."

"Well, hell, Jared. You can't make my job easy, can you."

"Look, this is all interesting, and I'd love to play

guessing games with you, but I *have* to get on that plane. It's a matter of life and death."

"Now we're in perfect agreement. We just found Criswell dead. Shot with a nine millimeter."

Jared's body numbed. He had to ask. "Was Derek there? Is he dead, too?"

"Derek Hines?" Blake's brow crinkled in question. "No one mentioned him, but I've got a half-dozen witnesses who saw you two come to blows and heard you threaten to kill him. I have a warrant for your arrest for the murder of Ned Criswell."

A loud gasp escaped from the back of the SUV. Jared winced at the sound. Blake had to have heard her.

"Who's in the back of the truck?"

Jared wasn't about to have Courtney show her face. He pushed open the door and stepped onto the pavement.

Blake placed his hand on his weapon. "Whoever's in the back of the SUV, I want you out of the car, now. Hands up."

"She can't." Jared opened the door, held up his hands and stood toe-to-toe with the sheriff. "Damn it, Blake. You've known me since we were in high school. I wouldn't kill in cold blood."

"I thought so, too." Blake frowned. "You've been a pain in my butt the last month with your theories about all those strange occurrences at your ranch. With no proof, I had no way to arrest Ned, and then you go and take things into your own hands. I expected more."

"You're not making any sense."

"How about if I spell it out. I have a list of complaints about sabotage on your ranch that simply stopped a couple of days ago. Not only that, you pulled every complaint and told my office they weren't valid. Even after the arson fire, not one request. But I know better. I saw the destroyed fences, the damage. We both know Criswell was probably involved. I even had a suspect. The guy's son, Chuck. And you go and refuse to assist in the investigation. You've never backed away from a fight in your life, and you just gave up. I've been wondering why."

Jared tilted his Stetson back and eyed the son of the man who'd tried to help him save Alyssa. He and Blake weren't really friends. More like acquaintances. Not that he had anything against the sheriff, but he avoided anything that brought back those five-year-old memories. "Why did you pull me over?"

"Anonymous call that you were heading to the airport." The sheriff scowled at him. "You think I like doing this? I got word you've set your place up like a fortress, given guns to all your hands. Everyone's walking around armed, including the men delivering stock across state lines. What the hell's going on? If you tell me, I can help."

Jared shook his head. "You can't help. Any more than your father could five years ago. You have to trust me, Blake. I need to go. *We* need to go."

The sheriff pursed his lips. "Who's in the back of your truck?" he repeated.

"My nine-month-old son and his mother, and they're in danger."

Jared knew he couldn't have surprised Blake more if he'd said he had a bunch of pink elephants in the backseat.

"Since when do you have a kid?" Blake said. "Now you have even more explaining to do."

"And I will, but right now you have to trust me."

"I'm sorry, Jared. I can't. Not with a warrant."

Jared leaned back against the car door and it clicked closed. "It wasn't me."

Blake pulled out his notes. "Look at it from my point of you. I have a fight over water, a confrontation, and the man was dead within a half hour of your leaving his ranch."

Jared let out a low curse. "Who the hell is doing this to us?" He glanced back at the SUV and took a couple of steps closer to the sheriff's vehicle so Courtney wouldn't hear them. He lowered his voice. "Look, I'm laying this on the line because I trusted your dad and by extension you. Someone threatened to kidnap and kill my son unless I paid a ransom. I have dozens of dead cattle, shots fired, an unexplained fire, and Velma was just attacked and is in the hospital. This is bigger than you and me. CTC is trying to help, but even they can't seem to pin this guy's identity down." Jared met Blake's gaze. "I know you have a family, and that you understand when someone is after them. I need you to let me go, Blake. I need to save *my* family."

The sheriff let out a low curse. "You're putting me in a tough position. I don't think you killed Ned, but we received a phone call from a witness who states he saw you do it. The judge issued the warrant. He's a fishing buddy of Ned's."

"What witness?"

"Anonymous call." Blake rubbed his temple. "I get it, but if I let you go, they'll arrest you somewhere else, and then where would your family be? At least here you have friends in your corner."

"No way. This guy has too much intel, Blake. I have to get Courtney and Dylan out of Carder. If I don't I'll lose them."

"Bring them in. I'll help protect them."

"Five years ago I tried the right way." Jared shook his

head. "This time I contacted a sure thing. All my men, CTC and high-tech surveillance couldn't protect them. I'm not sure why they're even still alive. I came too close to losing them. I can't trust anyone. I'm sorry."

The squeal of tires caused Jared to spin around. Léon's SUV peeled out and down the road.

"Courtney!"

"Let's go," Blake shouted. He rounded his vehicle then skidded to a halt. All four of his tires were flat.

"What the hell?"

Jared froze and squinted after the SUV. His entire body numb. Devastated, he looked over at Blake. "He has them. Damn it, Blake. Courtney and my son are gone."

THE SUV's DOOR SLAMMED.

"Jared?" Courtney asked.

He didn't say anything, just gunned the accelerator. When the SUV took off, Courtney toppled backward. Dylan wailed and she grabbed the baby.

"Jared, can you slow down?"

"Your lover is long gone," a familiar whisper said.

She rose to her knees and peered over the middle row of seats. Her stomach plummeted. The back of the ski mask covered his hair.

"Stop. Please, let us out. I won't tell anyone."

"You should know better by now. My plans are not yours." The man looked over his shoulder and pointed a gun directly at her. "Sit down and shut up or you and your kid are dead. And don't bother trying to call Jared. I have a jammer blocking service. No one can help."

Would that stop the CTC team from tracking her, too? Maybe not. She'd leave the phone on, hoping they would find her. But she couldn't count on being rescued. She needed a plan.

Courtney made a show of backing off. She sat flat in the back of the SUV, holding Dylan close. The vehicle swerved and the road became rough. She bounced several inches off the floor. Where were they going?

Think, Courtney. Think.

She felt for her waist. The knife was there. She measured the distance between her and the man driving. The space was awkward. He would shoot her before she could cut him. In the vehicle the knife was useless.

If she could get his gun, she might have a chance. She'd simply have to look for an opportunity.

She pressed Dylan close to her and rocked him, but she couldn't calm him. What did she expect? Her own heart raced, her nerves were shot. She knew this man might very well kill them both.

The vehicle stopped. Courtney tensed. What was happening now? Was this the end?

"Don't move," he whispered. "You do, I kill the kid and leave you alive to know your mistake caused his death."

She shivered. He exited the car and locked them in. He seemed to be searching all around the car.

When he was finished he opened the door and knelt down searching below the dashboard. He grinned. "Your ace consultants saved me the trouble of removing the GPS chip. Ironic isn't it. They were trying to protect Jared and you, and they ended up making themselves blind."

"Why are you doing this?" she asked. Maybe if she figured out why, she could convince him.

He said nothing and started the vehicle, reversing direction. The SUV made another sharp turn and a slurry of mud rose in an arc. Courtney could barely keep upright. Especially with Dylan in her arms.

When he stopped the SUV and opened the door she'd have to be ready.

She had no idea how long they drove, but the landscape hadn't changed. They pulled up to a small shack, the kind of isolated location where things never ended well.

Courtney gave Dylan a small kiss on his forehead. He looked up at her with so much trust. She prayed she could get them out of this alive. She prayed Jared would find her before anything worse happened.

The kidnapper exited the front and moved around the side. Courtney kept her hand at her waist and braced herself to attack. He yanked open the back end and she froze.

The man gripped an assault weapon in his hands.

She couldn't escape.

"Put the kid down," he whispered and threw her a rope.

"Get out of the SUV nice and easy," he said with a snarl.

She nodded.

"Excellent. You remember."

"Stand still and hold out your hands. If you try anything, I'll spray your kid with bullets."

She reached her hands out in front of her. He wrapped the rope around them and tied the knot off tight.

"Please, just let the baby go. He's innocent."

He slapped her across the face. "I told you no speaking. You have money and assume you don't have to follow the rules.

"Now walk."

She glanced at Dylan, hesitating. The spring heat was

mild, but with the sun shining through the windshield, he'd burn up. "Please, the car will get too hot."

He slapped her across the cheek again. This time even harder. Her head whipped back and her jaw throbbed.

"Don't give me a reason, because it'll hurt Jared just as much to spray this car with bullets and kill you both."

"He could fall."

He hit her a third time, but walked back to close the back door.

"Thank you."

The man raised his hand to hit her. She recoiled and he chuckled. "The kid is Jared's son. That makes him my most valuable asset. I've been waiting years to finish what I started five years ago."

She gasped in shock at the realization. Oh my God. This wasn't about her father at all. This was the man who killed Jared's wife and daughter.

Her throat clenched. No one had seen it. The money must've been a diversion the entire time.

And now he planned to kill her and Dylan.

"I see in your eyes you've finally figured it out. That's better than Jared ever did. He never understood. Never realized I should have had everything."

He lifted the weapon. "Now walk."

She made her way to the door of the shack.

"Open it."

Using both hands she twisted the doorknob and the rotting wood swung inward. She turned her head sideways, trying to see behind the mask, to make out who would do this. She couldn't tell except that behind the ski mask his eyes were flat and dead. He showed no mercy in his expression.

"Go inside and sit in the chair."

She walked in and sat down. The knife burned at her waist, but in her head every scenario she came up with ended in Dylan's bullet-riddled body.

There had to be a way to save her son.

"Stay in the chair. If you move, I kill your son. If you speak, I kill your son. If you beg, I kill your son. Do you understand?"

She nodded.

He returned a few moments later with Dylan and the car seat. He strapped the baby in and left him to cry.

She winced, but he seemed impervious to her child's screams.

Courtney worked her hands against the sturdy rope as surreptitiously as possible. At one point he whirled around and glared at her, staring at the tie.

He picked up the weapon and walked over to the car seat. She sucked in a deep breath and he smiled at her.

She got the message. He controlled everything.

Courtney couldn't move. She couldn't call for help. She couldn't try to convince him to let her go. She couldn't reach the knife.

She and Dylan were well and truly trapped.

Chapter Twelve

His ranch house had turned into a mausoleum. Every instinct screamed to search the roads, the mountains, the ranch, everywhere, but he had no leads.

He wandered from room to room, but in every square foot a crisp memory of Dylan's laughter or Courtney's smile would haunt him. He stopped by the guest room. His eyes closed in pain at the view of the crib. He moved down the hall to the kitchen. A plate of snickerdoodles sat there, lonely and pathetic.

Finally, he pushed through the large mahogany study doors. Where she'd shared with him the danger she and Dylan were in. Where he'd vowed to save her. Where they'd made love for the second time.

Courtney and Dylan had changed his life the moment she'd driven onto his land in that powder blue Mustang. He'd been dead inside for so long, he'd never even realized it. She'd dragged him kicking and screaming back to life. Right now he wondered if that was a good or a bad thing.

Velma would say good. Roscoe would say bad. For Jared, the jury was still out.

What Courtney had done was make him feel again. She'd brought him hope, he'd dared to believe in the possibilities, and now she and Dylan were gone. The feelings remained, though, except instead of a warmth inside, it was dark and ice laden.

The worst part, they'd been a half mile from getting out of Texas and regrouping. So close. Jared had been standing just feet away.

How had the guy pulled it off? Jared should have been able to protect them. He might never be able to forgive himself. When he and Blake had realized they wouldn't be able to follow, and that the nearest deputy was twenty minutes away, Jared had known he'd been beaten. That he'd failed. Despite the planning and preparation and the determination.

He was at a madman's mercy.

Jared circled the room, but there wasn't an inch that Courtney and Jared hadn't touched.

He had to get them back.

He stopped at the coffee table across from the couch. The cell phone the kidnapper had left with Courtney lay there, taunting him. Jared stared at it unblinking. Would the man even call?

He slipped the phone in his pocket. It was a call he couldn't afford to miss. "He must have seen me leave with Courtney and Dylan and decided to switch up his plan, though I don't know how." Jared looked over at Léon. "What's your gut tell you?"

"That's why we're looking at an inside job with a high tech expert. Too much has gone wrong. I've got my men interviewing every member of the staff again. Zane's executing a deep dive. If there's something there, we'll find it." The operative frowned and Jared's gut twisted in fear.

Jared rubbed his eyes. "I hope the guy's just greedy. He can have the money if he'll let Courtney and Dylan go."

"Me, too, Jared. Me, too."

But Jared could read the man's eyes. They were cautious and wary. Jared wouldn't ask for odds. He didn't want to know because he refused to let himself consider the alternative. He *would* find Courtney and Dylan. He would bring them back safe and sound, and then he'd send them as far away from Last Chance Ranch and Carder as quickly as possible so they could live their lives in peace.

"How long have we been waiting?" Jared asked, rubbing the back of his neck.

"Two hours."

Léon's tone didn't evoke optimism. They all knew the truth. Unless they caught a break, the guy was in charge. They needed him to call.

A knock sounded at the front door. Léon left the study to answer it.

"Can I see him?"

Jared tensed at Blake Redmond's voice. The man couldn't apologize enough. Jared wished he could blame the sheriff, but there was nothing the man could have done to stop the abduction, except to never have stopped the SUV in the first place. Okay, so maybe he blamed Blake a bit. But the truth was, Jared knew the only one at fault was himself. He should've taken them into the mountains when his gut was screaming at him to do so.

The sheriff entered the room, hat in hand. His boots scuffed across the floor. "Any news?"

Jared shook his head. "No note, no ransom, no call. No nothing."

"Damn, I'm sorry." Blake frowned. "I have more bad news, unfortunately. We found Derek's truck abandoned near the Criswell place. I'm sorry to say we found blood on the back of the seat."

"Not an accident."

Blake shook head. "Sorry."

Jared braced himself. God, how was he going to tell Roscoe? "And Derek."

"We don't know. My deputies are still searching. Maybe he wondered off, disoriented from his injury."

"Why am I not surprised?" Jared met Blake's gaze. "The guy has been ahead of us from the start. He's been toying with us since he wrote the note."

Léon entered the room with a duffel. "Here's the money. When he calls we'll be ready to make the drop."

Jared froze at the sight. He clamped his jaw shut. Five years vanished in the space of a heartbeat. Steeling himself, he opened the bag and stared at the bundles of cash.

"This still doesn't make sense. Did whoever come up with this scheme want money, and want Jamison to lose his family? Is this about revenge? Why focus everything on me."

"You've got the money." Léon twisted his lips into a frown. "But you're right. Nothing fits. It's all off. Zane investigated all the employees who lost their jobs because of the mill going under. No one lost a close family member."

"We're missing something," Jared said. "Something that's right in front of us."

"It feels like a diversion," Léon said. "Similar to the fire. He didn't leave any kind of trace evidence, either here or on the highway. He's a ghost."

Jared paced back and forth. A ghost. The déjà vu feeling made Jared nauseous. He glared at the phone. "Why don't you call?" he shouted.

The front door rattled with the sound of a key entering the dead bolt. Jared palmed his Glock and stood in the hallway waiting.

Tim escorted a limping figure into the foyer. Jared slipped the pistol back into the holster and strode over to the foreman. "Roscoe. Getting out of bed was a damn fool thing to do."

Jared patted his shoulder. "I know, but she's a survivor. She'll pull out of this."

"Of course she will," Roscoe said. "She's not through mothering the lot of us. Any news?"

Jared shook his head, avoiding his foreman's gaze. He wouldn't tell him about Derek yet. Not until they knew more.

Roscoe cleared his throat. "Courtney's tough and determined. She'll come out of this. So will that boy."

Jared tamped down his emotions. "I believe that, but I'm a little surprised to hear those words coming from you."

"City girls can grow on you," Roscoe said, glancing away.

"Since when?" Jared asked.

"Since a gal from New York schooled me on assuming the worst." He adjusted his cane. "She's a keeper."

If things were different, Jared would move heaven and earth to convince her to stay once he found her. But that wasn't where he saw the night ending.

He only saw an empty house, an empty bed and an empty life. He had every intention of saving her and then letting her go to keep her safe.

He lowered his head and rubbed the sting from his eye.

A grandmother clock chimed. Outside, dusk had begun to darken the sky. "Where are you? Courtney? Please be okay."

The phone in his pocket vibrated. The *kidnapper's* phone. He grabbed it and pressed the speakerphone.

"King."

For a moment he heard nothing.

"Jared King," the voice whispered. "It's been a long time."

His gaze flew to Léon's. "Do I know you?"

"Perhaps you'll recognize me this way." There was a pause over the phone. "You didn't follow the rules. Again. You haven't learned anything. Five years ago or now."

That mechanized voice. Jared's legs shook and he stumbled into the study. He sank into the chair so his legs would hold him. Impossible. Five years ago. It was *him*. The man who had killed Alyssa.

"Surprise," he said. "Did you miss me?"

"You son of a bitch."

"I like the title, but it's not true. My mother was a saint."

"Shall we return to unfinished business. I didn't receive my payment five years ago. I tacked on interest this time."

Jared glanced over at Léon. What the hell was going on? They'd figured out where the odd amount came from. Edward Jamison."

Léon shook his head.

"You're confused, are you? Don't be. I may have tweaked the numbers a bit just for fun when I realized our game wasn't over. You were a naughty boy, going to New York, falling for *another* girl. Getting her pregnant."

"Who are you?" How had he known? Courtney had only come to him a few days ago. "You don't have to do this. Courtney and Dylan are innocent."

The voice chuckled, and the inhuman sound made him shiver. "But you aren't."

Jared thrust his hand through his hair. "What do you want?"

"Oh, I'm getting exactly what I want. You know I could hang up and just let that be the end. I suppose you might find them. Someday."

"What about your money?"

"There is that."

A long pause made Jared want to leap through the phone and strangle the guy. Léon came up beside Jared and pressed the mute button. "I know you want to challenge him," the operative said. "Don't. He wants to be in charge. Let him. We still haven't identified him, and if Jamison isn't involved, Zane's search has been one giant waste of time. You need to do whatever it takes to have this meet."

Jared gave a curt nod. "I know. But when I'm near the guy, I'm not holding back."

"Jared. I think it's time we have a reunion. How about we take a walk down memory lane. Bring the money to the pier at Last Chance Lake. You have one hour. And leave your little friends at home. If I see the sheriff or those spies you tried to hire leave your house, she and your son are dead."

"Wait—"

The call ended. Jared sent Léon a desperate look. "Could you trace it?"

The CTC operative shook his head. "He timed it perfectly. We only needed three more seconds. We did get that he's probably in the county."

"Of course he is. He'll be at the lake in an hour." Jared shook his head. "We're out of options. He's looking for an excuse to kill them." He looked around the room from man to man. "Either I'm going alone, or it has to *look* like I'm going alone. I won't take any chances with their lives. Not this time."

León frowned. "We don't have much time to put any fail safes in place. He could be there already. Watching and waiting."

Jared's frowned deepened. "Which is why this time, I'm going to do exactly what he says."

A SLIVER OF red sky lined the horizon. It was getting dark. She could only make out the boat sitting near a platform at the center of the lake.

Her son was strapped to his car seat in that boat, the kidnapper sitting right beside him holding a pistol. Dylan was completely vulnerable, completely at his mercy.

So was she. Because she would do anything to keep Dylan safe.

Courtney sat in the wooden chair her masked kidnapper had placed on the end of the pier. Her hands were still bound and since he'd left her, she'd been working her wrists against the strong hemp. She could feel the blood dripping off her fingertips.

He'd strapped a heavy weight belt to her waist, but she could stand up if she wanted. Except the moment she moved off this chair, he'd shoot her son.

He was in control.

The baby had been screaming for close to an hour. She winced at the loud hiccups.

"Ma. Ma," he sobbed. "Ma. Ma."

They were in big trouble. She had to find a way to save herself and her son, but she had no idea how to do that.

The rumble of an engine dragged her attention away

from her thoughts. Her heart skipped a beat, reigniting hope within her.

Jared's old truck pulled up to the edge of the pier. He jumped out with a duffel bag.

His eyes widened when he saw her, and then his gaze whipped toward the sound of their crying son in the boat. He walked down the pier, his face obscured by the darkening sky.

Even then she'd never seen him so tense, strained, or so angry.

"I'm sorry," she said, not sure if he could hear her.

"Stop," the kidnapper's mechanized voice ordered through a bullhorn once Jared had made it halfway down the wooden planks.

Courtney kept working her wrists. With the man distracted, maybe she could reach the knife. The problem was, any wrong move and he *would* kill Dylan.

Jared lifted the bag. "Here's the money. I came alone. How about we end this now? You take the money. We forget this ever happened. Just let them go."

The man pointed the barrel of a pistol at the car seat. "I don't think so."

"No. Please don't," Courtney shouted, desperately wanting to stand and beg, but knowing if she moved, Dylan's life was forfeit. He'd warned her enough when he'd forced her to sit in that chair.

"Shut up," the kidnapper ordered. "Or I kill him anyway."

Her gaze flew to Jared's. *He's not bluffing*, she mouthed. *He's crazy. He will do it.*

"I know," Jared said as quietly as he could. He exuded a calm confidence she didn't think she would ever feel again. She prayed he had a plan.

He lifted his chin, his expression determined and in-domitable. He *did*. He had something in mind.

"Here's the way we play this game, Jared. A little different from five years ago, isn't it? You have two people you love. Two people you want to save.

"But you can't save them both." The man chuckled. "You have a choice. But first things first. There's a small boat right off the pier next to your lover. Put the money in it."

Jared walked the remainder of the way on the pier and lowered the duffel into the fiberglass craft.

He was within reach of her and she looked up at him. He was tall and strong and she couldn't imagine anyone she'd trust more to save their son.

"Excellent," the kidnapper said.

A small motor burst to life and the remote-controlled boat puttered across the lake, past the swimming platform, heading toward the opposite edge.

"You have what you want, let them go," Jared said. He paused. "Please."

"I don't have near what I want. We haven't finished our transaction."

Courtney's gut hurt at the malevolence in the man's voice. She closed her eyes. *Please. Save Dylan.*

"I control you. Your every move. I have what you want. Finally. What I should have had from the beginning."

"Who are you?" Jared asked.

"Your conscience. Your nightmare?" The man chuckled. "It doesn't matter who I am. What matters is you will always remember this moment. Because you will have to live with your choice."

Dylan's cries grew softer, more tired.

"Sounds like your kid wants this to be over. So do I. It's time to choose. Your lover or your son."

"No, you can't do that!" Courtney shouted.

"I'm in control. I can do whatever I want." His mechanized laughter filtered across the water from the boat. "You can save one of them. If you choose the baby. I leave him here on the platform for you to save, but you, you must push her in the water and let her go. If you try to save her, your son will die.

"If you choose her, I throw the kid into the water and he drowns."

He lifted a heavy dumbbell tied to rope. It was attached to the car seat.

Jared's entire body froze, but she could see the agony in his eyes.

"You don't have to do this," he said. "You have the money. Please. I'm begging you. What do I have to do?"

"I like you begging me, Jared. Makes you humble." The man laughed. "Would you give me everything you have? Your money, the house, the land, the oil?"

"Take it all." Jared's voice had grown desperate. "Whatever you want. Just let them live."

"Get on your knees. Beg me."

Jared didn't hesitate. He hit the wooden pier as if in prayer. "I'm begging you. Do whatever you want to do to me. Just let them go."

Tears streamed down Courtney's face. This wasn't what either of them had expected. There was no way they were getting out of this alive.

The man just laughed. Then suddenly he stopped.

"Choose. Now. If you don't make the choice, I'll shoot the boy, then her. You'll lose them both."

Jared stood up. He looked at Courtney, then at his

son. She could tell he was weighing his chances of saving them both.

The distance was too great. This was impossible.

"You betting I can't hit her? Think again. The pistol might suck for accuracy." The man held up a rifle. "It's not that tough of a shot."

The words ended Courtney's hope for herself. A strange peace swept through her body. She raised her gaze to the man she'd grown to love, the man who would sacrifice his life for them if he could.

"Jared." Courtney's voice was calm. "You have to save Dylan. He's all that matters. We agreed."

He stared at her, his eyes frantic. "I can save you both," he muttered under his breath. "I promise."

"I have faith in you." Courtney swallowed. "But I don't trust him."

She shifted slightly and her eyes welled. She blinked. "I never told you this, but I love you, Jared. From the moment we met."

"Courtney—"

"You're a good father," she said. "Please tell Dylan that I loved him with all my heart."

With that one statement, Courtney stood and jumped into the water, sinking like a stone.

Chapter Thirteen

Jared watched in horror as Courtney disappeared beneath the water. He knew with the weight around her waist she'd disappear below the surface and end up on the bottom of the twenty-five-foot expanse.

This couldn't be happening again. The man sitting in the boat cursed. "Damn her. I wanted you to make the choice!"

A shot rang out. The man fell to the side. Dylan screamed.

Jared's gaze flew to Léon's location two hundred yards as the crow flies. It had been an unbelievable shot, but Léon was a pro.

Blake Redmond raced from his hiding place across the lake and commandeered a waiting boat.

Knowing his child would be safe in moments, Jared yanked off his boots and dove into the water. The lake was lower than normal and murky. The last bit of light muted even more as he swam down to the cold depths. He squinted, barely able to make out strange shadowy shapes.

A horrifying sense of déjà vu nearly suffocated him. This time it would end differently. Desperate, Jared reached out for the base of the pier. She'd gone down right beside it. He could follow the post.

His hand encountered a thick wooden support and he used it as a guide. Down deeper and deeper he dove. His lungs protested but Jared wasn't about to go back up for air. Not without Courtney.

Darkness engulfed him.

No. This wasn't happening again. Not like before. Suddenly, out of nowhere he made out a murky figure hunched in the water. He kicked to her and clutched her arm. She shook him away and he realized she was using the knife he'd given her to free herself from the weighted belt. He shoved her hands to the side, pulled out his combat knife and finished the job.

The belt fell free. She slumped forward and grew heavy in his arms.

Don't do this, Courtney.

He wrapped his arm around her waist and kicked for all he could to the surface. He broke through the water and sucked in a deep breath. Her turned her in his arms and his heart sank back down to the lake's floor.

She was limp in his arms.

"Give her to me," Léon shouted above him. The CTC operative leaned over the pier, hands outstretched. Jared lifted her up and Léon dragged her onto the wooden platform.

He rolled her over just as Jared climbed onto the pier.

"She was moving just seconds ago," he shouted, moving to Courtney's side.

Jared bent over her. "Come on, Courtney."

He turned her head to the side and some water escaped her mouth. "That's it," he urged. He placed his hands on her neck and waited for the beat of life.

Nothing. He had to get her heart started.

He placed his hands over her heart and started compressions. Ten, twenty beats.

No. This couldn't be happening. He tilted her head back. "Courtney, you've got a son who needs you. I need you."

He breathed into her mouth. Once, twice, and felt for her pulse. Was that a small thready sign of life?

A bolt of energy washed over him. "You can do it. Fight. For Dylan."

He rested his cheek against her lips. Still no air movement.

He puffed in another two breaths. Then two more.

He turned her to her side and pounded her back.

Her lungs heaved. Water spewed from her mouth and she jerked against him. She turned on her side expelling the water from her lungs.

Léon looked at Jared a wide grin on his face. "Hallelujah."

Jared bent over Courtney and cupped her face in his hands. "Welcome back," he whispered softly.

She blinked up at him. "Dylan?"

"Safe." He pointed at the swimming platform in the center of the lake. Blake held their still-crying son in his arms.

She sagged against him, her shaky arms winding around him. "I—"

Jared helped her sit up and pulled her close. "Are you crazy?" He squeezed her tight. "Don't ever do that again."

She looked up at him again. "Wouldn't you have done the same?"

"That's not the point." He glared at her, then rocked

her close to him, kissing her temple, her cheeks and finally her lips. "I almost lost you."

"I know." Her voice was thick with emotion. "But you didn't. You saved our son. You saved us both."

She opened her clenched hand. The folded knife lay in her palm.

"You cut the way through most of the strap," Jared said. "I don't know if I could have gotten you out in time."

"I had to fight. For you. For our son. I knew you'd save Dylan even if I didn't make it, but the truth is, you need me. I haven't even showed you how to change a diaper yet."

She smiled at him and lay her head softly against his chest. "Thank you."

Jared nodded to Léon. "Tell Ransom, thank you."

"This will be one for the record books."

They all watched as Blake maneuvered the boat toward them. The soft growl of the drew closer, the remote control craft with the duffel of money floating behind.

The boat tapped the edge of the pier. Dylan reached up to Jared and he grabbed the boy in his arms, hugging him tightly before handing him over to Courtney.

She held him close, checking every inch. "Jelly Bean."

"Mama," he hiccupped.

"He's okay."

She held her son close and Jared wrapped his arms around both of them. His cheek rested against her hair. He closed his eyes and said a thankful prayer.

A thud drew his attention. Blake and Léon had moved the body to the pier. He lay there, still masked and anonymous, half the back of his head was gone.

"I had to take the head shot so he couldn't pull the trigger on reflex," Léon said.

"Who is it?" Jared asked. "Who hated me enough to kill the innocent."

Blake knelt beside the body and peeled the ski mask up.

Jared gasped. His knees gave way.

"No. It can't be." He shook his head back and forth at the very familiar face.

"Derek Hines?" He shook his head back and forth. "He was my best friend for years. I trusted him with my life. We had him guarding the house."

The lapping of the water against the pier was the only sound for several minutes.

"Why? Why would he do this?"

THE SMALL CARDER hospital was going to drive her crazy. Courtney lay in the bed. Every doctor, nurse and staffer had found a reason to visit.

A teenage candy striper poked her head through the door. "Do you need anything, ma'am?" she asked with a giggle.

"Thank you, no."

She fought not to snap. The residents of Carder were doing everything in their power to make her feel at home. Actually, it was too much of a good thing.

She glanced over at Jared and he chuckled. "I could put up a do-not-disturb sign."

"Do you think it would work?" She couldn't stop the hope from lingering in her voice.

"Not a chance. You're famous," he said. "The woman who was willing to give her life for her son." All humor left Jared's face. "I'm sorry I put you in that position. I should never have let it get that far."

"It's not your fault. It's his," Courtney said, wishing

she could wipe the guilt from his face. He'd made it possible for her to save herself and then he'd saved her. Didn't he understand they were in this together?

"Doctor says I can leave as soon as he finishes my paperwork," she said, hoping for a response.

Jared nodded and patted Dylan's back. He adjusted his position a bit. Dylan lay against his shoulder, perfectly content to be in his father's arms. "He looks good in your arms," she murmured.

Jared glanced down at the baby. "I can't stop looking at him, checking his fingers and toes, watching him breathe."

"I felt that way every day for a long time after I brought him home from the hospital."

"So I'll get used to it?" he asked.

She shook her head. "No. Because he's a miracle."

"You both are." Jared cleared his throat. "We've never talked about it, but I'm sorry I wasn't there for you, when you were pregnant, when you gave birth to him. I hope you know I would have been there. If you'd wanted me."

"I know," she said. "I'm sorry you missed out on so much."

Jared brushed a lock of hair from the baby's forehead. "He likes horses."

"I'm not surprised."

Courtney kept silent. She could see he wanted to say something, and her entire body shimmered with anticipation.

Were they thinking the same thing? How was she supposed to get around to asking the question she longed to ask?

She breathed in deeply. She'd just have to do it. If the last few days had taught her one thing it was not to wait, but to grab on to life with both hands and shove fear aside. Carpe diem. Seize the day had never become more real.

Before she could, a sharp knock sounded at the door and Léon walked into her room with another man.

"This is Zane Westin, CTC's ace computer whiz, in the flesh. He's been delving into Derek Hines's secret life. The man kept meticulous notes, obsessively so. I thought you'd want to know what we've discovered, but first I wanted to make certain you knew that the BOLO's been rescinded. You won't be arrested if you travel to New York."

Courtney's gaze flew to Jared. Even in the celebration of returning to the ranch, Jared had been tortured. Roscoe was inconsolable. Neither of them could understand why Derek could've been the man behind that ski mask.

"Secret life?" Jared asked.

"Everything he told you and his father since he left the military was a lie," Zane said. "He never earned a degree, but he did run some cons and he was good at ferreting out information." Zane glanced back and forth between Courtney and Jared.

"Tell them," Léon said.

"He's been obsessed for a long time with your family and your ranch." Zane pulled out a file folder. "Jared, he met your first wife in a bar the week before you did. From his writings he thought he was in love with her."

"Strange. I remember we went to the bar together when I met Alyssa." Jared's brow wrinkled in confusion. "He never said anything."

"Evidently, she fell hard for you, when his intention had been to show her off," Zane commented. "He wrote dozens of draft emails in his system, letters he never sent to her, begging her for a chance, threatening you to leave her alone. When he finally sent one of the emails, she didn't remember him. Once she chose you, it sent him over the edge. When you married something inside of him snapped. He blamed you for everything in his life that didn't work."

"This doesn't make sense. We were friends. We confided in each other."

"He kept a lot of secrets and they burned a hole in his gut. He never told anyone. He believed his father would rather have had you for a son. He became obsessed with taking everything away from you. When Chuck Criswell started his destruction campaign, Derek took a lot of pleasure in our investigation. He took the shot at Angel Maker to spook the horse. He had no idea the pin had been removed and the bull would get out. He found the irony amusing. He also salted the water and gassed the quarter horse barns."

"He almost killed his own father."

"Collateral damage would be acceptable, he wrote."

Jared rubbed his eyes. "Why didn't I see it?"

"He didn't want you to. And he wasn't around enough for you to pick up on the inconsistencies of his behavior. I called a few of the guys he hung out with. They said everyone talked about how the guy was just off enough to make them nervous."

"How did he find out about me?" Courtney asked.

"When your private investigator began the search for Jared, it clued Derek in. It's one thing he didn't lie about. He was actually gifted. Even Zane was impressed. Once he realized through your PI that your father was in financial trouble, his plan took shape. He hacked into the bank and adjusted their records. The bank believed a decision had been made to call in the loans. They believed the notes in the computer. Most people do. Derek manipulated the situation so you'd have to ask Jared for help. Derek hired a thug to kill Botelli because the PI was a loose end he couldn't risk."

"Derek set up this elaborate scheme just to get back at me?" Jared's incredulous voice was tinged with hurt.

"A five-year-long plan to destroy you. He was simply waiting for the right opportunity to hurt you as much has he had been," Zane said. "Impressive for a crazy guy."

Léon shot Zane a pointed look. The man shrugged. "What? It's the truth."

Courtney had a hard time processing all the information. She'd been a pawn in a revenge plot that had started years ago? She shifted in the bed. Everything they'd been through had been orchestrated by one man searching for revenge.

"One last thing you both need to know," Léon said. "His plan from the start was to get Courtney and the baby out to that lake to kill them both. He never wanted the money. He blamed his lack of money on losing Alyssa, but he actually wanted to drive you insane. Once you cracked after losing them, he planned to swoop in to take over the ranch.

"He wanted your life."

A small choked gasp sounded from the doorway. Roscoe swayed. Léon rushed over and propped the old man up.

Jared rose and placed Dylan in Courtney's arms. He walked over to Roscoe and stared at the foreman. The man's eyes were bloodshot and he looked ten years older than he had when she'd last spoken to him.

"I didn't know." He clutched Jared's shirt. "I swear. I didn't know."

Jared nodded. "Neither of us knew."

Roscoe stared at his feet. He looked at Courtney, to Dylan and back to Jared. "I… I'm so very sorry."

He limped out the door. Jared started to follow. Léon held him back. "Leave him be. It takes time when you discover you've been betrayed by those closest to you."

Jared thrust his hand through his hair. "The irony is, if Derek had wanted to run the ranch with me, I'd have let him. I loved him like a brother. What does that say that I couldn't see what he was. What he'd done."

"He was a functioning sociopath," Zane said. "He knew how society would expect him to behave, but the truth is the world revolved around Derek Hines and that's all he could see. There was nothing you could have done or said. He had no empathy for anyone."

Jared stretched out his hand to shake Léon's, then Zane's. "Thank you. Both of you. Tell Ransom I owe him more than I can ever repay."

"I'm glad we could help," Léon said. "I'm glad it turned out well for you all."

Léon smiled at Courtney and she glanced down at her baby boy. "Thank you for saving his life."

He gave her a kiss on the cheek before he and Zane headed out.

Jared walked back to Courtney.

"Are you okay?" she asked softly, gently rocking Dylan.

He sat on the edge of her bed. "No. I keep thinking back from the time Derek arrived on the ranch. I did trust him with my life. I would have trusted him with yours. I *did* trust him with yours, with everyone's life."

He met her gaze. "I'm so sorry for everything. For all the pain you went through." He swallowed. "I know you're probably ready to get out of Carder and go back to New York." He looked down at Dylan and placed his hand on the boy's head. "I… I'll do whatever you want, but I'd like to be part of his life. If you'll let me."

Courtney froze. She hadn't expected him to kick her out. She'd hoped… She turned her face to the side, away from him.

"Why are you doing this?"

"You have a life in New York. A career. Your father. Why would you want to stay here? It's just a reminder of how badly everything could have turned out."

Even as the words echoed from his lips, Courtney's back tensed. She looked him straight in the eye.

"Is this what you really want?"

"It's for the best. I'll talk to Ransom about using the plane to fly you back to New York. We'll figure out something."

"Jared. Why?"

"Because it's the right thing."

THE SUN WAS setting on Last Chance Ranch. Jared stood on the porch while Courtney packed. The plane was ready and he would soon say goodbye.

Roscoe guided Velma's wheelchair from inside. Jared knelt down in front of her. "How are you doing today?"

"Irritated," she muttered. "Can't button my clothes, can't cook. Can't stand up without getting dizzy." She gazed at Roscoe. "I'm sorry about Derek."

"I still can't believe it," Roscoe said with a weighed frown.

Velma patted Roscoe's hand. "He was sick in the head.

Something happened to him, Roscoe. It wasn't your fault. Don't forget that."

"I'm not so sure about that. I don't know if I'll ever be."

The wound was fresh and raw and they all felt it. Rain clouds filled the sky to the west. The perfect ending to what would be a horrible day Jared would remember until he was dead and buried in the ground.

"I'm walking over to the east," Jared said.

He didn't have to say where he was going. Roscoe and Velma would know. And understand.

Angel Maker snorted as he walked past the bull, but he ignored the stud. He was numb.

A white fence surrounded the small family cemetery. Jared stood in front of the two newest crosses. Alyssa's and his daughter's.

"We caught him, honey. God I'm sorry I didn't see it. I keep thinking back when I introduced you. Why didn't I see shock or anger on his face? Why didn't I see how much he hated me?"

He crouched down in front of the grave and pulled a weed.

"I wanted to save you, Alyssa. I wanted us to be a family." He sighed. "You'd have liked Courtney, though. You two could have talked shopping and shoes for days. I almost lost her, too. I don't know how she survived, but I know I have to let her go. Even though she told me she loved me, it's for the best."

"Do you really believe that?" Courtney's voice was laced with hurt and sorrow.

Jared rose to his feet and turned to face her. She was alone.

"Where's Dylan?" he asked.

"With Velma and Roscoe, eating a snickerdoodle."

"Are you packed?"

She lifted her chin. "No."

He blinked. "I don't understand."

"I've been up all night thinking about leaving you. I need to know one thing. Why. Why let us go?"

"I… I—"

"I thought so. You love us, Jared King. Deny it and I'll walk out of here without looking back. We'll do the court thing, the visitation rights and move on. You can see Dylan every other Christmas and a couple weeks in the summer."

He rubbed his face with his hands and led her away from the graveyard. The ranch house and barn loomed in the distance. "This isn't your kind of place, Courtney. Admit it. Would you have ever come to Carder if you hadn't been desperate?"

"If I'd known you'd lived here, I'd have at least visited." She frowned at him. "Why are you making all these assumptions? Since when did I deserve to be pushed into a cookie-cutter life because of who my father is or what hotel I like to stay or even where I work, because you know what, Jared. You're not *just* a cowboy. I learned that a long time ago. You're an entrepreneur, you're a risk taker, and when it comes to me and my son, you're a hero."

His mouth gaped.

"So I've decided you've been in charge for too long," Courtney said. "I think you could do with a shake-up in your life, Mr. King."

A flicker of hope ignited in Jared's belly, but he quickly tamped it down. What was she saying?

"You wouldn't have chosen to live here."

"Nope." Courtney looked around. "Until a few days ago I'd never heard of Carder, Texas. This was never my primary destination. But things change. People change. Do you recognize what you have in this small town?" She stepped closer to him. "When you were in trouble, no one bargained or even questioned whether they would help. They just did. Your men put their lives on the line to guard me and Dylan, two people they didn't even know."

She leaned into him. "I only knew one person in my building, and that was Marilyn. Her family won't accept my call. Even though CTC provided the police with the evidence I wasn't involved with her death. The rest of the building, except for the doorman, they probably don't even know my name. I could walk down the street right next to my building and no one would *see* me, much less know me.

"Look how everyone has rallied around Roscoe, despite what Derek did. You have a gift, and I want Dylan to be cherished the same way the people of this community cherish you. I've felt more like part of a family here on this ranch than I have since my mother died."

With a sigh, she placed her hand on his cheek. "I didn't know what I was missing without you in my life. Now that I recognize it, I can't go back to what I was. I've changed, Jared. Our son changed my life. And you changed it. I want to stay. Here. With you."

Jared could barely breathe. His legs shook and he cupped her face. "Are you certain? We lived through hell. Normal won't be exciting or intriguing."

"That's okay. I can do normal. I'd love to do normal."

Jared felt the ice around his heart—the barrier that had frozen him that horrible night five years ago—melt away.

He gripped her hands in his. "The night I met you,

I could barely speak. I needed a shot of tequila to give me the courage to walk up to you. It was the best decision of my life.

"I want you to know that you brought me back to life. I was dead inside until you lit a spark."

She smiled at him, her heart shining in her face. "Finally." She gripped his shirt. "And I knew you were different the moment you approached me. I just didn't understand why you were so much more than anyone I'd ever met." Courtney pressed herself against him. "I didn't know what I'd been missing." She smiled. "Then Dylan came along and he showed me. He and you are the best things that ever happened to me."

She slipped her arms around his waist and rested her head on his chest.

Jared sighed in contentment. "I want you to be happy."

She leaned back. "You're not responsible for my happiness, Jared. But know this. I can find happy here. With you."

"You're going to stay?"

"If I'm asked the right way."

Jared grinned. "Miss Jamison, will you stay with me on the Last Chance Ranch?"

She pretended to consider the offer. "I could be convinced."

She lifted her lips to his and his heart sang when he kissed her back. He held out his hand and she threaded her fingers through his. "So, we take this last chance together?" he asked.

"We'll make it work, Jared. I believe that."

"And I believe in you," he said, taking her lips once more. "Always."

Epilogue

The West Texas sunset flared with a mass of color, orange and pink, purple and blue painting the violet sky. Jared paced the front porch of his house. He couldn't stop the nerves from twisting his gut.

If he'd learned one thing about Courtney over the last few months, she liked to plan and she didn't always appreciate surprises.

"What was I thinking?" he muttered under his breath. The entire event had seemed like a good idea at the time.

Now he wasn't so sure.

He tugged at his shirt collar.

"Are you going to cut and run, my friend?" Léon posed, dropping any pretext of hiding his accent.

"No more hiding," Jared said. "But I may have made a mistake. Maybe a trip home to New York…"

"Do you love her?" Léon asked.

"More than my life." More than he'd ever imagined. She deserved something more extravagant.

"Then it's no mistake. If I've learned anything over the last few years, it's that home isn't a place. For you, or for her. Besides, didn't she say she wanted to stay."

Jared shoved his hands into his pocket. "After she got

out of the hospital. She was grateful. She could change her mind. Why wouldn't she?"

Léon let out a strange word, but even if Jared didn't understand the language, he knew a curse when he heard one.

The screen door opened and Courtney peeked outside. Her gaze landed on Léon. "Weren't you heading back to Dallas?" she said.

"Thought I might hang around, see if I can't find a place to rest my hat for a while," the man replied, his unique accent melting away, being replaced by a perfect Texas drawl. Léon let very few into the secrets of his life.

He briefly met Jared's gaze and wandered toward the barn.

"Is he okay?" Courtney asked, slipping into Jared's embrace and wrapping her arms around him.

"Someday, I hope."

He swallowed and tightened his embrace. He rested his cheek against her hair and inhaled the fresh scent. Her softness sank into him. He never wanted to be a day without feeling this way.

"He deserves it. He's lonely, isn't he?"

Jared pulled away slightly and met her gaze. "You see to the heart of people, don't you?"

"Not really," Courtney said. "I have a lot of flaws, Jared."

"I don't recognize them. Besides, you saw through me, no matter how much I tried to protect myself from you and Dylan."

"You were hurting." She sighed and met his gaze. "Is Roscoe still planning to leave?"

Jared scowled at the barn. "I can't convince him to stay. Velma's beside herself. She's done everything she can, but he blames himself for not seeing how twisted Derek had become."

Courtney clasped his arm. "You have to stop him. He's family."

"Well, I disabled his truck, so we have one more shot."

Her eyes widened "You didn't."

"He's not leaving without a fight."

"That's what I love about you, Jared King. You don't give up without a fight." She reached up to kiss him.

Jared closed his eyes and returned her touch. His heart raced. It was time. He held out his hand. "Come with me?"

She placed her hand into his. "Where are we going?"

"A surprise," he muttered beneath his breath. He led her over to the barn and slid open the door.

"Surprise!"

A cacophony of shouts greeted them. Courtney's eyes widened with shock. She gripped his hand tight. Her eyes teared up. Her gaze moved across all their family and friends. Blake Redmond and his wife and their children. Ransom and his family, the rest of the CTC operatives. Léon stood in the corner, alone but with a slight smile on his face.

She opened her mouth to speak when her gaze fell on the man Jared had flown in just this morning.

Courtney's father peered behind Ransom, his face healthy once again and his smile bright. His eyes clear and sober.

"Daddy." She ran over to him and hugged him tight. "I don't understand."

The entire group of men, women and children were grinning. Roscoe held Dylan in his arms and walked over, Velma at his side.

She beamed at both of them. "Welcome to forever, dearie."

Courtney smiled at her son. "Hey, Jelly Bean."

"Ma…ma." He grinned. He turned to Jared. "Da."

Jared took a deep breath. It was now or never.

He knelt down on one knee in front of Courtney and looked up at her. "Courtney Jamison, I know you never imagined yourself living on a ranch in Texas. But if anyone deserves honorary cowgirl status it's you. You're tough, you're determined, you love our son. I'd be honored if you would be my wife, stay with me and let me prove my love for you every day of our lives."

He dug into his pocket and pulled out a small velvet box, and flipped it open. The old-fashioned ring rested against the black, simple, the diamond small. Maybe he should have bought her something glitzy.

"It's beautiful." Tears rolled down her face. "Perfect, and like nothing I would have ever chosen for myself. You see into my heart like no one ever has."

She stood there, silent, staring at him. He squirmed under her gaze.

"Courtney?"

She smiled, her eyes bright with joy. "Of course I'll marry you."

A loud cheer rang out. Jared stood and slipped the ring on her finger. He couldn't help himself, he lowered his lips to hers, slowly, gently, tenderly. Trying with actions to show her what he had so much trouble saying in words.

His heart thudded in his chest and he entwined his fingers with her. "If you don't like the ring—"

"It's mine now. You're mine." She squeezed his hands. "Haven't you learned by now, I don't need the trimmings. I'm only interested in your heart, Jared King."

His heart overflowing, Jared sent a prayer upwards. Courtney's love had broken the curse of the Last Chance Ranch.

"You have it. Forever. For always."

* * * * *

THE DEPUTY'S BABY

TYLER ANNE SNELL

This book is for Marjorie and Annmarie. You two have been by my side, rooting for me since before I could remember. Even now you two are my own personal cheerleaders, and I couldn't ask for anyone better! You might have a dedication in this book but know that you help me write every single one. Love you!

Prologue

"Listen, I need you to buy me a drink."

Henry Ward put his beer bottle back on the bar's top and glanced at the couple next to him. Well, considering what the woman just told the man, he guessed they weren't a couple at all. It was well past the afternoon, but the bar hadn't yet filled up. If he hadn't been so focused on mentally prepping for what he had to do the next day, he probably would have noticed that he and his bar stool companion weren't alone.

"Say what?" the man next to Henry asked. He had a slight slur that sounded like he was trying to talk through a coat of syrup. That wasn't exactly surprising considering Henry had watched him down four very potent drinks within the last hour. Ones that had no color other than dark brown and could be smelled a few feet away. The woman must not have had the chance to catch on to the fumes yet or just hadn't registered the slur. Or maybe she didn't care. Either way, it wasn't his business.

Yet he couldn't help keeping an ear turned to the conversation.

"I need you to pretend that you bought me a drink, I should say," the woman was quick to add. There was some hesitation in her words, but she took the bar stool on the other side of the man, three seats down from Henry.

He glanced over to see the blond of her hair, curled and running down the length of her back, but couldn't get a good angle on her face. He turned his gaze back to the TV over the bar area and fingered the label on his bottle.

"My, uh, sister Kristen just told me she's bringing one of her coworkers over to meet me. She's been trying to set us up for a while now and…well, she won't take no for an answer. So I thought I'd take the option off the table." The woman waited for him to respond. When a moment stretched on, she laid it out simply. "Can I just sit here and talk to you for a few minutes? Maybe throw in some fake laughing every once in a while for show?"

Henry snorted but then covered it up by taking another pull of his beer. Even though he'd been sitting in the Eagle longer than the man a stool over from him had been, he'd only had the one drink. The only reason he'd even left his hotel for the bar was nerves. He had a job interview the next day.

An important one at that.

"Sure thing, hon," the man finally answered. The slur went past the subtle side and right to blatantly obvious. "I'll be your shoulder to lean on *all night long*. You're such a pretty little thing."

Henry glanced over at the two again in time to see the woman's hand, rising to grab the bartender's attention most likely, stall in midair. There was no denying the man between them was drunk now. Henry knew she'd heard it clear as day.

And it had bothered her.

"Oh, you know, *thank you* for that," she hurriedly said, hand already back on the bar's top. "Really. But I just…

well, you know I just realized how rude it would be to lie to my sister. I mean, she's a pain, believe me, but I should just be honest with her. So thank you again, but I don't think this was the best idea." She was off the bar stool faster than the drunk man could probably process the movement. "I'm sorry for the interruption. Enjoy the rest of your night!"

"I don't think so, sweetie," the man managed to rasp.

Henry tensed as his neighbor started to turn around.

"You can't just leave me hanging like that. It isn't nice."

Henry was a second away from making the man turn around on his stool, with more than a few stern words, but the woman beat him to the punch. Her voice, sweet as honey moments before, took on a sharp edge.

"If you think I'm not nice, then you wouldn't like my Taser," she said simply.

It did the trick.

The man mumbled and then was facing his empty glass again.

Henry smirked as the woman walked away. He didn't look after her. He didn't need to be doing anything other than worrying about his interview. Though admittedly he wanted the man next to him dealt with. Instead of minding his own business again, he caught the bartender's eye and waved him over. He pointed his thumb at the man now cursing all women beneath his breath.

"I think this one needs a cab called in right about now," Henry said.

The bartender, an older gentlemAn with no hair on his scalp but at least a year's worth of hair on his chin, nodded. Without looking at the man in question, he sighed.

"One's already on the way," he said. "Gary gets pretty

foul after four of his drinks. If I don't send him off after that, he won't pay the cabdriver when they get him to his place."

"Good policy," Henry admitted, impressed.

The man named Gary swore at the two of them but nothing that made sense.

"If you get him into the cab so I don't have to, next drink is on the house," the bartender added, annoyance clear in his voice. "I'd rather not deal with him tonight."

Henry felt the now-room-temperature beer between his hands. It would be nice if he had a cold one. "Deal."

He spent the next five minutes or so trying to get Gary to calm down. Even without the woman coming over, Henry would bet Gary could still have managed to get riled up all on his lonesome.

During the last two years, Henry had worked alongside men like Gary, known them like he knew himself. They were angry no matter the drink in their hand or the people at their side. The way they held themselves, the way they dressed, spoke and even held their glasses or bottles showed Henry men who were unhappy and, for whatever reason, wanted to stay that way.

Being around them was more than a job. It was an exercise. One that had worn him down to the point of exhaustion.

Which was why his interview the next day was important.

He needed a new routine.

Gary, however, didn't seem to want anything other than his current mood. He grumbled and cursed as Henry took him to his cab. Henry watched after him for a moment. The night air was cool and apparently rare, according to the manager from his hotel. Henry almost considered going back to his hotel room and trying to get a good night's sleep. But just as quickly, he realized that wasn't going to happen. He had too much on his mind. Not to mention a free beer back inside.

It wasn't until he had that free beer between his hands that a new wave of night air rolled in around a small group of people that Henry thought about the blond woman again.

It might have been a Wednesday, but apparently that did little to diminish the bar's popularity. Ten or so patrons had eked in and were already either playing pool or sitting around, drinks in hand and conversations going strong. Finding the one person without either was fast work.

Henry wished he'd looked for the woman sooner.

Standing from a booth she'd commandeered in the corner, one of the most beautiful women he'd ever seen was waving at the new group of people who'd just come in. The long, curly blond hair he'd already seen was half pinned back, showing an open face made up of high cheekbones and a long, thin nose. Her lips were rimmed in pink. Even from this distance he could still see the green of her eyes as they moved from who must have been her sister Kristen to a man who must have been her arranged date. Despite what Henry had heard her say about the man, he was impressed to see her expression gave none of her distaste away. Instead she was exuding nothing but enthusiasm and politeness.

It made something in him shift and before he had time to be surprised at himself, Henry did something he wasn't expecting. With one look at the empty second pool table in the corner, he straightened his shirt, ran a hand through his hair and started to walk over to the group. His sights set squarely on the woman with green eyes.

The sister picked him up on her radar the moment he was a few steps away. It didn't stop Henry. He felt a smile pull up his lips and hoped it was pleasant enough.

He also hoped the blonde hadn't already committed to her arranged date. Or else things were about to get awkward.

"Hey, sorry, about that," Henry started, eyes locked on target. "Work called and I had to answer." He motioned back to the pool tables. "But one of the pool tables is open now if you wanted a rematch."

The group turned to him as a whole, but the blonde didn't miss a beat.

She grinned. "If you really want to lose again, then who am I to stop you?"

Henry didn't have to fake the grin that stretched one corner of his lips higher.

"Wait." The sister butted in. For a moment Henry thought the jig was up, but then she laughed. "She actually beat someone at pool?"

Henry shrugged.

"Believe me, I'm not proud about it," he said. "I even owe her a drink because of it. A drink that's past due now."

The woman, once again, didn't skip a beat. "Then let's fix that, shall we?"

She smiled at her sister, said a quick, "Excuse me," and followed Henry to the bar. Without another word between them, she ordered a drink. It wasn't until the group she'd left behind settled into a booth that she spoke.

"I'm assuming you overheard my conversation with the man at the bar," she said, voice low. It was back to honey.

"I did," he confirmed.

Her smile returned.

"Thanks for helping me out," she said. "In my sister's words, as the baby of the family, I never know what's good for me. She thinks that's Stanley, and I think she has too much time on her hands."

Henry snorted. "My brother plays that age card on me from time to time, too. I know the pain."

The woman laughed.

It was a very attractive sound from a very attractive woman.

"I'm Cassie, by the way. Thanks again for being quick on your feet. You saved my night."

"The name's Henry. And I wouldn't thank me yet." Riding a genuine wave of excitement, he leaned closer, careful to keep out of her personal space but just close enough that he smelled her sweet perfume. He felt the new grin seconds before he heard it in his own voice. "I'm actually *really* great at pool."

Chapter One

Henry was looking through the passenger's side window at the Eagle, trying to pretend he wasn't thinking of a beautiful woman.

"This is one of three bars in Riker County worth their salt," explained the driver and temporary tour guide, Sheriff Billy Reed. His cowboy hat sat on the center console between them. It was a reminder that Henry was in the Deep South now where cowboy hats could be normal even if cowboys in Alabama were few and far between. "The owner, nicknamed Hawk because nothing gets past him, also runs the bar and does it well. He makes a mean drink and doesn't put up with any nonsense. Also has a memory of steel. Go to him once or twice and he'll know your drink for life. And when to send you off." The sheriff cut a smile. "I suggest you don't force him to do that, though. Getting on his bad side wouldn't be the best thing to do if you want to fit in with our crowd. This is one of local law's favorite haunts."

Henry grinned, deciding not to tell the man he was sure he'd already met the famous Hawk and seen up close how he operated. Seven months ago he'd been in the bar the day before interviewing for the Riker County

Sheriff's Department deputy's position. One he had now held for a week.

The night after the interview he'd left town fast and hadn't been back since. However, Henry was sure he'd been there long enough to peg the man next to him as one of the good ones. Quick to laugh, quick to teach, more pride than most men showed in their entire lives just while staring at one bar within his jurisdiction. It was crystal clear that Sheriff Reed loved his job, his home and the people he had sworn to protect.

The only thing Henry hadn't seen yet was how quick Billy went from fun-loving to business when something serious went down. Sure, Henry had read and seen news stories where the man and his department had been quick on their feet, but he was a man who preferred to deal in firsthand experience. Though, thankfully, no calls that week had been worthy of straining the department, the deputies or its sheriff.

But Henry knew it was only a matter of time.

Bad guys never took breaks for long.

The sheriff took the Tahoe out of Park, backed out of the street-side parking spot and into the two-lane. It was a little after nine in the morning and the small town of Carpenter was mostly sleepy. The Eagle and its surrounding businesses especially, since they catered to the nighttime crowds. Still, Henry kept alert as they drove through, trying to catalog everything he could about Carpenter.

Or maybe he was just trying to keep his focus anywhere but on the bar. Even though he'd only been there once, his thoughts had been sliding back to the place for months. Back to the night when he'd met a woman with honey in her voice and a smile in her eyes.

Back to the night when they had played pool, laughed a lot, and things had been anything *but* sleepy.

A pull of regret momentarily tightened his stomach. He only had one thing to remind him of that night outside of his memories. The small piece of paper tucked into his wallet was a constant reminder of one of the best nights he'd ever had.

And how a man like him shouldn't have anything beyond that.

"Now that we've had a look at where some of the nightlife of Carpenter takes place, I want to show you a few spots of interest during the day," the sheriff said. He paused before continuing and seemed to consider his next words. "Listen, Henry, I know that you're used to fieldwork and that this 'touring the county' thing is probably driving you a little up the wall, but while sitting in a car as I point at stuff might not be exciting, it's hard to serve a county you're flying blind through."

Henry didn't dispute that.

He'd spent the last five years in Tennessee, bouncing around when the job called for it. Not too far a cry from South Alabama but enough of a difference that he couldn't pretend to know the county's flavor just yet.

Henry pulled his mind away from the blond-haired beauty he'd rescued from a blind date, and tried to refocus on the task at hand. This was the first day he'd spent out of the sheriff's department. One of several days to come that he'd spend touring with the sheriff and the chief deputy before getting partnered with another deputy. Then, after a while, Henry would finally get his own cruiser and be able to get back to working alone.

He hoped.

It had been a long time since he'd had a partner, and

he wasn't itching to get back into the swing of being one of two.

Sheriff Reed's guided tour took them through the whole of Carpenter, one of three small towns in the county but, according to Reed, they were barely scratching the surface of his hometown.

"Carpenter has been through a lot in the last decade or so. Heck, the *county* has been through a lot," he said later when they pulled into the parking lot of a small diner across the street from the department. Apparently, it was also a law-enforcement favorite, and not just because of its close proximity. "It's made the community stronger, but it's also made the people that make trouble smarter. Trickier. Carpenter, and Riker County as a whole, has a lot of nooks and crannies, country roads and open land, not to mention a good deal of abandoned properties scattered throughout the towns and city, that all make it harder to do our jobs. To keep the community safe, to keep the bad guys from getting the upper hand. Which means we get to work harder and adapt so that never happens."

He put the Tahoe in Park and cut the engine. Henry couldn't help noticing the temperature on the dash read ninety degrees. Though that wasn't counting in the humidity.

Billy glanced at the temperature, too, and smirked. "Which means after lunch I'll start showing you the juicy stuff. Until then you're about to experience one of the best burgers in town and one of the most powerful commercial air conditioners, too."

"And I won't turn that down, either," Henry was quick to say. It wasn't like they were allowed to wear shorts on the job to help fight the heat. Plus, it had been a long time since he'd had a good burger.

They got out of the Tahoe and started across the parking lot. It was summer and the heat kept sticking to its guns. The air was hot and heavy, pressing against his uniform without hesitation. Tennessee had its moments of uncomfortable, but one week in Riker County and he thought he understood the meaning of the word *melting*.

"You weren't kidding about this place being popular with the badges," Henry observed after trying to memorize their surroundings for later. He noted two cruisers at the corner of the building and, if he wasn't mistaken, there was also a personal vehicle of Chief Deputy Suzy Simmons parked in front of the entrance.

"The power of good food in a small town is second to none," the sheriff responded, seemingly not surprised by the turnout. "Though today it's less about the food and more about celebrating." Billy pulled open the door but paused to explain himself over his shoulder. "One of our dispatchers is finally back from an extended vacation. We love all of our department, but I don't think I'm being too sentimental when I say she's close to the heart of it."

Henry had heard that one of the night-shift dispatchers was out of town, but he hadn't thought any more on it. Carpenter might have been a small town, but Riker oversaw two more towns and one city. He hadn't had a chance to meet all the deputies in the department, let alone all the support staff. He hadn't even personally met the dispatchers currently working.

"Plus," the sheriff continued with a smirk, "I may be a man of the law, but I'm not one to turn down a chance at cake."

Henry laughed and followed him inside. It was a small

room but efficient. Booths lined the right wall along the windows while a counter stretched across the other with stools in front. In the back corner three booths were filled with deputies, Chief Deputy Simmons, and even one of the detectives, Matt Walker. Some were off duty; others wore their uniforms. All were seemingly in good moods.

Henry spied the half-eaten cake in question sitting in the center of the middle booth, but the woman of the hour wasn't across from it. Even without knowing it was a celebration for her, Henry could have guessed easily enough. Everyone seemed to be leaning in toward her. She stood at the head of the closest table, a gift bag in one hand and tissue paper in the other. Henry couldn't see her face, but he had an uninhibited view of her hair.

It was blond and curly and familiar.

"Deputy Ward," Sheriff Reed announced as soon as they were close enough to the group. Everyone quieted and turned their attention to their leader. Including the woman of the hour. "I'd like to introduce you to our very own Cassie Gates."

Two beautiful green eyes found Henry's and widened.

The woman Henry had spent months trying to forget wasn't just a dispatcher for the department. According to the sheriff, she was the heart of it.

On reflex alone Henry outstretched his hand.

"Nice to meet you," he said. There was a distant tone to his voice. Even he could hear it. Like someone who had just been blindsided. Which, he realized, was exactly what was happening.

Cassie's long lashes blinked a few times but she collected herself quickly.

"Nice to meet you," she repeated. Her tone also sounding dull, hollow.

At least he wasn't the only one who had been caught wholly off guard.

The change in both of their demeanors didn't go unnoticed, either. The sheriff raised an eyebrow. He didn't have time to comment.

The sound of glass shattering filled the air.

And then, right in front of Henry's eyes, the sheriff took a bullet to the stomach.

BETWEEN THE SPACE of two breaths, all hell broke loose in the diner.

Cassie dropped to the floor, a scream caught in her throat. Almost simultaneously the weight of someone else was on top of her, sandwiching her flat against the tiled floor.

Yelling followed by more glass shattering kept the noise levels high and heavy. What was once a celebration had turned into terror. Like a light switch had been flipped, bathing them in a whole new array of shadows. Whoever was covering her tightened around her body, making a cage.

More gunshots sounded overhead. So close, her ears rang in protest. Her colleagues, her *friends*, were returning fire.

Memories of being in a similar situation years before filled her head.

She'd done this before.

She'd been here before. Under fire...

When she thought she was supposed to be safe.

Cassie sucked in a breath, panic thronging her body. If her hands had been free, they would have gone straight to her neck. A gut reaction she'd honed in the last two and a half years. Her fingers would trace the scar at the side of her neck. She'd remember the blood and terror. However, now she couldn't go through that routine. Not when the weight of someone was keeping her to the floor.

So she did the best thing she could. She squeezed her eyes shut and waited.

What felt like an eternity went by until silence finally cut through the madness. It was brief but poignant. As if the diner as a whole had decided to take a collective breath. She couldn't have been the only one whose heart was trying to hammer itself out of her chest.

The body holding her didn't move.

Then, as quickly as the shot had invaded the diner in the first place, the yelling started again. A collective muddled sound where everyone spoke together, canceling one another out with no real progress.

It wasn't until one voice climbed its way above those of the patrons and staff that the chaos was curbed.

"Billy! Billy's down!"

Cassie's personal cage loosened around her enough so that she could look toward Suzy. The chief deputy dropped to her hands and knees next to the sheriff, hands already pressing into the gunshot wound in his stomach. Cassie couldn't look away as blood began to flow onto Suzy's dark hands.

Billy didn't complain about the shot or the pressure.

He didn't even move.

"Are you okay?"

A new voice was at Cassie's ear. The weight on her eased off until a man's concerned expression swam into view. Still, she couldn't look away from the sheriff. She could almost smell the blood.

"Are you okay?" the man repeated. "Cassie?"

Two warm hands came up to cradle her chin. He was gentle as he forced her to look away from the anguishing scene no more than two feet from them. Her boss. Her friend.

"Are you hurt?"

It was like he reached out and slapped her. The shock, the fear, the panic turned analytical. Cassie focused on her body, a new kind of worry coursing through her.

Had they been hurt?

Other than her racing heart, nothing felt different.

"Cassie?"

Clear eyes implored her. She finally recognized them as Henry's. If they had been in any other situation, she would have been fighting a storm of emotions just at the sight of him. Instead she answered him simply. "I think I'm okay."

Henry dropped his hands from her face to her shoulders. He pulled her up but not to her full height. Instead she let herself be led behind the counter that ran the length of the diner. Two waitresses were already huddled there, a reflection of the fear Cassie felt in their faces.

"Stay here," Henry ordered. "There could be more than one shooter."

She nodded and watched as he disappeared. Without his weight keeping her arms down, Cassie was able to reach up and touch the scar on her neck.

Then she dropped her hand to her stomach.

Henry's voice joined the chorus of law enforcement in the diner. It had been so long since she'd heard it like this. Panic and determination. Fear and anger. Uncertainty and planning.

And then here Henry was, among them, adding to

the group. It had been over seven months since she'd seen him. Now here he was after no contact whatsoever.

And still he'd tried to protect her.

Cassie rubbed the bump beneath her loose-fitting shirt.

Henry Ward had no idea he'd just protected his unborn child, too.

Chapter Two

The man who had shot Sheriff Reed had been killed on sight by Chief Deputy Simmons. She hadn't even needed to leave the diner to do it, shooting through the shattered window from next to the booth. Though the man had taken a hit or two from Deputy Dante Mills and Detective Walker in the process.

As for who the shooter was? That wasn't answered until that night inside the department. Suzy, as everyone called her, straightened her back and addressed a room filled to the brim with staff on and off duty. With the sheriff out of commission, she was next in line to lead, and from what Henry had seen of her so far, he more than believed she was ready for the job.

"I just got off the phone with Mara," she began.

Henry knew she was talking about the sheriff's wife. It wasn't a secret how much the man loved his wife and two children. It had been a point of envy for Henry when Billy first talked to him. Now it did nothing but make him feel even more for the man. He knew he wasn't the only one.

"She said that according to the doctor, he isn't out of the woods yet. The bullet missed any vital organs, but he lost a lot of blood."

The woman paused, pain crossing her expression before she could rein it in. Billy had also not kept it a secret that his chief deputy was his best friend and had been for years. They were even godparents to each other's children. He was her family just as the rest of the department was. That closeness was apparent in how the room around Henry seemed to be hanging on her every word.

He couldn't deny he missed that feeling.

Camaraderie that was familial.

"But the doctor also said he's optimistic," she continued. A small smile pulled up the corner of her lips. "And we all know how hard-headed Billy is. Knowing him, he'll be giving out orders by the end of the week from his hospital bed, fussing for his cowboy hat."

There was a chorus of laughter and agreement.

It didn't last long.

Neither did Suzy's smile.

"The reason we're all here is a man named Darrel Connelly," she started again, her tone sharp, serious. A leader addressing those who followed her. "He had no ID on him, but a local police officer recognized him. We ran his name and found that he hadn't been arrested before, but his brother, Tanner, had been for the attempted murder of his girlfriend. Billy's testimony sent Tanner to jail, where he was killed in an inmate-led riot. He was Darrel's only family. So I don't think it would be going out on a limb to say that Billy was targeted out of revenge."

The same group who had laughed in agreement a minute before cursed in unison.

Henry joined in.

"However, until we complete an official investigation, no one in the department will comment to the press. Understood?" Suzy didn't wait for an answer. Instead she took a quick breath and gave a small nod. "While Billy is out, we will continue to do our jobs with the best of our abilities. Any and all questions in the meantime can be addressed to me or Captain Jones. When I know more about Billy's condition, I will update you. Until then, let's continue to make the sheriff proud."

The room's mood swung into a cheer before they started to break up. Suzy stayed up front, talking to those who stopped at her side. Almost like a widow after a funeral. Henry just hoped the analogy didn't come true.

He stayed to the outskirts of the room, hanging back while the bulk of people filtered out. He looked through the crowd, hoping to see the woman he hadn't ever thought he'd see again.

Cassie Gates.

One of Riker County Sheriff's Department's dispatchers.

Henry hadn't even gotten a chance to talk to her since the diner. After they had secured the area, she'd left with one of the deputies and his wife. She'd been visibly shaken. They all had been, though, if he was being honest.

"Hey, Ward."

Henry turned as Detective Walker came up to his side. He ran a hand through his blond hair and let out a sigh. It was tired.

"Not how you pictured your first week," he commented. It wasn't a question. "Wasn't how I pictured my week, either, to tell the truth."

Henry nodded. "Bad guys don't take breaks for long," he said. "My partner used to say that all the time."

"I hate that it's true but it is." Matt ran another hand through his hair. He'd been the one doing the legwork on

Darrel since they got back. Henry imagined he'd have a full, exhausting day tomorrow, too. "One minute we're eating cake and the next—" The detective cut himself off, anger rising to the surface of his expression.

Henry let him have the moment in silence. He took another visible breath to calm himself.

"I just wanted to say thank you for what you did today."

Henry couldn't help his eyebrow rising in question.

The detective elaborated. "You covered Cassie without hesitation," he said simply. "Made sure she was safe before we could get a hold on the situation. Good instincts can't be taught, but they can be thanked."

That surprised Henry. For two different reasons. One, trying to protect Cassie was a gut reaction. One his body started before his mind could even catch up and act on. He'd heard and seen the shot and then trying to protect her had been his only priority. He hadn't done it for praise or thanks and was surprised he was getting both.

Two, being thanked was strange enough, but being thanked by the detective raised a few questions. The first and loudest was why was Matt invested in her safety? Or, more to the point, was it more personal than colleagues and friends? Did he care more for the woman than the rest?

And why was the mere thought of the two having more than a working relationship bothering Henry so much?

He'd only known Cassie for the one night—and the following morning—and then they'd parted ways. The slip of paper in his wallet was the only connection he'd had to her past then. It was foolish to think she was the same woman. He hadn't seen her in over seven months.

A lot could happen in less time.

Henry shouldn't, and couldn't, be surprised that she might be in a relationship. Heck, *they* hadn't even had one to begin with.

"I was just doing my job," Henry said dutifully, locking down any conflicting emotions that might be splaying across his expression. "Nothing the rest of you wouldn't do in my place. I'm just glad we kept anyone else from getting hurt."

Matt nodded, accepting the statement as true, and started to walk off.

However, Henry couldn't help himself. "I actually wanted to talk to her," he blurted out, surprising himself. "Cassie, that is. I never got the chance at a proper introduction." It was a lie, but Henry wasn't about to admit to the detective that he had already met the woman… At a bar before going back to his hotel room. Especially if the two were involved. "Do you know where she is? I haven't seen her since we left the diner."

Matt's brow furrowed. "She went to the hospital afterward, but now, if I'm not mistaken, she's back at my place. I told her not to bother coming into the department tonight. Technically she doesn't start back until next week."

Henry's gut dropped more than it should have. He had just confirmed the theory that Cassie and Matt were involved. Some of that emotion must have showed in his expression.

Matt gave a small smile. "You know, I'm about to head there myself but need a ride. If you give me a lift, I can trade you a home-cooked meal. I don't think any of us has had anything to eat yet. Plus, I'm sure Cassie will want to thank you for earlier."

The offer felt genuine. Matt hadn't picked up on any of Henry's thoughts.

But even those thoughts gave him little ground to argue with. Though Henry had to admit he didn't like the idea of Cassie with someone else, he knew it was for the better.

People around him got hurt. Plain and simple.

But that didn't stop him from accepting the offer.

He still wanted to see her. If only to make sure she was really okay.

They said goodbye to Suzy, asking again to be kept in the loop, and were on the road to Matt's house within minutes. The detective gave directions, but other than that their conversation was light. Henry wanted to get to know more about him but decided he already knew enough. The lead detective was good at his job, nice to his team and loyal.

He reminded Henry of Calvin, his old partner.

A good man.

A man that Cassie deserves.

The thought popped into his head so quickly he couldn't brace himself for it.

How had a woman he'd known for such a short time affected him so much? It made no sense. And was dangerous. Henry needed this job. He needed a new start. Banishing any and all thoughts of Cassie Gates past professionalism wasn't something he wanted. He *needed* it.

Get a grip on yourself.

Henry loosened his shoulders, put on a polite smile and was ready when they finally pulled up to the detective's house.

"Home sweet home," Matt said over the hood of the

car when they got out. "I don't know about you, but I'm ready to eat a horse."

The house was a good size with a nice yard. Simple and quaint. Two cars were parked in the driveway. One Henry recognized as the detective's personal vehicle, the other he'd not seen before. Lights were on in the dining room, the curtains open enough that Henry got a clear view of the table.

And Cassie sitting at its end.

She must have felt his stare. She looked out the window and met his eyes.

She didn't smile.

Maybe coming hadn't been a good idea.

"I should also probably warn you," started Matt, walking up the sidewalk that led to his front door. He paused at it, hand on the handle. "You're about to meet a very loud, slightly intrusive woman. I mean, don't get me wrong, I love her, but sometimes she can be a little overpowering when you first get to know her." There was a smile in his voice. "She calls it curiosity."

Henry didn't remember Cassie being loud, certainly not intrusive. At the bar she hadn't kept poking around when he'd said he couldn't talk about his current job and, in fact, hadn't asked too many really personal questions at all. He'd treated her in kind.

Still, he had to remind himself he didn't know her past their one shared night of passion.

That passion.

Even months later his body remembered it. Craved it.

Henry cleared his throat and followed the detective inside. He was just about to agree with his earlier thought that coming had been a bad idea when they made it to the dining room. Cassie was staring up at them. She looked tired. It reminded him that there were more important things than their past. She'd been witness to one of her friends almost dying across from her.

"I invited Henry to join us for dinner," Matt greeted. "Since…well, today didn't go as planned."

Cassie looked between them. It encouraged Henry to respond.

"It's nice to officially meet you," he lied again. If she was with the detective, he didn't want to make anything awkward. Not when Riker County was his chance to start over. He didn't want to make enemies his first week on the job. And judging by the look she was giving him, he could only assume she was trying to figure out what to say herself. The least he could do was try to help her out.

Cassie's green, green eyes widened, but she didn't get a chance to respond. Sound from the other room turned into a flurry of motion that converged on the detective next to him within seconds. Henry tensed, but Matt was laughing into the hair of the woman whose arms were wrapped around him.

"My God, Maggie," he said, reciprocating the embrace. "Ever think about playing football?"

The woman covered his mouth with hers in a quick but strong kiss. She wasn't smiling when she pulled away.

"I'm glad you're okay," she said. "If something had happened to you, I would have hurt you myself."

"Of that I have no doubt." Matt reached up and squeezed her shoulder. He turned to Henry. "This is Maggie Carson. Apparently my linebacker of a fiancée. Maggie, this is our newest deputy I was telling you about. Henry Ward."

Maggie's gaze lifted to his. Her handshake was firm.

"Thanks for bringing him home," she said, sincere. "My car's been acting up and I stole his to pick Cassie up from the hospital."

Henry felt his eyebrow rise. He turned to Cassie. "I thought you said you were okay."

He wouldn't have left her alone otherwise.

She gave him a polite smile, one he'd seen when he first met her at the Eagle, and stood from her seat.

Henry's eyes zipped downward.

Right to Cassie's stomach.

She placed a hand over it, protectively.

"I was," she said. "But I wanted to make sure he was, too."

Chapter Three

"You're pregnant."

It wasn't a question but it wasn't a statement, either. It felt like a confused in-between. Henry Ward had been thrown for a loop and was still trying to find his way back to solid ground. Cassie tried to help, even if she was also looking for some better footing herself.

It wasn't every day that the father of your child appeared out of thin air for the first time since the night he'd spent with you months before, then potentially saved your life and pretended he'd never met you before.

It was all confusing.

"I am," she confirmed, though it wasn't needed. "Seven months, give or take."

Cassie would bet Henry was doing some of the fastest math he'd ever done in his life. All while staring at her pregnant belly. Since she'd never had kids before, she wasn't showing as much, but there was no denying the bump once she brought attention to it.

The man wasn't stupid. If his math was even in the ballpark, he'd guess that he was the father. However, he didn't ask the question. Then again, she didn't think he would. Not after he'd made it clear they didn't know each other.

You didn't speak up, either, Cassie pointed out to herself.

The weight of the day erased thoughts of Cassie's personal life for the moment. She moved her hand across her stomach.

"The doc gave the okay, though," she said. If Maggie, the ex-reporter, or Matt noticed anything off about the two of them, they didn't say a word. "But you can never be too careful. Plus, I wanted to be there for Mara."

Henry tore his eyes off her stomach.

"That's good," was all he said.

Matt put a hand on his shoulder and steered the deputy into the kitchen. Cassie settled back into her chair while Maggie followed the men. She was soon back with the dinner they'd just finished making. Nothing too fancy, just something to kill their hunger. Cassie doubted any of them could take any real pleasure from a meal until Billy could, too.

Like her hand had a mind of its own again, it moved up and touched the scar at her neck. Maggie didn't miss it. She took the seat next to Cassie and patted her back.

"You're okay," Maggie whispered. "You *both* are okay. This will all get sorted out. Have faith."

Cassie felt herself nod.

Maggie started a volley of questions as soon as the men were back and seated. More than anything Cassie wanted to pay attention, to learn more about Henry, a man at times she'd wondered if he was even real. Yet there was a rising feeling of overwhelming vulnerability in her chest. It tightened her stomach and pulled out some of the fear and anger she'd felt at the diner.

She didn't know if it was because she was pregnant, because the man she'd spent the last several months hoping would call had showed up, or because she just hadn't had the time to process everything, but suddenly she couldn't just sit there anymore.

"If y'all hadn't have been at my party, this wouldn't have happened," she said, cutting Matt off midsentence.

He was quick to shake his head.

"Cassie, you know as well as I do that you and your party had nothing to do with this," Matt said in defense. "That man was angry, probably out for revenge. Location doesn't deter someone stuck in the mind-set that they're going to try to take on the law."

"But it did give the bastard the opportunity, didn't it?"

She felt the heat that surged through her words seconds before Matt's eyes widened a fraction. She'd bet Maggie's were probably wider, too. It wasn't every day that Cassie Gates had an outburst. She was the sweet one. The Southern girl who always smiled and was agreeable. The one who stayed optimistic when things went badly.

Her cheeks stung now that she'd broken out of her normal character. It didn't help that Henry was there, staring at her with those eyes of steel. The same eyes that had traced her lips seconds before he'd kissed her for the first time. The same eyes that had traveled across her bare skin sometime later in the night.

Cool, hard steel she hadn't seen since.

And she hated that she was thinking about that night right now. After the day they'd been through, it didn't seem so important.

Yet she could feel the tears of being rejected starting to push themselves forward.

"Cassie…" Maggie began, but her tone was what finally broke the dam that Cassie had put up to keep herself sane after the diner.

The chair scraped against the floor as she pushed

herself back and stood. With one hand on her stomach, Cassie met no one's gaze. "Sorry, I'm just tired and hormonal," she declared. "I don't mean to be rude, but I think I'd like to go home now."

Maggie, bless her, must have caught on that Cassie meant what she said.

"Okay," she said, a reassuring smile lifting her expression. "That's fine. Let me at least make you a plate before we go, though, all right? Tired or not, you *two* still need to eat something."

There was force behind her words. A mother mothering a soon-to-be mother. Practically the lifeblood of the South. But she was right.

Cassie nodded and collected her plate. "I'll help."

Without looking at the men, or the one in particular, Cassie fled to the kitchen, a storm of emotions battling it out in her chest.

THE WOMEN WERE out and gone before Henry could think of a reason to pull Cassie aside, alone. Not that it would have changed anything. Cassie could have medaled at the Olympic sport of avoidance with how she'd skirted him on the way out.

Instead of asking her the million-dollar question, he'd been left watching through the dining room window as she slid into Maggie's car.

Not that he blamed her.

He'd just burned any normal bridge they could have had, announcing that he'd never met the woman before in front of her coworkers. Her friends.

Henry resisted the urge to slam his fist down on the tabletop.

Seven months give or take.

That give or take could make the difference.

Had she met someone after him?

Or was he the father?

How had he missed that detail at the diner?

Why had he lied?

And why hadn't Cassie corrected him?

Too many questions and no one to ask them of. At least, not right now.

"I'm sure Billy already told you, but we've been through a lot as a department the last few years," Matt said, breaking the silence they'd fallen into. He moved his food around on his plate before dropping his fork and taking up his beer. "Stuff that scars. But I guess with your last job you know that better than most of us."

It wasn't a question. Few had been aware of the finite details that went along with his last job. The detective hadn't been one of them, but Henry knew he wasn't stupid. It was public knowledge that his partner, Calvin Fitzgerald, had died during an undercover operation.

Henry took a long pull from his beer as thoughts about Cassie were momentarily replaced by the one part of his past he'd been forced to leave behind.

"Scars are par for the course in this field," he said. "Everyone seems to get them, no matter which side they're on. And even if they aren't on a side at all. A damn shame, if you ask me."

Matt picked up his beer and tapped it against Henry's bottle with a *clink*. "Amen to that." He paused, his bottle hanging in midair. "But some of us have literal scars. Ones that came from calls that were way too close. Cassie's one of them. So I'm sure she's swimming in a sea of bad memories right now. When the dust settles and *when* Billy heals up, you'll see us all in a better light."

Matt smirked. "Until then, try not to take any general grumpiness personal."

"Deal."

Henry didn't have the heart to tell the man that any ill feelings he might get from Cassie were more than deserved.

Instead they finished their dinner just as Maggie returned to help clean up. The way she and the detective moved in tandem without even realizing they were doing it was refreshing to see. The only relationships Henry had been around in the last few years had been dangerous, toxic and unpredictable. Ones that were filled with uncertainty and almost always sank his world into trouble.

Which was why he'd come to Riker County in the first place.

He wasn't looking for redemption and he sure as hell wasn't looking for a second chance at his old life. He didn't want to make things better. That was another bridge that had already burned.

All Henry wanted now was a big heap of nothing.

He wanted a clean slate.

But could he do it? Could he start over? Or had his last job rubbed off on him too much?

Henry sat heavily in the driver's seat of his car after saying 'bye to the couple. He waved at Matt, who retreated into his house, Maggie at his side.

What about Cassie?

And her unborn son?

THE HEAT WAS THICK. Heavy. Unforgiving.

He didn't care.

"What was that?" His voice wasn't low. He was yelling. Again, he didn't care. "You all had one job. *One job!*"

With a flourish he swept his arm over the desk. Everything on its top flew off and crashed to the floor. The man across from him winced. The woman holding his hand did not.

"We saw an opportunity and snapped at it," she hissed, all venom.

"You could have ruined everything," he yelled back. The keyboard that clung to the desktop by its cord didn't last long. He put more feeling into his swing and it, too, crashed to the floor. This time the computer went with it.

The man across from him flinched again like he'd been the one struck. His woman didn't bend.

"We have been waiting for you to put your plan into action for months," she retorted, fire in her words. In a detached sort of way he noticed the tension that had tightened her muscles. He'd bet she was doing everything in her power not to throw her entire body into her anger. Her rage. Under different circumstances he might have been impressed.

At the moment he was not.

"What we're doing, what *I'm* doing, isn't planning some stroll through the park or setting up some simple con," he said, pulling some of his own frustration back into himself. With Darrel's death he'd already lost one of his players. He wasn't willing to lose any more. Not yet. Not when they were so close. He straightened his tie and ran a hand over his hair to smooth it down. "It isn't a plan at all, really. It's a vision. One that will only work if *we don't do whatever the hell we want to.*"

His calm shattered in an instant. He grabbed the lip of his desk and pulled up. If it had been his home office desk, it wouldn't have budged, but this one was cheap. The desk flipped over without much resistance.

Paula was quick. She was up and out of her chair in a flash, long legs graceful in their movement. Her poor excuse for a boyfriend, Jason, wasn't as fast. The weight of the desk pinned the top of his foot. He yelled out in pain.

Again, if it had been his personal desk, Jason's foot would have been broken by the weight.

"Things are about to get crazy," he continued, voice lost to the strain of trying to figure out if he should keep his tantrum going. "And that chaos *is* the goal, the end game." He fixed Paula with a look that kept whatever she was about to say behind her lips. "No more acting out of line in the name of revenge. No more taking shots because you have the opportunity. You're here for more than something so insignificant."

Paula crossed her arms over her chest. She made no move to help Jason free himself. It was as if she'd already forgotten him.

Which was even better.

"What's more significant than revenge?" she asked, cool and calm. "What's better than making the people who wronged us and ours suffer?"

He was quick to answer. "The power to prolong both."

For the first time since he'd summoned them both into his makeshift office, Paula's expression went blank. Then, slowly, she smiled. "Then let's go make some chaos."

Chapter Four

The night ended without any more fuss. Cassie went home, showered and then took comfort in the arms of her padded duvet. But only after dropping the air-conditioning down a few degrees. She'd had a good pregnancy so far when it came to morning sickness, but she never stopped being amazed at how hot she got.

Her sister Kristen called her a walking furnace.

Cassie lived up to the name the next morning. She woke up sweating. It wasn't until she made it to the kitchen for a glass of water that she fought through the haze of sleep and remembered everything that had happened the day before.

She downed half the glass and went in search of her cell phone. It had also spent the night tangled in the bedsheets. Which meant her battery hadn't been charged. A notification showed it was less than 15 percent. The one below it listed two new text messages. Cassie perched on the side of the bed. She didn't give herself time to worry about what each message said before opening and reading both.

The first was from Denise, the Caller ID reading Mrs. Beadle. Several hearts were on either side of the name. Cassie smiled. Her eldest sister and sibling was just as maternal as their mother. She'd actually been the first person Cassie had called after getting to the hospital to make sure everything was okay with the baby.

Which hadn't made Kristen happy, since she was local and Denise lived in Colorado. However, it was a force of habit to call the eldest Gates sibling and had been since she'd moved out of the house when they were younger. Denise had a gift for worrying about a person with all of her being while simultaneously helping comfort that same person with all of her being. And that was what Cassie had desperately wanted. Comfort, released of the fear and uncertainty that had just crashed back into her life. Both sisters said in their own ways to call them when she was up and moving around.

Cassie sighed.

It was only a matter of time before word got out to the rest of the Gates clan. Then her brothers would be the ones filling her inbox.

It came with the territory of being the youngest of six siblings. The baby. Which, by default, meant she received the full weight of their worry and less and less of their confidence. Never mind Cassie was twenty-nine, had a mortgage and was a few months shy of becoming a full-fledged mother.

She placed a hand on her swollen belly.

A love she didn't think was possible consumed her entire heart and soul at the touch. Relief cascaded down until she felt like crying.

The sound of gunfire shot across her thoughts.

If anything had happened to her son at the diner…

Cassie fisted the sheets in her hands, suddenly as angry as a kicked hornet's nest.

Then she was picturing gray eyes and feeling the warmth of a body protecting hers.

Henry. Henry Ward.

The rage at the most horrific what-if about her son lessened into a different kind of anger. One that, if she was being honest, was backed up by insecurity.

After a night of connection so deep with the man that it had surprised her, he had promised to call when he got back home.

Yet he never had.

No call. No text. No anything.

What's more?

He'd told her his name was Henry Smith.

How idiotic she found that now. Of course the gorgeous man she'd had a wonderful night of passion with after meeting in a bar had given her a fake name. She should have taken it as a hint he didn't want to see her again after he'd told her he couldn't give his number out because he didn't have one yet. But, boy, if she hadn't believed him then. Hung on his every word.

She had been a sheep, like normal. He, a lion.

Embarrassment began to burn in Cassie's cheeks. She shook her head.

"Nothing's changed," she said out loud, stern with herself. "You have this baby and this baby has you. You don't need strangers who lie. No matter how sexy that stranger is." She patted her stomach. "You can do this, baby mama."

It was a good little talk that mostly did the trick.

She went around the house trying her best to get back into any semblance of a routine. She ate, she cleaned and she cooked, all while making calls to her family and friends. The former she assured she was okay, the latter she asked for updates on the sheriff. Maggie was the only person she could get hold of who knew anything substantial about Billy's condition. He was stable but still unconscious. Once he did wake they'd be able to go from there. It was good news, all things considered, yet it wasn't enough to erase the fear that had taken root.

It wasn't until she finished strapping a pan covered in aluminum foil into the passenger seat of her car that Cassie realized she was going to try to help alleviate some of that stress for her friends by delivering a platter of lasagna to the department. Just in time for lunch like the Southern woman her mother taught her to be. Sure, it wasn't a normal lunch meal, but she blamed that on the baby in her stomach. She'd been craving cheese and tomato sauce for days. Two birds, one stone.

The dish didn't budge as she drove to the heart of Carpenter. Since she was alone she said a few curses under her breath about the weather. Furnace or not, their South Alabama town was just plain old miserable. A blanket heat, a choking humidity and a baby in her belly were not complimentary details that made the situation better. By the time she pulled into the parking lot at the sheriff's department, she was ready to sprint inside for the lobby air conditioner if she had to.

The day shift had most of the lot filled, but Cassie couldn't help noticing a car she didn't recognize. Which probably belonged to Henry, she realized.

The father of her child.

No amount of lasagna or air-conditioning was going to smooth over that particular stress. Despite her feelings, reservations and insecurities, she couldn't sidestep the man forever. Especially if he was a deputy.

That meant that she was going to have to decide sooner or later if she was going to tell him the truth.

Guilt pooled in her stomach, but she was quick to combat it with the facts.

As much as she wanted to believe that the man she'd had a connection with months ago was great, she couldn't escape the reality that he had lied to her about his name and then disappeared completely from her life.

He had been a one-night stand, albeit a great one. That was what it boiled down to.

One night.

That didn't seem like a lot when contemplating letting him possibly have a place in her unborn child's life.

Cassie cut the engine and patted her stomach.

"No matter what, it's going to be all right," she told her son, though she knew it was more to herself. With a sigh that she was sure even he felt, Cassie got out of the car and pushed into the heat.

She wasn't two steps behind her car when her plan of action to escape the heat was halted.

"Excuse me."

Cassie turned in time to watch a man walk out from between two of the cars. He immediately held his hands up in defense and pointed behind him.

"I was on the way over here from the coffee shop," he explained. "Now I realize how creepy it must look, me just popping out from the back of the parking lot."

The man managed to look sheepish. He was well dressed, she guessed in his early thirties, and had a shock of dark red hair that was trimmed neat to the scalp. Cassie had never seen him before, but nothing about him screamed hostile. The smile left behind from his laughter put her at ease.

"I assume you work at the department?" This time he motioned to the building behind her.

She'd been with the sheriff's department for years and knew it like the back of her hand. It stood between the county courthouse and the local television station, a two-story wrapped in faded orange brick and concrete. It was wider than its neighboring buildings but shorter. The second floor was vacant minus a room used for storage. Still, the department had spent years cultivating efficiency in the first floor's space. Cassie was particularly proud of her dispatcher's area.

"Yes, I do," she answered, mimicking his smile. "Though at the moment I'm off duty. But I'd be glad to try to help you."

"I really do appreciate that, but I'm afraid I have a bit of a weird request." He pulled a plastic sandwich bag from his pocket and held it out to her. There was something inside it. A ring. "Sheriff Reed made a stop into the Carter Home yesterday and a deputy who was with him left this behind."

Cassie took the bag, her heartbeat already quickening.

"I never caught his name, so I figured I'd just bring it in and let you all sort it. Maybe you could return it to its owner?"

Cassie might not have been back at work, but she'd learned of Billy's intended tours for new recruits. In this case, that meant Henry. Which meant fate was having a good ole laugh at her right now. It looked like she'd have to talk to the man sooner rather than later.

"Of course I will. I even know the deputy in question," she answered. "Why don't you come in with me? I'm sure he'd be grateful for you returning this." Maybe she could use the man as a buffer until she decided what to do.

The man shook his head. "I'm actually in a hurry." Again he motioned to the building that butted up to the back of the parking lot. It was a strip mall that housed several businesses, including the best coffeehouse in town. "Would you mind giving it to him instead? I have a friend waiting for me plus a cup of coffee with my name on it."

Cassie was nothing if not accommodating. "I can do that. No problem." She readjusted her purse. Sweat was already forming above her brow. "Can I give him your name so he can at least know who to thank later if the occasion arises?"

"Michael." He held up his hands again, an apologetic look across his face. "I really have to go now. I hope you have yourself a great day."

Before Cassie could press for a last name, he turned, effectively ending their conversation.

Maybe she wasn't the only one in a hurry to get out of the heat.

"It's not ideal." Suzy's mouth tightened. "But it's what I'm saying."

Henry looked across the top of the woman's desk and was trying his best not to look petulant. He knew a very bad thing had happened the day before, but he didn't want to get benched because of it. Not when he'd done nothing but key himself up with thoughts about his future in Riker County the night before. He knew change was inevitable, but that didn't mean he had expected it to start so quickly after joining the department.

"Listen, I get it, I really do," he returned, trying. "I'm the new guy. It only makes sense that the sheriff's case takes precedence over taking me around town and explaining the lay of the land. But isn't there some way I can speed the process up? Maybe have someone write down the places I need to know and I can go when I'm off duty?"

Suzy gave him a flat stare. She looked as tired as he felt. "The idea was to pair you with people who have grown up in the various towns and city in Riker County. It's a process Billy started up when he was elected sheriff and one that I truly believe has helped every new addition to the team. Even support staff has been paired with one of us or a senior deputy to learn, as you said, 'the lay of the land.'" She pointed to herself. "Billy and I were your guides along with Deputy Mills, but now… Well, now plans and priorities have shifted, and as much as I hate it for you, you're going to be sitting at your desk until all the dust settles."

Henry didn't like that. Not one bit. Billy might have stabilized, but regardless of his condition he wouldn't be back to work for months. Which meant Suzy would hold the title of acting sheriff until then. Which meant there might be some shifting around of the deputies, picking up the things that might fall through the cracks of a sudden management shift.

Which meant he might be saddled to his desk a lot longer than he wanted.

"What about Cassie?" The words left his mouth out of desperation. It wasn't until he saw them register in Suzy's face that he himself wasn't keen on the idea. Still, desperation bred desperation. He pushed on. "She's not due back to work until next week, right? Maybe she wouldn't mind showing me around, all things considered. I heard she grew up in the county."

Henry wasn't about to say he'd heard that from the

woman herself, months ago and in between the sheets at his hotel room. The bottom line was that he'd made a point. One Suzy seemed to be considering.

"She spent a few years in Darby, but yeah, the bulk of her childhood wasn't spent too far from where Billy and I grew up." Suzy made a pyramid with her fingers, then tapped two of them together in thought. "Truth be told, I would like to get you out into the field sooner rather than later. I know Billy probably already told you this, but you've got an impressive résumé. I'd rather you use your skills out there trying to keep the county safe than stuck behind a desk."

Henry felt a stab of guilt in his gut. He was proud of his career, sure, but in his mind that career had all but died when his partner had. Being praised for any of it now felt wrong. It hadn't mattered how good he was at reading people, how fast his reflexes were, and how good a shot he could be, at the end of the day, none of it had saved his friend.

And if he couldn't save Calvin, what made any of them think he could save anyone else?

That thought scorched across his mind so quickly he nearly stood from his seat to distance himself from it. Doubting his role as a deputy would *definitely* get someone hurt. Even him.

No. He needed to be ready for anything.

That included Cassie Gates.

"Let me give her a call and feel it out," Suzy declared with a nod. She grabbed the phone but paused before picking it up. "But if she isn't up for it, you'll go to a desk until we can find someone else. Understood?"

There was no malice or annoyance in the woman's

tone. Just a boss needing to make sure her charge was on the same page.

And he was.

"I won't push the issue," he said. "Scout's honor."

She smirked at that and dialed Cassie's number without another word. Henry was wondering if he should leave the room when a song started to play out in the hallway. They both looked to the open office door as the song got closer.

"You rang?" Cassie said, popping her head into the room, surprising them both. At seeing Henry there, she faltered but finished her thought. "Or are ringing, I should say." She held up her phone as Suzy hung up hers.

"You're here? Is everything all right?"

Cassie nodded hurriedly. "Yeah, I just thought I'd bring in some lunch for everyone." Her cheeks reddened a little. She groaned. "Which I left in the car. Because pregnancy brain is real." Her eyes flitted to Henry's. Instead of looking away, she held his stare. "I was also distracted by someone in the parking lot looking for you."

"For me?" Henry asked, once again surprised. Outside of the people who worked in the department, he'd made no friends in Riker County. He didn't even know if he could give the people he worked with that title yet. Not to mention no one from his life in Tennessee even knew where he'd gone. At least, no one who would have bothered to visit. And surely if it had been his brother he would have called. "Who was it?"

Cassie pulled a plastic bag from her purse and passed it over. "His name was Michael. He was at the Carter Home yesterday when you came by with Billy. He didn't know your name but knew you were the new deputy."

She shrugged. "He was in a hurry, so I said I'd make sure you got it."

There was curiosity in her voice. Henry heard it plain as day. Yet it paled in comparison to his own.

He looked at the bag between his fingers. He didn't open it. He'd recognize the ring anywhere. A warmth that had no business belonging to him started to spread in his memory. Just as quickly it turned ice cold. He looked back to Cassie. If her expression was any indication, she'd caught on to the unwelcome change in his demeanor. Apparently she wasn't the only one.

"Deputy," Suzy said, breaking their stare, "what's wrong?"

Henry met his boss with an even look that he hoped gave nothing away but the facts. He held up the bag. "The last time I saw this ring was a year ago." That cold feeling began to spread as he took a moment before finishing. "It belonged to Calvin Fitzgerald."

By the change in *her* demeanor, Henry knew Suzy recognized the name. And why it was significant.

"A year ago…" she said, fishing.

Henry took the bait.

"The day of the fire," he offered. "The day he died."

Chapter Five

Henry and Suzy went out to the parking lot in search of Michael but found no one. Cassie went to look at the security footage that covered the lot and had a deputy pause the tape for them until they came back.

"Do you recognize him?" Suzy asked. Thanks to budget cuts, the footage wasn't grade A, but it was enough to make out the key features of the man Cassie had talked to. Red hair, general build and well dressed.

Henry took a moment but shook his head. "No. I don't. Not from Tennessee and not from yesterday, either. If he was at the Carter Home, I didn't see him."

"And you're sure that's the same ring?"

There was a noticeable pause. Cassie glanced over at Henry. He didn't look at the bag or the ring inside.

"There's a chance it could be a different one." Henry met Cassie's gaze and looked away just as quickly. "Maybe this Michael guy was mistaken about who dropped it. I can go after my shift to try to talk to him."

Suzy had opened her mouth to, Cassie assumed, question the shift in certainty when Detective Ryan Ansler moved into the doorway. His brow was drawn tight.

"Matt needs to see you," was all he said. Though his

tone added an understood "as soon as possible" to the end. It rallied Suzy instantly.

"I'm coming. Deputy Ward, keep me updated on what you find out about the ring." She turned to Cassie. "And, Cassie, I have a favor to ask of you. Could you walk with me?"

Cassie nodded without another look at Henry. Part of her wanted to avoid him so she didn't have to worry about their past, present or future just yet. Another part wanted to ask him why he had just lied to Suzy. Because she had no doubt that was exactly what he'd done.

Turned out that other part of her was about to get the chance. Not only did Suzy want her to help show Henry around the county, she wanted her to start today.

"But I can't make you do it," Suzy reminded her as they hovered outside the conference room door. Cassie could see Matt and Captain Jones talking inside, heads bent toward each other, clearly concerned. It put an ounce more urgency in Cassie's gut. "This is strictly a favor. One I'll understand if you turn down."

Cassie couldn't believe herself as she nodded. "The department is under a lot of stress right now," she reasoned, more for herself than for Suzy. "I was on vacation for too long. I'm ready to help out now."

Suzy gave her a smile. It was fleeting after she glanced at the men in the room. Her shoulders pushed back even more. She gave a curt nod. "Thanks, Cass."

And then Cassie was alone in the hallway.

She contemplated staying there for a while or maybe finding a place to hide from the responsibility she'd just accepted. Or, rather, the man she'd just agreed to saddle herself with. Instead she patted her stomach and walked back to the bull pen to find Henry at his desk.

He looked surprised to see her. So much so, it almost was offensive.

"I'm ready when you are," she greeted, trying to stay as friendly as she normally was. And no more or less than that. If she was going to work with Henry Ward, she might as well embrace it. "We can take my car, since you don't have a cruiser yet. If that's okay with you."

Henry looked like he was about to say something but thought better of it.

"Sounds good to me," he said, standing. He scooped up the plastic bag with the ring and slipped it into his pocket. Then that smile was back. The one that had wholly captivated Cassie months before. The one that had pulled her from an almost-blind date and convinced her to play pool for hours with a man she didn't know.

The one that had led her back to his bed.

A warmth began to move up Cassie's neck to her cheeks. She turned on her heel to try to hide the blush, resigned not to speak to him again until she had better control. However, two steps out the front door and into the heat, she couldn't help herself.

"You lied to Suzy," she accused, still sure in her words. "Why?"

She felt his gaze turn completely on her as he fell into step next to her.

"What do you mean?"

"You said there was a chance that the ring wasn't Calvin's." She spelled out her thoughts. "But you lied. You're positive it is. Why tell Suzy differently? And how are you so sure?"

She turned to the man now. Cassie knew he was good at reading people, one of the few things she *did* know about him. She wanted him to see she wasn't backing down.

Cool gray eyes searched her expression. Two unbelievably soft lips turned up into a small smile. If she hadn't been walking for two, her knees might have decided to give out because of it.

"We haven't seen each other in months and now we're essentially partnered up to tour the county we both work for and the first thing you say when we're alone is that I'm lying." He said the last part deadpan. It wasn't a denial. "I didn't think this was how any of our conversations would start."

"There's a lot of things I'd like to say instead," she admitted, growing hot in temper and not because of former steamy memories. "But this is important. I've learned through years of being here that if the past reaches out to you, then sometimes bad, bad things follow. I'd like to *not* be blindsided twice in two days. That goes double for the department. What happened to Billy…" She shook her head. "I'd just rather be prepared."

Henry sobered. They were halfway through the side guest parking lot before he answered.

Cassie could feel the sweat already trying to form down her back.

"I know this ring because it used to be mine. I'd know it anywhere, anytime. But after I gave it to Calvin, I never expected to see it again."

"Because he died?" Cassie felt regret at not spending the morning learning more about the man next to her. Now that she had a real last name, she could have at the very least searched the internet for information. She had no idea who Calvin was, why he died, or anything else about Henry before yesterday. Instead of the last puzzle piece being just out of her reach, she felt like she was left holding only one while the rest of the picture was gone. It wasn't a good feeling.

Henry nodded. "Yeah, he died. And his body was never recovered."

Cassie could almost hear him going tight-lipped. It was difficult to talk about.

"And who was Calvin to you?" She had to ask. She omitted the once again obvious fact that she didn't know anything about his past.

Henry kept his gaze straight ahead. "We worked together in Tennessee."

Cassie was given the distinct impression that Henry sidestepped the rest of the details on purpose but didn't get the chance to say so. They came to a stop at the back of her car, but not before movement on the sidewalk between the strip mall behind the department parking lot and them caught her eye.

"Hey," Cassie yelled. "That's the guy!"

Henry followed her stare to the red-haired man who had given her the ring in the first place. The man was leaning against the building but pushed himself off it at their attention. He was smiling.

"He's the one that gave me the ring," she added to make sure Henry understood. "Michael."

The deputy didn't need to be told three times.

"Wait here," he said, touching the small of her back on the way around her car. The unexpected contact sent her thoughts scattering long enough that she was slow on registering what happened next.

"Hey, you," Henry called out. "Could we talk for a—"

Michael turned tail and followed the sidewalk through the strip mall and out of sight faster than Henry could finish his sentence. The deputy didn't hesitate in following. His heavy shoes hitting the concrete echoed around the back of the parking lot. Then he was out of sight.

HE WAS FAST. Too fast.

What started as a few yards between them stretched to an even wider gap as Henry followed the sidewalk to the front of the strip mall. Michael used the open space to really lean into his pace. He weaved around a few pedestrians coming out of the coffee shop and then ducked around a well-dressed group going into an office farther down.

Michael might have been fast, but that didn't mean he was going to lose Henry. What he'd lost in a lead, he'd make up for with his stamina. And the way Michael was running, there weren't many places to hide or fully escape without being seen.

Henry might not be familiar with Riker County, but he'd at least figured out the few blocks surrounding the department. The one they were on housed a handful of offices and shops before turning into side streets that led one of two ways, back to the main street in front of the department or to the civic center and several streets that led to downtown. The way the man named Michael was running, he was about to make the decision of where he wanted to go. Either direction, he'd still have to cover a lot of ground to lose Henry.

Or maybe not.

Michael ran across the street, taking a right toward the civic center and downtown. Henry followed suit but had to hit his brakes as a driver refused to hit his. He resisted the urge to bang his fists on the hood as the car drove past. He just wanted to talk to Michael.

Why was he running?

What did he know?

Henry cursed beneath his breath and kicked it back into high gear. By the time he was across the street and following the sidewalk up and right around a tall building that housed a small office complex, the man had once again spread the distance between them.

However, he stopped before Henry could eat any more of it up. Chest heaving but in no way hesitating, Michael opened the passenger's side door of a car stopped by the curb.

He paused, but only long enough to give a parting speech. The mystery man met Henry's gaze with a wave of his hand.

"Find me if you can," he yelled.

The door shut and the car was pulling away from the curb before Henry could catch up. Adrenaline was coursing through his blood as he skidded to a stop at the curb. The excitement of the chase was making it almost impossible to stop his muscles from readying to keep going. There was no way he could catch the car on foot. And even if he did go back for his car, they would probably already be long gone by the time he made it back.

"Son of a—"

"Get in!"

Henry turned on his heel to see a car stopped a few feet behind him. Not just any car, it was Cassie's. A cloud of curly blond hair stuck out the window as she eyed him.

"Come on," she called. "Get in or we're going to lose them!"

Like she had trained his body by simple command, Henry wasted no time in jumping into the passenger seat, careful to keep his eye on the fleeing car. It was at the end of the street now, executing a left turn. If they didn't hurry—

No sooner had he had the thought and was inside the car than Cassie hit the gas. The tires actually squealed.

However, Henry's focus abruptly changed directions.

"What *is* this?" he yelled, feeling something warm and soft against the seat of his jeans.

Cassie whipped her car around a stopped truck, dipping into the empty oncoming traffic lane before coming back.

"What?" she shouted back, volume level matching.

Henry reached down as whatever was beneath him shifted.

"Cassie, what am I sitting in?" he asked, voice higher than normal. "It's *warm*!"

"Oh, no, Ms. Moye!"

"Ms. Moye?" Henry jumped up and reached down in an awkward attempt to rid himself of the unsettling sensation seeping into the seat of his jeans. His hand hit a hard container. For one wild moment he imagined some kind of urn. When his hand hit foil and then something red, he almost left the car altogether.

"My neighbor Chelsea's lasagna!" She turned the wheel to follow down the street to the left. It put Henry off balance even more. The mushy sensation against his backside became even more pronounced.

"Well, I made it, but it's her recipe. I brought it to the department for lunch but forgot about it because, again, pregnancy brain is real." She glanced over. "I guess I forgot it was there again. Sorry!"

Henry finally managed a glance down. Sure enough, he'd sat right in a food dish. The aluminum foil had saved some of the lasagna from spilling out, but not all of it.

"I hope you like lasagna with your car, because I'm getting it everywhere," he muttered, pulling the dish out from under him and putting it on the floorboard.

"I need to get it detailed anyways," she said dismissively. Her tone had an edge to it. Concentrated. It reminded Henry of what they were doing.

He adjusted his gaze out the windshield and forgot all about his backside covered in lunch.

"There are no plates on the car," he noted. "I don't recognize it, either. And, again, I didn't recognize the man. There should be no reason he's running. Or, at least, I don't know one."

Henry brought out his phone and started to dial the department.

"Well, for men you don't know, they sure seem intent on losing us." Cassie had to slow as the few cars between them and the black one got caught in a construction zone. "If you're calling this in, let Myra know that we're headed toward the civic center. Wait. Scratch that."

Henry looked up in time to watch the car in question hook a right.

"Where does that street lead?" There was hesitation in her answer, yet Cassie didn't stop her pursuit. "Cassie?"

"That's Keller Avenue," she answered.

He glanced over to see her brows pinched in thought.

"Old houses, an auto shop and then a whole lot of nothing. A weird place to go if you're trying to lose someone following you. It would be easier to lose us in lunchtime traffic near the civic center or downtown."

At her words, or maybe the way she said it, Henry's gut started to yell. But he kept quiet.

The last time he'd listened to his gut, Calvin had died.

He wasn't about to make the same mistake again.

Chapter Six

There were three cars, two trucks and one tractor driving along Keller Avenue. Cassie maneuvered around each with caution and speed. One of the cars honked at her. The man driving the tractor shook his fist. She didn't care. She was in the zone, tunnel-visioned on the black car in the lead. Soon it would take the bend of Keller and disappear from view if she fell any more behind.

Either way, she wasn't stopping.

It was a surprising sensation. One as a dispatcher she rarely dealt with. Sure, she'd had calls and incidents where all hell felt like it was breaking loose, but typically that was on the other end of the line or radio. In those times she had to be the calm one. Steel in her voice and concentration that rivaled that of the best of the best deputies in her department. It was easy to do when sitting behind a desk. However, now that she was operating on more than just a hint of urgency, she was surprised that she not only wanted to catch the man and get answers, but felt like she needed them.

Maybe it was just her picking up on Henry's desire to know what was going on. Maybe she subconsciously thought it would make her feel better about her current uncertain situation with the man sitting next to her if he at least found what he was looking for.

Or maybe it was just pregnancy hormones craving something other than salty-sweet.

"What does this road turn into?" Henry asked, re-adjusting himself in her periphery. He seemed to still be distracted by the lasagna he was now wearing. He opened up the glove box without permission but was rewarded with a handful of napkins she kept in it just in case.

"It can turn into a county road that runs to the city of Kipsy or, if they take the next turn, they go into an old neighborhood called Westbridge." She thought for a moment. "And, honestly, either option won't be fast. It's a mostly straight two-lane to Kipsy and the neighborhood isn't small, but it all leads into a dead end with no other exit. Whoever Michael and his driver are, they aren't making the most progressive choices if they're trying to run away."

Cassie kept on the gas. If she couldn't lessen the gap, then she was determined to at least be close enough to see which choice they were going to make. She hated to admit it, but their black four-door was faster than her older Honda. She'd had the car since she'd moved out of her parents' house. It wasn't meant for high-speed chases. In its old age it was barely meant for normal-speed anything. Getting a new ride had been on her to-do list since she'd found out she was pregnant. Though she might not have a choice than to go car shopping after this episode. There was a slight rattling in her dash, but she couldn't decide if it was any different than the random sounds that came with the car's age.

"The opening to the neighborhood is right after this

bend." Layers of trees blocked her from seeing anything other than the road right in front of them. She sat straighter as she turned with the road.

"If they do go into the neighborhood, I don't want you to follow."

That caught her off guard.

"Wait, why not?" she asked, indignant.

Henry's voice was calm but authoritative when he responded. "When people run like this, they usually have a good reason they don't want to get caught. Or, at least, it's a good reason in their own minds."

Cassie glanced over long enough to see his jaw harden.

"And I have a feeling that this Michael wants me to catch him *and* get away at the same time. Which makes him even more unpredictable. So, no, I'm not about to ask a pregnant woman to drive headfirst into what could be a trap."

Henry didn't know it yet but he'd just had the misfortune of walking right into a wall of hormonal anger from said pregnant woman. Cassie's face heated like someone had just turned up her personal oven burner.

"Well, good thing you don't have control over this pregnant woman, Deputy *Ward*," she shot back.

"Cassie, that's not what I meant," he started, too oblivious or too smart to touch on the fact that she'd just put a nasty amount of emphasis on his name. A name that was different from the one he'd given her. "It's just that—"

However, Cassie wasn't having it. Her internal burner was on high. "You think you can just walk back into town after absolutely no contact and then have some kind of hold over me because we spent *one* night together. My being pregnant or not, that doesn't give you the right to decide what I should or shouldn't do!" The bend was finally evening out. Cassie's anger was not. She almost missed the one glaring detail ahead of her on the street. Or rather, the lack of one.

"They must have gone into the neighborhood," Henry said, staring out the window at the empty street.

There was no time to comment on her outburst, Cassie knew, but still couldn't deny she felt a sting at his not acknowledging that he hadn't reached out to her once in the last several months.

"And we're not following," she intoned instead of continuing her rant.

Henry nodded.

He motioned to the shoulder of the street across from the Westbridge neighborhood sign. Cassie put on her flashers and pulled off onto the dirt, angling the car so if they needed to she could floor it right back onto the street. More trees stretched a few feet to their left, closing in the shoulder, while the neighborhood across the street looked like it was being swallowed by them. That was the beauty of Southern Alabama. Not only did you get farms and fields; there were the occasional woods thrown in, too.

"So what? We wait until they come out?" Cassie put the car in park but kept her gaze on the entrance to Westbridge. "What if they don't? What if they go into a house or ditch their car and run through the trees? I think there's a county road that runs parallel to this one they could get to. Or maybe—"

Henry opened the door. The sudden sound made her jump. "Wait, what are you doing? You said we weren't going in there!"

Henry didn't answer until the door was shut and he

had walked around to hers. Cassie rolled down the window. The heat pushed against her face. It didn't improve her mood.

"Call the chief deputy sheriff and let her know what's going on. Tell her we followed that same man who gave you the ring earlier."

"And what about you?" Cassie asked, already feeling disgruntled at his show of authority. She'd been with the sheriff's department for years. *He* was the new one. "I thought we weren't going in there."

Then Henry did that thing he had done all those months ago that spelled trouble for Cassie. With a capital T.

He smirked.

It was like his lips were connected all over her body. In her stomach she felt the warmth of memory across her chest, the pain of longing beneath her waist and the irrational fear of being left again by a man she didn't know. Combined, it made for a distraction wide enough to hide the man's motive until he had to spell it out for her.

"You aren't going in there," he said. "But I am."

AT FIRST GLANCE, the neighborhood of Westbridge seemed normal enough. Henry kept his hand on the butt of his service weapon, touched his deputy's badge to reaffirm his decision to follow the lead past the entrance sign, and stalked cautiously past the third house before he understood that his earlier assumption was wrong.

Westbridge was quiet.

Sure, it was a weekday and not yet time for the normal working class to be home, but still it was *way too quiet*. The type of silence that wasn't intentional. No. It was the product of abandonment. Cassie had said the neighborhood was old.

What she hadn't said was that it was a relative ghost town.

One-and two-story houses, some with siding covered in mildew and others in faded brick, sat sentry on either side of Henry as he moved deeper inward.

The driving force of curiosity started to cool in his chest thanks to the nearly overpowering yell of his gut.

This has to be a trap, it said.

But for what? And why? the less rational part of his mind answered.

All the while both parts focused on the real reason he had rushed headlong into a situation he normally wouldn't have.

The ring.

It shouldn't have been in Riker County.

It shouldn't have been in Alabama.

It *definitely* shouldn't have been in his pocket.

Yet there it was. Like a weight was tied to it, dragging every part of Henry down.

He didn't want to find answers just to satiate his innate curiosity that came with the territory of being in law enforcement.

No. He'd sure as hell earned them.

The road curved enough so Henry couldn't see if the car they'd been following was farther up ahead. Though, by Cassie's estimation, Michael and his mystery driver weren't going to be able to just drive out using another outlet out back. So, instead of staying in the open on the sidewalk, Henry moved across the side yard, deciding to stick closer to the houses to stay more hidden.

Thunder rumbled in the distance.

It should have been a sign. One that foreshadowed the result of Henry's careless decision to pursue the unknown the way he had. Because he knew that was what it was. Carelessness. No backup. No real plan. Just a man hell-bent on understanding why the ring he'd given his best friend was now with him.

But Henry's steps never faltered.

The moment his boots touched the backyard's overgrown grass, he was staring at a man no more than twenty feet from him.

It was Michael. And he had his head thrown back in laughter. Henry took out his gun. It didn't faze the man.

"You know, out of all the houses and backyards, you chose to come into *this* one," Michael said, composing himself. His laughter died away but his grin did not. "I'd heard that you had a set of instincts that bordered on unnatural, but to see it in person? Well, that's a treat."

Henry took in the yard around them as quickly as he could. Tall grass, a privacy fence in disrepair, the side opposite him missing altogether and showing the next yard over. And, as far as Henry could tell, no one else was in the vicinity.

Where was the driver?

"Who are you?" Henry demanded. He pulled up his gun, aiming for the man. Lacking backup wasn't going to stop him from protecting himself if everything went south.

"I'm Michael," he said as if that explained it all.

"Why give me some random ring?" Henry asked. "And then run off?"

Michael was the sole recipient of a joke Henry couldn't even guess at. He racked his brain, flipping through a mental Rolodex of names and faces from what felt like his former life, trying to place the man once again. Yet he was coming up empty. Not a feeling he was used to.

Or liked.

"Trying to find the right answers by asking the wrong questions is an interesting, risky tactic," the man drawled. "One that I'm sure has worked on common criminals and those with less than average IQs, *but* here's the deal, Deputy Henry Ward." He moved his arms wide and smiled to match. "I'm not a criminal. I'm a broker. A smart one at that, too."

Henry had almost had enough of the man. He took a step forward, gun staying on target.

"A broker, huh?" He smirked. Just because he was focused didn't mean he couldn't also show some of the cockiness the mystery man was exuding. "That's a new one. What do you deal in? Let me guess… The cliché answer would be, what, information?"

A muscle in the man's jaw twitched. His smile faltered. But just for a moment.

"Sometimes," he admitted. "I like to wear many hats. It gives me an edge on my competitors. What keeps a client from shopping around more than if you're a one-stop shop?"

Henry couldn't help himself. Try as he might to leave his former life behind, he knew there would always be moments when his old life would bleed through.

"What are you? An infomercial?" he asked with a snort. "Do I have to give you two payments of $19.99 to get a real answer?"

Just as Michael's cockiness had caused Henry to answer in kind, Henry's new attitude had clearly rubbed the man the wrong way. His smile wiped off. His body tensed.

Henry made sure his grip on the gun was solid.

Not that it would matter.

"What I'm *really* good at isn't information," he said, voice taking on an edge so sharp it felt nearly visible. "It's connections. Creating new ones…and reuniting old ones."

His eyes flitted over Henry's shoulder. By the time he pivoted, gun swinging around with him, it was too late.

Henry froze, his blood turning to ice.

Despite years of training, a lifetime of honing reflexes and learning to listen to his gut, he couldn't move.

"I told him you'd be surprised to see me," the man said in greeting. "It has been a while, hasn't it, partner?"

The ghost of Calvin Fitzgerald smiled.

Though he didn't seem to be as much a ghost as he should have been.

"I know," he continued, taking a step closer. "Confusing, right? Don't worry. I'll explain everything later. For now, I need you out of the way."

Henry wanted to ask a lot of questions.

He didn't mutter a word.

Calvin reached out and patted his shoulder.

"I can't let them kill you, Henry," he chided. Then, like a switch had flipped, the face of Henry's former partner and best friend melted away. In its place was a dark, twisted mask of hatred. "Because *I* want to be the one who does that."

In hindsight, Henry saw the signs that the blow was coming. Saw Calvin make a fist, saw his stance change, and saw the pullback. He saw what was going to happen, seconds before it did. Why? Because he'd seen the man knock out a man before with a perfectly placed hit.

He saw it all.

However, hindsight was only good for the living. It rarely factored in the appearance of ghosts.

Chapter Seven

Henry remembered the first time he'd met Calvin Fitzgerald. They were both green and, according to their sergeant, had a lot of experience to gain before they could rise through the ranks of their police department. Henry saw it as being told he was beneath par, and *that* hadn't sat well with him. Still, he'd known the pecking order and that only in time would he get higher on it.

Keep your head down, put in the time, do the work.

So he'd kept his mouth shut as his then sergeant finished the speech about their lack of experience and dismissed them. As soon as the door shut behind them, Calvin had turned to Henry, grinned and wondered out loud how big the stick was that had taken residence in the sergeant's backside.

It wasn't called for, or professional for that matter, but it lightened the mood enough for normal conversation to take over.

One year later and Henry and Calvin were thick as thieves, best friends, basically brothers.

Then a year after that they were partners. Both heading into the unknown together, each promising to have the other's back no matter what.

One more year passed and then Calvin was dead.

But he's not.

It was the first thought that entered the darkness in Henry's mind. The pain waited for him to recall the twisted face of the man who had made a miraculous re-appearance in the land of the living before it descended on him. He opened his eyes, wincing but ready.

Though, once again, maybe not.

"Whoa there, deputy," came a woman's rushed whis-per. Henry's eyes adjusted to the darkness that hadn't just been in his head. He was leaning against a wall, staring at a strip of stained wallpaper curled and hanging next to his face. He winced again as he moved to get away from it, disoriented. Movement on the other side of the small room started to focus his attention.

Enough light was coming through the broken blinds over the lone window in the room to show him the soft concern across Cassie's face. She crouched down in front of him, one hand reaching out.

"You have a knot on the back of your head," she ex-plained without preamble. Warm fingers touched the spot in question. A sting of pain quickly followed. Her expression softened a little more.

"Calvin," Henry bit out, anger starting to take up the slots he'd let his surprise fall into.

How had he let himself be ambushed like that? How had he let the man get the upper hand when Henry had been the one armed? How had he let that happen?

"You mean Michael?" Cassie's eyebrow rose.

"Both."

Henry cursed. Cassie shushed him.

"I'm pretty sure they're gone, but still I'd appreciate some inside voices," she told him, stern. That was when Henry saw another emotion he didn't like in the woman.

She was worried.

It deflated his anger.

He needed to get his bearings.

"Are you okay?" he asked. He eyed her stomach before finding her gaze. "What happened? And where are we?"

He sat straighter and reached for his gun.

It was gone.

"I'm freaked out but okay." Cassie stood but kept her voice low. "After you left, I called the department like you said to tell Suzy what was going on. No one answered. The line was dead."

"The line was dead," he repeated, adopting her quiet.

"Not even a busy signal, just dead." A loud rumble sounded at the end of her words. Thunder. It seemed closer this time. Henry got to his feet. "So I called Suzy directly," she continued. "It was busy. That's not unusual, but both Matt Walker's and Deputy Mills' phones are either busy or going straight to voice mail?"

"That *is* unusual," he said.

Cassie nodded, following him to the window. Without pushing the blinds aside he could see a sliver of faded siding on the house next door. They were still in Westbridge.

"That's when I saw Michael drive out of the neighborhood. I got nervous, so I came in after you," she said. "It took me a little bit to find you, but when I did, you were knocked out cold on the grass. So, considering I can't get hold of any backup, I dragged you into the closest house so we weren't just out in the open."

Henry paused, hand in midair in front of the blinds. "Wait, so not only did you *leave* the car, but you knowingly walked into what could have been a trap?" His emotions split in two.

He was angry she'd put herself and the baby in danger.

He couldn't help liking that she had thought he was worth the risk.

Both thoughts immediately turned to a nearly overwhelming feeling of guilt.

He *wasn't* worth it.

Either way, he could see Cassie's indignation at his line of questioning before she even spoke.

"Don't forget I, the pregnant lady, dragged your mass of muscles up a set of back porch stairs, broke into a house and then managed to *gently* lay you down once inside," she shot back, hands going to her hips. "I mean, it wasn't like I could have called you anyways. Not that I'm confident about Carpenter's cell service, but if I remember correctly, you once told me that you *don't have a number.*"

Henry turned back to the blinds, jaw tight.

"We're going to have to talk about that, I promise," he said, voice detaching even to his own ears. "But right now we have bigger fish to fry."

He looked out at the house across from them and the yard between. It was the same one he had walked through. The same one Calvin had used to ambush him. The same Calvin that he'd watched get shot three times in the chest.

Henry shook his head, trying to clear the unnecessary details. It didn't matter *how* Calvin was still alive. What did matter was that he *was* and apparently he didn't want the same for his old partner.

"You said you only saw Michael leave in the car? Are you sure no one else was inside?"

Out of his periphery, a mass of blond curls shook side to side.

"Unless they were lying down in the seats, I didn't see anyone else," she answered. "No one else drove in or out, either. Which is another reason I thought it best for me to get us somewhat hidden. I don't know where Michael's driver went. Like I said, there's no easy way out of the neighborhood other than the entrance, and most of these houses haven't been used in years."

They quieted a moment. Henry was trying to think.

No gun.

He reached into his pocket.

Empty.

No cell phone.

Cassie had one but no one was answering.

Or either couldn't.

Henry's gut grumbled at him. It had already drawn several conclusions. His head injury, no doubt a concussion, was just making it slow to translate them.

"Also, I'd like to point out that *you're* the one who seemingly walked into a trap all willy-nilly, not me."

Henry looked over at Cassie, surprised. She kept her gaze out the window, but she still shrugged.

"All I walked into was a rescue mission, thank you very much."

Despite the situation, Henry smirked.

Their eyes met.

Cassie smiled.

And just like that, they were back in the Eagle, sharing drinks and looks over the pool table. Smiling at each other. Wondering what the rest of the night would bring. Wondering what each other felt like. Tasted like.

Another boom of thunder sounded. This time it felt like it was right outside.

Cassie's smile dropped.

"I also wanted to find you before it started raining," she said. "There are no working lights on this road and with how dark it's getting…" She shook her head. This time her hand went to her stomach, protectively.

Henry pushed his shoulders back again. The pain in his head pulsed at the movement. No gun, no backup and a storm moving in.

Not great to deal with but also not impossible, either.

"Listen, I want you to call everyone and anyone you know who could send someone out here. Including local PD," he ordered.

Cassie didn't seem to be offended by the direction. She pulled out her phone. "Tell them to come prepared. The man who could still be in here with us is smart, fast and extremely dangerous. His name is Calvin Fitzgerald."

Cassie's eyes widened.

"And be sure to let them know that instead of being dead like we all thought, he is very much alive."

RAIN STARTED TO pelt against the old house's roof. It was like nails on a chalkboard as far as Cassie was concerned. Grating against her nerves that were already starting to fray.

What she had told Henry was the truth. She'd seen Michael leave and couldn't get hold of anyone to alert them to what was going on. When Henry hadn't showed up after that, staying in the car or leaving hadn't been options for Cassie. So she had left her car and snuck around the street and its houses until she'd found the new deputy.

What Cassie *hadn't* told him was that her heart had been in her throat the entire time. That every time she'd turned a corner or rounded a fence, she'd imagined the worst. And that, even when she had finally found him, tears had sprung to her eyes as she'd seen him lying on his back, unmoving, in the grass. That, while she'd hoisted him up and struggled to move him to what she'd thought would be a safe place for both of them, she'd done so with a worry and fear in her heart unlike she'd ever felt before.

The entire world had fallen away in that time, leaving only three people who mattered. Her unborn son, her body that cradled him and Henry.

Now, after another one of her friends' phones went to voice mail and the rain continued to beat down overhead, the rest of the world was starting to filter back in.

And with it an uncertainty that made her want to cling to her belly and the man who had given her the very son she wanted to keep safe inside it.

"There's no movement from the houses on either side of us or across the street. If Calvin is around here, he's keeping low."

Cassie turned, startled, as the man from her thoughts walked back into what had once been a living room. His face was pinched. His brow lined with worry.

She wasn't about to help those lines, either.

"Unless everyone decided to turn off their phones or make lengthy calls, I think something is wrong with Carpenter's service," she said. "Or at least the department's. I can't even get the local PD to pick up. Which makes no sense."

The lines of worry deepened.

"Has anything like this happened before?"

Cassie shrugged. "Yes and no. While I was a trainee, we got a rough batch of tornadoes that caused an almost county-wide blackout. Landlines went down and a lot of people lost cell service." She motioned to the window and outside. "But this storm just came up on us. It couldn't have already done that kind of damage. Heck, I doubt even now it could." She let out a frustrated sigh. "So what *is* going on out there?"

Henry's expression went blank. His body subtly shifted to more alert. "I don't know, but staying here isn't helping us. I'm going to go get the car." He raised his hand to silence her before Cassie could open her mouth. "And this time you are staying put."

"You do remember how that turned out last time, right? You said it yourself that we don't know where Calvin is. He could be simply waiting for you to show up again."

Henry kept his hand up, unperturbed. "Last time was different." His voice took on a hard edge. Angry. But she couldn't tell at who or what. "Now I know who we're playing with. I won't let Calvin get the better of me. Not again."

He dropped his hand and knelt to the bottom of his pant leg. He pulled it up, showing off a knife holstered to his ankle.

"Calvin hates knives," he explained, unfastening it. "He was jumped by a perp with one when we were beat cops. Got messed up pretty badly. Ever since then he won't touch them. Won't hold them."

"So he didn't take it off you," she finished.

"A lot apparently has happened in the last year to him, but that fear seems to have held true."

He stood and handed her the knife. Cassie didn't like

them, either, but she disliked being defenseless more. She took it, but before she could pull away, he held on to her hand, his fingers against her skin. Their warmth spread from his touch across her body like a wildfire.

Cassie suddenly remembered what it was like to have those same fingers move across her body.

Nimble.

Strong.

Intoxicating.

"Don't come after me this time." Henry's voice thrummed, a soothing baritone. If he was struggling with memories, it didn't show. His expression stayed blank. "I mean it, Cassie."

She didn't want to agree, but then his eyes turned down to her stomach for the briefest of moments.

This time Cassie knew she would listen.

Henry must have seen the decision in her face. He let his hand drop.

"I'll come inside and get you," he said, already moving away.

Cassie wanted to stop him. Wanted to talk. To tell him how hurt she'd been when he'd never called or tried to contact her. To tell him that, even though he obviously hadn't wanted to be with her, now they would always be connected by their son.

But it wasn't the right time.

Would it ever be?

Did she ever *want* it to be?

She watched as the father of her child ran out the back door and disappeared into the rain. Now was the time to focus on danger, not feelings.

So Cassie gripped the handle of the knife and waited.

Chapter Eight

The rain washed the lasagna off most of Henry's pants. It was the only silver lining he could come up with as he drove into Westbridge and into the driveway of the house Cassie was in. If Calvin was around, he'd decided not to make his presence known. Or maybe he'd realized the rain, growing heavier by the minute, could just as easily be an advantage or a disadvantage.

One night, as partners, Henry and Calvin had discussed using weather as a cover for a raid. Calvin was for it, yet Henry hadn't liked the idea. Sure, rain caused low visibility, which meant the target couldn't be 100 percent alert. But, by the same token, that meant the one executing the plan couldn't be, either. Same with trying to get the drop on someone at night.

It was hard to keep your bearings if you never had them all the way down in the first place.

When you were dealing with armed, well-trained people, it was best to have as much control over the situation as you could. A stance that Henry and Calvin had disagreed on right up until the day that changed everything.

Henry's grip tightened around the steering wheel.

He didn't like the rain now.

Just as he didn't like the idea that Calvin could be lurking within it.

Cassie had the front door open before Henry was done jogging up. He was glad to see the knife in her hand still, but that she was also calm.

"No one made a peep," she confirmed, voice rising above the rain as they ran to the car together.

She went straight to the back seat on the driver's side. Henry took lead and slid behind the wheel.

"I don't like this," she added after he hit Reverse and then straightened on the street. "Did they say anything to you before Calvin attacked you?" Her voice softened. Honey. "And didn't you say that Calvin was your partner? What's he doing here? And alive?"

"I can only answer about half of that," Henry hated to admit.

"Then I'll take those answers."

Henry turned out of the neighborhood and directed them back toward the department. The sky behind them was almost black, but in the distance it looked like the clouds were wanting to part. Leave it to the temperamental Southern weather to keep everyone on their toes.

"The man named Michael said he was a broker, one who made connections," he started, keeping his eyes on the street ahead. The last thing they needed was to get into an accident while out of communications and drenched. "That's when Calvin showed up. Yes, we used to be partners, but then he was killed in the line of duty. Or so I thought. His body was never recovered, but—" Henry stopped and tried to find the right words to explain what had happened next. It was a hard task. "But with everything going on, there was a good chance the fire took care of it."

"The fire," Cassie repeated, hesitation in her tone. Still, she didn't form it into a question.

"He'd been shot in the chest three times and wasn't wearing a vest," he continued. "So when we couldn't find his body and he didn't show up..." Henry slammed his hand against the wheel. "I stopped looking for his body one measly month after everything happened. I should have kept on. If I had known there was a chance he was still out there..."

"It sounds like you had very valid reasons for assuming he wasn't. Anyone in your shoes probably would have done the same. Beating yourself up about it won't help us figure out what's going on *now*." Again her voice went to honey. Soothing and sweet. "Did he talk to you before you lost consciousness?"

Henry ignored the shame from the question but nodded. His jaw set. "He doesn't want them, whoever they are, to kill me—" he pushed the words through his clenched teeth "—because he wants to be the one who kills me."

Silence filled the small car. Henry kept his eyes forward, navigating back into traffic. The rain lessened. Sunlight could be seen breaking through the clouds in the distance.

It wasn't until they were going down the street in front of the sheriff's department that Cassie spoke again. There was no hint of honey in her words.

"I'm worried about my friends and the department right now and why neither seems to be picking up their phones," she said. "So we're going to make sure everything is okay. But, Henry? After that we're going to have a talk."

There was no room to interpret it as a request.

So he didn't. "Yes, ma'am."

EVERYTHING WASN'T ALL RIGHT.

There was a group of deputies standing at the back of the parking lot. Through the rain and distance Cassie could tell some were angry by the sets of their stances or the scowls on their faces. But that didn't mean she was about to go over to see what for. Cassie didn't want to stay in the rain to find out when she was on her own timeline, being possibly one of the only two people who knew there was a not-deceased Calvin and mystery man Michael in Riker County. With bad intentions to boot.

Henry seemed to be on the same wavelength as far as getting inside was concerned. After parking in the first open spot in the guest lot, he kept so close to Cassie that she ran into him twice on her way to the front door. His closeness would normally set off memories of their shared night together, if the last day was any indication, but Cassie found comfort in it now.

The lobby wasn't lacking in activity, either. Henry took lead and guided Cassie past deputies, civilians and a man she recognized as a reporter from the TV station next door. He didn't stop until they were in the hallway that ran past the main offices. Frustration could be heard clear as a bell through Suzy's open door. Cassie went straight for it.

"—can tell Dean Carver that if he wants to let everyone know it was intentional and start a panic, then by all means go ahead and make our jobs harder!"

Suzy slammed her open hand across the desktop while Captain Dane Jones nodded to the sentiment. They both looked like they had aged years since Cassie and Henry had left that morning.

Henry cleared his throat.

Suzy's demeanor changed so swiftly that the man hesitated in his opening.

"Where have you two been?" Suzy asked, eyes scanning them with open concern. It probably didn't help matters that both were soaked to the bone. "Mills said he saw you peel off in your car."

Cassie hoped she hid her embarrassment at what, in hindsight, hadn't been the smartest idea. Still, she wasn't going to lie. "The man that gave me the ring—Michael—was in the parking lot. Deputy Ward tried to talk to him, but he ran off." She tried an indifferent shrug. "So I pursued them both."

Suzy opened her mouth but Henry butted in before she could get a word out.

"He had a driver and we followed them back to the neighborhood of Westbridge," he hurriedly related. "I went in after them and was knocked out."

"But not before he identified the second man as Calvin Fitzgerald," Cassie added.

Dane raised his eyebrow.

"Calvin as in—" he started.

"That Calvin," Henry finished.

Cassie didn't feel like recapping this same conversation, so she moved to the part she didn't understand.

"We tried to call it in, but the phones aren't working here?" she asked. "And everyone else's were off or busy."

Suzy flipped back to angry.

"The fiber optic cables that run to the building were severed," Dane said with a good dose of the same anger. "It took out our internet and phones."

"Since then our personal phones have been tied up by each other and the public," Suzy added. "It took me twenty minutes just to get a call out to James and the kids."

"Wait, fiber optic cables are buried in the ground," Henry pointed out. "They just don't get severed on accident."

Suzy and Dane both tensed, the latter's hand fisted.

"Unless someone *accidentally* brought in an excavator to the back of the building and cut them, I'd say it was intentional," Dane said.

A moment of thought stretched between all of them.

First Billy, then Calvin and Michael, and now this? What was going on in Riker County?

THE RAIN MIGHT have pelted the houses in Westbridge, and even fallen at a good enough clip to hide the ruckus and the sight of an excavator digging at the department, but not even one drop had fallen at Cassie's house. Her hanging plants, on either side of the front door, were drooping something awful.

"One thing you can count on about the weather in Alabama during July is that you can't count on the weather in Alabama during July," Cassie told herself as she parked her car in the driveway and sighed.

The day had not gone the way it should have, not at all. Instead of her bringing some much-needed cheer to her colleagues and friends that morning, the department was now trying to keep its head above water without communications, ghosts apparently were walking free through the town with evil intent and her front seat was covered in lasagna.

She rubbed her belly.

And she was still hungry.

Movement outside the car finally coaxed Cassie to get out. Another item to add to the list of things that had taken an unexpected turn was the continued appearance of Deputy Henry Ward. She watched as he looked at her house. One-story, boxy and painted a calming light blue, it was small but had gotten the job done for the last five years. Then again, she'd lived alone during those years. Add in a baby and the home she loved dearly might become the home she wished had another bedroom.

"This is one of the newer neighborhoods in Carpenter," she found herself explaining, sidling up to the man. Their clothes had had enough time to dry to the point they weren't dripping everywhere like faucets. Still, Cassie would bet his personal car parked at the curb was just as wet as hers. "It was built to be its own miniature community with a fancy pool and clubhouse in the middle, kind of like what Florida does with theirs, but the developer's funding still hasn't gone all the way through yet." She motioned down the street. Her house was one of six in the area, beyond which were empty lots with For Sale signs staking out each plot. "You're looking at the crazy few who took a chance. Though I think maybe we just all really wanted a pool."

Henry smiled but didn't laugh. His thoughts weren't hanging around the small, undeveloped neighborhood, she knew. Still, it bothered her.

"Do you live in Carpenter?" she ventured. "Or do you commute from one of the other towns?"

"I'm staying in a hotel until I can find something," he answered.

It sounded rehearsed. She guessed he'd been asked several times already.

"Can't beat the location and it's way better than what I was used to back in Tennessee. That's one good thing about undercover, it makes you appreciate the simple joys of a somewhat normal life." Henry's demeanor changed in tandem with Cassie's eyebrows rising clear to her hairline.

Did he just say he'd been undercover?

"But you know, again the hotel is only temporary," he hurried to tack on. "It even has some good food, so I can't complain. So, does your sister live here with you? Didn't you say she lived in Carpenter?"

It was an attempted switch of topics. One Cassie wouldn't have stood for normally. However, being reminded of Kristen was enough to get her on board with the change.

"She doesn't live with me, but she *does* live close." Cassie pointed to the house across the street. "And she works from home mostly, so I suggest we hurry inside before she walks past her windows and sees us. Plus, I'd be lying if I didn't say if I don't eat something soon, things are going to turn dangerous for you and anyone else around me."

Cassie thought her bit of humor would do the trick, lightening the deputy's mood enough that whatever walls he had up around him would drop. Or, at least, create a doorway for her to go through. But no sooner had they gotten inside her front door than it was like someone had set his feet in concrete.

His jaw was set. Hard.

Like he'd just realized he'd made a mistake.

Cassie couldn't deny it stung.

"I can't stay," he said, resolute. "I need to help with the department, but I just wanted to make sure you got here okay… And I promised you we'd talk. I'd like to keep that promise."

Every question Cassie had for the man flew through her head in quick succession. She *knew* what she wanted to ask, yet, as she stared up into eyes that cooled the Alabama heat that had followed them inside, all she wanted in that moment was to be in his arms. To touch him. To kiss him. To know what she had felt all those months ago was real.

Yet he didn't give her the chance to utter a word.

"I can't do it right now. But before I can leave this house, I have to ask—" Henry broke his invisible mold long enough to take a step closer.

Cassie's thoughts scattered, leaving her utterly unprepared for the one question she should have seen coming.

Henry squared his shoulders and, with a look that was nothing but vulnerable, he finally asked it. "Cassie, am I the father?"

So, standing in her entryway with what felt like a town-size number of questions just outside her door, Cassie decided it was time for them to have at least one answer. Even if she had to give it herself.

"Yes."

Chapter Nine

One word.

That was all it took.

One word turned Henry's mind from worries about the surprise that was Calvin, from worries about the two men who were still at large for crippling communications at the department, and even from thinking certain charged thoughts about the woman standing in front of him.

The woman carrying his child.

A son.

Henry liked to think he was an honorable man. One who would say the right thing, do the right thing. Or at least who had the workings where he could eventually be that person. When he was younger he thought he knew what he wanted in the future. To be a cop, to fight for the people who couldn't, to meet a great woman, settle down and have a family.

Since then none of that had changed. Instead the only thing that had shifted was his belief that he deserved any of it. Henry had spent the last several years in between long stints of working as an undercover cop.

He'd toed the line between right and wrong, all in the name of trying to get justice. He'd seen bad and he'd seen worse. He'd done some of his own to keep his cover intact, turning his back on the lesser crimes to help build a case against the bigger ones. Calvin had been there, too, making the same day-by-day choices, weighing the good against the bad. The bad versus the greater good.

Sometimes it had torn Henry up to pretend he was just like the people and groups he'd had to infiltrate. Mean men and women. Greedy and selfish. Angry.

Sometimes he'd felt like he was losing himself, drowning in grown-up make-believe where every action had a potentially dangerous consequence.

Other times it had been easy.

He'd been able to play the role of "bad guy" even better than some of those he was trying to take down.

Too easy.

It was because of those times that Henry now felt shame burning in his chest. He didn't have to have known Cassie for years, like her friends did, to know she was one of the good ones. She knew where the lines were and stayed on the right side of them.

Soft skin, pink lips and green, green eyes that probably tried to see the best in everyone.

Cassie Gates was too good for him.

So how could he be good for their child?

The internal war of thoughts Henry's mind exploded with only took seconds. If he was being honest with himself, he had already known the moment he'd seen her protruding belly. Getting confirmation from her had only given him permission to finally listen to what he'd already thought about the night before.

Still, he let the silence almost suffocate them until Cassie had had enough. Her expression pinched, her nostrils flared and the very lips he couldn't get out of his mind thinned.

"I would have told you, but as it turns out, I don't know you." With one graceful movement she reached around him and opened the front door again.

Henry should have said something—anything—but the words never came. He took Cassie's lead and left, chest filled with regret this time.

TRAVIS NEWMAN WAS caught trying to shimmy down a drainpipe off an office building like some kind of trained monkey. All Deputy Maria Medina had had to do was reach out and grab the man's pants before slinging him to the ground. There he'd put up a fight, but it had only been a halfhearted one. It was hard to tussle with your pants ripped right across the backside.

The excavator Travis had stolen and then used at the sheriff's department had been linked to a construction company in the town of Darby, just beyond the town limits. The office manager had been able to get footage of the nighttime robbery off a well-hidden security camera. It had been the lone one not destroyed by Travis's accomplice, a woman wearing a ski mask and boots. She had stood on the outskirts of the property while Travis did the heavy lifting, so to speak.

From there tracking down Travis had been easy enough. He was what the sheriff's department called a frequent flier. They knew his face, his name and where he lived. Not including or limited to his predilection for prescription pills, public intoxication and domestic violence when it came to his on-again, off-again girlfriend, Sara.

"And now suddenly he wants to take an excavator to

the back of the sheriff's department?" Henry shook his head. "Doesn't seem to fit with what you all have told me about the man."

Henry was leaning on the edge of his desk in the bull pen, one of three deputies making up a half circle around him. Caleb Foster was the most severe of them. Henry had no doubt he knew things weren't adding up. He turned to his partner, Dante Mills, with a frown. "I know I haven't been here as long as you, but am I wrong to say that I didn't think Travis even knew what fiber optics were? Let alone where to dig to get to them and cut them?"

Dante shook his head.

"That's some out-of-the-box thinking for a Newman," he confirmed. "His lady might know a thing or two more."

Caleb's eyebrow rose at that. "Last I heard, Sara left Travis high and dry for that McGinty kid over in Bates Hill. You know, the one who got naked and ran through the parade last year."

Dante shook his head again. "My grandma said Rebecca, over at the salon, heard that her sister talked to someone who saw Sara necking with one of the Marlow brothers at the drive-in in Darby."

"Oh, you mean the ones who opened that new hardware store in Kipsy?"

Dante gave him a thumbs-up. "That's them."

Caleb looked impressed.

"Good for Sara," he said approvingly. "I heard both brothers are good guys. Alyssa had to meet them for work and said they were really respectful and seemed to know their stuff."

Henry watched their back and forth like a tennis

match. Other than Alyssa, Caleb's wife, he didn't recognize the other names. That wasn't unusual for a community like Riker County. Small towns, tight-knit communities and gossip that stayed as strong and steady as a river's current. One day he'd be able to get into the lingo with the best of them, but for now it made him feel very much like the new guy he was. The useless, beneath-par new guy who had already broken protocol that morning, getting the pregnant dispatcher to chase danger.

Though Henry doubted he could have stopped Cassie from doing just what she had done.

Then again, he should have at least tried.

Henry cleared his throat and pushed off his desk.

"So, guessing that Travis was given orders to follow isn't a far-fetched notion," he offered. Both men shook their heads.

"He has a sister, but she lives out of state. Tennessee, I think," Caleb said. His attention caught on Captain Jones across the room. While the sheriff was openly charismatic and personable, the captain was openly gruff and introspective. He carried a box now, head bent and eyes not caring to take in the bustle of deputies and personnel around him. His mind was clearly on something else. Caleb seemed to be interested in that unknown topic. He was already turning his body away as he finished his thought. "Matt is tracking her down, though. I think Maggie is helping from home, too, since our internet and phones are on the fritz. Hey, Jones!"

Caleb took off, Dante on his heels. Henry surveyed the bull pen, but his thoughts went straight out of the building and to a small box house on a street with five other small box houses.

Cassie Gates. Soft skin, lips that tasted as good as they felt, and hair that he'd been happily tangled in. A woman who had wielded humor, compassion and a quick wit with ease the night they had met.

A woman who had taken a grieving man and given him hope that he could still find some happiness.

If only he deserved it.

Henry shook his head, growing angry at himself. Not only did he think he didn't deserve the touch of a woman as pure as Cassie, but he didn't need to even think about that touch. Not right now. Not when the department he had pledged himself to was going to hell in a handbasket.

He needed to focus. Distractions had already cost him his best friend and partner. Though, after running into that same best friend and partner, Henry wondered what else he had missed about the man while they were undercover.

Thunder grumbled above the building. The sound of heavy equipment and ground crews outside trying to restore what Travis had destroyed didn't waver. All calls from the sheriff's department jurisdiction had been temporarily rerouted to the local police departments in each town while deputies on patrol kept their cell phones close at hand. Still, even the workers outside knew the precarious situation they were in.

Having no communications was one thing.

Having your trusted law enforcement have no communications was another.

"Hey, Ward."

Detective Walker stood in the open door of his office and waved him over. He was shaking his head already.

"Detective Ansler just finished his sweep of Westbridge with a few other deputies," Matt told him as he neared. "The only person they found was a female squatter we're familiar with. She said she didn't see anything or even know you and Cassie were there earlier. I'm inclined to believe her, since we've never had an issue with her honesty before. *But* Ansler is bringing her in anyways. She might know something she doesn't even know." Matt shifted his attention to the cell phone in his hand. "Suzy should be bringing our friend Travis back to the interrogation room for round two right about now. I couldn't be present for the first time, but for this one I want to see his reaction when Suzy asks him about Calvin."

"She hasn't asked if there's a connection there yet?" Henry was surprised at that.

"No. Suzy has her own system when it comes to getting answers, though." Matt clapped him on the shoulder reassuringly. "She's a grade-A button pusher. I'm pretty sure she learned half of her interrogation skills from her nine-year-old." He smiled at a memory Henry wasn't privy to, but then sobered. "Why don't you come along and watch with me? I'd like to have you in there when she throws out Calvin's name. Him showing up at the same time a no-brain like Travis attacks the department is a coincidence I don't like or accept. If there's a connection, I want to make sure we're looking at it from every possible angle."

"Yeah, I'd like to come," Henry agreed. "Thanks."

Matt gave him a smile as they moved back through the bull pen. It was brief but true enough. "I don't know how you're used to working in your undercover stints, but here we rarely go lone wolf to get a job done."

A laugh bubbled up behind them.

"Yeah, none of us has ever gone lone wolf in this

department," Suzanne Simmons deadpanned. A look passed between the chief deputy and Matt as she fell into step at their side. "I can't even recall any one instance where one of us decided to figure out things by ourselves."

Matt put his hands up, obviously guilty.

"Okay, so *sometimes* a few of us have decided to err on the side of keeping information close to our chest until we get better bearings," he admitted. He pointed at Henry, mock sternness pulling his brow tight. He shook his finger like a teacher would when instructing a student. "But when things got too hairy, we always knew to call in the cavalry. Standing alone in the face of danger when you have a building full of people to back you up isn't always the smartest decision."

Henry couldn't help grinning. "That sounded like something you would read in a fortune cookie."

Suzy snorted. Matt shrugged.

"Doesn't make it any less true," Matt said.

The moment they walked into the hallway that led to the interrogation room, the humor dissipated. Like they'd shucked invisible coats and were about to be forced to enter the cold.

"Travis's lawyer should be here by the end of the hour," Suzy said, voice lowering the closer they got. "Pay attention to everything and anything. He's not the smartest guy in the county, but after what he pulled, maybe we haven't been giving him enough credit the last few years."

Henry had started to agree when voices and footsteps pulled their attention to the end of the hallway. Deputy Medina rounded the corner, directing a man who must have been Travis at her side. She nodded to them, totally unaware of the change in her perp's expression.

A shock of adrenaline charged Henry's system as the man met his eyes.

"Gage?" the man called Travis rasped.

No hint of suspicion, betrayal or anger colored the twenty-something's face. All Henry could read was surprise. Sincere surprise.

It was because of this surprise that several things happened at once.

First and foremost, Henry's thoughts went to his clothes. He was wearing a pair of jeans his brother had often said made him look like some kind of cowboy doing a Levi's ad. Women in the past had more or less given him the same comment, though their attention to the details had been less analytical and more on the sensual side. Henry wasn't above trying to entice the opposite sex using a pair of jeans, but that wasn't why he loved them. They fit well, were the color of worn denim, and always made a pair of boots look good.

He'd had them for years but hadn't thought to break them out at his new job. That had been Cassie's fault. Or, at least, her lasagna. Once he'd gotten back to the department, he'd changed out of his soiled uniform and into his plain clothes. Since there were more important issues being addressed, no one had ordered him to change.

Which was good, considering that what he was about to try to do required him to *not* be in uniform.

The second and third things that happened next did so in quick succession. Henry stopped in his tracks so suddenly that Matt bumped into his elbow. Suzy, a step behind, stepped on the back of his boot.

There was no time to explain himself.

He just hoped he wasn't about to get fired.

Or worse, shot.

Riding the wave of confusion, Henry turned on his heel and fisted his hand.

Matt never saw the punch coming.

Chapter Ten

"What?"

Kristen Gates's mouth hung open like she was trying to catch something. A few seconds before, a noise escaped the open trap that Cassie couldn't easily define. It wasn't exactly a shriek but not a yell, either.

Maybe screech was a more applicable descriptor.

Either way it made Cassie fight the urge to cover her ears.

Maybe telling someone about her day hadn't been the best idea.

Or, maybe, it was her choosing her older sister to tell that hadn't been the right call. Kristen was already dramatic in her own right. Never mind adding *actual* drama to the mix.

"I'm fine," Cassie reassured Kristen again. They were sitting in her living room, untouched sweet and decaf tea beside them. The rain had stayed away from their houses, but Cassie had a feeling nothing now would have stopped Kristen from crossing the street to get to her. It was like she had a sixth sense for excitement. Even if it hadn't happened to her.

Cassie made a sweeping gesture to include her stomach. "Again, we're fine," she said.

Kristen, a woman made up of long limbs, wild blond hair and a nose that had earned her the nickname of Mrs. Beaks in middle school, was notably trying to hold in the rushing waters of sibling protectiveness. She opened her mouth, closed it, opened it again and started to turn red.

Cassie mused that the older woman looked like she was sucking on a lemon while simultaneously trying to scold an errant child.

She didn't know if she should be afraid or flattered. Or both.

However, she felt neither reaction.

If Cassie hadn't been emotionally gutted hours before by the brooding Deputy Ward and his utter lack of response when learning he was the father of her child, she might have been amused by her sister's overreaction. As it was, she sank even farther back into the plushness of her living room chair and waited out the storm.

"What makes you think that going after those men was all right?" Kristen finally said, landing on anger again. "They could have had guns! They could have shot at you! And chasing them in your crappy little Honda, too! That in itself is bad enough. Did you forget about that one time *when it caught fire*? And that was when it was going through Mom and Dad's neighborhood! Where it's like ten miles an hour! It's a miracle it didn't combust pushing eighty!"

Kristen's face reddened into a dangerous shade of crimson. Her chest began to heave. She had officially entered into angry-worried, an emotional state that Cassie was used to being on the receiving end of thanks to being the baby of the family. Her brothers entered that state every time she'd dated a boy they didn't like or been caught sneaking off to a party. Who needed parents when your big brothers were always ready to give you a stern talking to?

For once, though, angry-worried wasn't unwarranted.

Yet the part of Cassie that resented being babied, especially by someone only a year older than she, reared its head long enough to defend herself.

"It was *one* time and it didn't catch fire! It overheated and puffed out smoke. That was it."

"I saw flames!"

Cassie opened her mouth to attempt another defensive strike even if it was a halfhearted attempt. Once Kristen Gates had something to talk about, especially when it came to venting, she wouldn't stop until everything was out on the table.

But the older woman didn't give her the chance at a rebuttal.

"That's not the point, Cassie. Flames or not, you shouldn't have followed. You should have let that man go it alone."

Cassie had a moment of déjà vu. The fear and anguish at finding Henry unconscious in Westbridge hitting her like a ton of bricks again. If she hadn't been there? What would have happened?

Then again, if she had never showed up at the side of the street and driven them to that very same neighborhood?

Guilt extended the worry behind each *what-if.*

One or all of the emotions must have showed in her expression. Kristen took a beat, visibly restraining herself. She inhaled a long breath and sat on the edge of the coffee table. When she let the breath out, her face lost some of its redness.

"Cassie," she started again. Their knees touched. It

was the grounding Kristen must have needed. When she spoke, her words softened. "You have always been the sweetest, most compassionate out of the Gates kids. Something you no doubt learned from Dad. I mean, we don't just call you Daddy's girl for kicks. Your desire to see the best in everyone and even encourage it is a trait you and Dad have become pros at. You two put all of us above yourself.

"I mean, even when we were kids you always made sure we were happy before even thinking about you. What normal eighteen-year-old skips her own prom to throw her, at times admittedly ungrateful, older sister a surprise birthday party? Or who turns down a once-in-a-lifetime date with the hot, sexy fireman Marcus Guiles to drive over a hundred miles because you knew Davie didn't have anyone to help him move?"

She grinned. "At the best of times your heart and capacity to empathize and help the people around you have kept you from getting something you want." Kristen reached out and purposely touched the scar at Cassie's neck. "At the worst of times it has nearly cost you your life." She dropped her hand.

Cassie took the moment to touch the same scar.

"That was different, and you know it," she reminded Kristen. "I was trying to protect Billy's little girl."

Once again Kristen's expression softened.

"I know," she said. "But what about today?"

They both lapsed into silence.

Cassie didn't want to break it. She didn't want to admit why she had done what she had. Why she had wanted to help Henry.

Kristen took the silence as contemplation. She continued when it was clear Cassie wouldn't. "You can't help everyone, Cassie. Especially not strangers with troubled pasts." She smiled. It was a warm look. "There're two of you now. That's double the danger in everything you do."

Cassie let out a sigh of defeat.

The willpower she had long held on to since she'd found out she was pregnant had just cracked. While she hadn't kept her pregnancy a secret from her family and friends, she had censored the part about the one-night stand with a stranger. Instead she had said the father was a friend and one who didn't want a family. A decision they both had decided was best. No hard feelings.

It hadn't mattered, of course. Cassie's brothers, and most of her sheriff's department colleagues and friends, had roared. Threats and promises of pain had swiftly followed. Even her parents, even a parent as kindly as her dad, had had very bad words for the mystery man she refused to name.

But now that Cassie had found Henry?

Now that he lived in the same zip code?

Now that he worked in the same building?

Now everything was different.

"His name is Henry and he's not a stranger, Kristen. At least, not in the ways that count." Cassie let her gaze drop to her stomach.

Kristen's eyes soon followed. They widened when she understood. "Oh."

Cassie rubbed her stomach. "Oh is right."

A moment passed. Then Kristen stood, grabbed her glass of sweet tea and started to retreat into the kitchen.

"What are you doing?" Cassie asked, worried she'd somehow broken her sister.

"I'm exchanging this for two glasses of wine," she

called over her shoulder before disappearing into the next room. "I feel like you need a drink."

"Kristen, I'm seven months' pregnant!"

Kristen's mass of hair floated into view as she popped her head around the corner. "I know! I'm drinking for both of us!"

HIS JAW WAS THROBBING. There would be a bruise across his skin. If there wasn't already one. If he could have, he would have touched the tender spot. Instead he slid his jaw back and forth with a grunt.

He also tasted a little blood.

Suzanne Simmons had one hell of a right cross.

"You know, they ain't supposed to be able to do that," Travis said.

Henry looked across the interrogation table. Travis eyed the spot where Suzy had hauled off and hit Henry in retaliation for punching her lead detective. It had happened so fast that Henry genuinely didn't have time to dodge it, for show or not.

The surprise and pain had coupled to make him stagger. He'd barely regained his footing when the newly recovered Matt had jumped in to subdue him. But not without a fight from Henry. He'd bucked against the detective all the way into the interrogation room and didn't stop until his hands were cuffed behind the chair.

Even then Henry had used his words to fight. Calling Matt and Suzy a lot of not-so-great things.

By then he'd hoped they'd understood what he was doing.

If not, he was definitely fired.

Or really under arrest.

"They can't just touch you like that and then lock

you away," Travis restated. His eyes shifted to the mirror behind Henry. Suzy, Matt and Deputy Medina were all watching, he was sure. "That's what they did to Ricky, 'member? Jumped him and got all crazy when he fought back." He shook his head, disgusted. "Self-defense! That's all it was! How is that right that they locked *him* up and threw away the key? Tell me that!" Travis shook his head, hair slapping the sides of his head. It was shorter than it had been the last time Henry had seen him.

"These pigs think they can do whatever they want," Henry agreed, slipping into a heavier Southern twang. "Think they're above the law."

Travis ate it up. His head switched movements. He nodded so hard it made his cuffs *clink* against his chair.

"It's supposed to be innocent until proven guilty," he railed. "Just wait. My lawyer will get here and sort it out." The questions Travis should have had at seeing someone from his past finally seemed to dawn across his expression. His thin face almost caved in on itself, pinching in confusion. "Wait, what did you do? Why're you here?" He lowered his voice to a quick whisper, eyeing the glass behind Henry. "Last I heard, you'd got a new job."

For a split second Henry worried that Travis had figured it out, that he was a deputy, not the small-time drug runner Gage Coulson. But if there was one thing he was certain about, it was that Travis wasn't smart enough to hide what he did and did not know.

He *knew* Henry as a man he'd worked with for a year.

He *didn't know* that Gage wasn't real. Just a persona and an identity that had been created as a part of a task force to stop a dangerous organization from getting traction in Tennessee.

What *Henry knew* was that Suzy had been wrong. Not only was Travis not smart enough to bluff; he wasn't clever or organized enough to cripple the sheriff's department's communications. Not by himself.

He was more of a paint-by-numbers kind of guy.

And even then Henry had seen him mess that up from time to time.

Still, he needed to be a little cautious. Considering the last time he'd seen the man was right before the ambush.

"You heard what went down at the warehouse?" he asked, searching the man's expression for any tells. "After the fire?"

Travis nodded then shrugged.

"Everybody heard about that," he said. Again he eyed the two-way mirror. He'd been arrested enough to know that people were watching. Still, he wasn't smart enough to know that whispering wouldn't keep the people on the other side from hearing them. Or that maybe he should just keep his mouth shut altogether. "They said it was a trap, got swarmed by cops after I took off. Grabbed a group of y'all. Even nabbed some of those Richland fellas." He spit off to the side, a curse to the Richlands. "Ain't gonna lie, I was okay with that." He managed to drop an almost apologetic look. "Was sorry to hear about Parker, though. No way to go, I suspect. Burning alive like that. Heard they never found his body."

Henry didn't have to pretend that the memory pained him. To keep their partnership intact during their time undercover, Henry and Calvin had been named as brothers. Gage and Parker Coulson had become friends and business associates with the very people they were trying to take down. Calvin had been better at being friendly. Maybe *that* was how he'd escaped.

Because he surely hadn't used Travis's help.

The man seemed genuine in his belief that Henry *wasn't* a cop and that Calvin had died that day.

Which meant Calvin hadn't included the small-time crook in his plan. At least, if he had, not directly.

"They said the fire did the job," Henry said, careful in his words. "No remains left but ash."

Travis shook his head in sympathy. Curiosity soon replaced it. "What happened to you? Heard you was let go and left town."

"Yeah, those cops couldn't find nothing on me." Henry scrunched his nose like he smelled something disgusting. "They tried, though, but you know how smart Parker was. Dead or alive, he wasn't about to let his little brother get locked up." Henry lowered his voice to the point where he questioned whether Suzy and the rest of their audience *could* hear him on the other side of the mirror. "I had enough alibis to squeeze out of town. The Richlands, not so much."

Travis let out a hoot of laughter. His handcuffs *clinked* against the metal of his chair again.

"So I came to 'Bama, thinking the change in scenery would be good," Henry continued. "Then there I am, just checking out the situation with the local black-and-whites, when *bam!* I get grabbed again. Something about being a suspect. Calling me a thief and conspirator." Henry mispronounced the last word, adding enough Southern twang to make it seem like he was barely capable enough to know what it meant, let alone be it. His goal of getting down to why Travis had attacked the department would only be met if he stayed true to the most important principle of what had made him a successful Gage Coulson.

Travis had to be able to relate to him. Get on the same page. Henry had to show the man that even though time had passed and their situation had changed, Henry was still of the same mind.

The same side, too.

"Said someone took out their phones here," he added, sure to put some awe in his tone. "Now they're all running around like chickens with their heads cut off."

Travis couldn't help himself. He grinned.

Not only was it important to be able to relate to a dense criminal, it was also important to inflate their ego sometimes, too. Henry couldn't resist the latter.

"Told them it wasn't me, but I'll tell you what, that must have taken a lot of brains to pull that off." Henry gave him a wink. "Got them scrambling around like crazy. Believe you me, that's someone I wouldn't mind working for."

Pride, clear as day, pushed Travis's chest out.

Then something unexpected happened.

That pride was replaced with worry, followed swiftly by fear. It creased his brow and sagged his body down.

"You always been nice to me, Gage. So I'll keep it fair between us." Travis leaned over as far as he could.

Henry mirrored him, another surge of adrenaline starting to swirl inside his chest. When the man spoke again, his words were so low Henry almost had a hard time following.

"Might be time to leave town again. The people running this thing got a big plan for everyone here. As soon as it gets dark, all hell will be raining down. You don't wanna be around when that happens."

It wasn't a threat.

It was a promise.

Chapter Eleven

"He's not that dumb."

Henry dropped into one of the several seats around the conference room table. Luckily, he was neither in cuffs nor being fired. At least, not yet.

"Even Travis knows he pushed the limits with what he should and shouldn't have said," Henry continued. "With how quick he buttoned his trap closed just now, I think he's done talking."

Suzy kept standing next to the head of the table. Matt, Caleb, Dante and Deputy Medina took the open seats around him.

"I think you're right," the chief deputy agreed. "I don't think I'm going out on a limb here when I point out that man was afraid. Whether that fear is for the people he's answering to or for the supposed rest of the plan, or both, I'm not sure. But yeah, I think he's done."

"Even if he wasn't, his lawyer will make him shut up," Medina added. "We got lucky enough that he was caught in traffic and it added a few minutes to his commute. We definitely couldn't have pulled off that little show otherwise."

Henry agreed with that. After Travis had shut down, his lawyer showed up. Deputy Medina had explained why Henry had been thrown into the room with Travis by blaming the chaos of everyone running around, trying to do their jobs without their normal tools. It was vague and really didn't make that much sense, but Maria had sold it with a flair of anger. It had been enough to throw the lawyer's attention off Henry and onto his client.

Though Henry made sure to struggle against Caleb and Dante when they had come in to take him away.

"Sorry about the hit, by the way," Henry added for the first time. There was a mark on Matt's jaw, roughly the same spot where Henry was currently feeling pain. "When I realized who Travis was and that I wasn't in uniform, I thought we could use my old cover to our advantage." He managed a grin. "And Gage Coulson wasn't known as the type to *not* resist."

Detective Walker snorted. "You kidding me? It was well worth the hit just to see Suzy here nearly lay you out." Matt turned to the two deputies who hadn't seen the incident. "I mean she hit him so hard *I* almost saw stars."

There was a moment when everyone shared in the humor of what had happened. Even Henry joined in with a little laugh. The truth was he had been impressed with not only her strength, but how quickly Suzy had figured out what was going on. She had been made privy to his background but hadn't known the individuals he'd run into while working.

She'd taken a chance on him and it had paid off.

Which was the reason why the room sobered considerably right after their shared humor ended.

"All hell will be raining down," Suzy repeated, voice hard and cold. "It wasn't an accident, taking down our communications. It was a part of a larger, more menacing plan. One that is run by people, not just one person."

She looked to Henry. "I don't know Travis like you do, but am I right in thinking that if he had been in contact with Calvin, he would already have known you were a deputy?"

Henry nodded.

"You probably guessed it already, but Calvin was undercover as Parker Coulson," he explained. "Brother to Gage Coulson, aka my undercover identity. Even if Calvin *had* already met with Travis but, for whatever reason, hadn't given away who I really was, I'm pretty sure Travis would have told me he'd seen my supposedly dead brother. Calvin and I wanted to keep our cover as close to reality as we could when it came to our partnership, so brothers worked out well for us. It was no secret that Parker and Gage were close."

Again, that familiar pain of losing someone who was just like a brother ached in Henry's chest. He glanced across the table at Caleb and Dante. It wasn't a secret, either, that they had also gotten close in their time at the department. Dante had been best man for Caleb's wedding. Partners to best friends to basically brothers.

Henry fought the urge to warn them there was still a chance they didn't know each other at all.

However, projecting his past on them wasn't fair. It also wouldn't do a thing to help their present.

So he continued. "Bottom line, Travis would have told me about Calvin. If only to score some points of gratitude with me. I don't think he *could* have kept it a secret even if he'd wanted to."

"It still doesn't make Calvin's sudden appearance and threat less unsettling," Matt pointed out. "I'm still hard-pressed not to believe they're connected. Maybe this all has something to do with the undercover work you both did in Tennessee?"

Henry had already thought long and hard about that. He'd come up relatively empty-handed. "The last long stint of undercover work that we did before Calvin's death—well, what we thought was Calvin's death—involved us infiltrating a small but growing group of gun runners and drug dealers operating through a recreational ranch in Tennessee. He took a job as part of the security and I was an extra set of hands for the hard labor parts of keeping the ranch going. The task force wasn't sure who the main players were, so we divided and conquered until Calvin got his foot in the door. What we thought was a small operation with maybe twenty men ended up being two *competing* operations vying for the top spot in the area."

"I'm guessing by Travis's reaction that the Richlands were one of the opposing factions," Suzy said.

Henry nodded. "Not that I have a lot of love for Travis—who, by the way, we only knew as Glen—but he was right. The Richland family was a bona fide smorgasbord of awful men and women ready and willing to do awful things. There were many times I wished I could arrest them on the spot just for *talking* about the things they had done." He fisted his hand on top of the table, angry. "But we realized the main aggressor, Arnold Richland, was our golden goose. If we could catch him in the act or tie him to the shipments of guns his people were responsible for, we would potentially stop a mounting gang war before it started. Not to mention keep an influx of unregistered and very dangerous guns off the streets."

"What about the other side? The other faction, they didn't run guns?" Dante was leaning forward, attentive.

Henry was used to other law enforcement being interested when he talked about his undercover work. Especially in Riker County. Their undercover work wasn't as in demand as it had been at his former job.

"They were into drugs, meth and pills mostly," he answered. "But their matriarch, Nora, was trying to change that. She had started with negotiations to try to convince the Richland crew to combine forces. It didn't end well. Which is what brought our attention to the ranch in the first place."

"Sounds like a lot of chaos going on," Suzy commented. "And not the good kind."

"We thought we finally were getting the hang of it." Henry snorted. There was no humor in the sound. "We were wrong.

"The night we thought we finally were going to catch Arnold, his family, and Nora and her cronies in talks with their product in tow, everything went south. Quick. A group of Richland's guys ambushed the task force before they could take position. Didn't hesitate opening fire. It was a domino effect that ended in Nora trying to destroy the evidence and get the heck out of Dodge. Before I knew it, the warehouse around us was engulfed in flames. We were trapped. I lost consciousness before we could find a way out. Next thing I know I'm waking up in the hospital, a member from our team having barely pulled me out before the building was too far gone. He said he never saw Calvin."

"But that was the last time you saw Calvin before today," Matt said, trying to confirm. "That's why you thought he'd died in the fire."

Henry nodded. "That and the fact that one of the Richland men trapped with us shot him three times in the chest before the fire let loose and I passed out."

"Well, that would definitely convince me," Matt said.

Henry tightened his fist.

"But I was wrong," he growled. "Not just about Calvin's death but him in general." A thought Henry hadn't had until that moment finally occurred to him. It was nearly overwhelming, pitting his thoughts squarely between more anger and betrayal. "When I saw Calvin today, he didn't have a burn mark on him."

Henry looked to Suzy, the leader of the group, standing tall and ready at the head of the table. Her expression softened. She'd already made the connection. Still, she'd let him voice it.

"Which means, if Calvin's death was for show and he escaped the building before our guys could get in to grab me, he left me to die there."

A silence swept through the room. Matt looked sympathetic as he broke it. "If he faked his death, then there's a good possibility that he could have tipped off the Richlands in the first place."

Each new theory was a dig to Henry's side. Partly because he hadn't thought of them until now. Partly because, if they were true, he hadn't seen Calvin's true motives back then. He'd been blind.

What did that mean for him now?

How could the people sitting around him trust his judgment?

How could they trust him period?

"People suck sometimes."

They all turned their collective gaze to the open doorway. None other than Cassie Gates looked back at them.

More aptly, looked back at him. Her eyes were as fierce as ever. Two green orbs that commanded all his attention and held it without contest. "We can account for a lot of stuff with this job, but at the end of the day, some people just choose to suck."

She took a step farther into the room, unflinchingly unapologetic for interrupting. "And there's not anything we can do about it but get back out there and work hard for those who don't suck. Sure, your partner probably ended up being one of the bad guys. Doesn't mean you stopped being one of the good ones. Okay?"

Henry could get lost in those eyes.

And had done so once before.

"Okay," he answered.

Cassie nodded once, like she'd accomplished what she'd come for, and then turned to Suzy. "To be totally honest, I just eavesdropped most of that conversation," she started. It was a bold move, admitting that to the boss. However, Suzy didn't appear to be angry. Instead she waited for an explanation she must have realized was coming.

Henry was starting to see that normal rules didn't always apply to the family that was the Riker County Sheriff's Department. They really were an all-in-this-together kind of group. "But the door was cracked and... well, I think I have some information that might not be so great."

Suzy motioned to the closest chair.

Henry watched as she sat a little awkwardly, minding her stomach.

A baby boy cradled inside.

Which was why what she said next made his blood boil.

"A man showed up at my house just now." She held

up her hand, as if knowing they all were a second away from barraging her with questions. "It wasn't Calvin, but it *was* Michael."

THE ROOM EXPLODED in noise. It made her already twisting nerves knot further. Like wind-whipped hair with no brush strong enough to conquer it. Cassie ran her hands through her own hair. It brought little comfort. She hoped no one notice how her hands had a small shake to them.

"I'm fine," she said, collecting her nerve. "He didn't *do* anything other than talk. I don't know if that had anything to do with me being pregnant or Kristen being there, but he left. I was able to get Detective Ansler on his cell and he said he'd go ahead and notify local PD." Cassie didn't meet anyone's eyes. "Still, it spooked me enough that Kristen drove me here. She's in the break room. I hope that's okay?"

Suzy nodded. Out of Cassie's periphery she saw Henry move forward in his seat, anxious.

"What did he say?" His voice was clipped. Like he was holding back.

Cassie wondered if the others heard the difference. She wondered if there really even was a difference. Or was she just interpreting his concern for something more?

"What did he want, Cassie?"

She exhaled and fanned her fingers across her stomach. Rubbing it, she felt some sense of comfort as she spoke.

"Honestly, I don't know what he wanted," she admitted. "But he apologized. For the 'runaround' earlier. He said he hadn't thought I would get involved but complimented my driving." She remembered how innocent the conversation had been. Michael had been even-tempered, polite and, unless she had misread him, *sincere*. Then there had been a shift in his stance, his tone, too. "After that he told me that it might be a good idea to get out of town for a few days and visit my parents. Said it would be good for me…and the baby."

This time Cassie chanced a look at Henry. The deputy was strung so tight she would bet she could have played him like an instrument had she wanted. Though she would rather have known the thoughts running through his head.

"Then he got into the same car he was in this morning and left. That's when I called Detective Ansler."

Henry's frown nearly rolled in on itself.

He wasn't the only one.

"He threatened you," Matt said.

Cassie shook her head.

"He seemed genuinely concerned," she admitted. Henry started to open his mouth, so she hurried to finish the thought. "Which, I know, doesn't make sense, but, honestly, I think it was just a warning."

"One that Henry more or less received himself from Travis Newman." Suzy's voice had gone steely. Analytical. They were dancing around something very real. Something much more ominous than a storm in the distance. Something they didn't fully understand.

But desperately needed to.

Despite his anger, or maybe because of it, Henry was the voice that rang loud, clear and steady throughout the conference room. "We don't know who is pulling the strings, but I think what Travis did was the start of something. Something that's going to hurt. 'The people running this thing got a big plan for everyone here.' I don't think the 'here' Travis meant was about the county, or the town, for that matter. I think he was talking about the sheriff's department. Or maybe the people who run it."

Cassie let out a small gasp.

"Billy," she realized.

Henry nodded.

"I think we're about to have an all-out attack against us," he said. "And what better way to start than by getting the sheriff out of the picture and then taking out our communications?" Henry jabbed his finger down on the table's top, capturing everyone's attention even though it was already on him. "'As soon as it gets dark, all hell will be raining down.'"

Suzy straightened, standing tall.

Tall and angry. "So, whoever they are, they're going to hit us tonight."

It wasn't a question.

Chapter Twelve

"Are you kidding me?" Suzy said, twenty minutes after their meeting in the conference room had ended.

Henry didn't bother keeping his voice low. There was no point. Not when the department around them was one long stream of bustling noise. "You said it yourself. There's a good chance that the department *will be attacked* tonight! And you want to send me home? I know I'm technically new, but you've seen my résumé, you know what I've done." He let his hands fly around the air in front of him, physically broadcasting his frustration. "You know what I *can* do."

Suzy kept her expression tight and guarded. She was in planning mode. He'd caught her right before she was headed in to giving her troops the battle plan.

The troops he'd been told he wasn't included in.

"Listen, I know you're more than capable of helping, but I think the best way you can do that is by not being in or around the department." She pointed outside her office.

For a moment Henry thought he was being told to leave.

She continued. "Travis Newman would never have talked to us, at least not in time if there really is an attack. He *did* talk to Gage Coulson. What if he isn't the only one who's a part of this who thinks that's who you really are? Every minute you are here, you are further risking us losing the ability to use that if we need to again. As much as I admire and empathize with what you have done and been through, the fact of the matter is that right now the department needs Gage. If it wasn't for him, we wouldn't even have an idea of what might be happening."

Henry ran a hand through his hair. He cursed.

Suzy didn't mind.

"What about Calvin?" he had to ask. "And Michael? I think it's pretty safe to say they both know that Gage was just a cover. What if that's already blown and Travis was just the last to know? Even in the criminal world, there are just some people you don't trust with the important details. For all we know, this could be a giant trap. One you are asking me to leave you all to walk into."

Suzy had been indulging him up until that moment, he realized seconds too late.

"I am not asking you do to anything. I am *ordering* you to leave." She leaned forward, resting her fists on the desktop. It was a power move. One she pulled off well. "If this *is* a trap, then having abled-bodied men and women out there will only help us in the long run. But you're right, Travis may not know whatever plan is out there. Heck, we could all be jumping to one big conclusion. And if that's the case, I'm going to need you to be Gage again to figure out what really is going on. Which is why you're going to leave your uniform off and lie low until we figure out what is and isn't a plan or trap."

Henry didn't speak. He was angry.

Angry that he was effectively being benched.

Angry that the reasoning made sense.

"Is that understood?"

Henry met her gaze and nodded. "But I'm not leaving Cassie's side."

The words came out before he knew he was going to say them. Yet he stood by them, resolute. "Michael knows where she lives, which means Calvin could, too. If he thinks that he can hurt me by hurting her, he could use that. Let me make sure that doesn't happen."

Suzy's eyebrow arched high. "I want to point out that Cassie has showed that she can handle herself. She doesn't need any hero or savior to watch over her. I mean, she did come to your rescue earlier. She's clever, quick and resourceful when she needs to be."

Henry had opened his mouth to protest what he thought she perceived as a request—when he fully planned on doing it with or without permission—when she held up her hand in a stop motion.

"However, today there are a lot of unknown pieces on this particular chessboard. Ones I don't like. So I'd like to have a few of our own in place. Ones we can control. I am not her keeper, but I will suggest she consider having you around until we know what is or isn't happening."

Suzy was done with the conversation. She grabbed a file on her desk and headed for the door.

"And if she doesn't want me around?"

Chief Deputy Sheriff Simmons didn't so much as hesitate in her response. "Then you do it anyway."

THE SKY WAS the perfect blend of blue and gray, caught somewhere in between calm and dreary. The humidity was less pleasing. It made the air heavy and wet. Uncomfortable and unforgiving mixed with the heat. It fused clothes to skin and tempted all moods into souring.

Not that Cassie's mood needed help in that department.

She cast her gaze away from the sky.

Rain was on the horizon, but it wasn't promised. The change in pressure was pricking at her sinuses. A wicked headache would certainly be in her future. Another problem she'd have to endure.

It was much smaller in comparison to the rest.

At least a headache she understood.

The rest?

Calvin and Michael?

A possible attack against the department?

A man she barely knew with the power to completely and utterly derail her thoughts with ease?

Those were things Cassie was having a harder time wrapping her mind around.

Suzy had made a case for her protection that she had and hadn't appreciated. One that involved the walking conundrum that was wrapped in a pair of mouthwatering jeans. Henry had stood by stoically, like a Southern bodyguard waiting in the wings for her to try her hand at either fight or flight.

Instead she'd fallen somewhere in between.

"He can come home with me, check out the house and hang around while I get some things, but then I'm going to Kristen's for the rest of the afternoon and night," she'd said. "After that he can hang outside in the car if he thinks it's a good idea."

Suzy was pushed for time, but she paused long enough to add in another two cents, even using a nickname she'd heard Cassie call herself from time to time. "Better safe than sorry, baby mama."

Suzy had left then, face grim but ready. Henry's expression was also dark yet alert. He didn't speak as they went to the break room to get Kristen. Which was good for Cassie. Two steps inside the break room and she had a crisis of conscience so severe she didn't speak for a moment.

The department might be attacked that night by a formally deceased undercover cop, a self-proclaimed information peddler, and potentially more unknown faces and motives. Not that Calvin's or Michael's motives were clear.

What did they stand to gain going against the Riker County Sheriff's Department?

What was the point?

Cassie wanted to ask her sister that question, to brainstorm possibilities with her built-in best friend, but what good would that do? Telling Kristen everything that had happened was one thing. Telling her everything that might happen?

One look at Kristen, with her head bent over her phone and brow pulled tight, and Cassie made up her mind.

Her sister, plus her family as a whole, had already been through a lot in the last couple of years. Some of it had been personal; most of it had had to do with the scar that would forever be on Cassie's neck.

The bullet that had almost killed her, shot by a man who had simply missed his original target.

If someone was *actually* trying to target her?

Cassie fanned her fingers across her stomach. Protecting her unborn child.

Trying to keep her nerves from overwhelming her. Some what-ifs were better left unsaid.

"You okay, Kristen?"

Kristen was startled but recovered with a scowl. "Yeah, but no." She stood, agitated. "Work drama. Apparently the Danvers finally want to look at the Banana House out in Darby. I asked to reschedule and then Candice swooped in, fangs out."

"Banana House?" Henry asked at their elbow as they moved into the hallway. The department was still bustling from trying to get their communications in order. How would it be when Suzy told them to ready themselves for potential battle?

"It's this yellow monstrosity of a house about an hour from here," Kristen answered. "It's been on the market for three years and this older couple from Florida expressed interest in it a while ago. I've been trying to *gently* push them to look at it and they decided today was the day."

"And Candice is her work nemesis," Cassie added.

"Think of me as Luke Skywalker," Kristen said, spreading her arms out dramatically. "And Candice as Darth Vader, who's determined to steal all my clients out from under my nose."

Henry snorted.

"Before you ask, yes, she's seen all the *Star Wars* movies," Cassie intervened. "She knows she just basically said her nemesis Realtor is her father."

Henry laughed again but didn't say anything as they made it outside. Even out of her periphery, Cassie saw his body tighten. Reality was closing in on them again. The next time they stepped foot in the same parking lot, everything could be different.

Cassie thought about Billy holed up in the hospital.

She rubbed her stomach again.

"You know, Kristen, call the Danvers back and tell them you're on your way." Cassie rallied. She focused on keeping all her fears and worries from her voice.

Still, Kristen started to shake her head. "I'm not leaving you, especially not after that man walked right up to your front porch! Banana house, be damned."

Cassie pushed her thumb back at the deputy close behind them.

"He isn't just here for show," she said matter-of-factly. "He's going to be my shadow for the next few hours, just in case. Nothing but a lot of just sitting around and being bored. Plus, you've already done your due diligence in getting me here."

They stopped next to Kristen's car. Cassie had already made up her mind. She wasn't going to leave with her sister. No, she wanted her out and gone from Carpenter for now if she could swing it.

However, Kristen's jaw was set firm. "Cassie, that man knows where you live. What's to keep him from showing up again? No, I'm not leaving while you willingly go back like you've forgotten that fact."

Cassie opened her mouth, though she didn't know how to respond. Kristen was the only relation she had in the area, and her house was a stone's throw away. Cassie wasn't about to try to stay with friends, especially considering most were her colleagues or either their loved ones. If she *was* a target?

She would never forgive herself for willingly putting her friends and their families in danger.

"She can come stay at my place until you're done."

The certainty and surprise of Henry's baritone sent

a wayward shiver of feeling through Cassie. She hoped the smile she threw on covered it.

"Only a few people in the department even know where I'm staying. Not even my brother knows exactly where I've been laying my head. I doubt Michael, or anyone, could track me down easily."

Kristen looked between them, uncertain.

"And if they did?" she asked, protectiveness clearly thronging through her voice.

Henry returned the feeling with some of his own. "Then I'd make sure they got what was coming to them."

It was a promise.

One that Cassie believed with all her being.

One that Kristen seemed to believe in, too.

She nodded, but not before throwing her arms around Cassie.

"I want you to text me every half hour," she said into her ear. "Got it?"

Cassie smiled into Kristen's wild hair. "Got it."

They shared another embrace before Kristen got into her car. Henry stayed at Cassie's elbow, silent, as they watched her drive away. It wasn't until they were sitting inside his personal car that he spoke again. "You don't want to be around her just in case you're a target."

His gaze slid to her throat. Once again the scar at her neck burned. For the first time since she had met the man, Cassie realized there was a chance he had no idea where it had come from. After they'd gotten close, and she believed they were about to get closer, all those months ago, Cassie had almost told him.

But she hadn't wanted his pity.

She hadn't wanted to relive it, either.

Now, though?

Now she found she wanted him to know.

And not just because it would explain the grisly scar, but because it might show him the severity of what could happen when meaningless anger and violence were directed even at the places where they felt the safest.

Cassie slowly touched the circular scar and spoke around the lump forming in her throat. "Before Billy married his wife, she became the target of some really bad people. They didn't play by any rules of decency and targeted Billy and Mara's daughter. While everyone was trying to figure out what was going on, I offered to watch her. We were in the conference room when a shooter took aim at a witness inside the department."

Cassie tapped the scar. The fear of that day threatened to burst through her defenses. She held strong. "The first shot found me instead of the mark. I managed to pull Alexa into a corner and cover her until Billy and Mara could get her to safety. I lost consciousness after that and almost bled out."

Henry's jaw hardened.

His eyes narrowed.

His nostrils flared.

It helped her continue.

"I made it through everything, and I absolutely don't regret helping Billy and Mara. You see, I love them and the rest of the department. They're friends. They're family. But there is one thing I do regret about everything that happened."

"What your family went through," Henry guessed, surprising her.

Nevertheless, he was right.

"They won't say it, but it nearly destroyed my parents. They stayed by my side for months while I recovered.

My brothers and sisters weren't far behind. They all tried their best to get me to move away from Riker County, even offering up their homes to me. But I didn't want to move. I've made this place my home. One I want to grow old in. One I want to raise my family in."

She averted her eyes for a second. Was Henry now included in that family? Did he want to be? Cassie sighed and finished her story. "It wasn't until Kristen moved to Carpenter that everyone backed off. If you ask why she moved here, she'll tell you that she wanted a change and had fallen in love with Carpenter when we were young. That she's too self-involved to uproot her life to keep an eye on her baby sister since everyone else is married or has careers that they can't just leave. But the truth is, after I nearly died, something in my family changed and she's had the hardest time dealing with it. I don't think she'll ever leave my side."

She straightened in her seat and cleared her throat.

She had finally made it to her point, even if she hadn't known what it was when she'd started. "People can do awful, awful things sometimes and within the space of a moment everything can change. Whatever it is that Calvin, Michael and whoever else might be out there has planned, I won't let it hurt the ones I love. If that means keeping them in the dark and keeping a low profile? Then so be it. You won't get any resistance from me."

Henry started to speak but Cassie cut him off.

"But I'm here to tell you that I'm not some pregnant damsel in distress," she added, words heated. With them she felt a surge of adrenaline and decisiveness. Cassie looked into the true-blue eyes of a man who had given her the best gift she'd ever received in her entire life and gave him her ultimatum. "Whatever you choose to do in regards to being in my child's life, I will support. If you want to be a part of his life, I will be on board. If you don't want to be a father, then I can make that work, too. But only if you help me do one thing. Help me figure out why Calvin Fitzgerald is in my town, why he wants you dead, and how the sheriff's department plays into it all before anyone else gets hurt. Deal?"

Henry's face was blank. She couldn't read his thoughts let alone any feelings he'd had at her words. It didn't matter. What she needed now was his word.

And she got it.

"Deal."

Chapter Thirteen

"You're staying *here*?"

Henry pulled into the hotel parking lot and followed it around back, the Eagle in his rearview mirror. Cassie's lips settled into a frown. Even without lipstick they were a luscious red. The same lips he'd gotten acquainted with in the very same hotel he was parking behind.

"I liked it well enough the last time I was here. I figured why roll the dice on trying to find a new one?"

Cassie didn't respond. In fact, after giving her grand speech at the department, she hadn't said a word during the drive over. It wasn't like he had, either. The blonde had a way of throwing him off his game.

First, she'd opened up about the scar he'd always wondered about. That alone had his blood boiling—when everything settled down, he'd make sure to pull that report and read it personally—but then she'd switched gears on him so fast he'd barely been able to keep a straight face.

If you want to be a part of his life, I will be on board. If you don't want to be a father, then I can make that work, too.

Just like that, she'd given him a choice. Two, actually. To be in his son's life or not.

Was it that simple?

He knew which way his heart was leaning, but then there his brain was, pulling the other way.

He'd led a dangerous, mostly solitary life for the last several years. One that already had consequences threatening his new home.

Calvin.

Henry fisted his hand as he got out of the car. Cassie was right. They needed to figure out the now before he could even think about the future. *That* was his choice. Protecting the beautiful woman a few feet away and the child she was carrying, and stopping whatever Calvin intended to do.

The hotel was a five-story box. No pool, no mints on pillows and a small staff. Nothing fancy. However Henry enjoyed it. Mainly for its proximity to the Eagle and several restaurants and shopping farther down the block. At night the sounds of pleasant chatter rose to his window. It was a far cry from what he'd been used to undercover.

Cassie followed him like she had blinders on. She didn't look at Mike as they passed through the lobby. The potbellied day manager had his favorite classical music station playing from a small Bluetooth speaker underneath the front desk. He gave them a friendly wave, which only Henry returned. Like the staff of the Eagle across the street, Mike made it no secret that he was a fan of local law enforcement. He'd even gotten Henry a deal on his room.

Which Henry realized might have been one of the reasons Cassie's brow was furrowed deeper than her frown. Something that was confirmed when she took one look at the sign across the elevator's closed doors.

"Out of order," she deadpanned. "Does that mean I have to walk up five flights of stairs?"

She placed her palm over her stomach. Her cheeks took on a rosy tint. Henry wasn't sure if it was from the weather or something else.

"I'm not staying in the same room as last time, if that's what you're asking." Memories, hot and sizzling, soft and sweet, all threatened to come back as he thought about Room 504.

Not the time, Ward, he thought to himself. A second later he found himself wondering if she was struggling with the same thoughts.

Or, judging by her tone, maybe her memories of their time spent there hadn't been good ones.

That was another thought that didn't sit right with him.

"I have a bigger room this time," he said, steering her toward the stairs in the corner of the lobby. "It's a suite on the second floor."

Cassie nodded. He chanced a look her way. The lines across her forehead began to smooth.

"Good. Because if it was on a higher floor I might just stay down here." She made a grunt and kicked out one of her feet. "One perk of pregnancy that has stuck with me has been swollen feet. They're trying to break out of my shoes like a pair of inmates wanting to flee prison."

Henry stifled a laugh.

He had zero experience with pregnant women, but he had a feeling laughing at their pregnancy pains was a big no-no.

So instead he kept quiet and pulled out his key.

The smell of lemon cleaners and fabric softener filled his senses the moment they stepped into the second-floor hallway. Another reason he'd chosen to stay at the hotel while he searched for a place to live was in part how clean the place was. After spending years doing undercover work and staying in less than desirable locales, Henry found how much he valued a well-kept place to rest his head. Not to mention a relatively safe place. The simple layout of one long hallway with rooms off to each side and another stairwell at its end was also a bonus in his eyes.

Hard to be ambushed when you could see everything in one glance.

Room 201 was on the corner and because of that fact gave them three sets of windows instead of the two that all the suites had. The living area had one over the TV and its stand that looked out at the employee parking lot and the offices next door and another on the connecting wall that showed a clear view of the Eagle across the street. The third window from the small but efficient bedroom had the same view. Cassie took a moment to look through each but stopped short of the open door that led to the third. Instead she redirected herself to the couch.

When she looked back up at him, her expression was expectant.

"Now let's talk about Calvin," she said.

Henry caught himself smiling.

"You want anything first?" he asked, motioning to the minifridge next to the TV stand. "All I have is bottled water, but I was thinking about calling in some food to the front." On cue his stomach groaned. He patted it, hitting muscle. "I don't think I've eaten today, to be honest."

Cassie perked up a little. She mimicked his stomach-patting. "I already ate but I'd be lying if I said I couldn't do it again." Her cheeks flushed rosy once more. "Do you think you could call in some pizza?"

He nodded. "Yes, ma'am."

CASSIE DECIDED NOT to push on about Calvin until after their pizza was delivered. In truth her ultimatum had caught even her off guard, especially when she'd been ready to pull the trigger the moment they'd stepped into the hotel suite. Then again, she hadn't been prepared to be back at the scene of the crime, so to speak.

The room might have been plain, small and on a different floor, but Cassie felt like she was surrounded by hot spots of memories. The elevator had been the first one. The pale blue room door had been another.

The bed, with its king-size frame and white linens, was like something someone had stuck a blinking, neon marquee light over with an arrow pointing at its top.

She'd had to sit to ground herself, her thoughts. Her body.

Because, no matter what her mind said about Deputy Henry Ward, her hormones were steadfast in their thoughts about him.

He was a tall drink of sexy.

With and without his clothes on.

Though Cassie found herself almost drooling about the latter. Running her hands over the flat, muscled stomach as it hovered over her. Moaning while his lips caressed the side of her neck, moving down across her exposed skin. Feeling the hardness behind his zipper, pressing against her own desire.

"They said to give them about fifteen," Henry said, coming back into the living area. "Mike will call me down when they get here. I told him I didn't want anyone knowing where I was staying. Old habits, but I guess they're working out for us so far."

Cassie felt the scorching heat flash up her body and into her cheeks. She'd gone and let her hormones get the better of her and, boy, had they done a dang good job! Just remembering the start of their night months ago had put her entire body in a state of lust.

One that was holding even as her brain was shouting that this was a different situation. A different time.

"You okay?" Henry asked before she could even fumble together a response to what he'd said before. Every part of her seemed to be warring between reaching out to the man a few feet from her and the idea of running right out of the hotel and never looking back.

"Oh, yeah, I'm just a little warm." She scrambled for words, standing quickly. "You know I used to be good with the summers here and…well, I'm not anymore. If you excuse me, I think I might go to the bathroom for a moment."

Henry's eyebrow arched and then his expression was covered in concern.

That same concern only started to ignite more fires within her.

She wanted him to hold her. To soothe her. To touch her.

Which was why she nearly ran to the bathroom. Shutting the door with a little too much force, Cassie rounded to the sink and turned the water on high. She splashed the coldness on her face for a good minute.

Yet it barely made a dent in the sheer amount of desire coursing through her.

"Pregnancy hormones," she whispered to herself. "That's all this is. Biological. Normal. That's it."

Her words and rationale did little to settle the swell of her chest. Her heartbeat was starting to gallop just at the thought of Henry's fingers moving along her body, stopping only to tease her. How her nipples had hardened into pearls as his tongue had followed behind, sending her nearly to the brink without even getting to the main event yet.

How the warmth of him had moved against her, both swollen with desire.

How he'd captured her mouth when she bowed up against him, wanting—*needing*—more.

Cassie could still remember how she'd balled fistfuls of the sheets in her hands as he'd pressed against her opening, teasing.

Then, slowly, he'd moved inside enough for them both to feel the beginning of what could be fantastic before pulling back out.

"Not yet," he'd said, voice thrumming low and heavy. Cassie had moved her hands up his biceps and wound them in his hair. She had gotten a good grip and pulled his mouth down to hers, hungry.

It had been a move he clearly hadn't anticipated.

One he couldn't fight, either.

He'd parried her tongue with hers, grabbed her hips and had thrust deep inside her.

Cassie had moaned as Henry's movements slowed. The heat and hardness filled her, pushing her closer and closer to the edge again. When he'd picked up speed, she'd barely been able to keep it together.

Two bodies in want. Feeding off each other's desires. Playing off each other's pleasures.

Then together they'd both let go.

As far as Cassie was concerned, nothing aside from that room had existed that night.

And now?

She looked at her reflection. It was easy to see what she wanted. Just as it was hard to deny the attraction she felt for Henry would still be there with or without pregnancy hormones.

A knock sounded on the door.

The low baritone that had once washed over her naked body soon followed.

"Cassie?"

Her fingers curled around the edges of the sink. She felt her nipples harden beneath her bra.

How could he affect her so strongly?

His voice alone seemed to be tied to every part of her.

Before she could clobber up a response, another knock sounded.

It wasn't on her door, this time it was farther away.

"Turn out the light and stay in there," came Henry's voice. It was harsh. Quick.

It took every feeling of desire, lust and a good deal of the unknown surrounding both to shut them down. Hard.

Cassie flipped the light switch. Darkness enveloped her.

Her heartbeat continued to gallop.

This time it was from fear.

She held her breath, straining to hear. They were probably both overreacting. Maybe the pizza man had been really close? And already had their pizza made and ready within the minute or so it had taken to order?

Cassie's stomach knotted.

Maybe it was someone from the department.

Henry had already said a few had known where he was staying.

Or, maybe, it was Kristen.

Though, with a sinking feeling, Cassie realized they hadn't even told her where they were going other than to some hotel.

Cassie took a step toward the door. She leaned her ear against it, hoping against all hope that her feat was unwarranted. That she was just being silly. That her emotions were all over the place because she was pregnant.

A loud *bang* sounded in the suite. The door shook against her face. Cassie covered the scream that tried to tear itself from her mouth.

She had to use both hands when another sound came through the door.

Something heavy had fallen.

Or someone.

Chapter Fourteen

The world spun.

Henry fell. The weight of the hotel door pushing him hard to the floor. His head whipped back against it. Spots danced along his vision. He was going to pass out.

The man filling the doorway was breathing in and out like a bull readying to charge. The whites of his eyes were wild and wide, contrasting against his dark clothes and complexion. He had on a pair of hiking boots that had no doubt helped him kick the door right off its hinges. If it had been a newer hotel, he would have had to try a lot harder. As it was, Henry currently had a hunk of aged wood against him.

Which he needed to remedy.

Fast.

"Where is he?" the man roared. "Where is Matt Walker?"

Henry ignored his doubling vision and used his own boots to kick off the fragmented door. He reached for his hip holster, but the man stopped his questioning long enough to see the move. Henry rolled to the side as the Goliath ran forward and slammed his foot down, right where Henry's head had just been, like he was trying to crush a bug.

Again Henry's head threatened to spiral him into the darkness of unconsciousness but he rallied against it. Adrenaline pumped through his veins. He unbuttoned the clasp of his holster and pulled his gun. Goliath roared again. A meaty fist collided with Henry's jaw. The same one Suzy had already bruised. Bright, hot pain shot across his chin.

"I saw you two together last night," Goliath yelled, swinging his other fist around like an ambidextrous prizefighter. "Where does he live?"

Henry didn't have time to answer his questions. He rolled to his right, avoiding another blow. Whoever the man was, he was determined.

Henry just didn't know what he was more determined about. Crushing him? Or getting answers to his questions?

Either way, Henry wasn't about to take the time to suss it out. He got to his feet and had to do a quick two-step backward, just out of Goliath's raging wingspan.

One thing Henry did know—he was through playing defense.

Using as much power as he could put in his non-dominant fist, he repaid the man in kind for the pain now radiating across his jaw. The hit connected hard. Goliath staggered to the side but didn't fall.

Still, it created space between them and was enough of a window that Henry could use.

He brandished his gun with enough adrenaline backing him that he almost felt like he could take the man on with one hand.

But with Cassie hiding in the bathroom, he didn't want to take any chances. "Freeze or I'll shoot!"

Goliath roared.

And did something Henry hadn't expected.

He did exactly as he was told.

Chest heaving and rage clear in his dark eyes, Goliath looked down his large nose at Henry and obeyed.

"Do you have any weapons on you?" Henry asked, reinforcing his stance. If the man so much as twitched in his direction, he'd take him out. No more chances.

"I *am* the weapon," he said with reverence. There was enough ego to choke a horse.

"Any knives or a gun?" Henry pushed.

The man blew out a snort through his nose. Again, reminiscent of an angry bull. In this instance Henry was the red flag. "Where is Matt Walker?" he asked instead. Malice dripped off each syllable.

Henry didn't understand the question. Or, really, why *he* was being asked and how it fit into breaking down *his* hotel room door. "What's it to you?"

Goliath seemed to be close to bursting at the seams. Pent-up anger mixed with adrenaline and, by the glaze of his eyes, probably narcotics of some kind. Henry recognized that destructive energy. He'd been around it on the ranch undercover. He'd felt it himself once or twice, too.

Whatever was in the man a few feet from him, he wasn't going to hold it in much longer. Gun pointing in his face or not.

Henry was already on thin ice. And only growing heavier with as each second went by.

"He ruined my life," Goliath said. "I want to repay him for that."

"And why are you here?" Henry couldn't resist asking.

Goliath's eyes trailed over his shoulder to the window behind him. Henry wasn't about to turn his back on the man, though.

"I can't find him. He doesn't live in the same house he used to. You were with him yesterday, but I couldn't follow you. So you know where he lives. Where he is now." He glanced back at Henry like he was a mild annoyance. "And it's almost time for—"

"You boys sure do talk a lot."

For one wild moment Henry thought it was Cassie who interrupted. But the woman who sashayed through the open door and around Goliath was definitely not the woman he'd had on his mind the last several months.

Henry ball-parked her age in the mid to late twenties. He didn't recognize her. Tall, thin and sneering, she had jet-black hair, braided in pigtails, wore a black tank top that showed her pierced belly button and a pair of dark jeans that were so tight they left little to the imagination. Not that Henry cared about any of that. What he was pinpoint focused on was the shotgun she held steady in her hands.

He met her aim with his own. She didn't flinch.

Instead she *tsk*ed at him.

"I'm quick," she said, her sneer widening. "And even if I'm not…"

Movement caught his eye but not his aim as another unknown entered the room. This time it was a man. Compared to the threat that Goliath and the woman obviously presented, he did little to compare. Short and wiry, he was sweating openly. Nervous. The handgun he moved in Henry's direction shook.

"Jason may be slightly useless, but he *does* know how to pull a trigger," she added.

If Jason was offended, he didn't show it.

Henry kept his aim on the woman.

Three against one.

He should have taken out Goliath when he'd had the chance.

"So how's this going to play out?" Henry kept his voice even. Calm. He aimed the question at the woman. She seemed to be the one in charge. "You threaten to kill me to get to Matt?"

Goliath actually smiled. Henry was talking his language now.

The woman, however, wasn't. She laughed.

"I don't care about Detective Walker," she clarified. "In fact, I don't care about you, either. I just need you to be here and be still for a little while. So, if you'd please, put your gun down before I let Kevin here rip you from limb to limb like he seems to want to."

Goliath, apparently named Kevin, swung his head around, already biting his words off in anger. "He said I could have Matt. This guy knows where he is. So he's mine."

The woman wasn't amused. Her sneer wiped off, replaced by thinly veiled disgust. "I run things here. He stays here *and* alive until I say." She snorted. "You shouldn't have waited so long to get your shit together, Kevin. You should have already done your homework like everyone else. Not my fault you're an idiot."

Kevin rounded on the woman so fast that Henry barely had time to clear the shotgun blast she sent into the big man's chest. Blood and bone and everything in between exploded along with sound through the small area. The woman might have been ready to shoot, but she hadn't braced herself properly. She flew backward into the small dining set in the corner next to the door. Kevin went in the opposite direction.

Henry's ears rang with the shot, but he wasn't about

to waste his opening. He turned his gun toward Jason. The man might have been nervous, but his boss had been right. He did know how to pull a trigger. He shot at Henry but missed, hand shaking like a leaf.

Henry could have ended him right there, but he refused to return fire. Not when his angle was all off. If he missed the man or the bullet went straight through him, its trajectory would be pointed straight at the bathroom. He wasn't about to chance Cassie or his son.

His son.

The thought flashed across his mind with such an intense feeling of protectiveness that it rallied Henry even more. He knew then that, no matter what, he'd take on anyone and anything to keep his child safe.

Rushing the small man who looked like he was about to unravel? A no-brainer.

Henry closed the space between them before Jason could get another shot off. He grabbed his wrist and pulled up hard. The man let out a cry and dropped his gun but not before Henry used the butt of his service weapon to strengthen his next blow. The hit dazed the man. He fell to his knees. Henry drew back and landed a knock-out hit. Jason crumpled to the floor with a whimper.

"Ah!"

Henry turned in time to see the shotgun discarded on the floor in the corner. The woman who had been wielding it, however, was not. With a twisted face filled with violence, she was on him within seconds. This time she was swinging a knife. He yelled as it sliced into his shoulder.

"I…can't…kill…you," she grunted against him as he

grabbed the hilt of the knife, keeping it from going in any farther. "But… I…can…*hurt you*!"

She kicked out and hit him in the groin. He brought his gun up to her stomach, but she used another move he hadn't anticipated against him.

With a wild cry she head-butted him.

Pain blossomed across his nose as blood instantly rushed out. The gun in his hand hit the floor, but he wasn't going to let the crazed woman get the better of him. He used his free shoulder and pushed her off him enough to get room to land a kick. It pushed her small frame backward and to the floor.

Henry bent to get his gun, but the woman recoiled like a gold-medaled gymnast. Maybe Kevin hadn't been the only one on something. If he didn't get her under control soon—

A gunshot ran out once again in the suite. The woman fell back once more on the carpet. This time she didn't spring back up. Instead she cried out, cradling her arm.

Henry laced his fingers around his service weapon and turned to take on whoever the new player was. It wasn't like there seemed to be honor among the group so far.

But this time Henry did recognize the shooter.

Cassie stood in a nearly perfect stance, gun held firmly and eyes set on her target.

"You come at him again and I'll prove to you that I was aiming to hit your arm," she said. Not a waver or a break in her voice. "Then I'll aim for something else."

"You've *got* to be kidding me," the woman said in response. Though she didn't make an attempt to move again. "Damn, Henry! You had a pregnant lady waiting in the wings as backup. I didn't see that coming." Despite her precarious situation, she laughed. Henry grabbed the knife in his shoulder and pulled it out. He tossed it behind him, angry.

"Who do you work for?" he asked, not caring how cliché it sounded.

The woman clenched her upper arm. Blood pushed out between her fingers. Still she kept her smile. "Don't tell me you've already forgotten about your partner, Deputy. Because I'll tell you what, he hasn't forgotten about you." She nodded to the dead body she'd created in the middle of the room. "All of this is really for you."

Thunder rumbled in the distance. The light in the room had dimmed since Kevin kicked down the door. It only added to a rise of foreboding in Henry's stomach. What was going on? What was Calvin's game?

"I don't understand," he admitted. "How is any of this for me? How is finding Matt part of it?"

The woman laughed. This time she flinched at the movement. "That was Kevin's target. *His* chance at revenge." She shrugged, flinching again. "You aren't the only one who's stepped on some toes during your career."

Another crash of thunder sounded. Closer.

She turned toward the window.

Henry chanced a glance out, too.

A blanket of clouds darkened the sky above the Eagle and the town behind it. More menacing than the earlier flash storm that had popped up. By the looks of it, this one had staying power.

That was when it clicked.

Henry's blood ran cold.

"'As soon as it gets dark, all hell will rain down,'" he said, repeating what Travis had said in the interrogation room. The woman turned to him, lips already curving up into a smile. "You weren't waiting for the night. You were waiting for a storm."

"That's how all this is really for you," she said, positively radiating some kind of sick satisfaction. It was unsettling an already anxious feeling, pulling his muscles tight in anticipation. "He said this would be your perfect nightmare."

Lightning flashed.

Henry backed away from the woman and moved closer to Cassie, never taking his eyes off the former. "Cassie, there's a flashlight in the top drawer in the nightstand," he rasped. "Get it. Now."

Henry sensed Cassie's hesitation. Judging by the woman's smile, they might not be able to afford it.

"Ah, there it is," she cooed. "Now you know what happens next." She turned her head to face the window. As if she didn't have a care in the world. "Out there is about to get crazy. Don't say I didn't try to protect you, Deputy Ward."

Henry heard the drawer in the next room open. Cassie had to have been maybe five steps behind him. It was too far away.

Another boom lightly shook the glass in the windows. This time it wasn't thunder.

Henry watched helplessly as the town of Carpenter's power slowly blinked out.

"Cassie?" He tried, but it was too late.

The lights didn't even flicker. They all just went out.

Chapter Fifteen

The AC whirled as it shut down. The air in the suite went from cool to stale in what felt like one second flat. It was such a loud silence by contrast that Cassie stalled by the edge of the bed. What had been the beginning of a storm in the distance was now a darkness that reached through the windows and created the void she had been thrown into.

The adrenaline high she'd taken advantage of after hearing Henry cry out in pain was dropping off.

Suddenly she felt like a child again, terrified of the darkness.

"Cassie."

She couldn't see him, but Henry's voice was enough to bring her out of the fear clinching her chest like a vise. She remembered the weight in her hand. The flashlight was small but illuminated her immediate area. Enough that she saw Henry's concern clearly.

Without being asked Cassie tossed the light over. He was fast to turn it on the woman who had attacked him. She hadn't moved from her spot. She was still smiling, too.

It sent a chill down Cassie's spine.

"The more you shine that thing on me, the faster he'll

end up finding you," the woman said, almost coyly. Like she was trying to flirt with Henry. Cassie didn't like it for several reasons.

"Cassie, can you keep a gun on her while I get my cuffs?"

Henry's entire demeanor was hard. He was channeling the law right now.

In answer Cassie lifted her gun and braced her feet apart again. She knew how to shoot and not just because she worked in a sheriff's department. Three Christmases ago, her eldest brother, Davie, had given each of his sisters shooting lessons and paid for their classes to get licenses to carry. She'd have to make sure to thank him again.

Henry propped the flashlight on the coffee table so the woman was in the spotlight and made quick work of cuffing her to a wooden leg of the entertainment cabinet. He left her wounded arm alone and free. Not that it would do much good. If she wanted to escape she'd have to flip the cabinet and the TV. Cassie doubted she could manage it at the awkward angle she was sitting on the floor.

But if she did, at least they'd hear it and have a heads-up.

The woman stayed quiet during the deed and didn't try to resist. It somehow made Cassie even more nervous than if she had tried. The woman was too confident, which made everything she'd said to Henry in the last few minutes even more terrifying.

Calvin, and who knew who else, was coming.

Could she shoot him, too?

Cassie's stomach twisted. She'd never shot someone before. She was a dispatcher, for heaven's sake. The most action she'd seen was when *she* had gotten shot.

Suddenly the rest of the hotel suite started to come into focus around the beam of light. The shadows of two bodies were in front of her. One unconscious, one dead. The scent of copper filled the air. Cassie felt light-headed.

Not copper.

Blood.

"I—I need to leave." Even to her own ears she heard her voice break. The silence before and after made the fragility of it even more noticeable. She wasn't the same woman who had just shot someone in the arm.

Both Henry and the woman turned to look at her. Only one was smirking.

"I think she just realized she's standing in Kevin's blood and guts," the woman said. "Might want to make sure if she passes out to do it backward and not forward."

Cassie wanted to reply with something witty but the woman was right. She *was* about to pass out. Her vision started to tunnel. Without the flashlight's beam she might not have noticed the difference. A cold sweat broke out all over her body.

Henry was at her side in a flash, picking up the flashlight in the process. Its bouncing beam did little to help her attempt to calm down.

"Why don't you go back into the bathroom?" he urged. "I'll call in to the department and come and get you when someone gets here."

He tried to gently nudge her back into the closet-size bathroom. It caused an almost overwhelming sense of anxiety within her.

"I don't want to be trapped in there again," she whispered. "It's too small. It feels like being backed into a corner." She reached out and took his forearm. Warmth spread between them. It helped anchor her thoughts. "And I already tried to get hold of someone while I was in there. No one answered." She squeezed his arm as dread began to pool in her stomach. *"No one."*

The woman laughed.

"You're all cut off now, honey," she said. "Now all we have is the fun."

Henry stiffened. The unmistakable sounds of voices shouting somewhere in the building floated through the open door.

"Don't look so surprised. I might not be a top dog, but one of them sure does like me."

"Oh, God, they're coming for her," Cassie related. That was why the woman wasn't afraid. Which meant she thought Henry and Cassie were no match. Cassie thought about her unborn child. "What do we do?"

Henry took less time to contemplate. He moved the beam over the woman's face one more time. When he spoke, his voice was low and thick with anger. "Tell Calvin only children play games."

Then he took Cassie by the hand and pulled her along with him into the hallway. He barely took a beat before cutting to the right and running. The flashlight beam did little to quell the fear of the dark around them. Whoever had been shouting in the lobby was now pounding up the stairwell behind them.

Luckily, they weren't going to be seen.

Henry opened the door to the second set of stairs and ushered her inside. This time he stopped for a moment, listening. Cassie tried to mimic him, but her heart was hammering against her rib cage so hard she wasn't sure if that was what she was hearing or thunder in the distance.

"The Eagle," he whispered when he was satisfied

with what he did or didn't hear. "Would Hawk have guns there?"

Cassie was surprised he knew the bar owner's nickname, but she answered. "Yes, and he'd be ready to shoot them."

Henry readjusted the flashlight and started down the stairs, careful not to pull her too much. Which was good; she was starting to get really winded. Since she'd found out she was pregnant, she'd been doing prenatal yoga and other exercises to keep her in shape the best she could, but running for her life hadn't been on the recommended list of daily activities.

Another roar of thunder shook the building. This time the rain wasn't far behind. Henry swore under his breath but kept on. When they got to the door leading out, however, he turned to face her full-on for the first time. As he aimed the flashlight down between them, Cassie could barely make out the blue of his eyes as shadows danced across his face.

"Do you trust me?"

It was such an odd question. Simple yet in no way simple. One yes or no answer that fundamentally changed how their relationship would work.

Did Cassie trust Henry Ward?

The man who had stolen her heart with no obvious plan to return it.

The man who had said nothing of the child they shared in her stomach.

The man who she'd known less than a handful of days and yet felt a connection with unlike any other she'd felt before.

Cassie already knew the answer. "I do."

"Good. Because I have a plan. One that you might not like."

THE SIDE DOOR led out to a covered walkway that looped around the back of the hotel. Since the front of the building began a foot from the sidewalk, anyone checking in used the drive there instead. Which meant as soon as they cleared the awning they were currently under, they'd be pummeled by the rain.

And lose most of their already limited visibility.

"Are you okay to run again?" Henry asked. There was no point trying to whisper when Mother Nature was all-out yelling around them. Thunder and lightning sparred in the sky. Too close for comfort. Just like Calvin's lackeys inside.

Caught between a rock and a hard place?

More like forced between a hard place and a hard place.

In the dark.

"Yeah, but I don't think I can go that fast." Cassie held her belly in one hand and her gun in the other. It was a sight that unsettled him yet made him feel a twinge of pride. Not only had she probably saved his life, she'd done it seven months' pregnant to boot.

"I'm going to let you go first just in case they decide to pop up behind us, okay?"

Cassie nodded. Another boom of thunder drew her frown in on itself. She reached out and took the flashlight from him. The storm was heavy but not nasty. Not yet, anyway. Without the streetlamps, the only light they had to pull from was the sky itself, and that was dim at best. If Henry hadn't been comfortable with the Eagle, he might not have attempted the trip. He reached out and took Cassie's shoulder. Together they moved out and through the rain.

Cassie went faster than he expected but did her due

diligence before crossing each street lane. The Eagle didn't get popular until around seven and the hotel was in one of its slower months. Not to mention, as far as he could tell, Carpenter had gone lights out. If anyone was in the hotel, he hoped they were sticking to their rooms after hearing the gunshots. He also hoped that Mike the manager was still alive. Henry had a feeling the man wouldn't have let the woman and her goons upstairs without a fight.

Now the question was if Hawk the bar owner was in his bar and would willingly help.

They made it to the front double doors without any people or cars coming at them. The bar was dark, like the rest of the block save for the small light in Cassie's hand. She waved it across the glass. Henry stopped her before she opened the door.

"If anything goes sideways, I want you to run and hide," he said, angling down so his mouth was next to her ear. The rain had only intensified the smell of her shampoo. Citrus and spice. An intoxicating mixture against the wet skin of a beautiful woman. "Okay, Cassie?"

She nodded against the rain, hair darkening as it grew more wet, and let Henry pull her behind him. She kept the flashlight over his shoulder as they moved inside. Henry kept his gun low but wasn't for a second going to let them be ambushed.

Again.

Like the hotel suite, the inside of the Eagle was so quiet it was nearly deafening. The air was still cool from the AC but felt stiff in the open, dark space. Cassie swept her light ahead and across the bar. No one was behind it or at any of the tables or booths. The main room was empty.

"The door was unlocked," Cassie said, this time at his ear. Without the rain beating down on them, she went back to a worried whisper. "Hawk has to be in the back."

Henry turned and put his finger to his lips. Cassie fell silent, eyes widening. He would bet Hawk *was* in the back. It was just his condition Henry was concerned about. What if the woman and her goons had looked for him at the Eagle first?

He walked Cassie to the corner, out of view from the windows if the lights did come back on, and pressed his fingers to his lips one more time to push his point home again. If he could, Henry wanted to keep Cassie a secret like he had done in the hotel room. There were too many unknown variables. He couldn't guarantee her safety if all hell hit the fan. It was that thought alone that had made up his mind to run across the street in the first place.

Cassie handed the flashlight to him. He put the small light in his mouth and pulled out his gun. He moved as quietly as his wet boots would allow across the hardwood until he was behind the bar at a door that led into the kitchen.

No one jumped out or said anything. The silence from the main room stretched all the way past the grill and cooler out into another door that led to a small hallway. Henry tilted to look toward the front of the building. The hallway ran to the front, passing two small bathrooms. He moved his chin around to face the other end. The beam lit up two doors. One led, he assumed, to the back alley. If he had to guess, the other led to the office. The door was open.

The sound of rain pelting the one-story building intensified. Henry moved down the hall, muscles coiling in anticipation. His brother's voice echoed through his head.

You are good at a lot of things, Henry, but stealth isn't your strong suit.

Hopefully he'd gotten better since Garrett had made the comment. Though the moment he swung around the open doorway, gun and flashlight high, he realized that maybe his brother was still right.

"Don't move or I'll blast a hole through your chest," the man said, eyes narrowing in the light.

For what felt like the umpteenth time in the last two days, someone had a gun pointing at Henry.

And, boy, was it getting old fast!

Chapter Sixteen

Henry lowered his gun slowly. With his free hand he took the flashlight from his mouth, also slowly. The man nick-named Hawk had been waiting in the dark for him. He surely wasn't going to loosen his stance any time soon. Better not to spook him.

"My name's Henry Ward," he started, keeping the flashlight pointed ahead. "I'm the new deputy at the sheriff's department. I was in here several months ago and—"

"And helped get Gary to his cab in exchange for a drink," he interrupted gruffly. "I'm bald, not dumb. Why are you here in my business, lurking around with your gun out?"

Henry motioned toward the hallway. He needed to be honest. If the sheriff and the department seemed to trust the bartender, then he would, too. Especially considering his own track record with apparently misplacing trust. "I've been staying across the road. A few minutes ago we were ambushed by three perps before the lights went out. One's dead and the other two were incapacitated, but more came into the building. I didn't want to take any chances of a shoot-out, since my friend's pregnant.

I thought she'd stand a better chance being here until things got sorted out."

Hawk's demeanor barely shifted. He didn't lower his gun but his eyes went over Henry's shoulder. "Who's your friend?"

"Cassie Gates."

It was like her name was the magic word. The hardened man across from Henry lowered his gun and took up a look of such great concern that he felt a shot of adrenaline go through him.

"Is Cassie okay?" Hawk asked, bending to pick up something.

Henry was relieved to see it was a camping lantern. A soft fluorescent light flooded the room. It was small but powerful. "She could probably use a place to rest, but I think she's okay."

Henry stepped into the hallway and they started back to the front.

"You know, I thought I heard a few shots, but with the weather, I chalked it up to thunder," Hawk said, trailing behind him. "Then my cell phone lost service and the lights went out. Knew it was trouble."

"It was intentional." Henry gritted out the words. Anger flared hot in his stomach. Calvin had done it. Or gotten someone to do it for him. Either way, this was him.

And he would pay.

"I figured as much. I don't think the storm is the only thing that's come into town angry."

Henry walked into the main room as a shock of lightning lit up the space. Cassie stood from the corner booth he'd set her next to.

"I found Hawk," he was quick to say. "He's okay,

and you were right, he is ready to do some shooting if needed."

Hank held up the lantern long enough for Cassie to cross the room. Henry watched the front windows and door.

"I locked the front door," she said, getting a quick hug from the bartender. "I hope that's okay, Hawk."

"Sounds good to me. It might be better if we pretend we're not home right now, anyways."

Henry nodded.

He didn't want Cassie as exposed as he felt they were just standing around. The rain was still falling in heavy sheets, but if there was a chance Hawk's lantern could still be seen from the street, he wanted to make sure they were at least in a different room.

"Actually, do you have some water I could have? I know I'm drenched, but I also haven't run around like that in a while."

"Sure thing. I have some bottles in the kitchen. Then I think I have some hand towels in the storage room. Might not do the trick, but they'll help."

Henry wanted to be the one who got her water and dried her off. He wanted to be the one who sat next to her and asked if she *really was* okay. But if Calvin was gunning for him, then they weren't safe.

She wasn't safe.

Their son wasn't safe.

"I'm going to stay here," he declared, eyes never leaving the darkness outside the door and windows.

Henry felt Cassie hesitate even if he couldn't see her.

"You think they know we came over here?" Cassie asked.

"There's a plan everyone seems to be following. One

that I don't fully understand yet. I can't guess at their moves because I don't know their full motives."

"The big guy wanted to hurt Matt, not you," Cassie offered. "But the woman wanted to keep you in that room. She wanted to keep you safe."

Henry nodded. He didn't know if either could see it outside their circle of light.

"Two different agendas, a town-wide blackout and somewhere out there Calvin is up to no good." Henry felt his nostrils flare, anger burning through him again. "It's hard to guess at what happens next when you're still hung up on what's happening now."

Hawk grunted in, what Henry guessed, was agreement. Cassie didn't say a word. The two walked back to the kitchen. Henry turned off his flashlight and set it on the bar in front of him. Complete darkness washed over the room.

Henry didn't want to admit it, but Calvin being hot on his heels was bad, bad news. The man wasn't just smart, he was clever. But what was worse came from the fact that he had always been a man able to adapt. He thought as quickly on his feet as Henry did. It had been one of the reasons they had been paired up and sent undercover in the first place. If Calvin really was pulling the strings, he might pull his puppets right on over to the Eagle.

Because that was where Calvin would have gone if he had a pregnant woman he was protecting. At least, the old Calvin would have.

Was he the same person now?

Had Henry just been blind?

He balled his fists on the bar top. The same one he'd been sitting at when he'd first heard the honeyed voice that was Cassie Gates.

If he'd only known what he knew now…

…He still would have walked over to her sister and pretended he was her date.

Another surprising revelation.

One that was short-lived.

Lighting flashed outside. Then it flashed again.

Henry stiffened.

It wasn't lightning.

Two beams of light strobed in front of the building, getting closer.

Had the goons already figured out where they'd gone?

Henry ducked low and hurried through the door to the kitchen.

"Hawk, lights out," he hissed, rushing to Cassie's side. He took her hand as the bar owner followed instruction without question.

"This is getting old," Cassie muttered.

Hawk beat them to the office and picked up his gun. He turned the lantern back on, low, and put it in the corner. Henry directed Cassie to a chair next to it.

"If that woman is with them, she made it pretty clear that Calvin wanted you alive," she said. "That's good, right?"

"No, it's not."

In the low light Cassie's brow turned in on itself.

He didn't like the explanation he gave. "She didn't say anything about keeping you alive."

Cassie let his words sink in.

He was right.

She hadn't mentioned keeping her or *anyone* else alive.

No, Calvin had wanted Henry, and Henry alone.

Cassie rubbed her stomach as she watched Hawk and Henry readying their weapons. They were talking quickly, quietly. Tackling what-ifs and bottom lines, she was sure.

She felt useless sitting there but wasn't about to argue. She might have spent the last twenty minutes or so being heroic and ready for action, but the truth was, she was exhausted. Adrenaline surge after adrenaline surge and being soaked from head to toe, she couldn't ignore the fact that she was seven months' pregnant. She couldn't keep up the pace of running for her life. It wasn't good for her or the baby.

"Henry," she called out when it appeared to be go-time. Even in the low light Cassie marveled at how attractive he was. Built for strength, molded by conviction. Sharp angles, soft lips. A storm of a different nature swirling in his eyes. The same eyes that held all of her attention in his gaze. "Be careful. Both of you."

Hawk dipped his head in acceptance of the order. Henry didn't. Instead he issued his own back at her.

"Shoot anyone who comes through this door that isn't us."

And then they took his small light and shut the door behind them.

Cassie blew out a long, low breath, trying to steady her nerves. She grabbed her gun and prayed she wouldn't have to use it again. Last time had been enough to last the rest of her days.

The rain hadn't lessened its onslaught against the roof above. It made it impossible to hear what was going on in the other room.

Maybe nothing would happen.

Maybe Henry was overreacting or trying his best to be cautious.

A warmth in her chest started to expand as she thought of the man taking her hand earlier.

He was doing his hardest to keep her and their child safe.

Did that mean he wanted to be in their life?

Or was he just doing his job as an officer of the law?

Like she was going through déjà vu, a sound in the other room cut off all current lines of thought.

However, this time Cassie could place it.

Someone had shattered glass.

Cassie pulled her gun up. She might be cold, tired and worried, but she wasn't about to let anyone harm her or her child.

THE DARKNESS BETWEEN Henry and Hawk was still thick, but two flashlights were eating up the space on the other side of the bar behind them. Heavy shoes crunched over the broken glass that had once taken up the top half of the front door. Now the feet squeaked along the middle of the room as two perpetrators surveyed the space around them.

Henry might not have been the king of stealth, but neither were the people behind them. After their lights could be seen moving to the kitchen door and the hallway, they had no problem talking to one another.

Loudly.

"Don't look like anyone's here," a deep voice grumbled.

"Yeah, they would have come out by now," another answered. Also male. Henry recognized neither. "Baldy would have already been in our faces if he was here, that's for sure."

"So what you wanna do?"

There was a pause as the other must have been thinking.

Henry couldn't see the bar owner next to him but knew he was ready to start the fight as soon as the signal was given.

"Well, I'm not about to go tell Paula we didn't search the whole place. She's already pissed enough with the bullet in her arm."

The other man agreed with a "Humph."

Henry reached out and touched Hawk's elbow. He didn't wait for a response. Taking a beer glass from behind him, Henry started to slowly stand, readying to throw it as far away from them as possible. It would be the distraction that would get them the upper hand.

Henry arced back, still hidden in the dark while the men's flashlights kept on the hallway ahead of them, and felt his muscles tighten as he focused on mentally picturing the spot in the corner he wanted to hit.

Then, just like that, the bar's overhead lights cut on.

The pumped-up alternate rock from the stereo, some sports game on the overhead TV and the building whirl of the AC unit were all background noise as two armed men stood staring at Henry and his beer glass.

"Well, this is awkward," Henry stated.

Henry followed through with his plan and threw the glass hard. Both men danced away from it, but only one took a shot while doing it. The bullet embedded somewhere over the pool tables to the left of the bar. The beer glass shattered and the second man readied to shoot his own gun.

Hawk was faster.

He shot the second man in the leg while Henry made sure the first didn't get any more ideas. Much like Cassie had done with the woman, named Paula according to the men a few feet from him, Henry clipped the first man.

He yelled out in pain and dropped his weapon.

"Drop yours or I'll shoot again," Hawk ordered.

The man was slower than his friend to fall, but he did lower his gun long enough to slump to the floor, cussing.

"Push the guns away," Henry yelled. "Both of them."

The order did the trick.

Both men kicked and slid their guns away, the first man whimpering as he did so. The second kept to cussing.

Henry and Hawk worked quickly. They substituted plastic zip ties from behind the counter for cuffs. Soon both men were restrained.

"Nice job, Baldy," Henry joked. Hawk snorted. "Now let's see if we can't get hold of someone at the department."

The man shot in the leg spit to the side, earning a scowl from Hawk. Then he bit off some laughter.

Henry didn't like what he had to say.

Not one bit.

"Pretty sure they ain't coming," he said too calmly. Too confidently. "They got their own problems right now."

Chapter Seventeen

The power had been out for fifteen minutes.

In that time the Riker County Sheriff's Department waited. With their communications already dicey and the power gone, they were ready for an attack.

It never came.

At least, not where expected.

Henry touched the bandage the ER nurse had put over the knife wound in his shoulder. It didn't hurt. Then he felt his nose. Swollen, bruised, but not broken. It hurt, but nothing could compare to what he was currently feeling.

He wasn't angry.

He was furious.

He wasn't the only one.

Suzy threw her fist into the side of the vending machine Henry had positioned himself next to. It made a loud bang but didn't draw anyone's attention but his. Everyone else was busy bustling around. The backup generators had kicked on in the hospital, but because the rest of the town had been dark, there had been an influx of new patients. Some car accidents, a few self-defense incidents when a couple of geniuses got the idea to try to loot some local stores, and then some patients already in-house who'd had trouble before the backup generators could take over.

Billy had been one of the latter. He'd been in surgery after a complication had arisen around lunch. It had almost cost him his life, but the doctor had been fast on her feet.

But that still wasn't why Suzy was so mad.

"They never wanted us," she said, rage spilling out. She ran her hands through her hair and then down her face. "My God, we were so worried about them hitting us and then they went after *our families*."

It wasn't new information to Henry. After they'd gotten a call through to the department, one of the deputies had told him everything. Said how those who hadn't lost their cell signals because of the downed power had started to get calls from the outside world. One where their families were being attacked.

Four hours had gone by since then. In that time they'd found out that Caleb's house had been broken into and his wife had been attacked. The man had tried to get her to his car, but their dog had attacked, giving her time to run and hide. She had gotten stitches but was safely upstairs now.

Others who had been targeted but managed to escape or fight back had been Suzy's mother, Dante Mills's niece, Detective Ansler's brother and Captain Jones's father. All attackers had been since identified as men and women who Caleb, Dante, Ansler and Jones had directly affected by way of arrest, prison sentence or either a family member being arrested or sentenced.

"An eye for an eye," Alyssa's attacker had said while trying to put her in his car.

However, even though that had been the end of the

attacks, the main reason everyone was on edge had to do with Matt's fiancée, Maggie.

Even though Goliath had been killed, she'd still been targeted and taken from her home. Her young son had been with her. She'd fought tooth and nail to free him before the man had managed to put her in the trunk and drive off.

Currently the boy was in the room across the hall with a broken arm, Suzy's mother keeping him company.

Maggie had simply disappeared.

"What's the plan now?" he asked, trying to focus her anger.

"Local FBI have integrated into this madness and are helping to look for the people behind this, Maggie's attacker included. The local chief of police is covering the department while the rest of us are trying to get a hold on the situation. Once I go check on Billy and Mara, I'm heading back out there to meet up with Matt. We brought out our reserve deputies to help Ansler try to chase down the people we know are already tied up in this."

The stress Suzy carried wasn't just in her shoulders, it was everywhere. "I'm sheriff for less than two days and the department has been crippled, our families have been targeted and the entire town is put out of commission." She held up her hand to stop his attempt to comfort her. Which he was ready to do, since it was *his* fault that this had happened. He'd already told her everything he'd learned since the hotel room, namely that Calvin had most likely orchestrated the blackout and Paula had been sent to keep him out of harm's way.

Even though that in itself was confusing. If Calvin had recruited a group of angry people looking for revenge on the department, then why would they try to target Henry?

It was one of many questions they'd all had.

But there was no time to sit back and wonder.

"What's happened has happened," Suzy continued. "Now we need to focus on making sure we get Maggie back and bring our perps in. And make sure if another strike happens, we're ready." She pulled something out of her pocket.

Henry was surprised to see it was a key.

"You seem to be an extra-shiny target, which now includes Cassie. If Calvin wants to use Carpenter as his own personal chessboard, then I'm done playing. It's time to take a few pieces off the board altogether."

THE RAIN BARRELED on throughout the night. It only started to taper off once they had driven over the town line, through the city of Kipsy and finally into Bates Hill.

"It's the smallest town in the county," Cassie reported. Her voice came out tired, worried.

Henry knew both feelings well. The old him wouldn't have left Carpenter at all. Not when one of their own was hunting the man who had taken his loved one. Not when they might be subjected to another attack.

Then Cassie would let out a soft sigh or rub her stomach and Henry would remember that there *was* a new him. One who had a woman and unborn child to protect. It was the least he could do, since now, because of him, the off-her-rocker woman, Paula, had seen them together.

The men who Henry and Hawk had taken at the bar had only reiterated two facts before shutting their mouths entirely.

One, that Paula had been shot.

Two, that a pregnant lady named Cassie had been the one who shot her.

Once backup had arrived, Henry had gone through the hotel with them before being taken to the hospital. Mike the manager had indeed put up a fight but was still alive, albeit in need of medical care. Jason, the nervous man who had come in with Paula, had still been unconscious in the suite and Goliath had been just as dead as ever.

Paula and the cuffs were gone. The few guests staying at the hotel hadn't seen her or anyone else come or go from the second floor when the lights came back on.

It was the only reason Henry had agreed to, once again, trying to sit out and hide. Though, this time, he hoped it would actually work. He'd kept his eyes on their surroundings, looking for a tail. He still didn't know how Paula and her lackeys had found them so quickly at the hotel.

Unless they'd gone through his cell phone. It had been new and almost no information had been in it, but, still, maybe Calvin had looked at the recent calls and connected it to the hotel. Then Paula had staked him out? And Goliath had, too?

Henry ground his teeth at the thought.

What madness had he brought with him to Riker County?

"Bates Hill might be small, but it's really come a long way in the last decade or so," Kristen piped up from the back seat. When Henry had told Cassie the plan, she'd refused to go anywhere without her sister, especially since Michael had seen them together.

Kristen had driven to the hospital and as soon as she'd gotten into his car, Cassie had told her everything. This was the first time she'd spoken since Kipsy. "A certain, handsome-as-all-get-out resident millionaire has been helping make it into a great place. More and more people have made appointments with me to try to move out here. I even thought about it once or twice myself."

"Which had nothing to do with that certain, handsome-as-all-get-out resident millionaire who was single then, I'm sure." Cassie might have been tired, but she didn't let that dull her sense of humor. Or, maybe, she was trying to distract her sister.

Kristen snorted. "Hey, I'd like you to find me one woman in the entire zip code who wouldn't have changed addresses to get to James Callahan," she challenged.

Henry glanced over at Cassie. He didn't like being reminded that he didn't know many things about her, romantic life included. For all he knew, she could have been seeing someone.

Henry ground his teeth again at the thought of her being with another man.

He actively kept from gripping the steering wheel tighter.

"You got me there. James *is* a catch," Cassie admitted. "But I can also show you the *only* woman in the zip code who exists according to James."

There was a huff from the back seat.

Cassie smiled. She caught his eye and took pity on his utter lack of knowledge when it came to the personal intricacies of Riker County.

"That one woman is none other than our fearless leader."

"Suzy?"

Cassie nodded. "Her job is probably the only reason some crazed James fanatic hasn't tried to get in between the couple. Not that I think anyone could do that to start with." Her smile faded. Shadows covered her. The mood in the car shifted just like that. "It's his cabin we're going to. One that they've kept private. James even bought the land under his sister's boyfriend's name to keep people from prying. Unless they're local and friends with James and his family, I can't imagine anyone would even know it's there. I didn't until tonight."

Henry hoped that was true.

They drove in silence, following Kristen's GPS until it directed them to a dirt road on the very tip of the town. Rolling fields transitioned to thick woods of tall oaks and pines. The girls were just as alert as Henry felt maneuvering his car over the rough road. Both were leaning against their windows while he tried to survey their surroundings, looking for possible alternate escape routes or places where someone could hide a vehicle. He saw neither.

Two minutes or so into the drive, the road curved and the trees opened up. A small, true wooden cabin was nestled in a tight but clean clearing. No lights were on and no cars were parked in the small graveled parking area tucked next to the structure.

Henry left the car running and headlights on as he took the key Suzy had given him and went through the house. The cabin was less quaint on the inside but still cozy. It was also empty of any threats. The perfect place to let Cassie get some rest. Judging by the bags beneath her eyes and the slow gait she used between the passenger's side of the car and the living room, she truly needed it.

And apparently a hot bath.

"I've been rained on, twice, hidden in hotel bathrooms and back rooms of bars, not to mention walked through the aftermath of a shotgun blast." She crossed her arms over her chest. "If I don't get at least five minutes of sitting in a hot bath, I will probably throw a tantrum." She jutted her hip out and narrowed her eyes at Henry and Kristen. "Anything you need to do in there, you do it now."

In unison Kristen and Henry responded.

"Yes, ma'am."

The older Gates scurried off, brandishing her toothbrush while Henry put the bags she'd packed before going to the hospital in the bedroom.

Cassie sat on the edge of the bed and sighed. "Do you think Maggie is okay?"

The question didn't catch Henry off guard. He'd been waiting for it since they'd gotten the news. "I think she was taken for a reason." He straightened so he was opposite her. She looked up at him through her long eyelashes, worried and scared. It sent a shock through him at how close they were to each other.

And how much he wanted to be closer.

"Sometimes being taken for a reason rather than as an impulsive act can be a good thing."

"It might mean she's alive then," Cassie suggested. Henry nodded. "But if it's revenge these people are after, then the purpose she was taken for can't be good." Her shoulders sagged and her voice broke.

Henry lowered himself beside her and gently pulled her into his side. She didn't resist. The smell of her shampoo once again filled his senses.

In that moment all he wanted to do was to comfort her. "After the fire on the ranch, I was pulled from undercover work for a few months. I'd like to say it was for a lot of reasons, but mostly it was because I'd become difficult. All that work the task force had done, or I thought we'd done, and all I had to show for it was a few criminals behind bars and a dead partner. It didn't seem right."

Cassie kept her head at his shoulder but tilted her face up to show she was listening.

He continued. "I spiraled for a while. Drank some, then drank some more. Questioned life, my career, why I did what I did. Hit a low point and hit it hard. But, like I told you the night we met, I know what it's like to be the baby of the family. To be told what I needed rather than it being suggested. That's what my brother did. He drove eighteen hours straight out to my place, made me pack a bag and then made me drive the eighteen hours back."

He smiled. "In that time we talked about anything and everything. He didn't take no for an answer and pushed me to talk about stuff that I hadn't said to anyone. He made me face the pain of losing Calvin head-on. And then he made me face myself. You see, being undercover like we were wasn't just about lying. It was about making people believe." He fisted the hand not around Cassie. If she saw it, she didn't say anything. "I did some things I'm not proud of to keep my cover and that's just something I'm going to have to live with. But what had happened to Calvin was different. It changed me. So my brother asked me what I wanted out of life."

Cassie moved her head back to meet his gaze. Her eyes were shining but no tears stained her cheeks.

"I told him I wanted to protect people," he continued. "That's all I'd ever wanted to do. Help people and get justice for those who couldn't get it for themselves. And then he told me about a sheriff's department that had been in the news that wasn't too far from where I'd

been in Tennessee." He felt a smile stretch over his lips.
"The next week I applied. The week after that I drove
in for an interview." He paused, wondering if he should
keep going. But one look into those wide, clear eyes and
he decided against it. This story wasn't about absolving
him, it was about comforting her.

"I wanted and accepted the job at the sheriff's department because the part of me that has always wanted to
do good, to keep people safe, to get the job *done*, saw
that that's *exactly* what the Riker County Sheriff's Department did on a daily basis. They do good. They keep
people safe. They *get the job done*. No matter what, or
who, tries to stop them. You got that?"

A small but true smile lifted the corners of her lips.
Cassie nodded.

"Now, I also firmly believe you meant business about
taking that bath. So I'm going to leave you to that." He
stood and grinned. "I've seen just how good a shot you
are. I'm not about to tempt you to show me just how serious you are."

Henry went to the door, but Cassie spoke up.

Her smile was gone. "You gave me a fake name, said
you didn't have a phone number, disappeared for seven
months and then pretended not to know me when you
showed up again." There was no heat in her words. No
anger. Just statements. It was more effective than if she'd
yelled. "I know we've said we'll talk about it later, but
now that doesn't seem as important."

For the first time Henry saw Cassie ball her fist.

"I just wanted to say thank you for what you've done the
past few days... But, honestly, I'm still mad. And I don't
think there's anything you can say that will change that."

Kristen cleared her throat. Henry turned to see her

outside the door, toothbrush in hand. She was frowning. Henry moved to let her by. She looked almost apologetic as she shut the door to the bedroom behind her.

Chapter Eighteen

The bath was getting cold, the bubbles getting low. Kristen had laughed when she'd found the kid's bubble bath, but Cassie had been delighted. Sure, she liked soaking in the tub, but bubbles made it more fun. Or, at least, they had.

She leaned back in the shallow tub and moved the suds remaining around her like a blanket. Her body might have relaxed because of the heat, but her mind hadn't slowed.

From the attack to Maggie being taken.

From the fear of Henry being hurt to having to shoot a woman.

From Henry opening up and then to her letting him in.

Not to mention pregnancy hormones.

It was already a lot to take in without those making her emotions go haywire.

Part of Cassie wanted to cry in bed until she fell asleep.

The other wanted to scream and jump into a car in search for Maggie herself.

Another part, small but strong, asked for food. She'd eaten at the hospital, but that had been a few hours ago. It was now nearing one in the morning.

A soft knock rapped against the door. It startled her out of her thoughts.

"Come in."

The last person she thought would want to talk to her right now popped his head around the opened door. Despite her earlier flip from gratitude to anger at his speech, a thrill went through Cassie's naked body. She slid down into the water. Henry kept his eyes on hers, not looking down.

"I just wanted to check on you," he said, voice tight. "It's been a while. I was afraid you might have fallen asleep."

Cassie sighed. It moved the last of the bubbles across her chest.

"I thought I'd be more tired, I surely was earlier, but now all I am is worried, mad and hungry. It's like my mind and body won't sync up. How can I take what's going on seriously while all I can think of are doughnuts?"

Henry held up his finger. "Maybe I can help with that."

He disappeared from the door frame. Cassie checked her bubbles again. Her stomach stuck out of the water an inch or so, but the rest of her was hidden. Unless he decided to come stand over her.

Henry being so near her naked again sent a shiver of longing through her.

Another thing she'd blame pregnancy hormones on.

She wanted to be mad that he'd lied, left and lied again. She wanted to put distance between them so she could sort her thoughts and figure out how to move on from them.

But was that even possible?

Could she get over Henry Ward?

Just the sight of him filling the doorway with his masculine frame was enough to send her body into another fit of yearning. His eyes so blue and so true lit up as he shook a bag in each of his hands. Cassie momentarily forgot to be mad.

"Before we left the hospital I grabbed a few things from the vending machine. Suzy pointed out these are some of your favorites?"

The man was holding a bag of chips and a pack of M&M's and he had never looked so sexy.

She could have cried.

"I swear you have just answered my prayers," she said, meaning it. Henry laughed and, keeping his eyes directly on hers, let her reach for the chips. She settled back into the water and opened the bag. Only after she smelled the chips did she feel heat crawl up her neck. "I bet I look like such a slob right now," she quipped.

Henry shook his head. "You look like a woman who's had a hard day." It was a smart thing to say. "Which you have. If there was a hot tub, I might be in there right now with these."

He shook the candy bag she'd left him and started for the door. Cassie didn't like the thought of him leaving. It made her angry at herself. Then angry at him. Then angry at herself for being angry.

"Wait," she called. "If you want, you can stay in here for a little bit." The blush already burning her cheeks became hotter. Still she pushed through it. "I wouldn't mind the company."

Henry didn't argue. He shut the door and sat on the floor, back against it. For a minute they both ate their snacks in silence. It was enough time to sort her thoughts out. She finished off the bag of chips and rested it against her floating belly. With a sigh that had been one of many through the last seven months, Cassie finally got to the heart of what was bothering her.

All while sitting in the bathtub.

"Okay, so I guess it was my fault."

Henry's eyes found hers and held. His eyebrow arched high. "What was your fault?"

"I was naive," she started after a long exhale. She idly began to move a cluster of bubbles next to her belly with one of her hands. It weirdly helped her nerves. "See, my parents have been with each other since they were fifteen. During their life together they've had six kids. Of those six, four have spouses they're mad about. I mean, over the moon, would do anything for, and two even have those tacky, matching tattoos. Being around them, you can just feel it, too. Like they've found their purpose in life within each other. Just like how our parents are. So, it sounds silly, but all I've known of relationships is true and unending love."

She gave him a wry smile, trying to let him know that she realized what she said probably sounded cheesy. As usual, his expression was guarded. She could no more tell if he thought she was crazy than if he was even listening to her at all. But what she knew of the man, she was sure he was. "Now, I've dated and been with men before. But there was never a connection. Never anything that was like what my family had talked about feeling. That is until the night I met you."

The courage that had filled her chest the moment before started to wane. She averted her gaze but only for a moment. "That night I felt what I thought was a connection with you. A spark. That's why I came to your room, that's why I gave you my number and that's why I shared your bed. I broke character for the first time in my life because I thought I was following some kind of invisible road to what had made my family happy for decades. I didn't care that I had only known you for a few hours. It didn't matter."

A lump formed in her throat. Tears welled up behind her eyes. Cassie refused to stop for either. "But I... I was naive. And so I waited for a call, a text. Heck, I would have been happy with a friend request. But nothing came. That's when I realized that my family wasn't average. What they had was special and rare and beautiful."

The tears that had threatened now fell down her cheeks. "And that made me proud of them, of where I come from. But...but then I felt like a little girl who'd just been told Santa didn't exist. That love was more complicated than some magical connection. And then... then I found out I was pregnant and the most extraordinary thing happened. The heart I'd just been worried would never find someone to love was stolen by someone I hadn't even met yet." She touched her stomach, feeling the love for her child radiate throughout her. She smiled through her tears. "During the next few months I realized that, while my life had taken a different, maybe unconventional, path compared to my parents' and siblings', it didn't mean it wasn't special in its own right."

Henry's brows knitted together, his jaw hardened. "Cassie, I—"

She shook her head. She wasn't to the point yet. The real reason she realized she was so angry. "I also took that time to come to terms with the fact that I'd probably never see you again. I even got used to the idea. Then, all of a sudden, there you were. Walking into that diner wearing a shiny deputy's badge. And just like that I was back standing at that pool table, laughing at your jokes."

Henry got to his feet and started to close the gap between them. Cassie couldn't read his expression. She didn't care. She had to say her piece. She had to let them both know what she was feeling because, soon, there would be three of them.

"After everything that had happened, everything that was going haywire around us, and there you were. Smiling at me over that pool table with those baby blues. I guess I knew then I couldn't deny it anymore."

Henry got to his knees on the tile next to the tub. If he wanted, he could see all of her by just glancing down. But she knew he wouldn't. He wasn't that kind of guy. He didn't take without asking. Or, well, maybe he did.

Henry was so close she couldn't help reaching out. He let her trace the sharp line of his jaw as she continued.

"While my son might have taken all my heart, there was still something inside me that just wouldn't let go of you."

A breath barely stretched between the end of her admission and the beginning of their kiss. Henry moved over the lip of the tub so Cassie didn't have to move an inch. Not that she could. She hadn't been fishing for affection from the man. She'd just wanted him to know what she felt. With the madness of everything that had happened, it had been nice to say something certain.

Now what was certain was the hardness of his lips against hers. The prickle of his facial hair against her fingers. Her mouth parting so his tongue could delve deeper.

The way one kiss could somehow touch every fiber of her being.

Henry moved his hands to either side of her face and softened the kiss until he broke it. He was smiling.

"Cassie Gates, I want to show you something."

He released her, to Cassie's utter surprise, and pulled out his wallet. She couldn't stop her eyebrow from shooting straight up toward her hairline. He opened the worn leather and pulled something out from behind the plastic protector that held his license. It was a piece of paper. A small piece, ripped from the corner of a hotel notepad.

Cassie knew this because she'd been the one to do it.

Henry held the paper up. "The day you gave this to me, I interviewed for a job and was offered that same job on the spot. I accepted it and went straight home, resigned, and had to start tying up loose ends. I gave you a false last name on the off chance you tried to track me down before I could finish because I didn't want you to get tangled up in my old life. I had decided that after I was finished, and got a new number and officially was done with that life, I would call you."

His smile wavered. Cassie hung on his every word.

"But then my boss pulled me in for one last job that he said needed Gage Coulson. He told me it would be quick. It wasn't. I finished it up a month ago." With one hand he reached out and moved a wayward strand of her hair behind her ear. Then he was looking at her like she'd never been looked at before. "I should have still called or done something or *said* something when I did finally see you. But, Cassie Gates, I was a damn idiot." That smile found its footing again. "You're the most beautiful woman I've ever seen, and even though I'm an idiot, I kept this piece of paper with your number on it because I'd always hoped I'd see you again. If only to kiss you at least one more time."

Cassie dropped her gaze to her handwriting across the paper. He'd really kept it. For seven months. He'd kept it in his wallet.

"I know you said there isn't anything I could say to make you not be angry with me, and that's fine," he continued, voice lowering. "I just was tired of being quiet about something I should have already said."

Henry's face, for once, wasn't closed. The walls that he'd been guarding himself with were all gone. He'd opened himself up to her, finally, and now was waiting for her to set the new tone for them. His baby blues searched her face, his lips slunk downward and just when he looked like his was about to move away, Cassie decided what that tone would be for them.

"So," she started, trying to keep her expression neutral. "After seven months of waiting, you decided the best time to kiss me was when I was naked, sitting in a cold tub, surrounded by strawberry-scented bubbles, *completely* hormonal, and with an empty bag of chips sitting on my swollen belly? I have to say, Deputy Ward, I know we might have done this relationship a bit backward, but in the future I wouldn't mind some romance in my life."

Henry's smile resurfaced and then turned into a grin. "Yes, ma'am."

Chapter Nineteen

The rain was a fine mist outside, cooling the ground but not hurting the view. Henry was like a sullen child, pouting as he stared out the window. He'd been in the same state for almost twenty minutes, just watching the wooded area surrounding the cabin. It gave Cassie the time to watch him in turn.

Broad shoulders nearly blocked the window's width, filling out his flannel button-up to the point of where it was tight across his biceps. Whatever he had been doing in the last several months, she would bet lifting weights had been a part of his routine. Just as wearing those jeans must also have been on his docket. You just didn't get that shade of faded denim store-bought. That was true wear and tear. It was amazing it even kept that tush of his in.

Cassie's gaze had traveled over that very tush and down across his thighs and calves. She knew them just as intimately as the rest of the man. Taut, muscled and hard from an active lifestyle.

In fact, she didn't know if there was a spot on the man that was soft.

She traced his profile back to the line of his jaw where

stubble had sprouted. Then her eyes went to the last feature of the man she hadn't admired yet in detail.

There *was* a softness to his lips. After they had shared their feelings in the bathroom, they'd taken to the couch in the living room. There they'd touched on almost every topic under the sun. There he'd given her more than a fair share of gentle, sweet kisses. Ones that filled her with hope, comfort and had eventually made her feel safe enough to fall asleep.

Now, an hour or two after she'd woken, he had his eyes outside and his mind somewhere else. She wished she could make him feel better. Just like she wished she could help the men and women of the department who, according to him, hadn't had any luck in finding Maggie or the rest of the culprits.

Cassie kept her sigh close to her chest and let her eyes dance across the man who could put fire in her body just by standing still.

The same man who apparently wasn't as oblivious as she'd thought.

"You stare at me much longer and I might just have to charge you for it."

A muscle in Henry's jaw twitched, trying to keep in a smirk, no doubt.

Cassie felt heat start to crawl up her neck. That had less to do with being caught admiring the man's body and more to do with how hers had reacted to the memory of what it had felt like against hers. South of her waistline was already heated.

And was already wanting more.

There he was again, a fire starter wearing denim so well it was almost criminal.

"I was just wondering how long you were going to

sulk," she said, keeping her tone light. "You're acting like you were the last boy to be picked for kickball, and you know that's just not the case."

Another small twitch in his jaw let her know she'd hit on some of his humor. It was brief. Even if they'd made headway about the two of them, there was still a county of hurting outside the cabin's walls.

"I spent months trying to get away from my old job, an old life, and still, after a week here, I bring trouble hot on my heels." He moved over so she could take up position at his side. The sky was nearly crystal blue. If storms were coming, they were being slow about it.

"Trouble follows this job." Cassie touched his shoulder to underline the point. "It might have followed you, but it also followed Caleb and Suzy and a whole bunch of people. That's just the way of the job. You do enough good and you're bound to reap some of the bad you helped stop."

"But Calvin is my bad. And if he really did orchestrate the attacks yesterday…"

Cassie saw his frown. She felt it in her bones. Just as she saw the guilt weighing down his body. She felt it, too. She wanted to stop both. Or, at least, lessen them.

"No one is going to blame you for Calvin. No matter what he does, he did it. Not you. Plain and simple."

Henry looked down his nose at her, eyes the color of any woman's favorite pair of blue jeans. Which might just be the ones he was wearing, Cassie decided.

"You know you Riker County people have a habit of sounding like fortune cookies. First the 'some people suck' thing and now 'trouble follows the job'?"

Cassie made a face as he smirked.

"I mean no disrespect. Just saying you all might need

to look into designing those inspirational office posters. You know, the ones with cats hanging from things and nice words over pictures of sunsets. Might be a good source of extra income for the department."

Cassie couldn't help snorting at that.

It earned a small smile from the man.

Again, that didn't last long, either. He didn't have to say a word. Cassie knew he was still being eaten up from the inside. Memories of his former partner, worries of his new department and the giant unknown connecting both.

"Here, I know what might help." Cassie reached out and took the man's hand. Despite his inner turmoil he wrapped his fingers around hers, protectively. They were warm and strong.

Cassie directed the man through the living room to the kitchen and out its back door. The temperature had indeed cooled, but once the mist left over by the rain was completely gone, the sticky heat would make up for the change. Until then she marched them through the yard and right into the trees.

"We shouldn't be out here," Henry said, head already on a swivel. He didn't get out of her pull, but she heard the distinct sound of him freeing his gun from its holster.

"No one knows where this place is. We've been here for hours. If Calvin or Michael or anyone else manages to show up, then color me impressed." She gave him a little tug as he started to resist when she said Calvin's name. "Plus, isn't that a gun in your hand? If anyone comes out at us, shoot 'em!"

She heard him chuckle but kept on forward.

"You know, since I started, everyone keeps telling me how sweet and calm you are, but sometimes I think they don't really know you," he said matter-of-factly.

"Instead of honey, you're more like hot sauce. But the kind they try to hide in one of those bottles with the pretty wrappers."

Cassie dropped his hand as they moved through the trees, trying to keep herself balanced. The ground was filled with thick, twisting roots. The last thing she wanted to do was to face-plant in front of the deputy.

The deputy who seemed to think she was a bottle of hot sauce in a pretty wrapper.

"You don't think I'm sweet?" Cassie asked with mock offense. She placed her hand on a tree, trying to navigate around a few of its gnarled roots. It didn't work. One foot slipped off. It was enough to tip her entire balance off. Her stomach probably didn't help matters. All she had time to do was yelp.

One strong, solid arm looped around her waist. Henry stopped her fall by pulling her to him. Suddenly she could feel his warmth through the back of her shirt, feel his heartbeat thump between them. Cassie tried to laugh off her embarrassment and the heat that it brought to her body.

But she couldn't bring herself to make a sound.

Henry's hold on her didn't loosen. He didn't step back. He didn't try to turn her around. Cassie placed her hand on his arm. The fabric of his flannel was impossibly thick.

"You okay?" he asked.

Henry's voice had filled with grit, low and heady, near her ear. His breath skated across her skin. It didn't just stir feelings within her, it ignited them. Fire starter in denim, indeed. Cassie closed her eyes. Now wasn't the time.

"Cassie."

It wasn't a question. It felt more like a declaration.

Henry used the arm at her waist to slowly turn Cassie around. One look up at those soft lips and hers parted in anticipation. The deputy replaced his gun in his holster and then, slowly, closed what little distance there had been between them.

The woods around them quieted.

All there were was two people, each breathing heavy and searching for something the other might just have. Past and future be damned, Cassie wanted the man who'd given her her son right then and there.

Closing her eyes, she tilted her head up, anticipation tightening her entire body. All the man had to do was meet her halfway.

HENRY'S PULSE WAS RACING. His body winding up, ready for the woman he still held by the hip. Sure, they'd kissed the night before, but this was different. This feeling was almost carnal. This feeling was need.

One his body decided to give in to.

Her lips were soft, warm and inviting as Henry pressed against them. He laced his fingers into her hair, holding her fast. A moan escaped between them.

It unleashed the reservations inside Henry.

Moving carefully but pointedly, he pushed Cassie backward until she was against the bark of the closest tree. He braced one hand against that very bark. His tongue swept past her teeth and met hers, keeping the kiss. And then deepening it. Familiar territory.

But that didn't mean he was about to stop exploring.

He slipped his hand from her hair back to her hip,

meaning to pull her even more against him. To show her that his attraction to her hadn't lessened in their time apart. His jeans were already growing tight at the zipper with how much he wanted the woman.

However, she was two steps ahead.

Her hands found his backside faster than a canine unit could find drugs in a dealer's den. She cupped his cheeks hard, using the force to try to pull *him* closer. It was enough of a surprise that Henry couldn't help the laugh that bubbled up in his throat.

Cassie broke their kiss, eyes hooded and lips dark, but kept her hands firmly in their respective places.

"What?" she asked, breathless.

"Never had a woman manhandle me like this before."

Not even an ounce of embarrassment passed over her expression. Instead her eyebrow rose high. "Wearing jeans like this and you're surprised I'm admiring your *assets*? I never took you for the modest type, Deputy Ward. I surely never took you for a fool." She took the smallest of moments to straighten her shoulders and jut out her chin, resolute. "Plus, pregnancy hormones are a very real thing."

Another laugh leaped from his chest. It was loud, genuine and seemed to please the woman. A beautiful smile pulled up the corners of a set of perfect, sexy, plump lips.

It was those lips he caught again in a quick kiss.

"See?" he said, pulling away to speak. "Hot. Sauce."

The sound of a branch splitting somewhere behind them changed the mood in an instant. Cassie let go of him as Henry pivoted around, careful to keep her behind him, gun already being pulled out and up.

Kristen's hands flew up in surrender.

"Well, this is awkward," Kristen hurriedly said.

Cassie let out a sigh.

"What are you doing out here?" she asked her sister, heavy with the annoyance in her voice.

Henry put his gun back in its holster and angled his body so Cassie could get a better view of her older sister. The woman looked between them with a knowing expression.

"I would ask what *you* two are doing out here, but I think that's apparent," she shot back. "As for me, I heard you two sneak out and got worried. We *are* supposed to be keeping a low profile, right?"

The unmistakable thuds of car doors shutting sounded behind them, back at the cabin. Henry pulled that gun right back out. No one had called Cassie's phone. No one was supposed to show up.

And even if Suzy Simmons or James Callahan had wanted to, they shouldn't have brought so many people.

Before Henry could move Cassie to the other side of the tree they'd been against, he had counted at least six car doors shutting.

"Calvin?" she whispered.

Henry didn't respond. The sound of glass shattering seemed to be answer enough that whoever the guests were, they weren't friendly.

"We need to go," he said, already moving backward. He took Cassie's hand as Kristen hurried to their side. "Try to be quiet," he warned. His heart thrummed in his ears. One man he could take on. Two or three, maybe, depending on the situation. But five or six?

If he lost, Cassie and Kristen would be targeted next.

No, he would try to get them to safety first and then—

"Hey! I see something!"

And just like that, the plan changed.

Henry cursed and spun on his heel, dropping Cassie's hand.

"Go," he instructed over his shoulder. "I'll hold them off."

Cassie stopped, shaking her head. "I'm not leaving you!"

"I'll be right behind you," he lied. "I just need to scare them off to give you some time."

Cassie's face contorted into an emotion he couldn't place. He didn't have time.

"Kristen, take her," he ordered, voice going hard. Two figures in the distance were coming through the trees.

"Come on, Cassie." Cassie must have resisted. Kristen's voice had also taken on an edge. "Think of your son."

Henry didn't take his eyes off the men coming through the trees at them, but he was keenly aware of the sounds behind him.

The sound of Cassie running away.

Chapter Twenty

One man wore all black. The other also wore a ski mask. Both had guns. Neither was prepared for Henry.

Wanting to give the girls more time to escape, he checked his gun and ran straight toward the men. It apparently wasn't what they wanted.

The man wearing the mask hesitated, misstepped and toppled over with a yell. His friend in all black was more graceful in his surprise. His eyes widened, but his gun remained steady. He sent off two shots just as Henry took aim and fired his.

Bark next to Henry's head splintered and a quick burn of pain lit up the side of his leg, but all of his focus was on the man. Henry's bullet hit his stomach and down he went.

Now it was time to make sure his mask-wearing friend stayed down.

He closed one eye, pictured where he wanted to hit, and pulled the trigger.

Ski Mask gave another yell. This time in pain.

Henry was upon him in seconds, picking up his gun. The man in black was unconscious, but Henry wasn't going to take any chances. He put the new gun in the back of his jeans and hurried to the fallen pistol. Ski

Mask was angry. He cradled his shoulder but stayed on the ground.

"You son of a—"

A gunshot echoed through the trees. Henry ducked behind the one closest to him. He needed to reevaluate his strategy. Anyone and everyone at the cabin or in the surrounding woods would have heard the shots clear as day. The advancing shooter might be by himself now, but his numbers could quickly multiply.

Henry took a quick breath, adrenaline pumping hard throughout his system. He ducked low and swung around the tree. The gunman wasn't anyone he recognized, but he was admittedly a better shot than those who had preceded him.

The bullet tore through Henry's shirt, hot pain pushing into his skin. It threw off his trigger hand and aim. He shot close enough to make the man take temporary cover but not close enough to do any damage.

"You hit him," yelled the man in the mask.

Henry cursed something awful, wishing he'd rendered Ski Mask unconscious. His words alone rallied the man in the distance. He sent off another shot around the tree. Henry ducked to the side, barely clearing it.

He needed a better position to hold or else he'd be in real trouble sooner rather than later.

His arm burned, angry at being used after taking a bullet, as he pulled up his weapon, ready to stop the third unknown man.

He didn't get the chance.

Another gunshot filled the air. The man who had shot him made no noise as a bullet went through his head. Henry stalled in his current action, stunned.

Calvin stood farther behind the now dead man.

He was aiming at Henry but shouted an order to the world around them.

"No one take a shot at Henry Ward or I will kill them, too. Understood?"

Henry had thought his situation was already one-sided. Sure, he'd taken down two men, but he'd assumed there were more.

He'd assumed correctly.

Yells of confirmation sounded off in the distance, near the cabin. However, a few came from the one place he didn't need them to be.

Behind him.

"You're thinking about trying to shoot as many of us as you can," Calvin called from his spot several yards away. "But I promise you that I came prepared."

A woman's scream made Henry's insides go cold. He spun around, not caring that his back was to Calvin. Paula walked out from behind a cluster of trees smiling. At the end of her shotgun was Kristen.

Her eyes were wide, terrified.

"First you're holed up in a hotel with a pregnant woman and now you're traipsing through the woods with this one?" Paula shook her head. "And here I was hoping I'd get a chance to say the first thank-you for my new scar." She motioned to her shoulder. It was bandaged. Henry shared a glance with Kristen. She gave nothing away.

"Well, now that we have what we need, I think it's time we get started," Calvin said.

Henry turned to watch Calvin's smirk dissolve. "Like you said, only children play games. And now it's time to be an adult."

Henry's mind raced, filling with questions and fears and plans that might save them.

However, above the whirl of noise, there was one question that stayed loudest.

Where was Cassie?

"STOP *BITING* ME!"

Michael managed to free his hand, but Cassie was more than ready to try again. Hands tied behind her back or not, she had enough adrenaline and rage pumping through her that she was positive she could do some damage.

"Oh, I'm sorry, am I causing *you* discomfort?" she yelled. The sound bounced off the wall around them. Without the blindfold over her eyes she had to squint against the sunlight filtering through the closest window. "Considering you're the one who *kidnapped* me, *blindfolded and gagged* me, and now *have tied me to a chair*, that's truly rich."

Cassie struggled against the rope around her wrists. They weren't that tight. If she could slip out of them, maybe she'd have a fighting chance.

Michael took off his suit jacket. Wherever they were, along with not having any furniture, the place didn't seem to have air-conditioning, either.

"I had to get you out of there as fast and as quietly as I could," he said. "I didn't think you'd just believe that I was trying to save you."

Cassie felt her eyebrow rise. She snorted. "Trying to save me?"

Michael rolled his eyes and looked at the half-moon mark she'd just left on his hand. He sighed. "Despite what you may think of me, I'm not some cold-hearted thug. I was paid to find Henry Ward and get him to meet with Calvin. I knew he was looking for revenge, but I didn't know how far he would take it. He saw you drag Henry into the house to protect him yesterday. He decided he wanted to use you against the deputy. I tried to warn you, but that had the opposite effect, apparently."

Cassie tilted her head to the side, confused.

"Why?" she asked. "Why do you care about me? We don't even know each other."

Michael looked at her belly. His expression actually softened. "My wife's pregnant."

Cassie knew she could be naive sometimes, too kind at others. But in that moment, with those three words, she believed the man standing in front of her. Still, that didn't mean she had to be happy about it.

"Why didn't you grab my sister, too? Why not help Henry?" Fear gripped her chest. "What happened to them? Do you know where they are? Where are we? What happens now?"

Michael shook his head. "Paula was too close to grab you both. One look at you and I'm pretty sure she would have forgotten who her boss was and repaid you for shooting her. She doesn't hold that anger for your sister. Hell, unless they say something, I don't think they'll make the connection that you two are related. I was the only person who did my homework. That was only my job."

The pit of Cassie's stomach fell to the floor. "So Kristen is with Paula and Calvin? Is Henry, too?"

An emotion crossed Michael's face. She couldn't tell what it was. Regardless, it scared her.

"Yeah, Calvin and his band of merry men took them both, and as far as I know they're still alive. But…" He glanced at the window. "When I was leaving with you, he spotted my car. I knew if I tried to run he'd send someone after us. So I came back to where we've been hiding out. Luckily he was preoccupied or else he might have noticed I waited until they were out of sight before bringing you in."

Cassie didn't understand. "So you kidnapped me to keep me from getting kidnapped, or worse, but then brought me to the place I was originally going to be taken to if I *had* been kidnapped?"

Michael ran his hand through his red hair, frustration evident. "Nobody's perfect, Miss Gates."

HENRY HIT THE floor hard. Blood ran down his arm and shirt, hitting the wood next to him. Dust kicked up against his face. He groaned.

"Fun fact, those are your cuffs." Calvin laughed. "The ones, I'd like to point out, that I took off you probably a few feet from here. Give or take."

Henry rolled onto his side and then his back. He recognized the room. Though the last time he'd been in it he had been staring at the face of a beautiful woman. Now he was staring at the face of a sick man.

He only hoped that wherever Cassie had hidden, she was safe.

"Where did you take Kristen?" he asked, barely able to form words around his anger. She'd been put in the same car as him and used as a way to keep Henry from fighting. Once they'd entered the old neighborhood of Westbridge and parked outside the same house he and Cassie had taken refuge in the day before, Paula had taken Kristen in a different direction. Henry had bucked around then and earned quite the proficient beating from one of the seemingly countless lackeys Calvin had roped in. He'd also earned the being handcuffed at his back. "What are you going to do with her?"

Calvin leaned against the wall. He nodded for the man who had brought Henry in to leave. He didn't speak until the door closed in the next room over.

"She's fine for now." He was wearing the same grin he'd had on since he'd ordered Henry into the car. "But you know the drill. You do anything crazy and I go get her and make sure she's *not* fine."

Henry sat up, using the wall closest to him for support. The bullet had gone through his arm, but it didn't detract from the pain. Not that he had room to complain. He needed to find a way to get to Kristen so they could escape. Cassie wouldn't forgive him otherwise. And neither would he forgive himself if anything happened to her. Especially at Calvin's hands.

"I don't understand," he decided on proclaiming. He needed to buy time to gather back some of his strength. What better way than to try to get some answers? "I saw you get shot in that barn and now you're back terrorizing some small Alabama town with a whole crew of criminals? Why?"

Calvin laughed again. This time Henry heard the bitterness in it.

"You know, the first time we met I thought we had the potential to be a great duo. Heck, I *knew* it. When we were busting up fights on calls, chasing down idiots who thought they could get away, or just trying to find the lie some hapless druggie would try to pass off on us, we just had the right groove going. And then *bam!* we started going undercover." He clapped his hands together. "What do you know? We were just as good at being bad guys as we were at being good guys!"

"It was an act," Henry said defensively, shame and anger coursing through him. "It was a job!"

Calvin's face contorted. He slammed his fist against the wall. The window next to him shook.

"It was a goal," he yelled. "One that I realized we could achieve!" He spread his hands out wide. "Instead of spending every day watching as men and women with a whole lot less intelligence than us prosper from doing *a whole lot less* than we did, I saw an end-game. I didn't need to *pretend* I wanted it, and that only made it easier to get."

Henry felt like he was going to be sick. How had he missed the change in Calvin?

How had he not known?

"So, what? You're just going to be a crime show's cliché?" Henry asked. "A cop who went undercover and then blurred the line between right and wrong?"

Calvin laughed with no smile. His mood swings were throwing off Henry's ever-changing opinion of the man. Maybe he wasn't stable anymore. Maybe he was so far gone that trying to make sense of him was impossible.

"See, Henry, that's you to a tee," he said. "You sit there and think a thousand thoughts but won't say what you *really* think until you're pushed. That's what made you so great at going undercover. You could sit in silence trying to figure out your next move and everyone just thought it was a part of some dumb criminal. Right now I bet you're trying to figure out why I am the way I am. What happened? What signs did *you* miss when it came to my descent into—" he motioned to himself with a wave of his hands "—whatever it is I am now?"

Calvin crossed the room and stopped just short of Henry's boots. He bent over and jabbed his finger in the air, level with his eyes.

"I want you to listen, and I want you to listen good," he continued venomously. "This had nothing to do with what you did and didn't do. This is about me. See, there was never any blurring of lines. Never just one assignment that sent me over the edge. Henry, there was never even an edge to begin with. Do you want to know why?"

Henry kept his mouth shut. His fists were balled against the floor. The blood from his gunshot turned cold against his skin.

Calvin's face was red. He spit as he spoke. "I was *always* on the ground knowing exactly what it was that I wanted out of life. I wanted to be bad. It just took me a while to figure it out."

"Then why come here? Why come after me? You could have stayed off the radar. No one suspected you made it out of that barn. Definitely not me."

Calvin answered him with another question. "Do you remember why Arnold earned law enforcement's attention in the first place?"

Henry knew this answer. "He gained a lot of power really quickly."

Calvin snapped his fingers together. "Exactly! And remember how he did that?" This time he wasn't looking for an answer. "Arnold Richland inspired loyalty among almost everyone who worked for him through mass example. He promised power and money and delivered on both so quickly that, yeah, it brought him to our attention, but it also got him a small army. One that is majorly still out there."

Henry ground his teeth. "No thanks to you, I assume."

Calvin smirked again. "I wondered if you'd figure out it was me who tipped the Richlands off that night. Though, admittedly, I'd been aligned with them for a few months by that point. It took a *lot* of convincing to keep Arnold from killing you."

Henry was seeing red.

"Then why give me a show of you being killed if you were just going to leave me in the barn to die?" he yelled.

Calvin was unperturbed by the change in volume.

"Arnold told me about the beginnings of his rise to power one night," he continued. "Apparently a few of his first followers questioned just how far he was willing to go to see their group succeed. Especially when it came to his little brother, Reggie. Do you remember him?"

Henry didn't answer, but Calvin did. He continued, once again unperturbed by his audience's anger. "He was a preacher. Nice, humble and the direct opposite of what Arnold wanted to be. The yin to his yang. That's how he knew what needed to be done. He had to kill Reggie to prove himself."

Henry could have been sick.

"Is that what I am?" he asked. "I'm your opposite so you have to kill me to make some kind of twisted point?"

Calvin simply nodded. "When you were trapped in that burning building, I thought, 'Well, hey, that's easy.' But then I found out you were alive. And not only that, but you were trying to make a new home for yourself in Alabama." He shrugged. "What better place to start my own rise to power? There was definitely no short supply of anger and resentment when it came to the sheriff's department. It made it almost too easy to find recruits. All I had to do was promise them revenge. Heck, I even sweetened the pot by convincing them that if they waited, played the parts I gave them, I'd give them a plan that ensured not only revenge but suffering, too."

"It didn't work," Henry pointed out. "Not on the scale I'm sure you promised, at least."

Calvin shrugged, the very picture of indifference. "What I promised them was the chance to get what they wanted. If they failed in following through, that's on them. All they wanted from me was the tools to attempt it. Not my fault that the idiot Darrel decided to take out his rage on the sheriff before it was time. Some minds are too small to see the big picture."

"And what now? Waiting for another storm?"

Calvin shook his head. "My demonstration has already gained me interest. Now your death will gain me loyalty."

Henry's muscles started to tense. His mind hadn't stopped whirling. He thought of Cassie, of his son, of Kristen, Maggie, Matt, Caleb and Alyssa. He thought of everyone else he'd met since coming to Riker County. He thought of Hawk, a man he'd fought beside, and Suzy, a woman who had earned his burden by proximity alone. He thought of Billy and his family. He even thought of Gary, the man at the bar who had been too drunk to see just how amazing the blonde asking him to buy her a drink was.

But most of all, he thought of Calvin Fitzgerald.

A man who had been a part of his life for years.

He had been hilarious, smart, ridiculous, kind when it counted, thoughtful when it was called for, and an absolute lightweight when it came to tequila.

He'd been the best friend Henry had ever had.

And as far as Henry was concerned, Calvin Fitzgerald had never come out of that barn in Tennessee.

Instead of feeling another wave of mourning that had knocked him on his ass after the fire, Henry felt something else spreading throughout him.

"You say I never really knew you, and that may be true," he breathed.

It wasn't a statement. It wasn't a speech. It didn't even feel like words. He was talking, but everything was shifting in each sound. Slowly, Henry tucked his legs and stood. The Calvin in front of him, a man built on ego and a broken moral compass, gave him the room to do it.

He hadn't realized it yet.

For all his skill and experience, Calvin Fitzgerald hadn't seen the signs.

He didn't know he'd already lost.

"Memory Lane is a two-way street," Henry said. All pain and anger left him. All that was left was the promise of justice right around the corner. It was just waiting for him to take it. "I may not know you, but you *do* know me."

This time it was Henry that smiled.

"So, I ask you, *partner*, what would Henry Ward normally do in *this* situation?"

A second of silence moved between them.

Then Calvin's face fell. His glee and ego with it. Lines of worry stretched across his expression and his eyes widened to make room for fear.

Still, he answered, "He'd fight like hell."

Henry rolled his shoulders back. "I guess you really do know me."

Then he charged.

Chapter Twenty-One

Cassie swatted Michael away.

He rolled his eyes.

"I'm trying to help you, woman," he whispered. "Let me go in first."

They were standing at the back end of a decrepit deck, careful to keep out of sight of the car sitting out front. Michael had a snazzy revolver in his hand, while Cassie had pregnancy hormones. They weren't being nice, either. Since Michael had made her promise not to try to escape or, worse, try to take on Calvin by herself, he'd untied her and given her two options.

She could wait in the house, hiding until Calvin and his goons left and then sneak out, or he could sneak her into his car and make up an excuse to leave.

Then Cassie had given him two choices.

He could either sit by like a coward while potentially two women and a good, good man were killed, or he could set an example for his future child by helping to save the father of *her* future child.

He had said some not-so-good words and now they were about to sneak into a house where he'd seen Kristen taken. So, basically, he'd made the only right choice.

"Cassie," he warned when she still wouldn't retreat behind him. "They think I'm on their team, remember?"

She took a deep breath, annoyed, but nodded. He put his gun behind his back and stood tall. Cassie followed him and then ducked to the side as he knocked on the door. Footfalls stirred inside. Cassie didn't have time to evaluate just how terrified she should be. She put her hand on her stomach. All she knew was that no one was going to take any part of her son's family away from him.

The door opened, but she couldn't see the person on the other side. Judging by Michael's lack of pulling his gun, she assumed they knew each other. Then she heard her.

"Hey, Paula, how's the arm?"

The woman snorted. "Nothing a dead pregnant chick wouldn't fix."

Cassie's blood went cold.

Michael kept a straight face.

"Sounds like you have some issues to work out," he said with a good dose of annoyance. "Until then, Calvin told me to come talk to the blond woman. See if I could find anything out from her."

Paula huffed. "Good luck. I already tried to beat some sense into her, but she kept her mouth shut."

Cassie's rage nearly blinded her.

Michael took a small step forward.

"I have a way with words," he said.

Paula made a noise that Cassie was ready to bet was accompanied by her rolling her eyes.

"Whatever."

She must have turned away. In a move that was truly the epitome of graceful, he leaped forward through the doorway. Cassie didn't wait on the sidelines any longer.

She sprang in behind him, ready to do some damage, but came up short.

Michael had Paula in a headlock, one hand over her mouth. Cassie hurried and closed the door behind them, hoping no one outside had heard the scuffle. The dark-haired woman raged against the man, fighting him and unconsciousness. She kicked back and flailed until her heel came up right where the sun didn't shine.

Michael held in his groan of pain and his hold on her drooped. Cassie wasn't having any of it. She lunged forward and punched the spot where she'd shot the woman the day before.

That did the trick.

She cried out around Michael's hand but had lost some of her fight. It was enough to let the man get the upper hand. Finally, Paula went limp.

Michael was less graceful about dropping her unconscious body to the floor.

"I am not a fan of that woman," he said, out of breath.

Cassie would have agreed, but movement in the corner of the room caught her attention.

It was Kristen, tied up to a chair, but alive.

Cassie could have cried as she hurried to her older sister's side. She ripped the duct tape off her mouth.

"Are you okay?" Cassie asked, restraining her emotions to a low voice.

"Is there anyone else in the house?" Michael asked at her shoulder.

Kristen had a bruise across her face and blood on her cheek. There were also signs of a black eye. But she answered quickly with a voice that didn't waver.

"That horrible woman was the only one I ever saw in here. Everyone else went back out to the car or drove off." She turned her gaze to Cassie. "Maggie is in the next room."

Michael nodded and started for the door.

"Let Cassie go instead," Kristen advised hurriedly. "Maggie already roughed up two men. The only reason they didn't kill her was that Calvin stepped in." Her eyes moved back to Cassie's. They glassed over. "They separated me and Henry. I don't know where he is, but he tried really hard to save me."

Cassie gave her sister a quick kiss on the cheek.

"It's okay. We're going to save him, too," she said, resolute. "Michael, untie her, please. I'll get Maggie."

Bless him, he did just that.

HENRY SENT CALVIN crashing through the window. The force of the righteousness he felt in his chest, plus the running start and mass of muscle he had on him, helped break the glass against his old partner's back.

Then they were airborne.

Then the ground met them with a vengeance.

Calvin's breath made a noise as it left his body from the impact. Henry's body rag-dolled off him. Glass and pain were shared between them.

But then it was time to finish what Henry had started.

He rolled over onto his knees, grinding glass against the grass and dirt beneath him. Calvin might have been surprised and in pain, but if there was one thing they had established, it was that he *did* know Henry.

Which meant he knew he had to recover fast or else he'd lose.

He rolled onto his side, still wheezing. He was going to go for the gun at his back. The same one that must have hurt like hell to land on.

Henry leaned back to his ankle. His hands might have still been cuffed, but he could reach the one thing he knew Calvin hadn't taken from him. By the time Calvin was struggling to stand and pull his gun, Henry already had the knife in his hands and was on his feet.

Again he charged forward. He pushed his shoulder into the man and then spun around. Calvin saw it a second too late. The knife stuck into the side of his stomach. His pain and fear made him drop his gun. Henry kicked it to the side.

Calvin let out a wild sound that Henry couldn't quite define. The man swung his famous knock-out hit, but this time Henry knew it was coming. He dodged the hit but kept close.

Using a move he'd been on the receiving end of the night before, Henry executed one of the top five favorite techniques of his career.

He head-butted Calvin so hard that he heard the man's nose break.

It was the final blow.

Calvin fell backward again.

This time he didn't get back up.

Henry wanted to take a moment to enjoy knowing that he had stopped a madman, but just as he thought about it, he remembered that Calvin had been trying to inspire loyalty.

At the sound of feet hitting pavement toward the front of the house, he hoped that loyalty hadn't stuck.

He had no weapons.

His hands were cuffed behind his back.

His shirt was soaked from the blood pouring out of his multiple wounds.

But he had two women to save, another woman to find and a son he very much wanted to raise.

Henry spun around, ready to win every fight he had to, to see all those things come to pass.

"Henry!"

But it was Cassie who was running toward him, her sister and Maggie behind her. Michael was there, too. Gun out.

Cassie must have seen the look he was giving the man.

"He's a good guy," she told him, nearly closing the space between them.

Henry was about to question that when the red-haired man lifted his gun up and aimed it at them. Henry took a step forward, already imagining using his body as a shield to keep Cassie safe, when the world seemed to go into slow motion.

Green eyes, the color of a forest after a nice, cleansing rain, widened in fear. It wasn't at Henry. It was behind him.

Without turning around he realized he'd fallen for Calvin's deceit one last time.

The man who had pretended to die by gunshots in a barn in Tennessee had pretended once again that he had been beaten.

Henry turned, knowing that Calvin would wait until he saw Henry's defeat before he pulled the trigger. Then, when he was done with Henry, he'd just as surely shoot Cassie before Michael could do anything about it.

And Henry refused to let anyone else suffer because of his past.

Cassie was already yelling by the time Henry turned. That yell turned into a scream by the time Henry had run at Calvin. He was sitting up but armed, as Henry had already guessed.

A gunshot filled the air around them as Henry took the bullet in the shoulder.

He didn't let it slow him down.

With every ounce of anger, remorse and guilt left in him, Henry kicked the gun free of Calvin's hand and then kicked the man.

Henry heard the crack and knew it was the one that would end his old partner.

Calvin fell back onto the remnants of the broken window, neck at an odd angle, eyes open and unblinking, looking up toward the sky.

Henry hoped that his best friend had finally found peace.

Even if it was more than he deserved.

"Henry!"

The bulge of a pregnant belly brushed up against Henry's bound hands. Darkness might have tinted the edges of his vision, bullets and cuts and bruises might have been trying to work together to bring him down, but in that moment Henry finally felt his own version of peace.

Epilogue

Cassie looked down and sighed. The white fabric clung to a stomach that wasn't flat but definitely didn't have a curve to it anymore. She fanned her fingers across the beads Kristen had been so insistent about. The dress was gorgeous, but still she found her form was lacking.

Kristen laughed from the doorway. "You know, I'm sure if you asked nicely, that husband of yours might just put another baby in there."

Cassie rolled her eyes but couldn't deny the idea was appealing.

"I think it might be nice to wait until *at least* a day after the wedding," she said. "Don't you think?"

Kristen waved off her concern. "I mean, technically, the wedding *is* over." She motioned to the window. Through the slats in the plantation shutter a party of people could be seen milling around outside. "The reception *has* already started."

Cassie felt her lips curve into a smile. It was genuine and one of many that had taken place during the course of the afternoon.

Six months had passed since Calvin Fitzgerald had died on the grass in between two houses in Westbridge. Six months since a terrified Cassie had held a bleeding Henry in her arms until an ambulance had gotten to them. Six months since she had thought she might lose the love of her life forever.

That day the communications of the department might have been lacking, but it hadn't mattered in the end. Whether following his instincts or his heart, Detective Matt Walker had decided to revisit Westbridge in pursuit of his fiancée. He'd showed up to find her, Kristen, Michael and the two lackeys they'd incapacitated in the street. He'd sent the cavalry in as soon as he'd spotted the group. Until they arrived, Henry had stayed conscious and, somehow, had found enough left in him to scold Cassie.

"I'd appreciate it if you'd stop trying to rescue me," he'd said, a smile on his lips.

Cassie had shushed him. "I'm a Southern lady. We're only polite until someone threatens what's ours. You're mine, Deputy Ward. If you're in trouble, then know I'll always be right there trying to get you out of it."

He'd laughed. "I could get used to that."

She'd ridden to the hospital with him, Kristen in tow, and spent every day at his side as he'd recovered from his wounds. Then, two months later, their places had reversed. However, that was all thanks to a blond-haired, green-eyed baby boy named Colby.

If you asked Henry if he had cried the first time he'd seen his son, he would shake his head, but Cassie knew differently.

He'd been putty in Colby's tiny hands since minute one.

Cassie caught sight of her sister, Denise, homing in on the very man who had stolen her heart. She let out a sigh. "I suppose I should get back out there and save that poor man from being cornered by Denise."

Kristen came up beside her and put an arm across her shoulders.

"You know, if you really wanted her to, I bet she'd move back here if you asked," she said. "She *is* the responsible sister. I bet she'd make life a lot easier, since she has a bunch of kids, too."

Cassie shook her head and nudged the woman next to her. "I love her, just like I know you do, too, but I think the only sibling I need already lives across the street."

Kristen's cheeks dimpled as a huge smile stretched over her face. She squeezed her shoulders and then, just as quickly, she turned to teasing. "All right, Mrs. Ward. Stop being all emotional and let's go save your husband from the wonderful terror that is our Denise."

The dance floor was filled to the brim with people, just as the many tables were. Cassie had opted for a smaller wedding, but Henry had refused. He'd known how much her family meant to her and since they were their own large crowd, half the place belonged to them. The other half had been split between Henry's small family and the Riker County Sheriff's Department. Almost everyone had found a way to come or to stop by. Others had to ask for time off, considering they were in the wedding.

Cassie smiled from her spot at a table near the dance floor where she'd needed to rest. From there she got an uninhibited view of Billy dancing with his daughter while Mara danced with their son. Matt, Maggie and their son were getting down next to them while Suzy, James and their large family did their own version of getting down.

Cassie spotted Kristen near the outside, wondering if the woman was pining after the good-looking millionaire, but surprised to see all her attention on a different man.

"Oh, boy," she muttered to herself. Kristen was using her flirty smile on none other than Garrett, Henry's brother. *That* was going to be interesting. Especially since Garrett had just surprised Henry with the news that he was transferring to Darby.

"Listen, I need you to buy me a drink."

Cassie's smile doubled as the sound of her husband's voice brushed against her ear.

"I need you to pretend to buy me a drink, that is," he said, quoting what she'd said to Gary at the Eagle. It seemed like a lifetime ago.

"I don't know if my husband would like that," she said, watching him step around her and take the seat at her side. In his arms was the only other man who could ever look so good in a suit.

"I don't think he would mind. Especially since he probably deserves one after dealing with the particularly dangerous diaper he just changed." He gave her a smirk, the one that made every part of her stand at attention. If he'd been wearing his blue jeans, Cassie might just have melted completely.

Henry passed Colby over and then readjusted his chair so they both could look out over the dance floor.

Cassie ran her hand through her baby boy's soft hair while Henry stroked the back of her shoulder with his thumb.

"I could get used to this," she finally said, feeling the full force of contented happiness in being surrounded by her love, her heart and her family.

Henry smiled.

"Good," he said. "Because I don't intend to ever let you go. I might be an idiot sometimes, but I'm not *that* stupid."

And then that smirk came right on back.

Maybe she didn't need him to be wearing those blue jeans after all.

* * * * *